BENTON AND HAWTHORNE INVESTIGATE

LUCY McCAUL

FEATURING A FOREWORD BY JOHN LEVENE

CANDY JAR BOOKS · CARDIFF
2025

Editor: Philip Bates
Editorial: Shaun Russell and Keren Williams
Licensed by Hannah Haisman, Kate Sherwin, Crispin Letts, Jenna Letts and Guy Sloman

Cover by Neil Coe

Printed and bound in the UK by
4edge, 22 Eldon Way, Hockley, Essex, SS5 4AD
ISBN: 978-1-917022-23-1

Published by
Candy Jar Books
Mackintosh House
136 Newport Road, Cardiff, CF24 1DJ
www.candyjarbooks.co.uk

FOREWORD

HAVING AUTHORED my own first book, *Run the Shadows Walk the Sun*, I know all too well the pure effort, dedication, and time it takes to produce a worthy, well-written product – something to be embraced by the fans of any writer, actor, or television show that is adored, loved, and followed with great passion and loyalty.

As an actor from the *Doctor Who* franchise, I can personally validate just how powerful and unbridled that affection can be. To feel the connection that fans have for their favourite show or character is an extraordinary privilege.

Which brings me to the emotional point of this foreword by yours truly. I have been lucky enough to enjoy every aspect of being involved in a television show that reaches across the globe, watched by millions upon millions of devoted followers in dozens of countries. It still thrills me to say that *Doctor Who* is surely among the top five shows ever to earn such a place in people's hearts.

Over the years, countless stories, scripts, and ideas have been lovingly crafted by fans and writers alike, each driven by a deep passion for the world of *Doctor Who.* Yet only a precious few manage to capture that elusive spark – the spirit, heart, and soul of the characters we know and adore.

It was during a convention in 2022 that I had one of those rare moments. A very polite, unassuming lady approached me and asked if I might read her work. I agreed, and what I found was a revelation. Her words had a rare depth and understanding, her storytelling rich with the kind of thoughtfulness and emotional observation that transported me right back to those heady days when Britain led the world in television storytelling.

Her grasp of the characters was remarkable. I was especially touched by her portrayal of my own Sergeant John Benton of UNIT, and the wonderful scene-stealing Damaris Heyman as Miss Hawthorne. Her writing didn't just reflect the show's magic; it honoured it, staying true to the characters while breathing fresh life into their adventures, particularly in *The Daemons*, my favourite *Doctor Who* story of all time.

It is rare to come across a writer who understands the essence of *Doctor Who* so intuitively, and rarer still to see it expressed with such warmth, intelligence, and heartfelt affection.

So, ladies and gentlemen – and just as importantly, the wonderfully well-informed young fans from five to fifteen years old – thank you for continuing to hitch your hearts, your enthusiasm, and your imaginations to the Doctor's TARDIS.

And now, it gives me great pleasure to introduce to you a writer whose passion and talent shine brightly… Miss Lucy McCaul.

John Levene, 2025

To Claire;
Friend, reader, and sharer of adventures.

ᛟᛈᛖᚾ×ᛋᛖᛋᚨᛘᛖ

THE WYVERNS OF ADDERSHALL PARK

ᛏᚺᛁᛋ×ᛁᛋ×ᛄᚢᛋᛏ×ᚦᛖ×ᛒᛖᚷᛁᚾᚾᛁᛝ

BRIGADIER LETHBRIDGE-STEWART looked at the photographs from the file in front of him, spread out across his desk, and sighed impatiently. This hadn't been an easy decision, but the government was breathing down his neck and he felt he had nowhere else to turn. His doubts began to grow again. He was sure she was an intelligent woman – from what Sergeant Benton had said, she could keep her head in a crisis – but if UNIT HQ found out that they had a self-proclaimed witch on staff…? The sound of the intercom interrupted his thoughts.

'Yes?' he said, brusquely.

'Miss Hawthorne is here, sir,' came the reply.

'Right, show her in, Jenkins.'

'Yes, sir.'

The Brigadier shuffled the photos back into the folder and stood up to welcome his visitor. She was slim, grey-haired, and wearing a tweed skirt and jacket, with a polo-necked jumper underneath. A lady in what used to be referred to as her 'middle years'. She had an air of looking beyond her immediate surroundings, as if seeking something just out of reach, which some might interpret as a sign of absent-mindedness, although this would've been a mistake. She approached the desk and stretched out a slim hand to the Brigadier, which he shook.

'Brigadier! Such a surprise to hear from you,' she said. 'I came as soon as I could – once I'd arranged for my neighbour Mrs Brookes to look in on my cat.'

The Brigadier sat down, and gestured to the chair on the other side of his desk. Miss Hawthorne seated herself, placing her large handbag carefully near her feet. The Brigadier raised an eyebrow, remembering what his sergeant had told him she usually kept in the bag. *Must be stronger than she looks,* he thought, but then returned to the business in hand.

'Miss Hawthorne. We find ourselves in a position where... well...' The Brigadier began, then hesitated.

'Yes?' enquired Miss Hawthorne.

The Brigadier tried again. 'We have a case on our hands that is...'

'Yes?' Miss Hawthorne was beginning to wonder what the purpose of this meeting was.

'We have a case that seems to involve your particular... *area of expertise,* and we would be grateful if you would see your way to helping us with it.' There, he'd said it.

'My area of—? You mean *magic*?' asked Miss Hawthorne.

'It would appear so,' said the Brigadier, cautiously.

'Well! You astonish me, Brigadier!' exclaimed Miss Hawthorne. 'I shall, of course, be delighted to help. If you really feel I can be of use, in my unscientific way, that is. If perhaps you could tell me what it is you wish me to help you with...?'

'Thank you, Miss Hawthorne. Are you familiar with the works going on in Essex for the new university?'

'Yes. At least, I had seen it mentioned in the newspaper. Was there not some delay? I believe the paper mentioned that, but didn't say why.'

'Yes, well, they've rather wanted to keep quiet about what's been going on. When I show you, I think you'll see why.' Happier now that the meeting was getting down to brass tacks, the Brigadier opened his folder and turned it so his visitor could see the contents, then spread out the photos.

'It began with these symbols appearing on the building.'

Miss Hawthorne gasped and gripped the amulet she wore on a chain around her neck.

'Black magic,' she whispered.

'Mph. The builders cleaned them off, of course, but the marks kept coming back,' said the Brigadier.

'It would take more than soap and water to cleanse those marks! Did they see who was responsible?' asked Miss Hawthorne, her eyes still on the photographs.

The Brigadier shook his head. 'They appeared overnight. There's a night watchman, but it's a large site and the ground is so churned up from the works, it's impossible to identify specific footprints. The fence was checked, but there was no obvious sign of a break-in. Then, after the symbols came the snakes.'

'Snakes?'

'Adders,' said the Brigadier. 'That part of Essex is known for them, it seems. But they don't usually find their way into upstairs bedrooms.'

'Good grief!'

'The committee overseeing the university was staying over in the main house on site, Addershall Place. They dined together with some local dignitaries, then went up to bed. Each of them found a snake in their room.'

'And was anyone—?' asked Miss Hawthorne, nervously.

'Nobody was bitten, but it gave them all a nasty scare. Local police spoke to staff, but couldn't establish how the things had got there. Then, last week, one of the builders ran into the site office swearing blind that he'd seen a monster in the foundations and refused to go back to work. He was in early, by himself, so there weren't any witnesses. The police thought he must've been drinking; the other builders say he never touches a drop.'

Miss Hawthorne leaned forward to examine the photographs, but at this, she looked up.

'And did the police find any trace of this "monster"?' she asked.

'There were some scratches on the concrete.' The Brigadier pointed out the marks on the photograph. 'And this mark here looks like something was dragged across the fresh cement, so there was certainly something down there. But this builder, one of his friends believed him and went there one evening with a camera. By morning, the poor chap was babbling about a dragon. He did manage to catch this, though…'

The Brigadier pulled a photograph out from under the others. It was blurred and shadowy, but Miss Hawthorne could make out a definite shape: a squat body and long neck; a sharp-looking tail curling around its legs; unmistakable talons; and a horned, reptilian head.

'Great Heavens! That's a wyvern!' she exclaimed. 'Did they catch it?'

'No, but this man's testimony was enough for us to be called in,' the Brigadier explained.

'I see.' Miss Hawthorne looked at the photograph, then back to the Brigadier, 'And how can I be of assistance? It does look as if there might be black magic at work, but, really, I cannot claim any familiarity with snakes or fabulous beasts.' She paused. 'With one exception, obviously.'

The Brigadier smiled, for the first time in the conversation. 'We're of the opinion that someone is either trying to use black magic, or pretending to use it to hold up the university's expansion. The work's already seriously behind schedule; any further delay could lead to it being abandoned completely. That would be a disaster, for a number of reasons I needn't go into now. It's all in the file. It's unclear whether the people behind this believe in magic, but even if they don't, someone's going to a lot of trouble to make it seem like some kind of devilry is at play. You know magic, Miss Hawthorn, and, after that bother at Devil's End, you know our methods too. Do you think you could help us find out who's behind this?'

Miss Hawthorne looked past the Brigadier, seemingly

focused on a spot somewhere through the wall behind him. Then she looked him directly in the eye, with an intensity that took him by surprise.

'Well, I can't promise to solve your mystery, Brigadier,' she said, 'but I will certainly try.'

'Excellent. Thank you, Miss Hawthorne. Now, we can give you an office here, but I imagine you'll be wanting to get down to Essex pretty soon to have a look around. We can have transport arranged for you and a driver who can be on hand, should there be any rough stuff.'

'Heavens, I hope there won't be!' exclaimed Miss Hawthorne.

'So do I, Miss Hawthorne. So do I,' said the Brigadier. 'But one can't be too careful. I wouldn't worry though; the sergeant will look after that side of things.'

'Would that be…?' Miss Hawthorne left her question unfinished.

'Sergeant Benton? As you got on so well at Devil's End, it seems sensible for you to work together again.'

'How delightful! And does he know about our, erm, *mission* yet?'

'Not yet.' A tiny smile quirked the Brigadier's lips. 'I'm about to tell him now.' He pressed a button on his intercom.

'Sir?'

'Send Corporal Scott in please, and get a message to the range for Sergeant Benton to report to me as soon as possible.'

'Yes, sir.'

The Brigadier passed the folder to Miss Hawthorne.

'You'll find all the facts of the matter in here; at least as far as we've been able to establish. Anything else you need, let Corporal Scott know, or call the switchboard. The number's in there.'

'Thank you, Brigadier.' Miss Hawthorne took the folder, then paused. 'May I ask? Will the sergeant and I be acting in an official capacity, or are we – how can I put it? – "undercover," so to speak?'

The Brigadier cleared his throat, trying to resist the mental picture of Miss Hawthorne and Benton as undercover agents.

'Well, for the time being we aren't investigating in an official capacity. The chief constable will be kept informed, but the powers that be are keen to keep a lid on this for as long as they can. You'll be there to gather facts and report back. Any serious developments and we'll get the local police sent in. Or go in ourselves.'

She nodded her understanding and thanked him, before there was a knock on the door. Corporal Scott entered and saluted.

'Ah, Scott,' said the Brigadier, 'take Miss Hawthorne to her office; see she has everything she needs, then get onto transport to arrange an unmarked car for when she's ready to travel.'

'Sir.' The corporal turned smartly and left the room with Miss Hawthorne following her out. As the door closed behind them, the Brigadier leaned back in his chair. One of the benefits of rank, he reflected, was that, when events became as strange as they frequently did at UNIT, you could always pass a fair amount of that strangeness on to your subordinates or advisors. A further knock on the door woke him from this thought. 'Come in.'

The door opened to admit the tall and reassuringly solid form of Sergeant John Benton.

'Ah, Benton, at ease. In fact, you may as well sit down – this'll take a few minutes.'

Miss Hawthorne followed Corporal Scott through the corridors of UNIT HQ, hoping that she'd be able to remember the way out and not wander into anywhere she wasn't supposed to be. Eventually, the corporal stopped at a door that seemed identical to all the others and opened it, standing back to let Miss Hawthorne enter.

'Here we are, ma'am,' she said.

Miss Hawthorne thanked her then paused in the doorway to look around. The 'office' proved to be a medium-sized room that reminded her of a school chemistry laboratory. A blackboard occupied one wall, with a desk and chair in front of it and a workbench running along the wall under the windows, an enamel sink set into one end. Chairs were stacked in rows along the wall opposite the desk. Miss Hawthorne supposed it was an unused briefing room of some sort. She set her handbag down by the desk and Corporal Scott joined her.

'The phone is here, ma'am,' she said, indicating a complicated-looking telephone. 'Just dial 0 for the switchboard.'

'Thank you, Corporal,' said Miss Hawthorne, looking at the phone and hoping she wouldn't have to use it.

'Is there anything else I can get you for the moment?'

'Hmm, let me think a moment... Yes, please. As the sergeant and I will be travelling, ahem, incognito, I think perhaps I'd better arrange for our accommodation myself. Could you find me a guidebook with some addresses for hotels or bed and breakfast establishments near Addershall?' Miss Hawthorne asked.

'Certainly,' said Scott, cheerfully, 'I'll drop it by as soon as I can. There's an untraceable outside line you can use; I'll show you when I get back.'

'Ah, thank you. And, erm, about the cost?'

'You'll get an allowance from the cashier when you're ready to leave to cover the costs – no need to worry about that,' said Corporal Scott, quick to put her new colleague's mind at rest.

'Superb. Thank you. Well, I think that's all I need for the moment. I shall get myself sorted out and then consult the Brigadier's file.'

'Very good, ma'am. I'll fetch that guide and then you can give the switchboard a bell when you're ready.'

Corporal Scott saluted, causing Miss Hawthorne's

eyebrows to shoot up, then left. Miss Hawthorne crossed the room to open a window, then seated herself cautiously at the desk.

'Olive Muriel Hawthorne, what have you got yourself into?' she said, then shook her head. She was there to do a job and do it she would, to the best of her ability. Still, this place was far too stuffy. She reached into her handbag and drew out a small, round stand, followed by her crystal ball. She might not need to use it, but it made her feel at home to have it on the desk. This was followed by a ceramic dish, a bag of dried leaves, and a box of matches. She placed them on the bench near the window, pouring some of the leaves into the dish and then lighting them with a match. As the familiar scent of sage spread through the room, Miss Hawthorne settled herself more comfortably at the desk and opened the file, taking a small notebook and a silver propelling pencil from her pocket. She spread out the photographs and opened a map that was included with them, then leaned forward to examine them more closely, making a note in her book when she found something of particular interest.

A knock at the door turned out to be Corporal Scott, bearing a well-worn but up-to-date guidebook to North Essex.

'Thank you, corporal – that was very quick!'

'No difficulty there, ma'am: Sergeant Beacham is keen on birdwatching and he goes that way camping when he's on leave.'

Scott departed again, leaving Miss Hawthorne with this surprising insight into the life of Sergeant Beacham. Armed with the guidebook, she turned to the map again. She was on the point of reaching for the phone to call for Scott when there was another knock at the door.

'Hallo, Miss Hawthorne,' said Benton, his wide grin making his whole face light up – a joy entirely echoed by the white witch.

'Sergeant! I am pleased to see you. Do come in,' said Miss Hawthorne.

Benton entered, then stopped, coughing. 'Blimey, Miss Hawthorne, what've you been cooking up in here?' he asked.

'Sage, Sergeant, sage. It clears the mind and drives out malign influences,' Miss Hawthorne explained.

'Anything you say, ma'am.' Benton glanced at the desk, the organised chaos of documents, photos, and the map. 'Made any progress?'

'I believe so,' replied Miss Hawthorne, pensively, 'but it'll be easier to tell once we've arrived in Essex. I was about to make the arrangements for our accommodation actually, but I'm unfamiliar with how these things work. Are we to travel under assumed names?'

Benton noticed a slight thrill quavering her voice. 'I don't think so; just not to tell anyone who we work for.'

'Hmm, in that case, we'd better have another reason for our visit.' Miss Hawthorne considered for a moment, then said, 'I'll need to visit some churches and historical sites, so we can say I'm researching family history, or something of that kind. Perhaps I'm writing a book about it.'

'Right, and who am I?' asked Benton.

Miss Hawthorne looked appraisingly at Benton, who would, she thought, never be mistaken for anything other than a soldier, no matter how he was dressed. Then an idea struck her. 'Even these days people don't expect a lady of my age to be able to drive, so perhaps you can be my nephew, escorting me on my visits while on leave from the army.'

'Right!' Benton suppressed a smile. 'Auntie?'

'You'd better call me "Aunt Olive",' replied Miss Hawthorne. 'And you have a first name – I can't very well address you as "Sergeant"!'

'It's, er, John,' said Benton. The conversation had taken a strange turn.

'Good,' said his new aunt, 'that should be easy enough to remember at least. Now, if you can show me how to make a call on this contraption, I'll make the arrangements and then we'd better look at this file together and make our plans.'

The afternoon shift was coming to an end as Bill Murphy set out from the site office on his round. The mud sucked at his boots as he walked, sending his already low mood to flatline.

He muttered an expletive to himself, pausing to withdraw his left boot from a deeper patch. The sun hadn't set yet, but already the evening silence was beginning to settle. Bill walked on, his torch gripped firmly in his right hand, a whistle on a chain bumping on his chest. And that was another thing. Ruddy whistles. Ever since that fool of a chippy had got himself in a tizzy, they'd had to do more patrols and have these things hanging round their necks like ruddy traffic policemen. As if that would help if you got attacked by a monster. Fool was probably half-cut anyway. And he'd roped his mate in to back his story. Dragons, indeed...

A sudden noise on his left made him stop. He caught his breath, then relaxed. Probably a rat. Trouble was, you started hearing things. Then it came again. A hissing, grunting sound, from behind a pile of sacks. Gripping his torch more tightly, Murphy crept towards the sacks, trying to be quiet, and silently cursing the noise made by the mud, slurping around his boots. Closer and closer he crept...

'Flipping 'eck!'

A fox darted out from behind the sacks. Brushing against Murphy's legs as it passed him, it sped off across the site, teeth bared. Murphy shook his fist at the departing animal. And then he saw what it was that had made the fox run, and began to run himself. He blew on the whistle, again and again, the thumping of his pulse in his ears and the noise of his feet in the mud drowning out any sound of the creature behind him, but he knew it was there. At last, nearing the edge of the foundations, he turned to look and fell, his feet sliding from under him. The creature leapt at him and the world went black.

*

'There, that must be the park, Sergeant,' said Miss Hawthorne, pointing to a turning marked with a temporary sign.

'Yes, it looks like it from the... *hang on*!'

The car braked suddenly as an ambulance came around the corner ahead, lights flashing and siren blaring. Miss Hawthorne looked at Benton in alarm.

'Oh dear, do you think...?' She didn't finish the sentence.

'I'm not sure, but I'd better report it,' said Benton. 'I'll just pull over; there's a lay-by just up there.'

Benton parked the car and Miss Hawthorne got out, wanting to stretch her legs and get a sense of the place they'd come to. Benton opened the glove compartment, which contained a small radio set, a feature of all UNIT unmarked vehicles.

'Greyhound Four, calling Trap One. Greyhound Four calling Trap One, are you receiving? Over.'

'Receiving you, Greyhound Four. Go ahead, over,' said the voice of Corporal Scott.

'Have just seen an ambulance leaving Addershall Park in a hurry, over.'

There was a muffled crackling and the Brigadier's voice came through the speaker.

'Thank you, Benton. Any other signs of trouble? Over.'

'Not so far, sir, but I thought I'd better report it. Over.'

'Quite right. I'll check with the chief constable and update you as soon as possible. Meanwhile, carry on as planned. Over.'

'Yessir, out.' Benton replaced the handset and closed the glovebox. Hearing the end of the conversation, Miss Hawthorne got back into the car. 'Well, Sergeant, I hope we aren't too late,' she said, with concern.

'So do I, Miss Hawthorne,' replied Benton. 'So do I. Let's get to the hotel first, then we can take stock.'

'I agree. We'll be able to think more clearly once we've settled in and had some refreshments.'

*

The hotel in Addershall village was adequate, if a little old-fashioned. As befitted their roles of aunt and nephew, Miss Hawthorne went to the reception to announce their arrival, while Benton parked the car and got the luggage out of the boot. He came in as Miss Hawthorne was taking the room keys from the owner.

'Ah, John, there you are. Mrs Hobbs was just explaining about dinner and lunches; she can give us a packed lunch for our adventures,' she said.

'Oh, good, thank you – that'll be ideal,' said Benton, smiling.

'If you'll follow me, Miss Hawthorne and Mr…?' said Mrs Hobbs.

'Benton.'

'I'll show you to your rooms. Two bedrooms and a sitting room, like you asked for.'

Miss Hawthorne's cover story popped into her mind. 'You're very kind. And if I might impose on you again…? My publisher may call this evening about an urgent matter; I took the liberty of giving him your number.'

Mrs Hobbs assured her that she'd let them know if she received such a call as they crossed the lobby, passing an elderly man who was seated in a battered armchair near the desk.

'That yore car out there, boy?' he said, in a quavering voice.

'Yes, well, it's a hired job,' said Benton.

'Ah, flash job. Thought yew mighter been one a' them from the paark,' the old man went on.

'The park? Oh, you mean the university?' asked Benton.

'Yewniversity? Pah!' He almost spat the word out.

'Now, Dad, don't go on at our guests like that,' Mrs Hobbs cut in quickly and ushered her customers away from the lobby. 'I'm sorry about that. Dad's set in his ways and doesn't like change, especially close to home.'

'That's understandable,' said Miss Hawthorne in calming

tones. 'He must've seen a lot of changes in his day.'

Mrs Hobbs relaxed a bit and nodded her agreement.

'If I may, I'd like to interview him later? Nothing formal, you understand, but I feel sure he might know things that would be a tremendous help with my book.'

'Oh, well, if you think so. Is your book about Essex then?'

'Yes, I have a particular interest in folklore and local history. I gather from my research that this area was once well-known for witchcraft!'

As Miss Hawthorne said this, she looked sharply at Mrs Hobbs. Was there the tiniest flicker in her hostess' eyes? Nonetheless, their hostess didn't comment so Hawthorne pressed ahead. 'In any case, I want to consult the parish registers and look at the church – it seems charming and very interesting, at least from the description in the guidebook,' she said.

Mrs Hobbs seemed to relax again. 'You'll find plenty to interest you in there,' she said, stopping outside a couple of doors. 'Right, here we are. Dinner at half past six, remember – down the stairs and turn right in the lobby for the dining room.'

'Thank you.'

As Mrs Hobbs bustled away, Benton and Miss Hawthorne exchanged meaningful glances.

'I reckon you put the wind up her properly when you mentioned witches,' said Benton.

'Looks as if the case is closer to home than we might've thought,' she agreed. 'In any case, we must get ready for dinner.'

'Yes, see you later… Auntie!'

Benton went into his room and closed the door quickly before Miss Hawthorne could reply.

The dining room was, like the rest of the hotel, clean but old-fashioned. The tables and chairs were made of a dark, heavy wood and there were garnet-coloured, tasseled shades on the lamps and wall lights, which lent a slightly ghoulish air to the room. *On the other hand,* Miss Hawthorne thought, *given the lurid pattern on Sergeant Benton's tie, perhaps subdued lighting is desirable.* Was it being in uniform all his working life that made him want to indulge in such bright colours when in civvies? She contemplated the dessert, an uninspiring mixture of jelly and tinned fruit cocktail, but her train of thought was interrupted by her hostess.

'There's a call for you, Miss Hawthorne,' said Mrs Hobbs, quietly.

Miss Hawthorne thanked her, put down her napkin, and followed Mrs Hobbs to the lobby. The telephone was in a small booth near the reception desk. Miss Hawthorne went in and picked up the receiver, pulling the door closed behind her.

'Hello?'

'Ah, Miss Hawthorne, Lethbridge-Stewart here,' said the Brigadier.

'How good of you to call, Mr Stewart!'

'I've spoken to the chief constable; there's been an attack on the site. One of the security guards was chased and mauled by… *something*. He survived, but had to be sedated at the hospital, so he hasn't been questioned yet.'

'Ah, thank you for confirming that,' said Miss Hawthorne. There was nobody else in the lobby, but she thought it wise to maintain their cover story at all times. Nonetheless, she whispered, 'We must hope he makes a speedy recovery.'

'Yes,' agreed the Brigadier, 'and, in the meantime, the sooner you can get to work…'

'Of course,' said Miss Hawthorne. 'I shall be visiting the church tomorrow. John may go to the pub later, if he isn't too tired after the drive, but I shall be getting an early night.'

'I see. I never thought I'd say this, but the sooner Benton gets to the pub, the better! Get all the local gossip…' In his office, the Brigadier grinned wryly.

Miss Hawthorne smiled too. 'Quite. Thank you, Mr Stewart.'

'Good luck, Miss Hawthorne. Oh, and it's *Lethbridge*-Stewart.'

'Oh!'

'Report in as often as you can.'

'Yes, of course. Goodbye, Mr Stewart,' said Miss Hawthorne, before hanging up.

By the time Miss Hawthorne returned to the dining room, the dessert bowls had been cleared and coffee brought around. She looked at the contents of her cup and decided not to take a chance.

'All sorted out, Aunt Olive?' asked Benton.

'Oh yes, Mr Stewart has cleared the matter up for me.' Miss Hawthorne picked up her handbag and stifled a yawn ostentatiously. 'And now, I think I'll go to bed. It's been a long day.'

'Right you are,' said Benton. 'I think I'll go see what the local's like.'

'Don't be too late. You've driven a long way today,' said Miss Hawthorne, in what she considered to be the proper familial tone.

Benton avoided her eyes, trying not to laugh.

They parted company at their bedroom doors, Miss Hawthorne to make plans for the following day and Benton to change into a more casual outfit before heading off to find a pub.

The Spread Eagle on Addershall's main avenue seemed a likely place to find what Benton was after; that is, the word on the street (and a pint or two). The front door was propped open and a warm yellow light flooded out onto the drive. A couple of cars were parked at the front and four or five bicycles, in various stages of decrepitude, were propped against the wall under the windows. Benton could hear the sound of chatter, laughter, and argument coming from inside.

He walked in and wasn't surprised when an awkward silence fell. The men seated at the bar turned to look at the newcomer and he met their gaze directly as he walked over to order. Having listened to him ask for a pint of the local ale, the regulars seemed to lose interest and the chatter resumed as he made his way over to a vacant table near the door. Putting his glass down carefully on the sticky table, he wedged himself onto the bench behind it, so he was facing the room, then pulled one of Sergeant Osgood's birdwatching books out of his pocket. To all appearances, he'd buried himself in its contents. Of course, he was instead soaking up all that was happening around him.

He heard about post being wrongly delivered. A Mrs Cameron was getting up a petition about local bus routes. Three gentlemen were bemoaning what was on TV these days. Another was enthusing about a James Bond film he'd seen recently, and was particularly enamoured of Jane Seymour. If he could, Benton would've told the naïf chap that field-work wasn't always that exciting. With that in mind, he soon drained his glass and set his mind to getting an early night, thinking the evening a bust.

The sound of a stool scraping on the floor made him look up. A thickset man in his thirties was standing by the table. He wore overalls, and Benton noticed dried mud on his heavy, steel-toed boots. Without waiting for an invitation, he plonked his pint glass down on the table and sat down on the stool. Benton waited for him to speak.

'You staying up at the hotel then?' the man asked.

'Yeah.' (Why make it easy for him?)

'First time here?'

Benton nodded. 'My aunt's writing a book and I had some leave, so I said I'd help her out with the driving.'

'Writing a book, eh? What about?' the man asked, with a hint of suspicion.

'Oh, local history and legends and so on. She's got a bee in her bonnet about there being witches round here,' said Benton, calmly.

He glanced back down at his book; even so, his eyes caught a movement near the bar and he heard a sharp intake of breath somewhere close by.

'I mean, it's barmy, right? But her publisher likes it, so…'

He shrugged.

The other man seemed to have made a decision, and stretched out his hand. 'Tom Mullins.'

'John Benton.'

'Good to meet you, John. And what are you doing while your aunt's chasing witches?'

Under normal circumstances, Benton would've told him to mind his own business, but these weren't normal circumstances. Instead, he held up the book.

'Thought I'd have a go at this. One of the chaps is crackers about it and said this was a good place to start. Gave me a few tips.'

He looked at his watch and stood up. 'Anyway, I'd better get back.'

'See you again then?' said Mullins.

'Expect so,' said Benton, deliberately non-committal.

'Right, well, if you get bored of the birds,' Mullins dropped his voice, 'I might be able to help you out. Got some things you can *help with* around here. Maybe earn a bit on the side while your aunt's gallivanting about.'

Benton sat down again, slowly.

'How'd you mean?' he asked.

'Oh, never mind that for now – we can talk about it later. Just keep it in mind,' said Mullins, getting up from his seat.

Benton left the pub, his mind racing. What exactly was Mullins suggesting? Something underhanded for certain, or he wouldn't have been so cagey about it. From the look of him, he worked on the building site. Could it have something to do with the case, or was some other dodgy business going on? Either way, it was worth looking into. Mustn't seem too keen though. Leave it for tonight.

This train of thought took him to the door of the hotel. He let himself in with the night key he'd been given and closed the front door quietly behind him, then headed upstairs. Seeing a light under Miss Hawthorne's door, he tapped gently. A sudden rustling noise in the corridor made him turn around. It was Mrs Hobbs, in a nightdress and dressing gown, with a torch in her hand.

'You found your way back all right then, Mr Benton?' she asked.

'Yes, thanks, Mrs Hobbs. Just letting my aunt know I'm back. She likes to sit up reading,' replied Benton.

They bid each other good night, and Benton, presuming his co-conspirator hadn't heard him, went into his room, locking the door firmly behind him. Really, there was nothing unusual about a hotel owner checking on their guests at night, but he felt somehow disturbed at Mrs Hobbs' sudden appearance in the corridor. Benton wasn't the type to get scared or uneasy, but, somehow, the events in the pub and the nature of the case, together with his encounter in the corridor, added up to something he didn't like at all. Hoping that nothing would happen in the night, he got into bed and turned out the lamp. In the morning, he'd have plenty to tell Miss Hawthorne. Or rather, Aunt Olive.

And with a smile, he turned on his side and was soon snoring.

The darkened room was lit by a single lamp. A pale hand held a telephone receiver, one finger bearing a heavy silver ring with a curious design engraved on it.

'And he came back in before midnight?' said a cold, female voice.

'Yes, he just went to the pub. Arthur Wilkins saw him there.' Another female voice, younger and warmer in tone.

'Good. Perhaps we needn't worry about him. What about her?'

'She went up early, but her light was still on when he came in,' came the reply.

'But she hadn't gone out?' the first voice asked, insistently.

'No, I would've seen her,' said the second.

'Good, we must make sure that she learns nothing. Even if she's not here to snoop, we can't risk anything. We're so close, once more. They'll be gone and we'll have won. You must watch them carefully.'

'Yes, sister, I will.'

The pale hand put the receiver back in its cradle. And at the hotel, Mrs Hobbs hung up the phone on her bedside table and switched off the light.

Breakfast at the hotel proved to be as underwhelming as the dinner of the previous evening. Miss Hawthorne restricted herself to tea and toast and Benton, having started on what was described as a full English, was beginning to wish that he'd done the same. After breakfast, they repaired to the sitting room, and, having made sure the door was locked and drawn the draught excluder across to muffle any sounds, Benton brought Miss Hawthorne up to date with what had occurred the previous evening.

'How interesting,' she said, thoughtfully. 'I feel sure that there are dark witches here. The Doctor wouldn't trust my intuition, I'm sure, but I can feel evil at work. And the evidence seems to confirm my suspicions.'

'Certainly looks that way – there's something fishy going on at that site or I'm a Dutchman. You think there's a connection between these "wyverns", witchcraft, and whatever it is Mullins is up to?' asked Benton.

'It seems an unlikely coincidence,' she replied and the pair fell into silence as they ruminated on the possibility (and how surprisingly comfy the chairs were). Miss Hawthorne pulled them out of this reverie: 'I must be going. I've an appointment to interview the vicar at ten.'

'Shall I run you down there in the car?'

'No, I think I'll walk; the church seems to be quite close on the map, and one never knows what one might see in a village.'

'Then I'll get on with some "birdwatching",' said Benton with a smile.

'Yes, but do be careful, Sergeant,' said Miss Hawthorne.

'Don't worry; I'm known for my *swift* reactions,' he said with a wink that was met with raised eyebrows. 'Are we getting lunch from here?'

'It seems churlish to refuse... but, after breakfast and last night, I can't say I'm tempted. I gather from the guidebook that there's a tearoom in the village – suppose we meet there at three, then we can make up for lunch, or lay in supplies in case dinner is a repeat of last night?'

'Sounds good to me. We'd better get going then, hadn't we?'

'Indeed. You've got the offending documents in case you need them?'

Benton patted his jacket pocket. 'All safe!' he said.

'Excellent. Good hunting, Sergeant!'

They left the sitting room and went downstairs to the lobby to collect their packed lunches. Miss Hawthorne tucked hers away in her handbag; Benton put his in a BOAC flight bag that he'd slung over one shoulder. With binoculars around his neck, a folding stool in one hand, and one of Beacham's bird books poking out of his pocket, he hoped that he looked enough like a trainee twitcher to pass muster with any onlookers.

Miss Hawthorne and Benton parted on the hotel drive, she to walk down to the church and he to the fields that were opposite, but not too close to, the building site.

The air was pleasantly warm that day and Miss Hawthorne enjoyed her walk, listening to the birdsong and feeling the breeze on her face. The church of Saint Osgyth was set back from the avenue, surrounded by a brick and flint wall. Miss Hawthorne passed through the beautiful lychgate and the churchyard, noting with interest the dates on some of the tombs and headstones. The church itself was typical of the area, a rectangular building with a short tower and spire and a tiled roof. From her research, Miss Hawthorne had learned that it'd been constructed in Norman times, and retained many of its original architectural features, although, sadly, the wall paintings that would've adorned the interior had been painted out in a less enlightened age. Miss Hawthorne sighed at the thought of this historical vandalism, but then smiled as she saw the vicar waiting to greet her in the porch.

'Miss Hawthorne?' he said, exuding warmth.

'Yes, thank you so much for meeting me,' replied Miss Hawthorne. 'I know you must be a very busy man.'

'I'm always happy to greet visitors if I can. Welcome to Addershall and to Saint Osygth's!'

After her unfortunate experience with the alleged Reverend Magister at Devil's End, Miss Hawthorne had got into the habit of looking closely at any men of the cloth she encountered. The Reverend Butterworth, however, appeared to be an unthreatening example of his kind. Small of stature and wiry of build, with thinning fair hair and wire framed glasses, he smiled up at Miss Hawthorne as he held out his hand to her.

'Do come in. I gather you're interested in our witches and mythical monsters?'

'Well! News travels fast around here, I must say.' In her call to the vicarage, Miss Hawthorne had only mentioned wanting to look at the parish registers; clearly the village gossip mill was as lively in Addershall as it was in Devil's End.

'You must excuse my flock. Having an author arrive to research here is something of a novelty – some of them have got a little over-excited perhaps,' said the vicar apologetically.

Miss Hawthorne smiled. 'No harm done!' she assured Reverend Butterworth. 'I should probably have "come clean," as the young people say, when I spoke to you on the phone. I was worried that you might resent my incursion if you knew what my actual interest was. I can assure you that I'm intending to treat the victims of the Witchfinder General's campaign with the utmost sympathy and that my interest in wyverns' – she looked sharply at the vicar, but he seemed untroubled by this reference – 'and other local myths is purely academic and founded in an interest in how stories become part of local culture.'

'My dear Miss Hawthorne, you need not excuse yourself to me. Working in a rural parish, one becomes acquainted with all manner of tall tales and strange events that would make my urban colleagues' eyes water! I was only going to say, if you're interested in the local mythology, you should speak to Miss Forster, the librarian. She has that knowledge at her fingertips, not only in the library, but also in her personal collection. I'm sure she'd be delighted to answer any questions you may have.'

'Oh, that's most kind,' said Miss Hawthorne, 'I shall certainly look in there; I believe I passed it on my way down the avenue.'

'Yes, on the left, just after the Co-operative,' said Butterworth.

Her host ushered her towards a table, where several large volumes had been laid out. 'Now, I presume you'll want to look at the registers,' he said. 'I have them for you here.'

'Thank you,' agreed Miss Hawthorne, 'I've the names of some of the women persecuted by Hopkins and his ilk. I should like to find out if they were registered in this parish and whether they had any descendants who may still be in the area.'

This time, there was a definite reaction. The vicar flinched, ever so slightly, but recovered himself quickly.

'I wish you success with your search,' he said. 'If you don't mind me leaving you to it?' He gestured vaguely towards the lectern and altar, where preparations for a service were clearly underway.

'Not at all!'

Miss Hawthorne took her notebook and pencil out of her bag and turned to the page where she'd listed the names of the women who had been accused of witchcraft in the time of the Witchfinder General.

Alys Byrd, spinster, died 18th October 1630. Mary Cross, married, 17th September 1625 to … Matthew Foryster.

Miss Hawthorne made a note, turned to the deaths columns, and saw it listed as 1645. 'So, there could've been children,' she muttered to herself and continued to skim the records.

Her face lit up as she found what she was looking for: 'Aha!'

Henry Forÿster born 21st April 1626 … married to Elizabeth Greene … died December 1687… children?

'Mind you,' she continued under her breath, 'the plague must've taken a toll…'

Elizabeth and Arthur, born October 1641.

'Twins – good Heavens!'

Elizabeth married to Charles Rainbird … Arthur married to… Anne Hobbes.

'Hobbes. That's interesting.'

Miss Hawthorne worked her way through the registers, painstakingly tracing the Foryster family members and sketching a family tree in her notebook. While scanning records from the late eighteenth century, she spotted an interesting, if not entirely unexpected, development.

John Forster married to Mary Clegghorn.

Forster. Changes in names weren't uncommon, but what could that mean? Her interest sharpened, Miss Hawthorne carried on her exploration, following the Forster family through the nineteenth and finally into the twentieth century until she found:

Forster, Enid Elizabeth Alice, born 14th March 1920.

No sign of a marriage. So, if this were the Miss Forster from the library, that would mean that she was a descendant of one of the Addershall witches! And that could, Miss Hawthorne admitted to herself, mean nothing at all, but she had to start somewhere and the library was worth a visit in any case. She glanced at her watch. Half past twelve. The library would be closed for lunch, but that would still leave her time for a visit before meeting Benton for tea at three.

Miss Hawthorne closed the registers and put away her notebook, smiling to the vicar as she rose from her seat. 'Thank you so much for your time, Mr Butterworth – it's been most interesting,' she said. 'May I eat my sandwiches in your churchyard? I think I saw a bench on my way in…'

'You'd be most welcome to, Miss Hawthorne,' replied Butterworth. 'Have you managed to complete your research?'

'Plenty for the time being, at any rate,' said Miss Hawthorne, watching her host carefully. 'This village seems rather magical.'

Again, a slight twitch under the vicar's left eye betrayed him, but, as before, he recovered swiftly, and said, 'I'm glad to hear it.' He ushered Miss Hawthorne out of the door and locked it with an imposing iron key.

The vicar and Miss Hawthorne made their way through the churchyard to the bench. Behind the tower, Miss Hawthorne noticed a patch of ground where the turf appeared to have been scorched.

'Ah, I see your grounds man has had a bonfire. I must think about that myself when I get home; the leaves do pile up so,' she remarked.

'Er, yes, yes, quite. Well, good afternoon, Miss Hawthorne,' he said, inexplicably flustered.

'Good afternoon!' said Miss Hawthorne, pretending not to notice.

Miss Hawthorne sat down on the bench and reached into her bag for her lunch. As soon as the vicar was out of sight, she got up again and went back to the site of the alleged bonfire. Why should the vicar be so nervous about it? There wasn't a law against bonfires, even in churchyards.

Miss Hawthorne bent to inspect the ground. If there were bonfires here, they were frequent, her experience told her that the ground had been burnt repeatedly and recently too. Not wishing to arouse the suspicions of passers-by, she returned to the bench and to her lunch, which proved to be as unappetizing as she'd feared it would be. She abandoned the curly-edged cheese sandwich and made do with the apple, wondering, as she bit into it, how Benton had been getting on.

After he'd left Miss Hawthorne on the hotel drive, Benton had strolled off in the direction of the park. He whistled as he walked down the path at the edge of the fields, enjoying the fresh air and the rustle of the breeze through the wheat. Having reached what he felt was an adequate distance from the village, he unfolded his stool and sat down in the shelter of the hedge. He took Beacham's book out of his pocket, and a notebook and pencil out of his bag and laid them on the ground next to the stool, to be picked up quickly in case anyone came past. These preparations made, he took his binoculars out of their case and, finding a handy gap in the hedge, trained them on the building site. The binoculars looked like an ordinary pair that might've been carried by any birdwatcher, but were actually considerably more powerful.

As far as Benton could see, it looked much as any building site did. Scaffolding had been erected and work was going on all over, with the exception of an area surrounded by police tape, presumably where the attack had taken place. So far, so normal.

Benton moved slightly to look at the perimeter of the park, which also looked much as could be expected – until he spotted a dark coloured van, parked in a lay-by, with two men standing near the bonnet, deep in conversation. This wasn't, in itself, particularly suspicious. They might be lost, or delivering to the site, but the van was unmarked and there wasn't a map spread out. Benton focused on the faces of the men and realised that one of them was his new friend from the pub.

Benton put the binoculars back in their case and the bird book back in his pocket. He picked up his notebook and took a small hikers' map out of the bag and unfolded it. Time to get a bit closer to the action. Benton stepped through a bigger gap in the hedge and onto the road. He walked towards the van with his eyes fixed on his map, apparently oblivious to the van and the men. He hadn't got far when he was tapped on the shoulder. Benton gave a start and dropped both the map and the book.

'Gordon Bennett!' he exclaimed.

'Sorry, mate; didn't mean to make you jump,' said Mullins.

'Do you always creep up on people like that?' Benton asked, crossly.

Benton bent down and picked up his belongings. As he did so, a slip of paper fell out of the book and fluttered down to the road. He grabbed at it hastily, but was beaten to it by Mullins, who stepped back out of Benton's reach.

'Been having a bit of bad luck with the horses, have we?' asked Mullins.

'That's none of your business!' snapped Benton. He made to snatch the paper again, but Mullins dodged him.

'Given any thought to my invitation from last night?' he asked. Benton, looking flustered, just stared back at him, so Mullins continued: 'I could put a bit of work your way. If you're interested. Looks like you could do with the cash.' Mullins gave the betting slip back to Benton, who stuffed it into his pocket.

'All right, so what? There's no law against having a flutter, is there?' he said, huffily.

'Not that I know of, mate. How about it? Fancy earning some quick dough? For one night's work?' Mullins' voice was smooth.

Benton took a moment to consider the offer. 'Is it on the level though? If my C.O. found out…'

'And what if he found out about the horses, eh? Don't suppose he'd be impressed,' said Mullins.

Benton scowled, but nervously. 'Okay, okay, you've got me. What do you want me to do?' he asked.

'Oh, it's easy,' said Mullins, airily. 'Me and the lads are shifting some stuff off the site tonight, and we need a lookout who can handle himself. We've got some help for a distraction, but we need a bloke to keep an eye out for trouble while we work. Cash in hand once we've finished. You in?'

Benton looked troubled. His shoulders sagged. Then he sighed. 'Yeah, okay, I'm in. When do we start?'

'After dark. Meet me back here at nine and bring a torch,' Mullins said, briskly.

'Right,' said Benton.

'Good man,' Mullins said, then clapped Benton on the back and went back over to his van, signalling an end to the conversation. Benton turned and walked back towards the village, a slow smile coming over his face. *Got 'em. Hook, line, and sinker.*

Having spent a diverting, if not particularly productive, time examining the inscriptions in Saint Osgyth's churchyard, Miss Hawthorne made her way to the library. This was a modern-looking building, with large windows and a flat roof, somewhat at odds with the slightly calamitous but warm feel of the village. The afternoon sunlight flooded through the windows onto the metal shelving within.

Inside, an argument, or at least a ticking off, appeared to be taking place. A woman in her mid-fifties was seated at the enquiry desk. Her wiry, grey hair was pulled back in a plait and she wore a black, polo-necked jumper. A tweed jacket, similar to Miss Hawthorne's own, hung on the back of her chair. Miss Hawthorne couldn't see if she was wearing an identical skirt, but imagined this to be the case. The woman was glaring at a younger woman with dark hair and glasses, clad in a cheese-cloth shirt and well-tailored slacks, who was standing on the opposite side of the desk.

'May I remind you, Miss Wilson, that trousers are *not* considered appropriate attire for female members of the library staff? I won't send you home to change, but don't let it happen again!' the older woman said in a cold, sharp voice.

'No, Miss Forster,' replied the younger woman.

Dreadful old bat, thought Miss Hawthorne, then had to suppress a smile; clearly Sergeant Benton's vocabulary was rubbing off on her. Pretending that she hadn't heard any of the previous conversation, she walked into the library and trilled, 'Good afternoon!' in her cheeriest voice. The women at the desk turned to look at her, Miss Wilson with a naturally cheerful expression, Miss Forster attempting to transform her scowl into a smile, with limited success.

Miss Wilson spoke first: 'Welcome to the library! How may we help?'

'Thank you. If you'd be so kind as to guide me to your local history section…?' replied Miss Hawthorne.

'This way,' said Miss Wilson, gesturing to her right.

Miss Hawthorne followed her towards the back of the library. The local history section covered two bays of shelves against the back wall.

'Here it is. This is the general Essex section, then there's Rowchester town, and here are the books about Addershall,' said Miss Wilson, pointing out the relevant shelves.

'Thank you. Have you any maps?' asked Miss Hawthorne.

'There are some local maps here, and the OS are on the shelf by the window.'

'Thank you very much. I must say…' Miss Hawthorne glanced across at the enquiry desk where Miss Forster was glaring balefully at her computer screen. '…I do like your outfit. I couldn't carry it off at my age, but it looks so smart and must be very comfortable and practical for work.'

Miss Wilson grinned widely. 'Thank you! If you need anything else, I'll be over there.' She gestured towards a shelf where a half-empty trolley showed that she had shelving to do. 'Or ask at the enquiry desk.'

Miss Hawthorne thanked her and put her handbag on a chair.

She went to look at the shelves. The books were much as she expected them to be: no contemporary historical texts, but plenty of pictorial works and a few more scholarly tomes. She selected a couple of volumes and a local map and sat down at a nearby desk, taking out her notebook and pencil. She read steadily for about a quarter of an hour, making occasional notes. The histories of Addershall and Addershall Park were fascinating to her without her additional particular interest, and she always enjoyed the atmosphere of a library and the chance to consult works that were new to her.

Miss Forster came over, apparently feeling that she needed to make up for her unfortunate first impression. 'Are you finding everything you need?' she asked, in what she evidently hoped were friendly tones.

Miss Hawthorne looked up. Her eye was instantly drawn to the ring on Miss Forster's right hand. She suppressed a gasp when she recognised the design. It was a sigil. A sign of black magic. So she'd been right in her supposition. She hid her concern and smiled.

'You really do have some excellent books here. Of course, one can't expect to find original historical texts, but this section really is most helpful. I should introduce myself. My name is Olive Hawthorne and I—'

'Yes, Mr Butterworth called,' replied Miss Forster. 'He said you'd be visiting us.'

Did he, indeed? 'That was kind of him. He told me that you were the person to speak to about the local folklore.'

Miss Forster smiled. 'He flatters me, I fear,' she said, with a false modesty that made Miss Hawthorne wince inside, 'but I do have quite a collection of works about our local myths and legends. One or two of them go back to the seventeenth century.'

'Goodness!' Miss Hawthorne didn't need to feign her surprise.

'I wonder, would you care to come and see them?' Miss Forster suggested, as if the idea had just come to her. 'I'm free this evening and I'd be honoured to show them to a fellow historian, especially one who's so interested in our little community.'

Miss Hawthorne didn't want to appear too eager. 'I'd be imposing...'

'Nonsense! It would be my pleasure. I know you are staying up at the hotel.' Was there anything, Miss Hawthorne wondered, that the inhabitants of Addershall didn't know about their visitors? 'And Agatha serves dinner at half past six, doesn't she? So shall we say... eight o'clock?'

'That would be delightful. Thank you so much,' said Miss Hawthorne.

'That's settled then! I'd better give you my address.' Miss Hawthorne proffered her notebook and Miss Forster scribbled away, even sketching a small map showing how to find the house from the avenue. 'It's not far from here.'

'I'll ask my nephew to bring me in the car. I'm sure we'll have no trouble finding you.'

With a cheery adieu, Miss Forster returned to the enquiry desk and Miss Hawthorne looked at her watch. Half past two. Well, she could take a leisurely stroll down to the tearoom, but she should probably put in another fifteen minutes or so with these books. She turned to a fresh page in her notebook and pulled the map towards her.

The tearoom, *The Country Cottage*, proved to be a small but welcoming establishment, run by a capable young woman with the assistance of a lanky boy and a giggly girl. The food was a definite improvement on the meagre fare at the hotel, and Benton and Miss Hawthorne tucked into excellent sandwiches and freshly baked scones.

When he'd taken the edge off his hunger, Benton sat back with a sigh. 'That's more like it!' he said.

Miss Hawthorne smiled at him, but commented with what she felt was an appropriately aunt-like tone: 'Now, John, we mustn't be greedy! But I must admit, our hostess could learn some valuable lessons from here.'

'Not half!' Benton grinned at her. 'Did you have a good time at the church?'

'Yes, the vicar was most welcoming and I made real progress with the registers. Then I visited the library, and the librarian's invited me to her home tonight to look at some of her rare books.'

'Really?' Benton's eyebrows went up. 'Are you going to go?'

Reading the question within the question, Miss Hawthorne nodded. 'It's seems too good an opportunity to miss. If you don't mind running me down there later on?'

'Of course not!' said Benton.

'Thank you, dear,' Miss Hawthorne said, causing Benton to smile. 'Now I've talked enough about my day; how was yours?'

'Oh, pretty quiet. Didn't see many birds,' he said. 'I don't know how Beacham sticks at it for all that time. But I did have a bit of excitement.'

'Oh? You must tell me all about it on our way back. I'll settle up and we can be on our way.' She caught the waitress' eye and asked for the bill. On the walk back to the hotel, Benton told Miss Hawthorne about his meeting with Mullins and their arrangement for that night.

'And he didn't suspect anything?' she asked.

'I don't think so. I reckon he was just looking for a mug who he could leave in the soup, who wouldn't be able to identify his gang.' She considered this and nodded, then Benton went on: 'And what about the church? Did you find anything out?'

Miss Hawthorne gave him the details of her discoveries. By the time she'd finished, they'd reached the hotel.

Mrs Hobbs handed over their keys, and, seeing them both deep in thought, said, 'why, what's got into you two? You look as if you'd lost a pound and found a sixpence!'

Recalled to their roles, Miss Hawthorne smiled at her hostess. 'Not at all! It's been a very good day, but tiring. I'm sure we'll feel better after dinner,' she said, at which Benton suffered a sudden coughing fit.

Having changed for dinner, Miss Hawthorne and Benton met briefly in the sitting room to confirm their plans for the evening. Benton had nipped out earlier to a phone box to update the Brigadier and had received confirmation that UNIT troops would be ready to respond at a moment's notice and that, if no updates had been received by ten o'clock, they'd move in anyway.

Once the plans were confirmed, Miss Hawthorne did something which surprised her as much as Benton; perhaps it was the time they'd spent together that made her feel as if she and Benton really were related, but she placed a slim hand on top of one of his large, muscular mitts. 'Do take care, John,' she said, earnestly. 'If these people are prepared to use black magic as a diversion, they must be utterly ruthless.'

Benton, equally surprised at himself, squeezed her fingers briefly. 'You too "Auntie". I don't like the sound of that librarian at all. Or the vicar.'

There was a brief silence. Then Miss Hawthorne rose from her chair.

'Well, it won't do any good to meet trouble halfway – we'd better go and see what delights Mrs Hobbs has in store for us...'

Dinner passed largely in silence, a plate of chewy casserole and lumpy mashed potatoes followed by yet more tinned fruit cocktail. Having endured the after-dinner coffee, which was brown but singularly lacking in either flavour or caffeine, Miss Hawthorne and Benton returned to their rooms to get ready for the rest of the evening. They met again on the landing, Miss Hawthorne in her tweed suit, with handbag slung over one arm, and Benton in dark trousers, a jumper, scarf, and a bomber jacket, with a torch bulging in one pocket. A slight distortion of the material under his left arm told Miss Hawthorne that he was taking no chances.

They drove the short distance to Miss Forster's house in silence, Miss Hawthorne's notebook propped on the dashboard so Benton could follow the map. Miss Forster was looking out of the window as they pulled up. Miss Hawthorne got out of the car and turned to go up the drive, until Benton called out 'Aunt Olive! You'll want your notebook!' He leaned over from the driver's seat to pass it to her, his jacket falling open as he did so. Miss Forster turned from the window abruptly and went to open the door to her visitor. Miss Hawthorne turned to wave to Benton, then walked up the drive, steeling herself for what might come and fixing a smile on her face to greet her host.

'Miss Hawthorne, do come in!' she said.

Miss Hawthorne returned her smile and thanked her. Miss Forster closed the door behind her guest and ushered her into what was clearly her study. She gestured to a wing-backed chair, and busied herself with pouring sherry from a bottle which she fetched from a cupboard below the bookshelves.

'Oh, thank you,' said Miss Hawthorne, accepting her glass and raising it to toast her hostess. As she did so, she noticed a slight sediment in the glass, that spoiled the usual clarity of the sherry. Had it corked? Or was it…? While Miss Forster's back was turned, she raised the glass to her nose. Her long experience of herbs and distillation of remedies had sharpened Miss Hawthorne's sense of smell. As Miss Forster turned back to face her, Miss Hawthorne put the glass to her lips as if to drink, but kept her lips closed.

'I don't indulge often, but I do like a good sherry,' she enthused.

'Ah excellent. Now, let's look at my books and see what I have that will be useful to you.'

Miss Forster's collection was, indeed, impressive. Volumes of all sizes, some clearly of great age, bound in leather or in vellum, lined the walls of the study. Atlases of the ancient and modern worlds, books about myths and legends and on archaeology; works on natural medicine, including a massive tome on sixteenth century herbal remedies, and a series of small books with spines decorated with symbols that left Miss Hawthorne in no doubt as to the contents.

Miss Forster selected a seventeenth century bestiary and passed it to Miss Hawthorne.

'Oh, this is wonderful.' Miss Hawthorne set down her sherry glass and began to turn the pages, genuinely thrilled by the contents. She lighted on a picture of a wyvern and compared it with her memory of the Brigadier's photograph. Miss Forster came to look over her shoulder.

'I see you've found our local monster,' she said. 'There have been stories of wyverns in these parts for hundreds of years. They are said to appear in times of conflict, when evildoers need to be driven out.'

'How fascinating! I don't suppose you'd happen to have a map that's contemporary to this book?'

'Hmm, there's at least a small map in this volume, I believe…' Miss Forster turned to the shelf again, and Miss Hawthorne took the opportunity to empty some of her sherry into a potted plant that stood on the table near her elbow. She then raised the glass to her lips again as her hostess returned with the book.

'Here you are.' Miss Forster laid the book down on a side table.

Miss Hawthorne looked at the map, and said, 'So, this area is now Addershall Park?'

'Yes,' replied Miss Forster, in a curiously neutral tone.

'And this,' Miss Hawthorne pointed to an illustration of a clearing in a clump of trees, 'could this have been a sacred grove?'

'Very likely. Worship of the old gods took place here long before anyone had even thought of universities.'

Miss Forster's face was expressionless, but her voice shook with suppressed emotion. Miss Hawthorne pretended not to notice. Instead, she pressed one hand to her temple and handed the book back to its owner with the other. Miss

Forster leaned forward, with a concerned expression.

'My dear, are you quite well?' she asked

'I… I'm afraid I must have over-exerted myself today,' replied Miss Hawthorne, faintly, 'Either that or your sherry is stronger than I thought. I feel … rather …'

Her voice trailed to nothingness and she slumped in the chair, her head against one of the wings. Miss Forster lifted one of Miss Hawthorne's hands by the wrist and watched it flop back limply.

'Yes!' The word was hissed, rather than spoken. 'You have a nice nap and keep out of my way for a bit. I'll sort you out later on.'

She moved to the telephone, picked up the receiver, and dialled rapidly.

'It's me,' she said when the call was answered. 'Out like a light. She won't bother us this evening. Now what about him?'

Miss Hawthorne strained to hear, but the reply from the other end was inaudible.

'Of course, they're in it together. I saw him this evening with a gun. Off duty soldiers don't go armed when escorting their aunts, do they?'

There were more garbled squeaks from the other end.

'Mullins is a fool. Oh well, at least you can get word to him. It's his mess; he can sort it out. No, I'm leaving now. Don't be late. This last ritual is the most important.'

She banged the receiver back in its cradle and looked again at the apparently sleeping form of Miss Hawthorne. 'Just to make sure…'

She took the key out of the inside of the study door and left the room, closing and locking the door behind her. Miss Hawthorne waited until she heard the front door close and Miss Forster's footsteps recede down the drive, then she sprang out of the chair and scrabbled for her notebook in her bag. Finding the right page with a sigh of relief, she picked up the telephone receiver and dialled the number from her book. She waited for an answer, drumming her fingers on the desk in frustration. After what felt like an eternity, an answer came: 'UNIT HQ, Corporal Scott speaking.'

'Oh, thank goodness. It's Olive Hawthorne here, corporal – I must speak to the Brigadier at once.'

Miss Hawthorne gave her report in as few words as possible. With the Brigadier's assurances of 'We're on our way, Miss Hawthorne; hold tight' still ringing in her ears, she opened one of the study windows, dropped her handbag through it, and then clambered out herself, before setting off at a run towards the church.

UNIT might be on their way, but the ritual would've started by now. As she ran, her mind went to Sergeant Benton, who was surely walking into a trap.

After dropping Miss Hawthorne off, Benton had driven back to the hotel and parked the car. Torch in hand, he'd then walked around to the meeting place. He reached the lay-by and turned off his torch. There seemed to be nobody there. Was he early? No, the illuminated dial of his watch showed just on nine.

'Mullins? You there?'

Footsteps sounded on the gravel behind him. He turned and then froze as the cold metal of a gun barrel pressed into the back of his neck.

'There's been a change of plan,' said Mullins, grimly. 'Search him.'

Two figures appeared out of the dark and hands patted inside his jacket, removing the gun and torch.

'Now walk. Keep your hands where we can see them,' said Mullins.

Benton raised his hands to shoulder height and walked forward. He'd no idea how many were in the gang, or how many of them were armed; he'd just have to wait for a chance to get away and hope he was able to take it.

By the glare of dimmed torches and the builders' security lights placed around the scaffolding, the gang and their prisoner crossed the site until they reached a demountable cabin that was serving as one of the offices. The lights were on, so Benton was able to see at least five men, not including Mullins, who was behind him with the gun.

No time like the present...

As one of the gang went up the cabin steps to open the door, Benton turned suddenly, crouching as he did so and grabbed Mullins around the waist. He pushed with all his strength and the two men landed on the ground, Benton reaching for Mullin's wrist to try and knock the gun out of his hand.

'Get him off me, you idiots!' hissed Mullins, and the rest of the gang tried to pull Benton away. It took all five of them to haul Benton off Mullins and force him onto his knees in the mud. Mullins spat, then struck Benton across the face with the gun. Two of the gang dragged him up the steps and threw him to the floor in a corner of the cabin.

'Tie him up quick. And shove something in his mouth,' instructed Mullins. 'We've no time to muck around now.'

One of the gang yanked Benton's arms behind him and secured his wrists with some fuse wire from a roll on the floor, while another tied up his ankles. Benton's own scarf was crammed between his teeth. Mullins stood over him, mud layered across his body and a deep graze marking his cheek.

'This might take a little while,' he said, viciously, and lightly touched the patch of raw skin, wincing as he did so, 'but I'll still have enough time afterwards to make you pay for this.' Then he turned to his cronies: 'Come on, lads – the old bags will be getting going any minute. If they're right, this might be our last chance. We'd better make the most of it.'

Benton watched blearily as the gang left the cabin. He heard the key turn in the lock, then struggled to see if there was any give in his bonds. There was not. Frustrated, he collapsed back in the corner, trying to plan for some way, *any* way, to alert the authorities.

He could only hope that Miss Hawthorne had had more luck.

*

By the time Miss Hawthorne reached the churchyard, the fire had already been lit. She could see the glow from behind the church tower. She crept past the gravestones, finally crouching behind a larger, family tomb to watch the ritual.

The fire was surrounded by robed and hooded figures. The leader – who Miss Hawthorne identified by her voice as Miss Forster – was conducting a series of chants. The voices of the hooded followers rose and fell, undulating like the overwhelming ocean. In the flickering light cast by the flames, Miss Hawthorne could see smaller stones on the ground, almost embedded in the mud a little nearer the ritual. Dare she risk it? She had no choice, really.

She edged closer to the circle of robed silhouettes, making her way towards the stones. Were they what she thought they were? As she crouched lower into the dirt, her suspicions were confirmed. Runes. A simple communication method with other realms. The realms, perhaps, of the gods. Or of the demons.

ᚡᚠᛁᚱᛖᛖᚡᛖᛁᛚᛚᛖᚱ

She tried to understand them. Alas. She thought she'd had enough experience with runes, and she translated the first part as 'FAIR.' But then the next two runes were both 'E,' which didn't make sense…

No, wait!

We get the word 'wyvern' from the French, 'vouivre', Miss Hawthorne considered. Would that work? She took a moment to remember her GCE French, hastily translated it, and muttered her conclusion: 'To awaken!'

She was sure of it now. But what could she do?

The air around her started to crackle. She had to move, fast. She looked up and slowly a shape began to form above the flames.

It started as a blob, which resolved itself into…

Clawed feet unrolled themselves from the darkness. A tail whisked the air. Wings clipped at the night. The twilight began to coalesce into a mighty torso. And, finally, a long neck and dragon-like head raised in triumph. The beast opened its mouth and let out a rasping howl.

Miss Forster's voice rose above the chanting and the wyvern turned its head to look at her, as if listening to instructions.

No time to be scared now, Olive.

Miss Hawthorne scrubbed at the runes on the ground, dispersing some but leaving a few impacted into the mud.

ᚨᛚᛚᛖᚱ

Aller. That should do it.

Next, she reached into her handbag. In an inside pocket, she found, by touch alone, a muslin bag, tied at the neck with string. Leaving her refuge behind the tomb, she got closer to the fire.

The wyvern towered over everyone, its viper-fangs glittering in light cast by the flames. It felt as if a vast menace had weighed down the earth. And yet, it looked unsettled too, ripped from its own world but now welcome here, whether it liked it or not.

Having got as close as she could, she stood up to her full height and hurled the bag at the flames. A sudden, magnesium-bright flash went up from the fire. The coven recoiled, dazzled, as Miss Hawthorne spread her arms and cried:

'Foul beast of darkness! Begone! *I banish thee*!'

The wyvern twisted in the air and howled, pain wracking its body. Its edges seemed to blur, shining eyes dimming, and limbs falling back into the blackness, then—

Gone.

Miss Forster pointed to Miss Hawthorne and shouted to her followers,'Get her!'

The coven was still dazzled by the flames and moved slowly towards Miss Hawthorne as she backed away. Suddenly, the churchyard was flooded with light and a man's voice called out:

'You are surrounded! Stay where you are!'

Almost as mysteriously as the wyvern had vanished, soldiers appeared out of the shadows, a vast crowd of khaki-clad individuals with guns, their heavy drumbeat footsteps unfurling between the graves. One of them ran over to Miss Hawthorne, who was leaning against a headstone, breathing heavily after her exertions.

'All right, Miss Hawthorne?' he asked.

'Captain! Yes, I think so. But Sergeant Benton is in terrible danger—'

The captain offered her his arm for support as they walked to the gate.

'It's okay, this is a two-part operation,' he said. 'The Brigadier is at the building site; he'll find Benton and sort out that lot.'

Miss Hawthorne looked at the captain's bright, clean-cut face and sighed. 'Oh, that *is* a relief, I can't tell you.'

The captain helped Miss Hawthorne into a jeep parked a short distance from the church, and instructed, 'Back to HQ, Jenkins, and step on it.'

As the jeep pulled away, Miss Hawthorne felt herself relax at last. Her eyelids weighed down on her. With all this excitement, though, she doubted she'd have a good night's kip for quite some time. Not with visions of demons and dragons dancing in her head.

Jenkins glanced at the rear-view mirror and smiled. Miss Hawthorne was, actually, asleep.

There were soldiers everywhere. This wasn't what any of them had signed up for. Mullins had said it'd be a good opportunity to make off with some goods and palm them off. Heck, maybe they could've been cheeky enough to sell some of it back to the builders themselves. But now, Mullins had legged it and his followers found themselves carrying a bag of heavy tools through a graveyard in the dead of night while being hunted by men with guns.

'Stuff this for a game of coconuts,' one of them muttered

and dropped the night's gains. He brought his hand up to ruffle his hair in frustration and saw flecks of rust from the building equipment fall around his eyes.

'Halt right there!'

He was bathed in light as a torch focused in on him. Through the glare, he could see a silhouetted figure pointing his gun at him.

Ah. Caught red-handed.

Benton had lost all track of time. He didn't know if Mullins would make good on his threat to come back, or even how long it had been since the gang had left. He closed his eyes, to try and ease his aching head.

The next moment, his eyes snapped open.

Was that gunfire? Where from? Were those lights in the windows?

Someone ran up the steps and rattled the door handle. It couldn't be Mullins – he had a key. The cabin shook as repeated thumps landed from the outside. Finally, the door burst open and a figure in uniform was silhouetted in the doorway.

The figure turned and shouted: 'He's in here! Bring those wire cutters!'

Benton closed his eyes again. Only one person had a voice like that. The next moment, the Brigadier was leaning over him and pulling the scarf out of his mouth.

'Well, Sergeant, you seem to have been having more than your fair share of the action.'

Two days later and a small group had gathered in the Brigadier's office for a final debrief. Miss Hawthorne, restored to her usual poise, with her handbag at her feet, was stirring a cup of tea. Benton, on the mend, but with an ugly bruise across the right side of his face, sat next to her. The Brigadier occupied his usual position behind his desk.

'So,' said the Brigadier, consulting his notes, 'Mullins and his crew were using the coven.'

Miss Hawthorne set down her cup and saucer. 'Rather, they were using each other. The coven wished to drive the university away from what they saw as sacred ground. And the gang was stealing building materials to sell – simply using the confusion caused by the apparitions to disguise the thefts and distract the police and the site security.'

'And the painted symbols?' asked Benton.

'That was the gang at work,' explained Miss Hawthorne. 'They were all employed by the builders, so they knew how to avoid the watchmen and get onto the site. While some of them were engaged in theft, the others were repainting the symbols from the previous night.'

The Brigadier nodded. 'That Mullins fellow – he crumbled under interrogation pretty sharpish.'

'Very impressive, sir.'

'Oh, I wasn't the one to break him,' he said and looked to Miss Hawthorne. 'As for the wyverns... Our scientific advisor says they were probably being summoned from a parallel dimension, and that Miss Hawthorne here interrupted the energy transference with her... uhm, bag.'

'Really, Brigadier,' she corrected him, 'it was a simple concoction of basil and agrimony, with a clear quartz to bring balance. Not to mention the added runic instruction, to leave this dimension.'

'Hmm, yes, well, our chap says your concoction must've amplified the energy transference—'

'That would be the quartz.'

'—so the wyvern was overwhelmed. The whole system backfired.'

Benton thought he was following, but wanted to check: 'It blew up, sir?'

'It blew up, Sergeant.'

One thing didn't make sense to Benton though. 'What about the adders?'

But it was Miss Hawthorne who answered: 'One of the coven turned out to be Miss Forster's niece – she worked up at the big house. She asked their groundsman for help locating snakes. Told him her aunt had become interested in them after reading about them in the library.'

'Troublesome aunts, eh?' said Benton, winking at her.

She ignored this remark, however, and instead picked up her bag. 'Thank you for the tea, Brigadier, but now I must be getting home. I've had enough excitement in the last few days to last me a lifetime!'

'Oh?' said the Brigadier, with a mischievous glint in his eye. 'So this won't be the start of a new crime-fighting team?'

'I wouldn't mind, sir,' said Benton, plaintively, 'but every time I work with Miss Hawthorne, I seem to get beaten up. I wouldn't want to make a habit of it...'

THE WRINGFORD WORM

ᚠᛞᛞᛖᚱᛋ×ᚠᛟᚱᚲ×ᚠᚾᛞ×ᛒᛚᛁᚾᛞᚹᛟᚱᛘᛋ×ᛋᛏᛁᛝ

SERGEANT BENTON settled himself in his folding chair and sighed. This was more like it. The sun sparkled off the river and a gentle breeze stirred the leaves on the trees. He checked the position of his fishing rod, pulled his hat further down over his eyes, and sat back to watch the float bob gently in the current. He wasn't expecting to catch anything, really, but fishing provided the perfect excuse to sit quietly by himself and do absolutely *nothing*. His BOAC flight bag, holding sandwiches and a flask of tea, stood to one side of the chair and a well-thumbed copy of an Alistair MacLean novel lay open on the grass. Benton smiled. Not an alien or malevolent mythical creature in sight.

As he watched the float riding the sparkling wavelets, his eyelids drooped and he dozed off, the warmth of the sunlight prickling his cheeks…

Suddenly, he sat up with a jerk and looked around, bewildered. He was sure he must've heard something to wake him up, but all seemed peaceful and whatever the sound had been, it was already fading from his memory. He shrugged. Couldn't have been anything much. He reached for his flask and poured himself some tea. The sun had gone behind a cloud and the breeze had strengthened and turned chilly. Sipping his tea, Benton turned his gaze back to the river. The next moment, his cup was thrown aside as he jumped to his feet and plunged into the water.

A figure was floating downstream, face down, arms spread wide. As Benton waded in, he called out – 'Hang on, mate! Hang on!'

The centre of the river was unexpectedly deep and Benton floundered for a moment, but found his feet again and came alongside the man. He turned him over onto his back and towed him to the far shore, dragging him up onto the bank. Pausing for a moment to get his breath back, he got up on his knees and began to administer artificial respiration.

At first, there was no reaction, but, at the fifth attempt, the man began to cough, then sat up, retching. Benton shifted quickly to give the chap some space. He put a hand on the man's back, supporting him as he gasped for air.

Eventually the man spoke. 'Thank... Thank you...'

'Don't mention it,' replied Benton, continuing to rub the man's back to help him breathe.

'It... It pulled me in,' the man said, quietly, chest still heaving.

'Hooked a big one, did you?' asked Benton, half-joking, but the man appeared not to hear him.

'It pulled me in. The worm pulled me in,' he said.

'Come again?' Benton thought he'd misheard. *A worm?*

The man turned to face Benton, his eyes bloodshot and wide with fear. 'The worm pulled me in...'

It had been a quiet evening at UNIT headquarters. Corporal Scott chewed the end of her pencil as she considered her crossword puzzle. A buzz from the telephone brought her back to her duties.

'UNIT HQ, Corporal Scott speaking. Aren't you supposed to be on leave? What? Yes, he's in his office. Yes, half a mo.'

She flicked a switch on the board and waited until the familiar voice answered: 'Lethbridge-Stewart.'

'Corporal Scott here, sir. I've got Sergeant Benton on the line.'

'Benton? Isn't he on leave?' asked the Brigadier.

'Yes, sir, but he says it's important,' replied Corporal Scott.

'Oh, very well, put him through, Scott.'

The Brigadier waited while the phone buzzed, then greeted his sergeant. 'You're supposed to be on leave, Benton.'

At the B&B, Benton, clad in a dressing gown, adjusted the towel draped around his neck and manoeuvred a mug of hot soup into a more accessible position.

'I know, sir, but something really strange's just happened.'

In her sitting room at Devil's End, Miss Hawthorne was finishing her morning coffee while glegging through the newspapers.

She shook her head at the international news stories – always full of war and despair. The news from home was hardly more cheering, and Miss Hawthorne was about to close the paper in disgust when a picture caught her eye.

It was simply a photograph of three men by a river. Except one was in police uniform, and appeared to be questioning the other two, who were seated on the riverbank and wrapped in blankets.

'Sergeant Benton?' Miss Hawthorne gasped.

The headline proclaimed: 'RIVER MONSTER STRIKES AGAIN? Wringford Tragedy Averted.'

She could guess the hero of the hour…

Miss Hawthorne began to read the story:

'The so-called Wringford Worm has struck again, according to fisherman Bert Graves.

'Mr Graves (54) was fishing on the banks of the Wring, when, he says, a giant worm came out of the river and dragged him into the water. He was knocked unconscious and floated downstream, where he was rescued by sergeant and fellow fisherman, John Benton.

'The Wringford Worm has been a figure of local legend from as early as the sixteenth century and…'

Miss Hawthorne stopped reading and set the paper aside. 'Really, sergeant, what have you got mixed up in this time?'

She tapped her fingers on her chin, lost in thought, then went to one of her many bookshelves and took down a large and ancient volume, marked 'Bestiary'. Setting it down with care, she turned the crackling leaves. There, amid the basilisks, unicorns, and mermaids, was an engraving of what looked like an overgrown earthworm emerging from a river, with a furious expression in its boggling eyes and a large, fanged mouth open to devour its victim, who stood, aghast, on the bank.

'The worme of Wryngford lurks beneathe the waters of the river Wryng and devoureth the unwary withoute mercie.'

Miss Hawthorne looked thoughtful. Not much information there, but at least the existence of the legend could be proved. She put a scrap of paper in the book to mark the page and returned the volume to the shelf.

She was about to take another book down when the telephone rang.

'Hello? Devil's End 7895?'

'Miss Hawthorne? Lethbridge-Stewart here.'

'Oh! Brigadier! I've just been reading about Sergeant Benton's adventures in the paper!'

'Harrumph. Yes, journalists get everywhere,' said the Brigadier. 'Look here, Miss Hawthorne, there may not be anything in this story – for all we know the fellow could've been drunk and his imagination got the better of him – but it seems there have been two or three of these incidents...'

You wish me to join the sergeant and investigate?' asked Miss Hawthorne, feeling excited, in spite of herself.

'If it's... convenient. And even if it's not, we could use your thoughts on the matter. I'll ring the chief constable today and get things sorted out for Benton to liaise with them. There isn't a police station in Wringford itself; the case is being handled from the nearest town' – there was a pause as the Brigadier consulted his notes – 'Wringwold. Will you need transport?'

'Ah, no, thank you. I've a car and Wringford is not so very far from here. I must just speak to my neighbour, and pack a bag. Will you let Sergeant Benton know I am coming? I'd hate to arrive unannounced.'

The Brigadier smothered a chuckle. 'Certainly, Miss Hawthorne. He can arrange accommodation for you at the bed and breakfast.'

'Oh, yes, that would be most helpful. Well, I'd better start packing.'

'Thank you, Miss Hawthorne. I'll send a courier with some equipment for Benton if you wouldn't mind taking that along with you?'

They bid each other goodbye then hung up to get on with their respective tasks – the Brigadier was to phone the bed and breakfast to check whether his sergeant had recovered sufficiently from his unexpected bath, while Miss Hawthorn returned to her bookshelf to find a smaller bestiary. She tucked it under her arm with her notebook.

Her cat regarded her suspiciously from the window seat.

'It's no use looking like that, Gabriel,' she said. 'I'll be back before you know it.'

It was late afternoon when Miss Hawthorne's Austin pulled up outside the B&B in Wringford. Benton was waiting for her on a bench in the garden.

'Hello, Aunt Olive!' he called. It had been decided that, to avoid drawing attention to the investigation, Benton and Miss Hawthorne would assume the roles of nephew and aunt that they had used at Addershall.

'John, dear – there you are!'

Benton took Miss Hawthorne's bag from her and offered his arm.

'What a surprise it was to see you in the paper!' said Miss Hawthorne. 'Oh, and I've got the fishing gear you asked me to bring.'

'Thank you, Auntie. Let's get you settled in and then I'll tell you all about it.'

They entered the house, looking for all the world like an affectionate and concerned aunt and her large, capable nephew.

In a rented cottage on the outskirts of Wringford, a tense conversation was taking place. A man paced around the small sitting room, the morning paper in his hand. Eventually, he stopped marching up and down, then threw the paper down on the sofa next to his companion, who flinched.

'A sergeant? You know what that means? The ruddy military! That's all we need.'

The speaker was a tall man, with dark hair that flopped over his forehead from a side parting. His face, otherwise good looking, was distorted with anger into an almost devilish expression. 'We are this close' – he held up one hand, finger and thumb parted – '*this close* and that twit has to get pulled out of the river by some military man?'

His companion, a small, wiry man with short grey hair and a hunted expression, looked up at him. 'But he's only a sergeant,' he said. 'He won't have any stroke with the local coppers, will he?'

'We'll have to hope not,' his superior said. 'As it is though… you'd better keep an eye on him for the next few days. If he shows any sign of poking his nose in, put him away.'

The smaller man shivered inwardly at his boss' tone, but said, 'Yes, guv.'

'Good. Now get that map out and let's get on with it.'

Having unpacked her valise, Miss Hawthorne picked up her handbag and a curiously shaped bundle that had been in the top of her case and left her bedroom. Benton was waiting for her on the landing.

'Here you are, John. I hope this is what you wanted; such a shame your things got damaged in the accident.'

'Thank you, Aunt Olive.' Benton glanced inside the bundle.'I'll just put these away and we'll go and get some tea.'

Benton went back into his bedroom and closed the door carefully behind him, turning the key in the lock. He put the bundle down on the bed and unwrapped it. Inside were his gun, silencer, shoulder holster, and ammunition. He loaded the gun, removed his jacket, and put on the holster, then inserted the gun and put his jacket back on. He went over to the mirror to make sure the gun wasn't visible. He then locked the silencer and remaining ammo in his suitcase and picked up his hat from the bedside table before leaving the room.

As Benton and Miss Hawthorne walked the short distance to the tea rooms, he gave her an account of what had happened the previous day, and what he'd learned from the police later in the evening.

'So the newspaper wasn't exaggerating? This isn't the first incident?' asked Miss Hawthorne.

Benton shook his head. 'The inspector said there have been three now. In the others, the blokes pulled themselves out; this was the first one to be knocked out.'

'I see. How interesting. And they all said they had seen this worm?'

'Yes, they were all fishing along the same stretch of river,' he replied. 'I'll show you where tomorrow – it's a bit late today. Anyway, they were all fishing when their floats disappeared, then this worm thing came up to the surface. The next thing they knew, they were in the water.'

Miss Hawthorne looked thoughtful. 'And does the inspector have any explanation?'

Benton grinned. 'Anything but a giant worm!' he exclaimed. 'He reckons they were either drunk or half-asleep and fell in trying to get their lines in, then made up the worm story to cover their idiocy up.'

'And what do you think?' asked Miss Hawthorne.

It was Benton's turn to look thoughtful. 'Honestly? I don't know,' he said. 'Giant worms seem unlikely, but we know that kind of thing is possible. And that chap I pulled out of the river was properly scared by whatever it was. So, I suppose we are where we usually are. Either there *is* a giant worm or…'

'Or someone is using the legend for their own purposes. Quite. Well, we must gather all the evidence we can and try to find the answer. Oh! Is this the place? But how charming!'

Miss Hawthorne looked with delight at the cottage tea-room and its pretty garden, its lawn dotted with bluebells – a good sign, at least.

'They do a decent spread here,' said Benton.

Miss Hawthorne raised her voice slightly as a couple of hikers passed on the other side of the lane. 'Well, John, I know I can trust you as a good judge of scones!'

Benton grinned as he ushered her through the gate.

The meal was, indeed, excellent. Miss Hawthorne and Benton enjoyed a high tea of thickly sliced ham and eggs, followed by fruit cake. Much better than what they'd suffered at the hotel in Addershall.

While Benton settled the bill, Miss Hawthorne looked at a map of the area to see if the position of the incidents sparked any ideas. She sighed as Benton came back to the table.

'Anything?' he asked.

'I'm afraid not,' replied Miss Hawthorne. 'We must wait for the morning and see what we can find at the place. I take it the police have been over it with their usual fine-tooth comb?'

'Oh yes, but it's not the easiest place to find clues,' explained Benton. 'The ground near the bank is either bone dry or thick grass, so not much chance of footprints.'

Miss Hawthorne nodded, then stood up, Benton helping her loop her arms into her jacket. Catching sight of the waitress in the doorway, Miss Hawthorne reverted to her maiden aunt persona.

'Thank you, John. That was a delightful meal, but if you don't mind, I'd like to get back to the bed and breakfast. Driving's terribly tiring and I'd like to get an early night.'

'Of course. I'll walk you back, then I'll go down to the pub for a bit.'

'Oh? Don't stay out too late – you've had enough excitement yourself!'

As she cleared the table, the waitress smiled to herself at the sight of the big man being scolded (however gently) by his aunt.

Benton escorted Miss Hawthorne back to the B&B, leaving her in her room to pore over the map and a copy of the police report, with her bestiary to hand.

In his own room, he took off his holster and gun and locked them away. He was loath to leave them behind, but the pub was small and likely to be crowded – he didn't want to risk being spotted with a firearm. He tapped on Miss Hawthorne's door to let her know he was on his way out as he had done on their last adventure, and left, picking up the latch-key that the landlady had left out for him.

There were a few people out and about – mostly tourists, who Benton nodded to and bade a friendly 'good evening' as he went along. At least, he guessed they were tourists: sunglasses dangling from their fingers; backpacks slung over one shoulder; the remnants of ice cream drips splashed across 'I survived the Wringford worm' t-shirts. They certainly had that air about them. He was impressed at the speed of the t-shirt manufacturers; they'd got those out quickly.

The Rose and Crown pub was on the main road through Wringford. A truly ancient inn with white walls and a low roof, it seemed to hug the ground for safety. Benton opened the door and went down two steps to the bar area, ducking to avoid a low beam. The barman looked up at his entrance, grunted 'evening', then turned back to the regular he'd been talking to.

But one of the customers nudged his fellow drinker and called out, 'Hey, it's the lad who pulled Bert out the river! Come in, what'll you have?'

There was a general hubbub at this, a pint was poured, and Benton was steered to a stool near the bar, clearly a place of honour.

He looked around with genuine embarrassment. He hadn't expected a hero's welcome and this public recognition would cramp his attempts at quiet investigation. But it was too late for that now, so he accepted the pint gratefully and bashfully muttered his thanks to the assembled locals. As he sipped his beer, the other customers retreated back to their tables, leaving Benton at the bar with the regulars and a few people who were waiting to order.

The man who had hailed him spoke first. 'Young Bert was lucky you came along, mister. Fool to let 'imself fall in like that – he'd a been in real trouble if you 'adn't been there.'

Benton muttered that he was sure anyone else would've done the same.

'That's as maybe,' said another man, 'but you was the one 'oo was there.'

Another voice spoke, from behind Benton. 'Do they know what pulled him in?'

The two regulars laughed, then one said, scornfully: 'Pulled 'im in? Ha! 'Ee says it was that worm. I reckon 'ee tripped over 'is own feet, clumsy 'aporth!'

The new voice spoke again, this time to Benton. 'Did you see anything?'

Benton turned to look at the owner of the voice. A small, thin man with greying hair and a look about him that he didn't much like. He couldn't put his finger on it, but there was something about the way the man had asked that question that made it seem like more than a casual enquiry. *Luckily,* Benton thought, *he could simply tell the truth.*

'No, nothing,' he said. 'Not until he came along in front of me. That made me jump, I can tell you!'

'And you didn't hear anything?'

This time, there was no mistaking it. The question was asked in a casual tone, but there was a curious urgency underneath.

'No, nothing at all,' replied Benton, pretending not to notice the tone. 'Actually, I'd nodded off and I'd only just woken up when he came by.'

The man nodded and turned away at this, but stayed close to the bar.

The elder of the two regulars piped up again. 'I tell 'ee, Bert fell in by 'imself!'

'But what about the others then?' asked one of his friends.

''Ow should I know? None of my business. I'll leave it up to the polis,' said the old man.

Having settled the argument to his satisfaction, he banged his glass down on the bar to attract the barman's attention. Had the evening gone differently, Benton might've asked a few questions, but being in the public eye as he was, he thought it wiser to keep his mouth shut and his ears open, at least for the time being.

The other regular, who was holding a crumpled copy of the day's paper, looked up. 'I s'pose your lot won't be coming 'ere?'

'My lot?' asked Benton in careful surprise. 'Oh, you mean…' He nearly said 'UNIT', but held himself back. Still a secret organisation. Well, mostly. 'No, why would they? It's a police case. Anyway, I'm on leave and I can't see the police thanking me for mucking about in their business. Besides, sergeants don't do investigating, as a rule.'

He glanced at the back of the grey-haired man as he spoke and saw his shoulders relax slightly. Interesting.

Benton finished his pint and walked to the door.

'Won't you stay for another, lad?' asked one of the regulars.

'No, thanks, I've got to get an early night,' said Benton. 'Thanks for the drink though. 'Night all!'

The regulars chorused farewells and Benton left the pub. He paused outside the door and checked his watch by the church clock, then strolled in the direction of the B&B.

The road was deserted now, everyone either at home or at dinner. Still, he had this weird feeling that...

After he'd gone about a hundred yards, he stopped suddenly, and bent down as if to tie his shoelaces. As he did so, he heard, faintly, the sound of footsteps coming to a sudden stop.

Very interesting. Benton grinned. Whoever his follower was – and he had his suspicions – they would be disappointed this evening.

He stood up again and carried on strolling, his ears alert for sounds of his 'shadow'. Having reached the B&B, Benton fumbled for the key – thankfully, the gloom cast by the porch allowed him good reason to turn slightly into the light so he could see the road. A lone figure walked past on the opposite side of the street and, even in the twilight, Benton recognised the grey-haired man from the pub.

He unlocked the door and went in. In the upstairs corridor, he tapped gently on Miss Hawthorne's door to let her know he was back safely, then went along to his own room to think and take stock of the evening's events. Someone was up to something, that much was clear. And whoever they were, they didn't want UNIT paying attention to it.

Benton smiled. 'It's a bit too late for that, sunshine,' he murmured.

Feeling that he couldn't really get any further, Benton got ready for bed and picked up *Ice Station Zebra.* A bit of a distraction might help him think better – and it was nice to read about *other* people being hit on the head for a change.

*

For her part, Miss Hawthorne had spent the evening studying the map, the police reports, and various accounts of the mythical worm.

Eventually, she sat back in her chair and sighed, then got up to put the kettle on for another cup of tea. Sitting back down again with her cup, she looked over her notes.

It doesn't really make sense, she thought. Miss Hawthorne had started from the position that human agency was the most likely explanation for the dunkings, for the rather grisly reason that the worm would surely have eaten its prey. In the Addershall case, the wyverns had been summoned to delay building works and to drive people away. In this case, surely the appearance of the worm would have the opposite effect? Knowing what she did of human nature, Miss Hawthorne could imagine visitors descending on the village, much in the same way as they did on Devil's End, all agog to see signs of the mythical beast. So, while pulling people into the river might deter them from fishing in that particular spot, surely it would attract more attention from tourists and the police? Unless...

Miss Hawthorne looked at her watch. That was enough for one evening; she would save her hypotheses to share with Sergeant Benton the next day.

At that moment, there came a quiet tap on the door. Good – he was safely back.

Miss Hawthorne folded up the map, put away her notebook, and got a pack of cards from her bag. A nice game of patience would be just the thing. Silence settled over the house and over the village.

The next morning dawned bright and sunny. After breakfast, Miss Hawthorne and Benton returned to their rooms to gather their belongings for what they had told the landlady was going to be a day of sightseeing with a picnic by the river.

'Got everything, Aunt Olive?' asked Benton, in cheery tones.

'Yes, thank you, John,' replied his pseudo-aunt. 'Did you pick up the sandwiches?'

'Got them here,' said Benton, patting his shoulder bag.

Benton closed the garden gate behind them and they set off. In keeping with their explanation, they first walked to the village. A small group of tourists had gathered at the church and were listening to a guide who was drawing their attention to carvings and other points of interest. Miss Hawthorne and Benton stood a short distance away and listened as the guide described the history of the church building and then began to talk about the local myths and legends.

'And here you can see our local monster, the Wringford Worm,' said the guide, who pointed to a serpentine carving, winding its way up one of the pillars of the doorway. The visitors crowded around with their cameras ready. This was clearly what they had come for.

Benton and Miss Hawthorne watched for a few moments, then moved on, passing the baker's shop, where worm-themed Swiss rolls were prominently displayed in the window.

Miss Hawthorne smiled wryly. 'I can see that some of the locals are making the most of the worm's return.'

Benton nodded, then a thought occurred to him: 'You don't think someone's doing all this to boost local business?'

'It seems rather extreme,' said Miss Hawthorne, 'but I suppose we cannot rule it out entirely.'

They left the village and headed towards the river. From a distance, the conversation appeared to be of two relatives catching up and Miss Hawthorne and Benton were careful to keep an eye out for passers-by so as not to be overheard.

Benton recounted his experiences from the previous evening, trying to describe the chap who followed him back to the B&B, in case Miss Hawthorne spotted him too. 'We'll have to be careful.'

'So there *is* something going on,' she agreed. 'I hope you managed to allay his suspicions, but we must be on our guard, I'm afraid.'

'Did you get any further with the report?' asked Benton.

The path they were taking had risen by this point, and a bench had been placed at the highest point, giving a view over the river and some of the surrounding area. In one direction, the church steeple could just be made out beyond the trees, and in another, the roof of Wringford Grange, the local manor house, rose in the distance. The river wound between the hillside and the village, sometimes visible, sometimes concealed by undergrowth.

It was rather peaceful, actually. With the sunshine cutting neat slices of brilliant white into the surface of the water, you could see the wind's effects on the river. It looked both refreshing and warm, a small arc of paradise – that is, if they didn't suspect a giant worm to be concealed by the darkness underneath, threatening to pull any waders into the depths.

Miss Hawthorne seated herself on the bench. 'Ah, this will do admirably for our lunch,' she said, then: 'Yes, well, I do have some ideas.'

As Benton sat down and unpacked their sandwiches, Miss Hawthorne took her notebook and the map from her handbag. Benton placed the lunch between them on the bench and started on his sandwich as he listened.

Miss Hawthorne spread the map out over her lap. 'I began with the assumption that, as with Addershall, the legend of the worm was being used by some human agency to deter others from that particular stretch of river. But the more I thought about it, the more I realised that that simply wouldn't work.'

'Oh?' Benton swallowed a mouthful of sandwich, before pouring a cup of tea from his flask and passing it over.

'Thank you. Yes, well, as we saw, the slightest hint of the worm attracts all kinds of attention,' she went on. 'And then, there's the police. Even if it turns out to be a practical joke, pulling people into the river could be very dangerous and the police are likely, if not obliged, to become involved at some point.' Miss Hawthorne took a sip of tea and tried not to wince. Benton's preference was for very strong tea with a lot of sugar. 'So, the idea that anyone would use the worm to drive people away from the river seemed unlikely.

'I started to look at the question from the other way around. Was the worm being used to attract attention to that part of the river? Or to Wringford as a whole? Given the popularity of the worm with visitors, this seemed to be a possibility. But then I considered the unknown person's methods. Would anyone *really* be prepared to risk drowning others to bring in more visitors to their village? It's possible, I suppose, but it seems to me a dangerous and ruthless approach.'

Benton opened his mouth to speak, but Miss Hawthorne pre-empted him: 'Yes, you're right, of course – there's no shortage of ruthless people, however much one might wish otherwise.' She sighed. 'That left a third possibility. Supposing some person or persons wished to distract the police, and the local population from some illicit activity taking place near the river? Not at the place where the incidents have taken place, but somewhere else?'

'Misdirection?'

'Precisely. The police and tourists will all be getting in each other's way, while the criminals, or whoever they are, are free to get on with their work elsewhere.'

Benton thought back to when he was tied up by the gang at Addershall, and nodded his agreement. 'But how do we find out where they don't want us to look?'

'That is the question!' exclaimed Miss Hawthorne, ruefully. 'I'm afraid it gives us rather a large area to cover…'

'And what is it they want to do?' asked Benton, frowning.

There was silence as they finished their lunch deep in thought. Eventually, Benton spoke: 'Right. Let's try and narrow it down a bit.' Miss Hawthorne took up her notebook and pencil. 'We think the people doing this want everybody's attention on this bit of the river…' He pointed at the map. '…so we can take that bit out.' Taking a pen from his pocket, Benton cross-hatched the area where the attacks had taken place. 'So, what do they want to do and where?'

Miss Hawthorne considered. 'I think we can rule out interference by a corporation. The river Wring is hardly strong enough to be of use for energy production, and, as far as I am aware, there's no mining activity in the area.'

'I can check with HQ, but I'm sure you're right,' agreed Benton. 'We'd have seen it if there had been.'

'So that leaves either a gang or an individual. But it's hard to see what they would want.'

There was another silence, again broken by Benton. 'Supposing they were looking for something hidden, something they'd left, or something someone else had left here?'

Miss Hawthorne looked up from her notes, excitement in her eyes. 'Sergeant! That's it! It must be something sizeable, or they would be able to remove it quickly and have no need of the diversion. I wonder, would UNIT be able to find out if any large thefts or burglaries had taken place near here – say, in the last five or ten years?'

'I expect so. Ten years though… Are you thinking that a gang might've dumped the swag, done time, and are coming back for it now?'

'Perhaps not in so many words,' said Miss Hawthorne, 'but yes.'

Benton smiled, packed away the sandwich wrappers, flask, and cups, and then stood up. 'There's a public phone near the church. I can call from there and check back later for an answer, or they could call the B&B.'

'The latter might be better – making more than one call from a public phone might arouse suspicion.'

'Right, we can stop off on our way back through the village, on our way to tea.'

Miss Hawthorne smiled. 'An excellent plan. And now, you'd better show me where you had your adventure, in case any interested parties are watching by the river.'

They followed the path down to the riverbank and Benton pointed out where he'd been sitting when the incident occurred.

'I see,' said Miss Hawthorne, with an excited interest that was only partly feigned. 'And where did he fall in?'

'Just along here; he hadn't come very far.' Benton led the way along the bank, brushing through the patches of long grass and holding back the occasional branch for Miss Hawthorne to pass.

'My word!' remarked Miss Hawthorne, pausing to disentangle herself from a twig. 'It certainly is overgrown.'

'It is here, but it clears up a bit further on. Here we are.'

The path cleared and they emerged into a patch of short grass shaded by trees, similar to where Benton had been sitting.

For a moment, Miss Hawthorne stood and looked at the river in silence. Then, close at hand, there came a rustling noise. Without having given any sign of having heard the sound, Benton joined Miss Hawthorne at the water's edge.

'This is the place, Aunt Olive.'

'Goodness!' taking her cue, Miss Hawthorne held Benton's arm as she looked. 'How very alarming! And does the poor man still say he was pulled in by the worm?'

'That's what he reckons.' Benton ushering her away from the edge of the bank. 'Well, the police will find anything there is to be found, I should think.'

'I certainly hope so. Now, John, if you want to call your mother, I think we'd better get back to the village.'

'Oh, yes,' Benton smothered a smile at the thought of the Brigadier in a maternal role. 'Yes, we better had.'

They walked in silence, still arm in arm until they had reached the main path, then Benton said in a low voice, 'You heard?'

Miss Hawthorne nodded and replied, in equally low tones, 'And did you see in the river?'

'Yes. Pity we couldn't get it out, but I'll let HQ know and they can get on to the police.'

They walked on, both thinking of the river. A piece of wood with two rusting nails had become wedged between stones, a short distance from the bank. And, snagged on one of the nails and trapped by pebbles, had been a piece of dark material, thick and with a visible textured pattern.

When they reached the church, Benton went to the phone box to call UNIT and Miss Hawthorne went into the churchyard, appearing to examine the carvings on the church exterior, but actually watching for anyone who might be following them.

The call didn't take long and Miss Hawthorne came back through the gate to the road as Benton emerged from the phone box.

'All sorted out?' Miss Hawthorne asked.

'Records are onto it – they'll call this evening.'

'Good,' said Miss Hawthorne. Then, as a couple of sightseers approached, added, 'And how is dear Muriel?'

Benton coughed loudly and then replied, 'She's very well.'

'I'm so glad to hear it. Do come and look at this carving of the worm; it's fascinating.'

Miss Hawthorne went back through the gate and Benton followed her to the church.

Once they'd reached the door, he gave her some more details of the phone call. 'I spoke to Scott. She's going to get Records looking into local crimes and let the police know about the river. She'll call back about seven tonight, and hopefully we'll have a bit more to go on.'

'Good,' said Miss Hawthorne. 'In the meantime then, we'd better settle on where we will eat this evening, in case we need a reservation.'

After considering the options, they decided to try a small restaurant near the church. The menu was small, but the food was good and Benton thoroughly enjoyed his steak and chips, while Miss Hawthorne found her helping of Dover sole very much to her taste.

After the meal, they strolled back to the B&B, chatting about the scenery and the weather. For all intents and purposes, they really were like an aunt and her nephew; indeed, if it weren't for all this nasty business with the legendary worm, it would've been a nice relaxing break for both of them.

Having let their hostess know about the phone call – which would be, Benton had said, from his sister – the pair took their books into the garden and sat on a bench overlooking the road. At just before seven, Mrs Wilmott, the owner of the B&B, called Benton to the telephone. He returned after about fifteen minutes, tucking his notebook back in his pocket. Miss Hawthorne looked up and raised her eyebrows as he approached.

Benton looked around quickly, then sat down. 'They've come up trumps. It turns out there was a burglary at the big house six years ago. The police caught some of the gang, but they never found the loot. The gang members didn't talk, and the ringleader got away.'

'What did they take?'

'Some silver, but mostly china. The owner collects porcelain and lost some Japanese vases and…' Benton drew out his notebook. '…a Meissen statuette?'

'Ah,' said Miss Hawthorne. 'Well, the silver might be damaged, but porcelain would survive being buried in the ground, provided it was protected, or even immersed in water.'

'You think they might have hidden it actually in the river?'

'We must consider the possibility,' said Miss Hawthorne. 'Provided it weren't too much in the current, porcelain would be safe under water. Think of the plates recovered from shipwrecks after hundreds of years. Oh, and that reminds me, was there any news from the police?'

'Yes, they checked. It was a bit of wetsuit material.'

'Ah, then our suspicions were correct.' Miss Hawthorne mulled this over and continued, 'In a way, that might point to the, ah, *loot* being underwater. Would the gang have gone to the trouble of getting diving equipment just for a decoy?'

'I suppose so, but the worm?' asked Benton.

'Yes,' she said with a sigh, 'there's that too. The police will have a record of the robbery, of course.'

'Yes, but I asked Scott to give them a nudge, just in case.'

'Good. Now…' Miss Hawthorne unfolded the map on the bench between herself and Benton. 'Where might they have hidden their swag?'

Benton leaned forward, smiling at the description. They considered the map, then he pointed to a section where the river broadened and curved towards the manor house.

'How about here? It's pretty close to the house, and it looks like there's almost a pool here on the left side.'

'Out of the main current, yes – that could be the place,' agreed Miss Hawthorne, 'but would the police not have searched there at the time of the robbery?'

'I'd have thought so,' said Benton, 'unless some of the gang led them the wrong way while the others dumped the stuff. The question is, how long have we got before they finish the job?'

'Yes, I see what you mean,' said Miss Hawthorne. 'They've already used their decoy three times that we know of; the police have become involved, which they may or may not have intended, and one of the gang has been watching you. Well, I assume he's one of them at any rate. It seems to me they may be preparing to act, if they have not started already.'

It was still light outside, but the evening had grown chilly. Miss Hawthorne shivered and drew her cloak around her. 'It's a difficult problem, but I don't see what more we can do tonight. We've at least informed the police of our suspicions and—'

She was interrupted by the return of Mrs Wilmott.

'I'm sorry, Mr Benton, but your sister is on the phone for you again,' she said.

'Right, sorry to trouble you, Mrs Wilmott,' he said, 'my father's a bit under the weather at the moment. My sister was going over to visit him and she said she might call when she got back.'

'No trouble at all – better than you walking all the way down to the call box.'

Miss Hawthorne followed Benton and their hostess back to the house. Once inside, Benton picked up the receiver.

As she passed him to go upstairs, she heard him say 'Hello, Millie? How's the old man?' and wondered briefly if Corporal Scott's name really was Millicent.

In her room, she took off her cloak and jacket and plugged in the kettle for an evening drink, then opened her handbag and began to organise the contents. The kettle had just boiled when there was a tap at the door. She opened it to find Benton outside, a worried expression on his face. She moved aside to let him in and closed the door quietly, turning the key in the lock.

'Sergeant?' she asked

'That was Scott again,' said Benton, his voice as worried as his expression. 'She called the police station to try and talk to the inspector, but there was nobody there.'

'Nobody at all?' Miss Hawthorne asked, equally concerned.

'Well, only the desk sergeant,' said Benton. 'He said they've all been called to a suspicious fire at a cottage not far from here, and he'd take a note to give to the inspector as soon as he got back.'

'I see. Could it be the gang?'

'Seems likely, doesn't it?' said Benton. 'It could be a coincidence, but it's a bit convenient that all the coppers are suddenly busy away from the village after everything else that's gone on here.'

Miss Hawthorne bit her lower lip in thought. 'Yes, but what can we do? There are only two of us and we don't know how many members this gang has.'

Benton nodded slowly. He was used to having a much bigger crew, but he wasn't going to let this all slip away from him. 'I could go to the river and keep an eye on the place,' he suggested. 'If nothing happens, I'll come back, and if they do turn up, I can keep an eye on them until the police get there.'

'Are you sure? But what if they see you?'

'I'll just have to try and stay out of sight; there's plenty of bushes and long grass near the bank and I won't need to be that close,' said Benton.

Miss Hawthorne didn't mention that the grass would have to be very long indeed to hide a man of Benton's dimensions. She could see that his mind was made up.

'Very well. But if you aren't back here by…' She looked at her watch. '…half past ten, I shall call the police.'

'Right. It might be a good idea to do that anyway, in case the message doesn't get to the inspector.'

'Yes, if I haven't heard from either you or the police, I shall telephone.'

Benton unlocked and opened the door. Miss Hawthorne returned her attention to her handbag, but looked up to say, 'Be careful, John.'

Miss Hawthorne locked the door after him, then poured water from the kettle into the teapot. While the tea was brewing, she sat in an armchair near the window and took up her crochet.

She was accustomed to waiting, but, as she watched the swifts loop and swirl in the twilight in search of their insect prey, Miss Hawthorne felt that this might be a very long night.

After he left Miss Hawthorne, Benton went to his room and changed into dark coloured trousers and a jumper. He fastened his shoulder holster and checked his gun, then put on a jacket, slipping some spare ammunition into his jacket pocket. He didn't take a torch: although dusk was falling, there was still enough light to see by, and he didn't want to draw attention to himself by the river. Closing and locking his room door, he went downstairs quietly and left the house.

Even away from the street-lamps of the village, there was enough light in the summer sky to see by. The trees cast lengthy shadows on the street from the bright, full moon. Benton kept to the side of the road, moving as quickly and quietly as possible.

Leaving the road, he followed the river path, before moving away from the bank to approach the part where the river widened from a less direct route, in case the gang should already be at work.

He paused every now and then to listen, but he couldn't hear any sign of human activity – only the birds calling and the occasional rustle of an animal moving through the grass. As he neared the river bank again, he looked around for a place to conceal himself. A large tree surrounded by long grass seemed the ideal choice, so he settled himself, trying to get as good a view as possible of the river, while avoiding cramp or pins and needles. He might need to move quickly later on.

Miss Hawthorne's head jolted as her chin hit her chest. She sat bolt upright in her chair.

Goodness! How long have I been dozing? she thought. She looked at her watch. Twenty to eleven. She was sure that the sergeant would at least have knocked, if not tried to wake her, had he returned.

Miss Hawthorne opened the door and looked along the corridor to Benton's room. No light under the door. He hadn't come back.

Miss Hawthorne moved quickly. She put on her cloak, picked up her handbag, and went downstairs. She lifted the telephone receiver and dialled.

'Hello, Wringwold Police Station,' came the eventual reply.

'Hello, my name is Olive Hawthorne,' said Miss Hawthorne, 'I am, ah, a colleague of Sergeant Benton of UNIT. Is the inspector there?'

'Erm, yes, ma'am – he's not long come in. One moment.'

The line crackled and a different voice answered. 'Roper here.'

Miss Hawthorne told Roper what she and Benton suspected, and where Benton had gone. She could hear the scratch of a pen as Roper took notes.

Finally, he said, 'Okay, Miss Hawthorne, we'll get over there as quickly as we can. I had to leave some of the men at the cottage fire, but the lads here have had a few minutes' rest, so we'll be on our way.'

'Thank you, Inspector. Goodbye.' Miss Hawthorne replaced the receiver carefully and listened. The house seemed to be quiet still; it seemed she hadn't woken anyone. Good. Miss Hawthorne pulled up the hood of her cloak, picked up her handbag, and slipped quietly out of the front door.

At the riverside, Benton glanced at the luminous dial of his watch. They were sure taking their sweet time about it. Would they come, or were he and Miss Hawthorne barking up the wrong tree?

He shifted his position slightly and wiggled his toes inside his boots, trying to keep his circulation going.

A sudden noise close at hand made him freeze. Approaching along the bank was a group of figures. The tallest, at the front, was clad in dark clothing. He had a coil of rope over one shoulder and a tool bag in his hand. He was followed by three other men, all in diving gear and carrying air tanks.

The group stopped a few feet away from Benton's hiding place. He crouched as low as he could, hardly daring to breathe, but the men didn't seem to suspect that they'd been rumbled. The leader gave instructions in a low voice and the others put on their oxygen masks and goggles, then slid into the river from the bank.

They resurfaced almost immediately, and the leader passed two of them tools of some kind, while the third took one end of the rope, the other having been fastened to a tree. Benton watched as the leader sat on the bank and unfolded two larger bags that had been stored in the tool bag. Eventually, the divers began to pass objects out of the water, using the rope to steady the larger items, which the leader then hauled out.

It was too dark to see the details, but Benton could make out shapes that looked like vases. The leader wrapped the smaller items and packed them into the bags, leaving the largest to one side. Benton assumed there would be a van somewhere nearby.

As the divers surfaced again, Benton considered the situation. He had his gun and the element of surprise, but he had seen the moonlight glinting off a gun at the leader's hip and he was sure the other gangsters would be armed, if only with knives. He was no coward, but he didn't much fancy his chances with four against one.

But the decision was taken out of his hands. Lights appeared on both sides of the river, and voices shouted: 'Police! Stay where you are!'

Two of the divers clung to the bank; one of them disappeared beneath the surface, presumably in an attempt to swim away, but Benton could hear splashing from the shallower part of the river that suggested the police were making their way across to cut him off.

The leader dropped the rope he'd been using to haul up a vase and fled. Benton got to his feet and gave chase, as the police closed in on the divers and secured the stolen goods. It was very dark, but he could hear the man crashing through the bushes ahead of him and could just about make out where he'd forced a path.

About a hundred yards on, Benton stopped. He couldn't hear his quarry and the path forked, one way leading from the river, while the other followed the bank. He strained his eyes to try and make out which path the man had taken.

Then: a rustle of grass behind him.

Before he could turn round, a pistol was jammed against his back and a voice hissed, 'Keep still and don't make a sound.'

Benton obeyed, and a hand reached inside his jacket and removed his gun.

'Hands behind your head and walk,' the man continued. 'That's it – nice and slow, carry on…'

Benton was now standing right on the edge of the river bank. He tried to guess how close the man was to him, but it was impossible to tell. Then, from behind, came an odd yet familiar sound, followed by a gasp.

Benton was hit with a large and heavy weight and fell forwards, towards the water. He shoved his way out from underneath that weight… which, he realised, was the unconscious body of the gang leader.

As he pushed the body out of the way, a voice came from the bank: 'Oh! Sergeant! I am so sorry. I didn't intend… Here! Over here.'

Miss Hawthorne crouched on the bank with one hand held out. Benton took it and, with her assistance, heaved himself out of the water. He sat on the bank, breathing heavily, then looked at the gangster, who was beginning to float towards the middle of the river.

'I'll have to get him out,' he said.

Then came a flurry of noises behind them and the voice of Roper: 'We'll see to that, sergeant. You two – bring those hooks and tow him in.'

Two police officers, clad in waders and wielding boat hooks, climbed into the river and set about trying to steer the unconscious man back into shallower water. Roper and another of his men shone torches onto the surface to guide them.

Suddenly, Miss Hawthorne gasped and pointed. 'Inspector! Look, there!' she cried.

Roper moved his torch to the patch of water she'd

indicated to. The surface bubbled and heaved and then something burst through. A creature – snake-like but bigger than any snake they'd ever seen, fully five feet round – reared up out of the water, its scaly body glistening like wet pebbles in the torchlight.

Frozen for a moment in horror, Roper roused himself. 'Get out! Get out of there!' he shouted to his men.

The policemen abandoned their hooks and scrambled for the bank. Benton and Roper heaved them out of the water and then the whole party beat a hasty retreat from the river's edge.

They watched, in fascinated horror, as the creature caught the gangster in its mouth and swallowed him in a series of audible, sickening gulps, then disappeared beneath the surface again.

Characteristically, Benton was the first to speak. 'Blimey, it was real after all!'

No one else knew what to say for a second. The creature, whatever it was, had been engulfed by the darkness of the rushing river. Miss Hawthorne brought a hand to her mouth and muttered about it all being her fault.

'What's that, miss?' asked Roper, leaning in.

'I did this,' she replied. 'I hit him with my reticule.' She indicated her handbag, which lay on the ground a short distance away.

'I see,' said Roper. 'I'd rather have taken him alive, but that was rather out of our hands.'

'You saved me,' said Benton, laying a comforting hand on her shoulder. She smiled at him, the events of the evening taking their toll.

'One wonders how they escaped being eaten before,' murmured Miss Hawthorne.

'Perhaps it was hibernating,' suggested Benton. Despite his previous experiences, the whole thing was beginning to feel unreal.

Miss Hawthorne went over and picked up her bag.

Benton hoped that Roper wouldn't enquire too closely into the contents. He had a shrewd idea that Miss Hawthorne was still in the habit of carrying her crystal ball in case of emergencies. But she was speaking again.

'If you don't need us here, I think Sergeant Benton would benefit from some dry clothes and a hot drink.'

'Oh, certainly,' said Roper, then turned to the constable by his side: 'Smith, run Miss Hawthorne and Sergeant Benton back to their accommodation.'

'Sir. This way, please…'

An hour later, Benton and Miss Hawthorne were in Mrs Wilmott's sitting room. The bar heater was on and Benton, in dressing gown and alarmingly patterned pyjamas, was sipping a cup of cocoa. Roper had arrived and Mrs Wilmott, having made sure that her guests' needs had been provided for, had retired to bed again.

After hearing the news that the gang was safely behind bars and their loot under lock and key, Miss Hawthorne turned to Roper. 'And was it a member of the gang who was pulling those unfortunate men into the river?' she asked.

'Yeah, when they saw their boss split on them, they started to talk straight away. It was as you'd suspected. They used the worm to attract attention further down the river and keep us busy. One of them had some kind of mask, and they picked on people who looked like they were dozing off a bit, so they wouldn't see too much if they suddenly got pulled in. Even without them talking, we matched the bit of wetsuit you found to a suit in their van. Of course, they're blaming everything on the boss – I doubt we'll ever know who had the idea to begin with, but they won't get out of it.'

'And the fire at the cottage?'

'That was them too. They'd rented it under assumed names, then torched the place when they left.'

Miss Hawthorne shook her head then sought solace in her cocoa mug. 'And the worm?'

'I don't know what we're going to do about that. We'll have to get some scientists in to look into it, I suppose, unless you could give us any advice...?' He looked at his listeners hopefully.

Benton took a sip of cocoa to hide his smile as Miss Hawthorne said firmly, 'Oh no, Inspector, our work here is finished. The gang has been apprehended and the legend of the worm has been proved to be true. What happens next is your responsibility! Now, if you don't mind, I need a good night's sleep.'

As Miss Hawthorne retired to bed, Benton looked at Roper who was, like the poor chap he had pulled from the river not that long ago, very much out of his depth. He put down his mug and smiled. 'Don't worry, Inspector, I think I know someone who might be able to help you out.'

THE UNFORTUNATE FORTUNE TELLER

ᛒᚢ×ᛏᚻᛖ×ᚨᛚᛚ×ᛋᛖᛖᛁᛁᚾᚷ×ᛖᚢᛖ×ᚨᚹ×ᚨᚷᚨᛗᚨᛏᛏᚨ

THE 'SILENCE' sign flashed on in the TV studio. The floor manager, hearing the producer's voice ringing in his headphones, held out his hand to signal the countdown to the presenter, who shifted slightly in his chair and faced the red light on the camera. A welcoming smile spread across his face, with a suddenness that was slightly alarming.

The Autocue rolled as he opened his mouth to speak: 'Ladies and gentlemen, welcome to the show. My guest this evening is a young lady whose powers will surely make her a household name. She is part way through a national tour, and will be appearing at theatres in our region in the next few days. Please welcome Miss Iris Gladstone!'

The presenter rose from his seat, leading the audience in applause as his guest entered.

Iris Gladstone turned out to be a small, slight woman of about twenty. Reddish-brown hair curled around her pale face and cascaded over her shoulders. This, together with her outfit – a dark blue, full-length dress and a sea green, woven shawl – lent her a pre-Raphaelite air.

She approached the presenter, looking around with a wide-eyed, almost haunted expression, but when she spoke, her voice was steady, clear, and unexpectedly deep. 'Good evening,' she said.

'Good evening, Miss Gladstone,' said the host, warmly. 'And thank you for joining us tonight. Now, I won't ask you to give us a demonstration of your powers straight away, but can you explain to the viewers what it is you do and, perhaps, a little of *how* you do it?'

In her sitting room at Devil's End, Miss Hawthorne looked at the television screen with curiosity. She didn't usually watch this programme – she had turned the TV on early to see the news headlines – but the running order had been disrupted. As the young woman began to explain how she used powers of divination to help her audiences and guide them, the white witch snorted. 'Pah! Stuff and nonsense.'

But something about the girl was nagging at Miss Hawthorne's mind: something felt wrong – what was it?

She watched more closely, concentrating on the expression and posture of the young prophetess. Something about the expression bothered her. The young woman's voice was calm, but her eyes darted to the left, shooting frequent glances to someone or something just off screen. After some jovial hints from the host, Miss Gladstone allowed herself, oh so graciously, to be persuaded to do a reading for him. Miss Hawthorne watched for a few more minutes, frowning. Then she made a decision.

Moving from her armchair to her desk, she lifted the telephone receiver and dialled, turning so she could still see the television.

'Hello, Olive Hawthorne speaking. Yes, that's right. Yes. May I… Is the Brigadier available, by any chance?'

There was a pause at the other end of the line, then Miss Hawthorne was greeted in familiar tones.

'Miss Hawthorne? What can I do for you?'

'Ah! Brigadier,' Miss Hawthorne said, 'I'm sorry to trouble you. I don't suppose there's a television at headquarters?'

*

The following morning found Miss Hawthorne at UNIT HQ, in the Brigadier's office.

The Brigadier seemed to be lost in thought. Finally, he said, 'Well, Miss Hawthorne, I agree. Something was wrong on that broadcast.'

Miss Hawthorne nodded. 'What she described was the usual nonsense used by fraudulent practitioners, but, when she began to work on the man, I felt a distinct impression of power. And there was something else. The young girl was terrified.'

'I can't speak for any powers – that's beyond me,' agreed the Brigadier, 'but I saw how frightened she was. That was more than just nervousness at being on television.'

At that moment, there was a knock at the door, and the Brigadier admitted Sergeant Benton, who was carrying a tray with three cups and a teapot on it. Lethbridge-Stewart had begun to realise that a significant proportion of UNIT's funding would need to be funnelled into supplies of tea if Miss Hawthorne was becoming a regular presence there.

'Thank you, Sergeant,' said the Brigadier. 'Put it there and take a seat. Miss Hawthorne and I have been discussing a matter which might need investigation...'

Benton poured them all tea and sat in the proffered chair. While they drank, Miss Hawthorne explained their concerns about the previous night's broadcast.

Sergeant Benton looked thoughtful. 'So, *is* it magic?' he asked.

Miss Hawthorne frowned. 'It would've been called magic once,' she said. 'These days, such powers are thought of rather differently. Some people think that there are parts of the human brain that aren't used – or, at least, not regularly – and that psychics and mediums are merely accessing those areas.'

'Oh, I see,' said Benton, in a way that suggested that he didn't really. 'So, what's the plan, sir?'

'Seems to me,' said the Brigadier, 'that the most logical course would be to attend one of Miss Gladstone's performances and see if that gives you any clues.'

Miss Hawthorne, it seemed, had already done some research. 'The nearest performance would seem to be at Risinghurst. I've the paper here.' She reached into her capacious handbag and pulled out a copy of the local newspaper. 'I'll call and try for tickets. They're bound to sell quickly after last night.'

'Very wise.' The Brigadier dialled for an outside line, then passed the phone to Miss Hawthorne. As he did so, he reminded himself that although they were acting mostly on intuition, UNIT had been tasked with investigating unexplained phenomena as well as alien incursion.

The box office number was engaged, but Miss Hawthorne's persistence paid off and, after repeated calls, two tickets were reserved for the following evening – and, after more consultation of advertisements in the paper, two rooms booked at a small hotel in the town.

Miss Hawthorne made a note of the ticket price. 'That'll give us the rest of today and tomorrow to plan our strategy.' She rose and gathered up her cloak and handbag.

Benton also stood up. 'What about transport, sir?' he asked.

'Take one of the unmarked cars from the garage,' said the Brigadier. 'Miss Hawthorne, you're welcome to leave your car here while you're away.'

'Thank you, Brigadier,' said Miss Hawthorne, relieved. Her car was on the small side, and, while it was the right size for her everyday needs, it certainly wasn't big enough to accommodate Sergeant Benton's long limbs.

It was shortly before three in the afternoon when the UNIT unmarked car pulled into a parking space outside the Fairview Hotel. The name was slightly misleading, the immediate view being a supermarket on the opposite side of the High Street, but the rooms were clean and comfortable and the staff welcoming.

Once Miss Hawthorne and Benton had unpacked and settled into their rooms, they walked around to the theatre to collect the tickets and explore the town a little before dinner.

Risinghurst was a small place which hadn't yet been swallowed by the urban sprawl of nearby, larger towns. The architecture in the town centre was a mixture of ancient and modern – a half-timbered inn sat cheek by jowl with an imposing Edwardian bank and glass-fronted supermarket. Some of the side streets off the main thoroughfare were cobbled, and tubs of flowers and hanging baskets brightened the houses and shop fronts. All in all, it was a pleasant place to spend an afternoon.

The theatre was on a turning off the High Street. The jutting canopy and windows were typical of an early twentieth century regional theatre. The cloakroom and velvet-fronted bar could just be seen in the darkened foyer.

Miss Hawthorne collected the tickets from the box office window, while Benton looked at the posters advertising current and future events, then strolled a bit further on to look down the alleyway that led to the rear of the establishment. He took a couple of steps down the alley, then stopped as he heard voices coming from the other direction. He moved forward again, but more slowly. He'd almost reached the stage door when the two men came round the corner from the back of the theatre. Benton stepped back into the shadow cast by the building and flattened himself against the wall. Fortunately, the speakers were too intent on their conversation to notice him.

The taller of the two was slim but muscular, and seemed to loom over his companion. He was wearing dark trousers and a black leather jacket, and carried a sports bag over one shoulder. His fair hair was trimmed to almost military neatness. His companion was a short, stocky man with a crew cut, wearing a belted mackintosh over a tweed suit.

'Has she come up with the goods yet?' the latter asked.

Their voices were low, but just about audible.

'Not a thing. Claims she can't get a clear impression, whatever that means. That's why I called you – I thought you might be able to… persuade her a bit.'

The shorter man laughed, nastily. 'Well, I could remind her of her responsibilities; that might do the trick. How are the numbers tonight?'

'Sold out,' said the taller man. 'Told you the telly was a good idea.'

By this time, the men had reached the stage door and entered. Benton stayed still for a few seconds, then walked quietly back to the end of the alley, a serious expression on his usually good-natured face. He didn't know much about theatre people, but those men did not match his idea of what they would be like, either in appearance or conversation. Miss Hawthorne had been right: the young clairvoyant was being threatened.

Miss Hawthorne had finished her transaction at the box office and was waiting by the entrance, looking at the posters. She turned as Benton approached.

'There you are, John!' she said. 'Where did you vanish to?'

'Not far, Aunt Olive – I just wondered if that alley was a short cut to the High Street.'

'And is it?'

'As it happens, no,' he said, guiding her carefully away from the box office queue.

When they were far enough away for their voices not to carry, Miss Hawthorne raised her eyebrows at her companion. Benton told her what he'd heard at the stage door.

'So our suspicions were right,' she said, frowning.

'Certainly looks like it. But what could they want her to do?'

'Hmm. Perhaps we'll learn more from tonight's performance.'

Benton was silent for a moment, then asked a question which had been troubling him since the previous day. 'Can people really read other people's minds? I mean, *really*?'

Miss Hawthorne considered, then said, 'It depends what you mean by reading their minds. The human mind is a mass of conflicting thoughts and impulses. One person might be thinking of three or four things at once; they might think they were concentrating on their work, for example, but behind the scenes they might also be wondering what's for dinner, or whether it would be fine later for a walk, or... well, all kinds of things. So, even if one could see into a person's mind, isolating a single train of thought from the others would be nearly impossible.'

'Oh, I see,' said Benton, nodding slowly.

'It is possible to read a person's feelings,' Miss Hawthorne went on, 'but that isn't really a question of clairvoyance – it's more about learning to read expressions and posture and tone of voice, and asking leading questions. I've seen it done by any number of charlatans.'

'Body language,' checked Benton.

'Precisely.'

'And what about predicting the future?' Benton had met one person who could predict the future, but he cheated somewhat...

'Ah, now that is a more complicated question,' said Miss Hawthorne. 'There are techniques that those with a talent for clairvoyance can use to "see" a vision of the future. But, as I said, these are just snapshots, with no context, and the way to that future is rarely made clear. One might, for example, see a vision that suggests a great disaster, but it might transpire that the disaster was necessary to prevent an even bigger one. We must also consider the question of suggestion. An unscrupulous person might suggest to a client that their life were to take a certain course, in order to influence their behaviour.'

'Like Macbeth, you mean?' said Benton.

They'd reached the hotel by this time and Miss

Hawthorne paused on the front step and looked at Benton, astonished. Seeing her bewildered expression, Benton explained, 'Well, the witches knew Macbeth wanted to be king, so they knew if they told him he would be, he'd do the rest. I reckon they weren't seeing the future at all – they just had to outline what he really wanted and he was so ambitious, he made it happen.'

Miss Hawthorne was rendered temporarily speechless by her companion's sudden diversion into dramatic criticism, but recovered quickly. 'Yes, yes, that's precisely what I mean.' Then her curiosity got the better of her. 'I didn't know you were a fan of Shakespeare…'

Benton grinned.

'Read it at school. We got taken to see a production for an outing. That's when I realised what the witches were up to.'

Miss Hawthorne smiled to herself as she led the way into the hotel. One should never underestimate Sergeant Benton!

The conversation continued over dinner. Having steered a large forkful of steak and kidney pudding from plate to mouth without losing even a drop of gravy, Benton went back to his earlier question. 'So, it is possible to see into the future?'

Miss Hawthorne glanced around the dining room. From snatches of conversations from the other tables, it was clear that they weren't the only ones who'd be attending the performance that evening; it seemed safe enough to carry on with the subject.

'Yes, but only up to a point,' she said.

'So how do you think this Miss Gladstone does it?'

'That remains to be seen. There are many ways of channelling clairvoyance. Some use the tarot or the I Ching; others may use crystals…' Benton grinned at the memory of the other uses Miss Hawthorne had found for her trusty crystal ball. She continued, 'Mystics and soothsayers have used all kinds of things throughout history. Mirrors, animal entrails…' Benton lifted his fork, then set it down again. '…the alignment of the stars, weasels—'

'*Weasels*?' asked Benton, astonished.

His reply came at a momentary lull in the hubbub of the dining room and several diners looked at him in surprise. He blushed, then lowered his voice as the chatter began again. 'Sorry, but… weasels? You're having me on, aren't you?'

'No, indeed! In ancient times, the weasel was seen as a beast of ill omen, a warning of impending death, or the familiar spirit of a witch.'

'Well, I'm blowed,' he said with a chuckle, shaking his head. 'Weasels, eh?' But his mind drifted back to something even more consuming: dinner, which was, in fact, quickly consumed, between conversations about familiars, pets, demons and Daemons, and how tempting the apple crumble looked.

The theatre lobby was buzzing with conversation when Miss Hawthorne and Benton arrived.

While Miss Hawthorne went to deposit her coat at the cloakroom, Benton took up station near the side wall of the lobby, in a position that would enable him to keep an eye on the people coming and going.

A sudden burst of loud laughter drew his attention to the far side of the lobby, where a large, red-faced man in evening dress was standing with the taller of the two men from the alleyway. The latter was in a smart suit, but still, to Benton, looked shifty. Their conversation apparently at an end, the taller rogue gripped one of the red-faced man's hands in both of his to shake it. He did this vigorously and with an odd movement that would've been missed by anyone less observant than Benton. The men moved apart, the tall man slipping through a door at the back of the lobby, which, presumably, led backstage.

Miss Hawthorne threaded her way through the crowded lobby to where Benton was standing, a thoughtful frown on his face. 'Have you seen anything of interest?' she asked.

'Oh yes. If I'm not mistaken,' he replied, 'one of my friends from the stage door has just pinched that man's watch!'

Miss Hawthorne followed Benton's gaze, to where the red-faced chap was chatting to a small group, clearly unaware that he'd been robbed.

'But how extraordinary,' she said. 'Surely this can't be the purpose of these gatherings?'

'I wouldn't have thought so – you'd need a whole army of pickpockets to rob all these people. It wouldn't be worth the trouble, surely?'

'Hmm, so why steal that man's watch?'

'Opportunist?' Benton didn't sound convinced.

'Possibly...'

Behind the scenes, the stage crew was making the final preparations before curtain up. This sort of show didn't need a lot of scenery, but the lighting was complicated, as there was a need to spotlight members of the audience as well as those on the stage.

Unnoticed by the crew, the tall man walked along the busy corridor and entered a door marked 'Dressing Room'. Inside were Iris Gladstone, who was putting the finishing touches to her make-up; the shorter man from the alley, who was leaning against the wall and scowling; and a small, dark-haired woman, who was sitting on a chair next to the mirror, watching proceedings rather as a cat watches birds.

The tall man closed the door behind him, held out his hand, and gave a nasty smirk. He had, indeed, stolen the watch.

'There you are,' he said, holding it out. 'Just you have a try with that and see if it doesn't jog your "visions" a bit.'

Without turning around, Iris simply shook her head.

The man's voice hardened. 'I don't think you understood me. I'm not *asking* you to do it.'

'And yet my answer is still no.'

'Really? Okay then. Monica.' The man gestured to the

dark-haired woman, who stood up.

Iris cringed and held out her hand for the watch.

'That's better,' said the man. 'One last time and your dad's debts are all paid off. Then you can go and spread the good news – or whatever it is you want to do. Now.'

Iris held the watch in both hands and closed her eyes. When she opened them again, her pupils had shrunk as if she were staring into a bright light. After a few seconds, she spoke, her voice slow and sleepy.

'This watch belongs to a rich man.'

'Tell us about him,' Monica intoned. 'Where does he live?'

'In a big house. Lots of rooms. Ten of them… Ten rooms.'

'What's inside them?' Monica asked. 'Start on the ground floor. What can you see?'

'A big room. Paintings. A dresser with… with silver things on it. A fireplace…' She paused and Monica leaned forward.

'Yes? What's on the fireplace?' she asked, trying to keep her voice level.

Iris turned the watch in her hands, her eyes still fixed on some distant point. 'A clock, all gold and silver, under glass. Candlesticks.'

'That's good,' said Monica. 'Now try another room. Walk out of the door and into the hall, then go into another room. What do you see?'

'A chair. A big desk. Bookshelves. Another fireplace.'

'And are there any pictures?'

'Yes. The one over the fireplace looks funny. It's not straight.' Iris frowned, but her gaze didn't waver.

Monica shot a glance at her companions, one of whom nodded. 'Okay, and back into the hall,' she said.

'There's a dog. A big dog. It's barking. It's…' Iris' voice faded away and her head drooped to one side.

Monica took the watch out of her hand and gave it back to her taller companion. 'There you are, Vince. Good enough?'

'I'll say. The safe's where we thought it was and we can

get the crew ready to deal with the dog. I'll call them now.'

'And you'd better "find" that watch before he notices it's missing. If he hasn't already.'

'Half a mo...' The man – Vince – took a small pair of pliers out of his pocket and bent the fastening of the watch strap, to give the impression that it'd worked loose and fallen off.

'And you'd better get our leading lady ready to go on,' he said. 'There's the bell.'

Monica didn't answer him, but bent over Iris, a bottle of smelling salts in her hand. As the young woman came to, coughing, Vince slipped out of the door.

In the lobby, he greeted one of the ushers, who was checking tickets at the entrance to the auditorium. 'Yes, sir?' said the usher.

'Sorry to bother you, but I found this over there by the bar.' Vince waved vaguely in the direction of where he and the red-faced man had been standing. 'I don't know who it belongs to, but I expect they'll want it back.'

The usher took the watch and examined it. 'I should think so! Thank you, sir – we'll make an announcement.'

Vince waved his thanks to the usher and went out of the main door onto the street. Once outside, he walked to the nearest phone box, a short distance away.

After speaking to Vince, the usher had gone to the front of house manager, who made an announcement over the Tannoy: 'Ladies and gentlemen. A gentleman's silver wristwatch has been found in the lobby. If you have lost a watch, please speak to one of our ushers with a description and we will return it to you. Thank you.'

There was a general hubbub as the men in the audience checked their wrists and pockets. Eventually, the red-faced man signalled to an usher and spoke animatedly. The usher left the auditorium and returned moments later with the timepiece. From their seats at the rear of the auditorium, Miss Hawthorne and Sergeant Benton watched proceedings with surprise.

Benton leaned towards Miss Hawthorne and whispered, 'So they nick his watch and then give it back to him?'

A woman in the row in front turned around and shushed him. Benton subsided, and Miss Hawthorne could only raise her eyebrows and shrug. But as the curtain went up, she was deep in thought. What use could it be to the men to steal a watch and then return it after so short a time? Had they taken it for Miss Gladstone to use? What could she be using it *for*? Her train of thought was interrupted by a burst of applause.

Iris Gladstone came on. She bowed to her audience and then settled herself in the chair, placed centre stage. A table with a glass of water stood to one side, and she took a sip before she spoke, apparently composing herself. Once again, Miss Hawthorne noticed how clear and steady her voice was: if Miss Gladstone were nervous, no sign of it showed. And this time, there were no darting glances to the side – no fear to be abated or reassurance needed.

She gave a brief account of her family history and how she'd discovered what she described as her 'gifts'.

Miss Hawthorne listened with interest, noting the slight quiver in the voice when the woman mentioned her parents. Miss Hawthorne's notebook was open on her lap and she wrote in the words, 'Parents? Orphan?' then turned her attention back to the stage.

The account of her upbringing and training finished, Miss Gladstone explained the form the evening would take. She did not, she said, have a spirit guide and wouldn't be offering to bring messages from beyond the veil – the woman in front of Benton and Hawthorne sighed at this – rather, she'd sense the auras of those present in the hall and help people to see themselves and their problems clearly. This, she hoped, would help the audience find solutions to any difficulties in which they found themselves. Benton looked at Miss Hawthorne and raised his eyebrows questioningly. Miss Hawthorne shrugged and wrote 'Cold reading?' on her pad. Cold reading was a technique used by fraudulent mediums and psychics which enabled them to get information about their audience without them realising how much they'd given away. A person practiced in cold reading would make a series of guesses (chosen based on the profile of the audience) and then pick up on and respond to cues given by them in response to the initial guesses.

And it seemed Miss Hawthorne was right. Gladstone made some insightful guesses in the form of simple leading questions, eagerly picked up on by some audience members; these were followed up by more precise educated guesses.

Yet there *was* something else. It was a feeling. An impression of something sweeping across the auditorium, like an invisible search light. Miss Gladstone might be using the methods of charlatans, but she also had power. Interesting. If she was using the cold reading for her public persona, what was she using her actual power for?

Miss Hawthorne closed her eyes and attempted to clear her mind. She pictured a slate, with one word written on it:

'FRIEND'.

She concentrated on that word as hard as she could. As she felt the 'searchlight' sweep over her, Miss Hawthorne gasped. Her gasp was echoed from the stage, where Iris opened her eyes with a start and looked around with a bewildered expression.

The audience watched in consternation as a dark-haired woman came onto the stage and crouched down by the chair, questioning her charge urgently. Whatever Miss Gladstone said seemed to satisfy her, as she held out the glass of water, which Gladstone gratefully sipped. She re-composed herself, then closed her eyes again and began to speak, using the same technique as before. Eventually, she seemed almost to doze off, then raised her head and looked at her audience with a smile.

'I hope you've found this evening to be enlightening,' she said. 'Thank you for sharing your time with me.'

Then she bowed, a little unsteadily and walked off the

stage to loud applause and cheering.

Under cover of the ovation, Benton leaned over again to Miss Hawthorne and asked, 'Anything?'

'Oh yes. Definitely. I believe we made contact. I only hope I've not got her into any trouble. Did you feel it?'

Benton considered. 'I felt… something. It was – well, it's hard to describe. It was as if something or someone was looking for something, reaching out towards me.' He stood up and said, 'Honestly? It was creepy.'

'That's a very good word for it. And now, I must go and make some unwelcome advances,' said Miss Hawthorne.

Benton smiled. 'Right. I'll go to the cloakroom and wait outside. If you're not out in half an hour I'll come and rescue you!'

'I hope I won't need rescuing. I expect to be given short shrift. But yes, I'll see you outside.'

When she walked off the stage, Iris was met by Monica, who grabbed her by the arm.

'What was that about?' she asked, urgently and angrily.

'Nothing. It was nothing,' she said, in a dull voice. 'I was too tired after the remote viewing. I shouldn't have tried to do the whole room in one go.' Monica looked at her suspiciously, but Iris turned a clear face towards her. 'Really, that's all it was,' she finished.

'Hmm. Either way, we'd better hurry. You've got to debrief before we leave the building.' She quickened her pace, dragging Iris behind her.

In a small voice, Iris asked, 'Must I? I thought—'

'Of course, you must,' said Monica. 'Don't give me any more nonsense. The sooner we start, the sooner it will be over with. Come along!'

She yanked her victim by the arm, almost pulling her off her feet. By this time, they'd reached the dressing room. Monica, seeing a group of apparent well-wishers approaching, hustled Iris inside and slammed the door behind them both. There, the younger woman sat down in front of the mirror and buried her face in her hands.

Vince, who was lounging against the wall near the door, looked at her, and asked, 'Well? What is it? What's upset our little star tonight?'

'Says she's tired,' Monica answered. 'Something gave her a fright on stage. Says she thought we wouldn't need to debrief.'

Iris looked up at this. 'But you got what you wanted. Didn't you? Isn't that enough?'

Vince was about to reply when there was a knock at the door. He signalled to Monica, who got up and opened the door a crack. Iris couldn't see who was on the other side, but she heard a female voice.

'I am sorry to trouble you; I know I'm taking a terrible liberty coming to the dressing room, but I did want to say what a wonderfully fulfilling evening this has been for me.'

Monica thanked the owner of the voice brusquely and made as if to close the door, but the speaker didn't take the hint.

'My name is Hawthorne,' she said. 'I write a column now and then in the *Wiccan Gazette* and I was wondering if by any chance…'

'No,' said Monica.

'Oh. But I haven't asked you yet!'

'Miss Gladstone is not going to give interviews. She is worn out.' Monica tried to close the door again, but the person outside resisted.

'Oh, of course, I wasn't expecting to speak to her now,' she said. 'Heavens! No, I was only going to leave my card' – a pale, slim hand was extended through the crack with a small square of pasteboard in it – 'and say that I'm staying at the Fairview Hotel for the next few days, if Miss Gladstone wanted to get in touch. I had such a warm impression of her during the evening. Almost as if we were already friends.'

That last word made Iris start. She managed to keep her

face expressionless though, and, instead, reached out with her mind. There it was again. 'FRIEND'.

Iris' mind raced. Who was this woman? She couldn't possibly be as silly and twittering as she sounded. Why had she come? Could she actually be here to help?

Monica had accepted the card and closed the door on the still expostulating Miss Hawthorne. Without looking at the card, she tore it up and threw the pieces in the wastepaper basket.

'So much for her. Debrief time,' she said.

She pulled up a chair and sat opposite Iris, who was too tired to resist.

She heard Monica say, 'Look at me'. Saw a small, sparkling pendant hanging in front of her eyes. The world folded in around her.

As she slipped into a trance, Iris repeated to herself over and over again: 'Hawthorne. Fairview. Friend.'

Benton was, as he'd promised, waiting for Miss Hawthorne outside the theatre.

'Any luck?' he asked.

'Sent away with a flea in my ear, as expected,' said Miss Hawthorne, cheerfully. 'I think I spoke clearly enough to make myself heard, though. We'll have to wait and see if Miss Gladstone's able to make contact.'

'Mm. We'd better be getting back, I suppose. Not much point in trying to follow them; they'd spot us straight away in a quiet place like this.'

'I fear so,' agreed Miss Hawthorne.

They walked back to the hotel in silence, both of them frustrated by their lack of progress. Having wished Miss Hawthorne good night at the door of her room, Benton went to his own room to get ready for bed. But, unusually for him, he couldn't settle down. The events of the evening nagged at his brain and, in the end, he had to sit up and read, not knowing that Miss Hawthorne had to do the same.

*

In the dressing room, Monica took out a plan of the auditorium, and began to read the seat numbers aloud.

In a slow, entranced voice, Iris gave a word in answer to each number.

'F47.'

'Lust.'

'F48.'

'Guilt.'

'F49.'

'Curiosity.'

As they went along, Monica made marks on the plan. Once they'd reached the back of the stalls, she glanced at Vince, who nodded.

Leaning forward, she snapped her fingers in front of Iris' face. The reaction was instant.

Iris opened her eyes and sighed, then looked down at the plan with disgust. 'You got what you wanted?'

'Enough to be going on with,' said Monica.

A tap at the door alerted Vince to the time. 'We'd better be going.'

Monica stood up and made to take Iris' arm, but was shaken off.

'Don't touch me,' said Iris, coldly.

Vince smiled, unpleasantly. 'Getting independent?' he said. 'Don't even think about making trouble, or we'll put you under again and carry you.'

Iris' shoulders sagged momentarily, but she said nothing. Instead, she gathered up her shawl and bag and walked to the door. As she did so, three words appeared in her mind.

Hawthorne. Fairview. Friend.

Miss Hawthorne and Benton met again at breakfast the following morning, both noting the other's tired face and deciding not to mention it.

Benton had picked up a newspaper from the pile at the

door of the breakfast room and exclaimed as he saw the headline on the front page. 'Look at this! Would you believe it?'

He handed the paper across the table and Miss Hawthorne gasped as she looked at it. The front page showed a photograph of an angry looking man outside a Georgian villa. The headline read: 'Burglary shock for local businessman.'

The man in the picture was the red-faced theatre-goer.

'Could it be a coincidence?' asked Benton. 'Someone in the neighbourhood who saw him leave the house and took a chance?'

Miss Hawthorne was reading the story. 'I think not. It says here that the thieves drugged the guard dog and went straight for the safe and the silverware, ignoring the other rooms. This theft must've been planned.'

There was a short silence, then suddenly Miss Hawthorne said, 'Remote viewing! Of course! What a fool I am!'

Sergeant Benton looked puzzled. 'Sorry, you've lost me there…'

Miss Hawthorne recovered herself and looked quickly around the breakfast room, but they were alone.

'It just dawned on me. The watch. That was what the watch was for.'

Miss Hawthorne explained that some clairvoyants were said to be able to read from objects – they could tell a person's history, whereabouts or even their future from touching and holding one of their possessions. 'It is usually a scam, using the cold reading techniques we saw last night,' she carried on, 'but we know that Miss Gladstone is not a fraud.'

'So, you think she might've seen inside this chap's house, by holding his watch? That seems a bit unlikely,' said Benton, frowning.

'It does, but it also seems possible,' said Miss Hawthorne. 'Consider. The watch is stolen for a short time before the show and then returned. Why? Not for a prank. When Miss Gladstone arrived on stage, she was already tired. So much so that my small intervention caused her to lose her concentration. Could this have been because she'd already exerted herself in attempting to view the house, using the watch as a focus? The burglars knew where the most valuable items were, and they knew about the dog: they must have got that information from somewhere.'

'Yes, but… It's a bit…' Benton wasn't sure how to phrase what he thought.

'Far-fetched? Yes, it seems so. I wonder… We may be able to find a more definite link.' Miss Hawthorne reached for her handbag and fished out the page from the newspaper that she'd taken to UNIT. 'But we'll need either to visit the local library or contact UNIT for information. As time is against us, I suggest the latter.'

Light dawned on Benton. 'Oh! You mean to check for more burglaries in places where there have also been shows? Is that the list of venues?'

Miss Hawthorne passed him the newspaper.

'Right,' said Benton, 'there's a phone in the lobby and it's pretty quiet at the moment. I'll get in touch with HQ.'

He went quickly out of the room, grateful to be taking some positive action. Miss Hawthorne drummed her fingers on the table, deep in thought, then called the waiter and was happy to hear that the reception had a map of the area she could borrow. She went to the desk and secured the map, then seated herself at a table in the lobby, close to the phone, where Benton was talking to HQ.

When he'd finished the call, he joined her at the table. 'Spoke to Jenkins,' he said. 'He's going to get on to records and the local police and get back to us.'

'Good. That'll be better than us approaching the police ourselves,' said Miss Hawthorne. 'In the meantime, after last night's excitements. I feel I could do with another cup of coffee…'

*

They hadn't long to wait. The coffee had been drunk and Benton and Miss Hawthorne were discussing a plan of attack for the day, when Benton was called to the phone.

He returned after about fifteen minutes, a serious look on his face.

'You were right. Every place she's performed, there's been a burglary. See here...' Benton sat down and put his notebook on the table next to the page from the newspaper. He showed Miss Hawthorne how the dates of the burglaries matched with the dates of the performances.

'Same MO each time. Only the rooms with the most valuable stuff are touched; the rest are left alone. And there's something else.' He turned a page in the notebook, and continued, 'On the day of the performances, there's been a morning reception at the town hall in each place. All the victims also went to those receptions.'

Miss Hawthorne leaned forward and rested her chin on her hands. 'How interesting,' she said. 'Could that be where the gang – I think we must be dealing with a gang?' Benton nodded and she went on, 'Could that be where the gang identified their victims?'

'Must be. If they were local bigwigs, it wouldn't be hard to find out where they lived. Or they might've had to give their addresses to get a ticket. The gang could see which house they fancied the most from the outside and then later on, they'd pull the watch trick.'

'And their other victim would fill in the details.'

Benton gave her a questioning look. 'Oh yes,' continued Miss Hawthorne. 'I think there can be no doubt that young Miss Gladstone is acting under duress. The conversation you overheard proves it, if nothing else. Now, where could they be staying, I wonder?'

'I don't reckon they'd be in a hotel. Even if the gang weren't all in one place, they'd want to come and go without anyone seeing them.'

Miss Hawthorne nodded and went to say something –

then paused. A couple walked past on their way out of the lobby. She said, 'Perhaps we should continue this conversation somewhere else.'

Benton picked up the map. The hotel had been able to provide a private sitting room: a much better place to carry on their discussion.

Daylight streamed in through the blind as Iris woke. She remained still, pretending to herself that if she didn't move, the previous night wouldn't have happened; that, perhaps, she would open them again and be somewhere else. A brief tap at the door shattered that illusion and she sat up in bed.

She had expected Monica to arrive, but instead it was Vince's boss, the shorter of the two crooks. He was carrying a tray and had a newspaper under one arm. He set the former down on the bedside table and tossed the paper onto the bed.

'You did well,' he said.

Iris looked at the headline and shuddered.

'Don't look like that!' The man smiled, spitefully. 'You've been a great help.'

He went to the door, then turned back. 'I'd stay up here for today if I were you – we've got a lot of organising to do, and then there's all the phone calls to make after last night.'

Iris nodded, then gathered her nerve. 'Mr Barnes,' she said, 'you said this would be the last time. Once you'd been paid back.'

'Did I? Oh, I can't think what made me say that. Why would we stop now, when it's all working out so well? Make the most of your day off. You'll be busy again before you know it.'

He went out of the room and Iris heard the key turn in the lock. So that was that. They weren't going to let her stop. She had to get away.

She had little appetite for breakfast, but ate it anyway, without really noticing what she was eating. As she did so, she turned the pages of the newspaper, avoiding the story of the burglary and the review of her performance the previous evening.

The reviews page was followed by a page of advertisements for local attractions, events, and accommodation. As Iris idly scanned the page, a small advertisement seemed to almost jump out.

The Fairview Hotel, Lower Risinghurst.

That was it! But how could she make contact? The window was too high to get out of, and, even if she could, Iris had no real notion of where the house was located – they frequently travelled after dark and her view from the car was blocked. The lower windows and doors were all secured and she was seldom left completely alone, even when not confined to her room.

That left the telephone. It was risky. She would have to be very quiet and hope that she could get through before she was discovered. She hadn't tried to get to the phone before: Barnes and Vince had persuaded her that, if she tried to call the police, she'd be arrested – that, plus their insistence that she pay off the debt her father had owed them (not to mention the promise of terrible consequences if she didn't), had kept her quiet. Until now. Now, she knew they wouldn't let her stop.

She shuddered again at the thought. The phone calls Barnes had mentioned were the result of her cold reading and her mental sweep of the auditorium. Monica had noted the seats where the patrons had negative emotions – guilt, fear, lust, hatred. A list of telephone numbers, filched from the box office, provided the gang with a route to blackmail. Calls were made from public phone boxes, using the same techniques as the cold reading, to scare the patrons and make them believe that the gang knew their secrets, whatever they were. From there, the gang would proceed to tighten their grip on the victims, with repeated calls and, finally, demands for money. And Iris had been coerced into helping their horrible little scheme along, into giving them more victims.

She had to try to stop this, even if it meant the risk of getting caught. The nearest telephone was in the study. If they let her out later on, she would try and call from there. Her mind made up, Iris focused on the advertisement and began to memorise the telephone number. She dared not risk tearing out the page and the gang had made sure that she had no writing materials.

With the number lodged in her memory, she got out of bed and went to the bathroom that adjoined her room to get washed and dressed. That accomplished, she made her bed and sat on it, putting her feet up, then picked up the novel that sat beside the tray on her bedside table. Locked in as she was, she could do nothing but wait.

In their sitting room at the hotel, Miss Hawthorne and Benton had studied the map that had been provided by the receptionist. Using a pencil, Benton had lightly marked the locations of the theatres where performances had taken place, or were booked for the next few days, after which, presumably, the gang would change their lodgings. Plotting a line around the area, they looked at the possibilities for a hideout. Unfortunately, the area covered several small towns and villages, so even this initial narrowing down wasn't much help.

Miss Hawthorne sighed. 'I fear we're looking for a needle in a haystack.'

Benton frowned. 'Looks like it. It must be somewhere in this area, but where do we start? Let's think. What would they be looking for?'

'Somewhere remote? But not too far away from civilisation; they'd need to get food and other supplies, but they wouldn't want to be overlooked.'

'Right. So that would rule out the centre of the towns and villages. Somewhere on the edge – a farmhouse perhaps. Would it need to be a big house, do you think?' asked Benton, looking at the map.

'That would depend on how many of them are staying

there, I suppose,' said Miss Hawthorne. 'If it's just the two men and women, or even one man... Didn't you say that the shorter man had been called in?' Benton nodded and she continued: 'Well, if it *is* just those three or four people, the house wouldn't need to be large. But if the whole lot of them, the burglars too, are lodging there and possibly storing the stolen goods there...'

'Hmm. So that gives us a house of at least four bedrooms – assuming that Miss Gladstone isn't sharing a room with that other woman – and on the edge of, or just outside, a town or village. That's still quite a lot of ground to cover.'

'Yes, alas.' Miss Hawthorne looked at her watch. 'Just on eleven. Supposing we take a walk around the town? There may be some letting agents we could consult on the pretext of wanting to rent.'

'Sounds good to me,' agreed Benton. 'Better than sitting in here and stewing over this map at any rate.'

'Good, I shall see you shortly then.' Miss Hawthorne went to the adjoining door to her bedroom.

Sergeant Benton folded up the map and carried it and his notebook through to his room, where he put both into his flight bag. He paused for a moment, then unlocked a rectangular case that was concealed in the bottom of the wardrobe: his shoulder holster and gun. It wasn't likely that they'd run into trouble on a walk round the town, but if they were dealing with a gang of crooks, Benton preferred to be safe rather than sorry. With the firearm concealed under his jacket, he picked up the bag and went out to meet Miss Hawthorne in the corridor.

At just after two in the afternoon, Iris opened her bedroom door and looked out cautiously into the hallway. Most of the members of the gang had left to contact potential or existing blackmail victims, using public telephones so they couldn't be traced. Monica had brought up a lunch tray and then departed, leaving the door unlocked, so Iris guessed that she was no longer considered to be at risk of interrupting the gang in their planning, at least for that day. Nonetheless, caution was essential.

She closed the bedroom door carefully and walked quietly along the hallway, pausing at the top of the stairs to listen. She could hear voices from downstairs, but they were faint: the door between them must've been closed. Good. Iris, her book tucked under her arm, made her way to the study at the far end of the hall. It was a small room, lined with bookcases, some still full of a mixture of reference books and novels. Watery sunlight stretched across the desk and chair inside, casting shadows behind the telephone and blotter on the top. Iris put her book down on the desk; it was ready to be picked up, should she need an excuse for being there. She closed her eyes, briefly, visualising the phone number she had memorised earlier. Then she opened her eyes, picked up the receiver, and dialled.

After what felt like an eternity, a friendly voice answered: 'Fairview Hotel, Risinghurst, how may I help you?'

'Hello. I, er – I believe you have a guest by the name of Hawthorne staying with you. May I speak to her?' Iris fought to keep her voice steady.

There was a brief silence as the receptionist checked the register. 'Miss Hawthorne, yes. One moment please. Who may I say is calling?'

'A friend.'

There was another pause. The silence filled the air around her as she waited, hoping Miss Hawthorne would get to the phone before Vince and his cronies found Iris.

Then, there came the voice she'd heard from the dressing room the night before: 'Hello?'

'Hello? This… This is Iris Gladstone.'

'My dear girl!' The warmth and concern in Miss Hawthorne's voice made tears spring to Iris' eyes. 'Where are you? Can you tell me?'

'I don't know. Not in a town. There aren't any other houses nearby, but I can see a church spire and some rooftops from the window of my room.'

'Good. And how big is the house?' asked Miss Hawthorne.

'I don't know how many rooms there are altogether – I'm not allowed downstairs…' Iris became aware that she was speaking like a child. Perhaps it was the relief of talking to someone who sounded like they cared about her. 'But there are four bedrooms and a study on the first floor.'

'I see. And do you know the telephone number you're calling from?'

Iris looked down at the dial and saw the number printed on a piece of card set into the centre of it. She went to read it out—

The sound of footsteps from the hall outside made her stop. She put the receiver down slowly and quietly and began to speak more loudly. Not words, but vowel sounds, vocal exercises that she did every day to keep her voice healthy for the stage. As she did so, she picked up her book and climbed a set of library steps that stood nearby.

When Barnes opened the door, Iris was sitting on the top of the steps, studying the shelves and enunciating consonants in her usual clear, calm voice.

Barnes stood in the doorway. 'Getting some practice in? You'll want to go back to your room now though – the lads will be back soon.'

Rightly interpreting this as an order, rather than a suggestion, Iris chose a book and climbed sedately down, walking out past Barnes without saying a word. He escorted her to her room and locked her in again, tucking the key in his pocket.

Iris sat on her bed once more, hugging her knees like the child she felt she'd become. Would Miss Hawthorne find her? She had tried not to hope lately, to avoid the inevitable pain of disappointment, but maybe, this time…? Whatever the outcome, she'd done all she could. Iris laid down on her side and picked up the book she'd chosen, hoping it would give her some distraction while she waited.

When the call was cut off, Miss Hawthorne paused for a moment, then dialled again.

'Hello? Operator?' She read out the telephone number of the hotel, then went on: 'I was just talking to a friend a moment ago when we were cut off. No, no, you needn't reconnect me, but could you give me the number? I daresay some emergency has arisen and I don't want to bother her now…' The receptionist, guessing what she was after, helpfully passed her a pad and pen, which she used to scrawl down: '"Blakeswood 7345"? Thank you so much – that is most helpful. Goodbye.'

She hung up, thanked the receptionist, and hurried back to the dining room, where she and Benton had been having a late lunch. Benton looked up from the remains of his ploughman's as she approached.

'You all right?' he asked.

'Yes!' Miss Hawthorne lowered her voice so as not to attract the attention of fellow diners. 'That was Miss Gladstone. We got cut off before she could give me the number, but I believe we may be able to find where she's being held. I only hope she wasn't caught speaking to me. Either way, we've no time to lose.'

Benton got up and they rushed to the sitting room, where the map was spread out on the table. Miss Hawthorne looked at her note.

'The number is a Blakeswood one, and Blakeswood is…' she said, scanning the map.

'There,' said Benton, pointing to a spot a few miles from Risinghurst.

'My eagle-eyed sergeant! Now, she said that they weren't in a town, but that she could see a church and some roofs from her window…'

They pored over the map. Then Miss Hawthorne gave an exclamation. 'There! Could that be it?'

She pointed to a place on the map not far from Blakeswood. Benton read the name.

'Blakesfield Place? Must be quite big to be on the map by itself, and with that elevation, it should be close enough to see the church,' he said. 'Look, there's almost a direct line.'

They looked at each other in silence for a moment, then Benton continued: 'I'll get on to the police. Jenkins spoke to the local station before he called me; they know we're here and will cooperate if we need them.'

'If the whole gang is there, we may require considerable force.'

Benton didn't answer, but left the room to go and telephone the police. He was back in a few minutes.

'Got through straight away. Spoke to the inspector dealing with the burglaries and told him what we'd found out. They'll be ready to move in about half an hour and will pick us up on the way.'

'Oh, that is a relief,' said Miss Hawthorne. 'What did you say about Miss Gladstone?'

'Well, I did gloss over the remote viewing a bit,' he confessed. 'I wasn't sure he'd buy that, so I just told him that a gang was using her as a front for the burglaries and left it at that.'

'Very wise. He might've found that side of the case hard to believe.'

'That's what I thought.'

'Then we'd better get ready – or you had, at any rate. I suspect the inspector will want me to stay in the background.'

Iris lay dozing on her bed. The boredom and silence had been getting to her, lulling her into this state. Then a sudden sound woke her.

She sat up, her dreams fading in the afternoon light. All was quiet. Had she really heard something? She was about to settle back on the pillow when the sound came again. She slid off the bed and went to the window. On the road, she could see cars and a van had drawn up a short distance away. And was that…? Yes, a body of men were moving quietly along the lane towards the house. The police? But would there be enough of them to take on the whole gang?

Then she saw a second, smaller party, coming towards the house from another angle – three men, carrying a long ladder. Iris' heart had leapt into her throat. As quietly as she could, she opened the window to its fullest extent. She didn't dare lean out, but the movement of her opening it had attracted the attention of one of the men, whose head darted in her direction.

Iris gave a sob of relief. She might get out at last. She turned away from the window and saw Monica standing in the doorway.

'I heard you open the window. What are you playing at?' she asked.

Iris said nothing, but tried to move casually away from the window.

Monica crossed the room and grabbed her by the wrist. 'I said, what are you playing at? Look at me!'

'No,' said Iris, quietly, as she met the other woman's angry gaze with calm, blue eyes that seemed to blaze from within. 'No, you look at *me.*'

On the ground below, Benton and two policemen set up the ladder against the side of the house.

One of the officers gave a signal on his radio – there quickly came a loud call of 'POLICE! OPEN THIS DOOR!' – then repeated blows to the front door – then the back.

One of the policemen steadied the ladder and Benton climbed up. He was met at the window by Iris, who had to resist the urge to throw her arms around him in relief; instead, she helped him over the sill and into the room.

Benton looked at Monica who was lying unconscious next to the bed, but said nothing. Instead, he put a finger to his lips and positioned himself next to the doorway, his gun drawn. From downstairs came the sound of shouting. And gunfire. Footsteps thundered up the stairs and Barnes appeared in the doorway with a gun in his hand.

'*You little witch*! Bet this is your doing. You'll pay for—'

He fell silent as he felt the barrel of Benton's gun against his neck.

'That's better,' said Benton, pulling Barnes into the room and deftly handcuffing him with his other hand, before shoving him to the floor. 'That's no way to talk to a lady.'

He picked up Barnes' gun and kept him covered until two policemen arrived and dragged him away, while another removed the still unconscious Monica.

Benton smiled at Iris and received a tremulous smile in response. 'Well, it still sounds a bit noisy down there,' he said, cheerfully, 'so we should probably go out the way I came in. Do you feel up to climbing down a ladder?'

Feeling almost hysterical with relief, Iris nodded.

When they reached the bottom of the ladder, Benton offered his arm to Iris, and led her over the grass to the lane, where Miss Hawthorne was waiting with a blanket and a warm hug.

Miss Hawthorne helped her into the back of one of the cars and then pulled a flask from her bag. She got into the car beside Iris, and passed her a cup of steaming coffee. Iris accepted it with shaking hands, grateful to have something to focus on. Miss Hawthorne said nothing, but her calmness was immensely reassuring, as was the solid presence of Sergeant Benton, who stood next to the car.

Eventually, the inspector came over and spoke to Iris, telling her that he'd arranged for her to stay at the hotel in Risinghurst for the night with Miss Hawthorne and Benton; nonetheless, he'd need to speak to her the following day to take her statement. Iris agreed and thanked him. Then the inspector nodded to Benton, who got into the driver's seat and drove back to the town.

The hotel manager had arranged for a camp bed to be set up in the sitting room between Miss Hawthorne and Benton's rooms and provided a nightdress and wash kit.

'And now, my dear,' said Miss Hawthorne, after dinner, 'you'd better get some rest. You can tell us all about it tomorrow. I'll leave my door ajar, so if you need anything in the night, you can call.'

With that, she left the room and Iris, overwhelmed with her experiences and with the kindness that these two strangers had shown her, did as Miss Hawthorne suggested and was soon asleep.

The next morning, they were joined by the inspector, who accepted a cup of coffee, then began gently to question Iris. He raised his eyebrows at her description of her psychic powers, but – aware that something fishy had been going on, enough to warrant UNIT's involvement at least – he let that go for the time being.

Miss Hawthorne and Benton sat quietly and listened, the former reaching across to take Iris' hand when she showed signs of becoming upset.

The first thing they learned was that her name wasn't Iris Gladstone, but Iolanthe Grosvenor. The false name had been suggested by the gangsters, then insisted on when she was in their power. Her parents had divorced when she was ten years' old, and her father had later had problems with gambling. When she was fifteen, he emigrated to Australia. They'd stayed in touch, writing to each other frequently, but she never saw him again before his death in an accident a couple of years later. Her mother had died when she was in her first year at university. She had inherited a small amount of money from her parents, but the shock of her bereavement and the need to earn a living meant that she left university and began work as an assistant at her old school, where she'd been very happy.

A few days after her twentieth birthday, she'd been approached by Monica and Vince. They told her they'd been friends with her father in Australia, but it had taken them some time to find her. At first, she was delighted to meet them and to hear about her father, but then it became clear that they had an ulterior motive in seeking her out.

She had always been aware that she was, as she put it, 'able to see more than other people', but she'd kept that side of her personality to herself, although she'd been unable to hide it from her parents. Monica and Vince had found out – she never knew how – from her father. Vince, who had by then been joined by Barnes, told her that her father had started gambling again, so owed him and Barnes a large amount of money, which she, as his only surviving relative, would have to pay back. Iolanthe was horrified by this news; even more so when the idea of her becoming a performing psychic was suggested. She resisted for as long as she could, but had no one to turn to and eventually gave in after days of threats, bullying, and hypnosis – under which she signed a contract with the gangsters. After the first few burglaries and the television appearance, she still held out hopes that she'd be released after the debt was paid, but this hope began to fade until it was finally dashed by Barnes.

The inspector thanked Iolanthe and told her that her statement would be ready for her to sign later that day.

Miss Hawthorne let go of Iolanthe's hand and asked, 'Have the gang confessed?'

'Vince has, but Barnes is staying tight-lipped for now. He may crack when he learns that the others have given him up,' replied the inspector. Then he turned to Iolanthe and explained: 'I'm afraid I can't share too much more, but I can tell you this. There never was any debt. They had marked your father as a likely target for blackmail, because of his history of gambling, and befriended him in Australia. They haven't said yet how they found out about you—'

'Hypnosis,' Miss Hawthorne whispered to herself, thinking about how clever Monica had been.

'But either way,' the inspector continued, 'he must've told them enough to make them curious. Then the accident happened and they filed the information away. Once their income in Australia dried up and the police there started to catch up with them, they decided to come to England and seek you out.'

'It... was all a lie?' Iolanthe's voice quivered.

'Yes. You're under no obligation to them,' he said, firmly. 'You never were.'

Iolanthe slumped. Miss Hawthorne put a hand on her shoulder and looked at the inspector, who nodded and stood up.

'I think that's probably enough for today, Miss Grosvenor. We'll have your statement ready for you this afternoon and you'll need to give evidence when the case comes to court, so we will need to know where to contact you. Will you be going back to Sussex?'

Before she could speak, Miss Hawthorne answered for her: 'For the time being, Inspector, Miss Grosvenor will be coming to stay with me at Devil's End. My clients give me plenty of work providing them with herbal remedies and it is high time I took on an assistant. Then, once her affairs are in order, she can decide what to do next.'

Still speechless, Iolanthe turned to her and mouthed a heartfelt 'thank you'. Miss Hawthorne gave her a little wink in return.

Iolanthe wasn't sure what the future held, but she felt safe for the first time in months and, though she wasn't sure exactly what being Miss Hawthorne's assistant would be like, she rather thought she would enjoy finding out.

ENTENTE IN DANGER

ᛖᚡᛖᚱᛁ×ᛞᚨᛁ×ᛁᚾ×ᛖᚡᛖᚱᛁ×ᚹᚨᛁ×ᛁ×ᚨᛗ
×ᚷᛖᛏᛏᛁᛝ×ᛒᛖᛏᛏᛖᚱ×ᚨᚾᛞ×ᛒᛖᛏ

THE MOLVANIAN delegate woke with a start and looked at the clock on his bedside table. Three in the morning. He shifted awkwardly, trying to find a cool spot on the pillow, his face running with sweat. Then he froze.

A tiny sound, barely audible, came across the room. He closed his eyes – as if by not looking, he could make whatever it was go away. The sound came again. A tiny creak, then the door of the room began to open.

Slowly… Slowly… Unable to bear the tension anymore, the delegate sat up, suddenly, and looked towards the doorway.

And then he screamed.

Benton walked briskly down the corridor at UNIT HQ. He'd been summoned by the Brigadier and he was not about to keep his commanding officer waiting. Arriving at the Brigadier's office, Benton knocked on the door and waited for the 'come in' to give him leave to enter. As soon as he went in, he saw that the Brigadier wasn't alone.

Sitting by the desk was a small man in his late middle age, wearing a dark suit and a worried expression. His face was vaguely familiar, but Benton put that out of his mind for the time being and addressed himself to his CO.

'You sent for me, sir?' he said.

'Yes, at ease, Sergeant,' the Brigadier replied, then he indicated the gentleman opposite. 'This is Sir Giles Mulberry, of the Foreign Office. He's come with a request from the conference that's taking place in Stanswick this week.' Benton had noticed something about the conference in the paper, a meeting of representatives from two independent states, but he hadn't paid it much attention. Not that he'd let on.

Sir Giles looked at the Brigadier, as if seeking confirmation, then turned to Benton. 'Hello, Sergeant,' he said, and each exchanged a respectful nod. 'We've run into serious problems at the conference and we – that is, *I* hope that UNIT may be able to help.'

'Sir?' Benton kept his face carefully expressionless, his eyes fixed on a point on the wall just above the speaker's head. Sir Giles shifted in his seat, appearing ill at ease. Then he came to the point.

'The fact is, one of the delegates has come to believe that he's being persecuted by... well, by person or persons unknown. He's demanded that a neutral agency be engaged to provide him with security.'

Light dawned.

'And that means you, Benton.' The Brigadier opened a file on his desk. 'I've all the particulars here. We can go through them in a moment, but I wanted Sir Giles to meet you in person before you go to the conference.'

So that was it. Bodyguard duty. He shrugged mentally. Oh well, it would be a change.

Sir Giles continued: 'Yes, if you can fill the sergeant in with the details, Brigadier, I'll expect him at Stanswick Manor by this evening. Good day to you both.'

Rising from his chair, the diplomat gathered his hat and coat and departed with some speed. After the door closed behind his visitor, the Brigadier relaxed a little. Dealing with civilian authorities always put him on edge: one never knew what they were going to ask and they tended not to understand the complications of military operations. He turned the file towards Benton.

'Please sit down and have a look at this.'

'Thank you, sir.' Benton relaxed into the seat and picked up the file, turning the pages with an expression of concentration that gave way to concern. 'Sir, this... Mr Vornschawl? Is he...?'

Benton wasn't quite sure how to say what he was thinking.

'Mad?' asked the Brigadier, dryly.

'Well, er, no, I mean...'

'That's precisely what I asked myself when I read the file. Man wakes up every night in distress, reports seeing figures coming in and out of his room, objects moving around, hearing noises. But apparently not. He's been looked over by a specialist and they can't find any sign of mental disturbance, other than his being very, very scared.'

'Were there any witnesses?' Benton asked.

'Not to the nighttime... ah, *visitations*, but the objects that he claimed were moved definitely had been, though the rooms were locked and nobody has yet admitted moving them,' said the Brigadier.

'I see.' It certainly wasn't the wildest thing Benton had heard of. In fact, his mind briefly wandered to Auderly House, where they'd investigated reports of ghosts, which had turned into a battle with Daleks. He hoped this wouldn't be more of the same.

The Brigadier leaned back in his seat. 'The thing is, Benton,' he said, 'this conference is of vital importance. Molvania and Slokovia have been at daggers drawn for years. Getting them talking would not only bring stability to that whole area, but Sir Giles has intimated that an understanding between those countries will have a huge impact on trade too. So, when this issue arose, he went to the top. I've orders from Geneva to extend him every possible assistance. In the first instance, that means you.'

'Right, sir.' Benton sat up straight.

'It'll be plain clothes.' The Brigadier paused and closed his eyes briefly at the thought of Benton's ties, which, while definitely clothes, were in no way plain. 'So get yourself sorted out. Smyth will lay on transport.'

'Sir.'

Rightly interpreting this as a dismissal, Benton stood up, taking the file with him. He paused at the door. 'Sir? These… visions, or whatever they are, and stuff moving around, do you think…?'

'Sir Giles won't approve, but he's given me carte blanche to deal with the matter as I see fit, so I see no reason why we shouldn't make use of all the expertise at our disposal,' said the Brigadier.

'Right.' Benton opened the door. 'Will you call her, sir, or shall I?'

Miss Hawthorne was in her workroom, bottling a distillation of evening primrose, when the telephone rang. She put down the bottle and funnel she'd been holding with an impatient exclamation but picked them up again when the ringing stopped and she realised that her assistant had answered the call. Having filled and sealed the bottle, she set it on the shelf with the others and rinsed her hands at the sink. She then went down the hall to the sitting room, in case she should be needed.

Her assistant was still speaking when Miss Hawthorne opened the sitting room door. Iolanthe Grosvenor had changed since her first meeting with Miss Hawthorne four months ago. Her hair, previously long and flowing, had been cut into a bob that framed her pale face with chestnut-coloured curls. She'd quickly abandoned her mystic's clothing – long, shapeless dresses and shawls, forced on her by her kidnappers – and, instead, wore her preferred outfit of simple trousers and well-cut blouses. Some of the inhabitants of Devil's End, being on the conservative, not to say old-fashioned, side, looked askance at the trousers, but Iolanthe had not let the suspicious glances bother her and the villagers had soon become accustomed to the sight of her trim figure either walking or cycling round the village as she ran errands and made deliveries for Miss Hawthorne.

Her friend and employer watched her as she spoke.

'Yes, yes, I've got that. Stanswick Manor. Will you be able to—? Yes, I'll call back when we're on the way. What time are you leaving?' She looked at her watch. 'Yes, should be before then. I…' She looked round to the doorway where Miss Hawthorne was standing and continued: 'Yes, she is, did you want to…? Okay, that's fine – we'll see you then. Goodbye.'

Iolanthe replaced the receiver and made a final note on the pad in front of her, then turned to Miss Hawthorne, who was looking both surprised and curious. 'That was Sergeant Benton,' she said.

'Ah, I see. And does he have work for me?' asked Miss Hawthorne.

'For us, actually. He's been ordered to Stanswick Manor, to that peace conference, or whatever it is, to act as security to one of the delegates. The Brigadier wants us to go up there and stay close by so he can consult us if he needs to.'

Miss Hawthorne nodded: like Benton, she'd seen the conference mentioned in the papers, but paid little attention to it. 'How interesting,' said Miss Hawthorne. 'But why would he need us? We're hardly experts in security.'

'It seems that the delegate has been… seeing things,' said Iolanthe. 'He's been given a clean bill of health by a psychiatrist, so the next thing is to work out what is happening to him and who's behind it. That's where we come in.'

'Hmm. And did Sergeant Benton say what form these *visions* took?'

'Not really,' Iolanthe replied. 'I got the impression he didn't want to say too much over the phone. He's got the UNIT file with him though, for us to look at when we meet him.'

'Good. We'll need all the facts. He'll be staying in the Manor itself, I assume? It is a hotel as well, yes?'

'Yeah, he needs to be on call for his delegate. But it's been taken over completely by the conference, so we've got rooms booked at...' She consulted her notepad. '*The Red Lion* in Stanswick village. The sergeant says he'll try and get over to see us sometime this evening if he can.'

Despite her previous experiences, Miss Hawthorne was slightly breathless at the speed at which events were moving. 'We'd better get packed! I'll just check next door about Gabriel...' The cat's ears pricked at the mention of his name, then settled down when he realised that food wasn't in the offing.

Miss Hawthorne left to call at her neighbour's and make arrangements for feeding Gabriel while she was away, and Iolanthe went off to pack a bag with clothes, toiletries, and a selection of books that she thought might come in useful. Iolanthe returned to the sitting room to take the AA Road Atlas down from the shelf and begin to plot their route from Devil's End to Stanswick.

Miss Hawthorne quietly came back, hanging around the door, and looked at Iolanthe. She really had begun to change – from the shy, nervous creature who had arrived at Devil's End after months of mental torment, into the calm, confident young woman who'd been hidden underneath. A metamorphosis. She was not completely healed: that would take a long time. But the security and friendship that surrounded her had already done a great deal, as had the knowledge that she was not, in fact, indebted to her captors. The fact that they were safely behind bars certainly added to her newfound tenacity. Miss Hawthorne smiled and went over to the desk.

Iolanthe smiled too to see Miss Hawthorne. Olive.

'It looks like there's a fairly direct route if we take the main road here...' Iolanthe pointed to the map and Miss Hawthorne nodded.

'That looks straightforward enough. I shall go and pack; if you could call the sergeant, we can be on our way.'

Ten minutes later saw Miss Hawthorne's Austin Seven pull away from the house and follow the road out of Devil's End and towards Stanswick.

It was late afternoon when they arrived at *The Red Lion.* The inn stood on the main street, near a marketplace, where the merchants were dismantling their stalls after what had clearly been a busy day. The front of the inn was red brick and the roof tiled with slates; the sign which swung above the entrance showed the heraldic design of the animal from which it took its name. Tables and chairs stood outside, some of them in use by groups of men who Miss Hawthorne's instincts told her were reporters, waiting for the bar to open. She ignored them and led the way to the reception desk, which was just inside the front door.

Miss Hawthorne and Iolanthe were greeted by the landlord, a friendly man of about fifty who checked them in on his register and then led the way to their rooms. The accommodation was in a small annexe to the main building, across a courtyard that bore witness to *The Red Lion's* past as a coaching inn. The rooms were small but comfortable and the shared bathroom clean and well fitted out.

The ladies unpacked, then made their way across to the demure function room that Benton had engaged for their evening meal.

Benton arrived as dessert was being served, bringing with him a tall man in a dark suit, who he introduced as Inspector Dent of the Stanswick police. He and Dent declined the offer of food, but accepted coffee, which they drank while Miss Hawthorne and Iolanthe finished their meal. When the plates had been cleared, the inspector drew two files from his briefcase and placed them on the table.

'This is what we have so far. It isn't much, I'm afraid. The Molvanians won't release the medical report on Mr

Vornschawl, but they insist that he is not suffering from mental derangement,' he said.

'I see,' said Miss Hawthorne, turning the pages of the first file. 'His sleep is disturbed; he reported seeing a cowled figure in his bedroom, but when he called for help the figure disappeared; and his belongings seemed to have been interfered with.' She paused, then said, 'Well, Inspector, without the medical evidence, and from a laywoman's point of view, this looks very like a case of paranoia.'

Dent cleared his throat. 'I agree. There's the question of the personal items being interfered with. He says that some of them were locked away in a desk to which he has the only key, and others had moved when he'd left the room briefly and locked the door. But it's not a difficult matter to get a key copied, and I'd be tempted to think that someone is stoking the paranoia by moving things around.'

Miss Hawthorne considered this. 'I would say you were probably right, Inspector, although telekinesis is a recognised phenomenon.'

Dent looked at her in disbelief.

'Yes,' said Iolanthe, 'it's possible to move things with the mind, but it takes a huge amount of mental energy.'

'Could they move things while they were in another room, though?' asked Benton, 'I mean, if Mr Vornshawl didn't hear or see anyone moving his stuff…' He broke off, but Iolanthe understood.

'I don't know,' she said. 'I think usually the person is in the same room as the object. Depending on how strong their psychic field is, they might not need to have eye contact with the object, but that's how I…' She stopped.

'Do you mean you can actually do that?' asked Dent.

Iolanthe didn't reply. She sat up straight and stared at the salt cellar, which stood in the centre of the table. Her companions watched in silence. For a moment, nothing happened, then the salt cellar wobbled. Iolanthe leaned forward. The cellar wobbled again, then fell onto its side, spilling salt on the tablecloth. Iolanthe sighed and collapsed back in the chair. Miss Hawthorne looked at her with concern. 'I'm all right,' said Iolanthe, faintly. 'But you see what I mean. I only just managed to tip that over and I was right next to it too. When I was…' She paused, then went on quietly. 'When I was with the others, they tried to get me to do it, but it took too much out of me. Telekinesis is hard work.'

She smiled, faintly, and Miss Hawthorne returned to the other matter in hand. 'These manifestations at night. Have there been any witnesses to them?'

'Yes and no. One of Mr Vornschawl's regular security men was on duty outside his bedroom door. He heard a disturbance inside and a cry. When he and his colleague went in, Mr Vornschawl was pointing at the door asking if they could see 'it'. When they told him there was nothing there, he refused to believe them, insisting that there was something in the room, that then left through the door, which, he believed, had been open all the time.'

Iolanthe raised her eyes from the file, her chin on one hand. 'But it definitely wasn't?' she asked.

'No, it was closed and locked,' confirmed Dent. 'The guards checked the room and the corridor, but they couldn't find any trace that anyone other than Vornschawl had been in the room.'

Iolanthe returned her gaze to the file and Miss Hawthorne spoke again. 'Has he only seen this figure at night? I mean, have there been other manifestations during the day?'

Benton took a turn in answering. He shook his head and said, 'He doesn't see anything in the daytime – just at night. He says he feels fine, or rather he felt fine, until just after dinner and then he feels more and more panicky until the early hours, when whatever it is shows up.' Benton looked at the inspector. 'I suppose it could be that he is so busy with the conference he hasn't got time to panic in the daytime.'

Dent nodded. 'That was my assumption at first.'

Catching the inflection in his voice, Miss Hawthorne asked, 'But?'

'In his statement…' Dent turned the file towards himself, briefly skimmed it, then turned it back when he had found the place. '*Here*, he says that he felt ill at ease for at least two nights before the first, ah, vision. The feeling started in the evening, got worse through the night, but, for the first two nights, he was back to normal the next day. Once the figure started appearing, he had more trouble sleeping, but, if it is a mental disorder, it seems to be very punctual, and that makes me suspicious.'

There was a brief silence as the investigators considered the files again. Finally, Miss Hawthorne spoke. 'Well, as I see it, we have two trails to follow. Firstly, we need to establish the cause of these visions and… practical jokes, for want of a better word. I suggest that Miss Grosvenor and I may be best placed to pursue that angle. Then we need to find out who is behind these attacks and what they seek to gain from them. Sergeant, I think this is a matter for you and the inspector.'

Dent was slightly startled at Miss Hawthorne taking the lead like this, but he couldn't fault her reasoning, and said so. 'Unfortunately,' he added, 'that may be a ticklish job. We can run background checks on the hotel staff, but the Molvanian delegation are understandably cagey about letting us investigate their people. They've already threatened to invoke diplomatic immunity and I'd rather have them cooperative, even if we need to take a closer look at some of them. Unless…' He looked at Benton who guessed what he had in mind.

'I can try, sir,' he said. 'I've got to check in with the Brigadier this evening in any case – I can ask him to get on to Geneva to try and smooth things over a bit.'

'Thank you, Sergeant. One thing we can look into is who stands to gain the most by disrupting the conference. I take it we are all agreed that this can't be a personal attack?' The others nodded. 'Right, then my team will start there. There must be lots of vested interests that wouldn't want this agreement to be signed.' He got up and nodded to the others.

'Are the Slokovian delegation also under suspicion?' asked Miss Hawthorne.

Dent paused. 'It's tempting, but I'm inclined to discount them for a couple of reasons. One: the delegations are in separate wings of the manor, with little communication apart from in the conference room; any member of the delegation passing from one wing to the other would probably be noticed. And two: they're the obvious suspects. And when a case presents me with such an obvious explanation, I want to make very, very sure before I start making accusations. We will have to investigate them, but I wouldn't be surprised if someone were trying to set them up. Right, I must be off. Sergeant?'

'Yes, sir, I'll call you tomorrow – or sooner if anything happens in the night – and I'll get in touch with the Brigadier as soon as I get back to the manor. I expect someone from HQ will be in contact with you regardless.'

'Thank you. Good evening to you all.'

With a final nod, Dent departed. Once the door closed behind him, the others relaxed a little. Benton went to the bar for drinks and, when he returned, he found that Miss Hawthorne and Iolanthe were both making notes and discussing possible tactics. He set the glasses on the table and sat down.

'Where are we up to?' he asked.

Miss Hawthorne looked up from her notes. 'Ah, thank you,' she said, then sipped her sherry. 'Iolanthe and I were just speculating on the causes of this unfortunate gentleman's hallucinations.'

'Right. Any ideas?'

'One or two, but they're difficult to verify, I'm afraid. Still…' She looked at Iolanthe who fidgeted with her pencil for a moment, as if finding the courage to speak.

'It's possible to use hypnosis to make people see things,' she said, 'but it's hard to tell when someone has been hypnotised until the trigger is activated and they start seeing whatever it is the person who hypnotised them wants them to see.'

'And what would the trigger be?' asked Benton.

'It could be anything: a sound, a smell, even! But they would only be affected by the hallucination when they heard, smelt, or saw the trigger. The rest of the time they would be completely normal,' explained Iolanthe.

Benton took a sip from his pint and then set the glass down again. 'Difficult to pin on anyone.'

'Yes, because you don't know when the hypnosis was first performed. In here…' Iolanthe reached into her bag which was next to her chair, and pulled out a book. '…it says that the initial hypnosis could be months or even years before.'

'So, he could have been hypnotised before he even got here? That does complicate things. We could be looking for a suspect who's still in Molvania.'

'Yes. Then there's the panic symptoms. The inspector said the hallucinations didn't start for a couple of days, but he still felt scared. So, whatever the trigger for the visions is, it isn't also causing the panic.'

Benton rubbed his forehead. 'Poor chap. What else have they done to him?'

This time, Miss Hawthorne answered. 'I believe I may have an answer to that question, but, again, it will be difficult to verify. It may be that Mr Vornschawl has been dosed with a substance that accelerates the heart rate, causing excessive sweating and a feeling of panic.'

'He's been *doped*? How would they get it to him?' Benton was both startled and appalled.

'My guess is that his evening meal has been doctored.' Miss Hawthorne leaned her elbows on the table and steepled her fingers. 'The symptoms began in the evening and had dissipated by the next morning. That would suggest a small dose has been added to his food or drink – enough to bring on symptoms overnight, but not enough to have any lasting effect. Unfortunately, we can't be sure what the substance is, or even if it exists, without testing the food.'

Benton frowned. 'The meals come from the hotel, but they're served by his own staff, so the stuff could be put in either in the kitchen, on the way up, or just before it's served, if it is one of his own people...' He paused, then spoke more decisively: 'I'll just have to try and get some of it to test. I'm not sure how, but I'll have a go and pass it to the inspector. He can get his lab onto it.'

'Can you do it without being observed?' asked Miss Hawthorne.

'I'll certainly try.'

'Good. About the hypnosis, I suggest that Iolanthe and I go over the files again and see if we can find the trigger for these attacks.'

'Right.' Benton looked at his watch. 'I'd better get back. I'll be in touch tomorrow, if not before. You got the radio all right?'

Miss Hawthorne nodded and smiled. She'd felt faintly ridiculous having to carry a UNIT radio set, but she recognised that it was the most efficient way of reaching Benton. It was currently in its case in the bottom of the wardrobe in her room, until she could summon the nerve to unpack it.

'In that case, good night to you both.' Benton headed to the door then stopped with an exclamation. 'Oh! What about the things moving around? That definitely happened.'

Miss Hawthorne looked thoughtful. 'Indeed,' she said. 'Telekinesis *is* possible, of course, though as we saw, it requires immense mental powers. But I believe we should start from the inspector's point of view: that these objects are being moved by more straightforward human interference and work from there.'

'That seems fair. Good night, then,' said Benton.

His fellow investigators wished Benton good night in

their turn and they all left the room, the ladies to return to their rooms for the night, and Benton to make his way back to the manor.

In a modern, luxurious study, one end of a telephone conversation was taking place. The walls of the study were lined with shelves, mostly holding photographs in silver frames. A large portrait hung over the fireplace, depicting a tall, heavily built man of early middle age. The face showed signs of having been handsome, but heavy jowls and a forbidding stare made it unattractive. The subject of the portrait was sitting behind an imposing desk, turning from side to side in his leather chair as he spoke.

'Report.'

'We have made good progress. He is almost on the point of collapse. I believe three days, at the most, and he will crack,' said the voice at the other end of the line.

'Excellent. And he doesn't suspect?' asked the man.

'No. He believes that he's being set upon by evil spirits or by wizards,' the other replied, laughing.

'And the police?'

'Putting their noses in. There is one thing...' The voice hesitated and the man in the chair leaned forward. 'There is a new man. He was requested by Vornschawl. He's from UNIT.'

The man in the chair stopped shifting around abruptly. 'UNIT? Blast. That could complicate matters. What's he like?'

'Tall, strong. Not very intelligent.'

'Well, that's something. He will be reporting to his HQ though.' The man frowned, deep in thought. 'He can't stop us now, though; we're too far along. There isn't time for him to get on our track and if he does...'

'Understood.'

The line went dead. The man in the chair smiled grimly and drew a folder from a stack in one of the trays on his desk.

UNIT? It was too late to stop now. He had too much riding on this. His accomplice would just have to keep an eye on this UNIT chap and deal with him as necessary.

Another grim smile. He'd no doubt that his man was capable of dealing with this newcomer, however tall and strong he might be.

When Benton arrived back at the manor, he reported to the head of security for the Molvanian delegation. Commander Axel Schmitz was a short, energetic looking man, with greying hair swept back from an incongruously youthful face. He shook Benton's hand and asked him if the accommodation provided was acceptable to him.

Benton's confirmation was met with a warm smile. 'Good, good,' said Schmitz. 'I'm sorry I couldn't stay to talk when you arrived earlier. I trust my colleagues made you welcome.'

'They certainly did,' said Benton, then, cautiously, 'I hope you don't consider this an imposition, sir. I'm here to help in any way you need me.'

Schmitz smiled. 'You need have no fear of that, Sergeant,' he said. 'I'm certain you won't be... "in the way", is it? We are grateful for the assistance of UNIT. And now, if you'll come with me, I'll introduce you to Mr Vornschawl.'

Benton followed Schmitz out of the room, noting as he did so a couple of security men taking a break at a table near the door. As he passed by, one of the men looked around, then turned back and muttered something to his companion, who looked over with an expression that was anything but friendly. Oh well. Curiosity? Professional jealousy? Schmitz seemed friendly enough at any rate and he was in charge, after all. Benton stored the incident away in his mind for later and concentrated on his immediate surroundings.

Schmitz led the way along a corridor to a lift, where he turned a key to access the buttons for the private floor where the Molvanian delegation was staying.

The manor, a building in the Palladian style which had been the focal point of a Georgian country estate, was divided into a central building and two wings. The conference room, kitchen, and accommodation for the conference organisers were in the central part and one wing each had been allocated to the delegations, allowing them both privacy and security.

Once Schmitz and Benton had reached the upper floor, another corridor led to the delegate's suite. Benton noticed a trolley by the door, bearing used plates and dishes, covered by a cloth. Could he be in luck? It was worth a try, surely? As Schmitz knocked on the door, Benton moved over to the trolley and cautiously lifted a corner of the cloth. Underneath were a soup plate, a dinner plate with the remains of roast beef and potatoes on it, and a dessert dish with the remnants of what looked to Benton like Angel Delight, but which he assumed was something a bit more refined. A coffee cup and saucer stood next to the plates.

Schmitz was now standing in the doorway, talking to someone in the room beyond. Looking over his shoulder, but trying to stay out of sight, Benton could just see that a waiter was removing a coffee pot from the table that stood to the left of the door. Good. That meant that the detritus under the cloth was the remains of Vornschawl's dinner. Not knowing how long he had, or if he would get another chance, Benton picked up a napkin from the tray and wiped it swiftly over all the plates and round the inside of the coffee cup. Schmitz, hearing movement behind him, turned, but Benton stood quickly at ease, his hands behind his back, the napkin screwed up in his right hand, his face betraying no sign of the hurried activity.

'Sergeant?'

'Sir?'

Schmitz turned back and went into the room. Benton followed him, hastily shoving the napkin into his pocket and hoping that he wouldn't be expected to shake hands with anyone. He stood to attention as he was introduced and breathed a small sigh of relief when it became clear that Vornschawl was going to keep matters on a formal footing.

The delegate was, like his security chief, a relatively short man, but, ordinarily, he had an air of calm authority. Looking at him now, however, Benton noticed shadows under his eyes, and had the impression of a man struggling to keep up an appearance of strength under extreme strain.

As if he had read Benton's thoughts, Vornschawl smiled wryly. 'Yes, I'm very tired today, Sergeant. But no less determined!' He looked around the room as if daring someone to contradict him. 'I'm most grateful to UNIT for their assistance, and to the police. If it were just a threat to myself, I would be content to allow Schmitz and his men to investigate, but there is more at stake here than my personal security.'

'Yes, sir,' said Benton, nodding.

'Commander Schmitz will see to it that you have all you need for your investigation. As to my immediate security, I understand that you will be on duty tonight?'

'Yes, sir.' It had been arranged that two Molvanian officers would be on duty from nine o'clock until one in the morning, when they would be relieved by Benton and a Corporal Hesse, Vornschawl's personal bodyguard.

'Then I will not detain you further.'

Benton thanked him, turned smartly, and left the room, followed by Schmitz.

Outside the door, Schmitz once again shook Benton's hand. Luckily, he had already wiped it on his trousers. 'Thank you, Sergeant. Corporal Hesse will meet you here at 1am. I regret I cannot join you myself: I have other responsibilities at that time.'

'Understood. Thank you, sir.'

Schmitz walked briskly off down the corridor and Benton went to his bedroom. Once inside, he locked the door and wedged a chair under the handle to make doubly sure that he wouldn't be disturbed.

In the bottom of his holdall was a small box containing

what he laughingly described as his 'detective kit'. Benton opened the lid of the box and took out a plastic bag. He pulled the napkin out of his pocket – wincing slightly when he saw what the food and drink had done to the lining – and put it carefully in the bag, sealing the top and attaching a label with the date, time, and contents. He then used his radio to contact the police station and arrange for the bag to be collected and sent to the lab. The room was equipped with a telephone, but Benton avoided it on the grounds that it offered too many opportunities for eavesdroppers.

Once his rendezvous with the police had been arranged, Benton forced himself to relax with the distraction of the latest Desmond Bagley novel. After about half an hour, a phone call from reception summoned him to the ground floor where, under the pretence of receiving a file, he passed his bag of evidence to the police rider and then returned to his room, this time to sleep until his alarm woke him at midnight.

Neither Iolanthe or Miss Hawthorne had felt able to sleep that evening, but they had said good night and went to their own rooms. Iolanthe had got into bed and spread the contents of the police file out on the bedclothes and, assisted by a bag of chocolate limes, began to search for any trace of the hypnotic trigger. Miss Hawthorne made herself a cup of tea and sat for a while with her crochet, mulling over her notes.

The next morning, they met outside the door to Miss Hawthorne's room and crossed the yard together. Breakfast began in silence, until Miss Hawthorne, noting the dark lines under Iolanthe's eyes, asked, 'My dear, did you get any sleep last night?'

'Not a lot,' admited Iolanthe, then, carrying war into the enemy's camp, asked, 'did you?'

Miss Hawthorne sighed. 'No, and I fear that it was so much wasted time. I seem to be no clearer in my mind about the case than I was last night. Did you make any progress?'

'Possibly. I can't prove it without testing, but I may have found the trigger.' Iolanthe looked thoughtful as she buttered a second slice of toast.

'Really? That's definite progress!' replied Miss Hawthorne, hopefully.

Miss Hawthorne glanced around the room. Nobody seemed to be paying them any attention, but they couldn't be too careful. Iolanthe caught her look and understood. For the rest of the meal, they discussed the local area, with the help of a guidebook that Miss Hawthorne had borrowed from the landlord; anyone listening would have assumed that the slightly eccentric looking lady and her younger relative were planning a day out.

After breakfast, Iolanthe and Miss Hawthorne returned to the annex and Iolanthe gathered the file and her notes before joining Miss Hawthorne in her room. She sat on the edge of the bed while Miss Hawthorne sat in an armchair and leafed through until she found the page she wanted.

'It may not be anything, but I noticed that before every hallucination, he mentions being woken by, or hearing a sound, like a door creaking as it opened,' she said, eventually.

'And you think that could be the trigger?' asked Miss Hawthorne.

'It's possible. But it'd be difficult to prove without testing it on him.'

Miss Hawthorne frowned. 'I can't see how we would manage that, but it might be possible. We must inform Sergeant Benton and see what he suggests. Would you say that the sound is caused by someone actually opening the door?'

'I thought so, but both the guards say that the door was closed and locked when they tried to get in, so unless they're lying...'

'Well, we must consider every possibility, of course,' she said, then a thought came to her: 'One moment! Does the room connect with the rest of the suite?'

Iolanthe pulled out a roughly drawn plan of the suite. 'Yes, here, there's the bathroom on this side and this door goes through to the sitting room.'

'I think we can discount the idea of someone hiding in the bathroom; that seems unlikely,' said Miss Hawthorne, looking at the plan. 'But it might be possible that the attacker opened the door to the sitting room, either to make the door creak or to fake the sound in some way.'

'Yes, that would work – Oh, except it says that the door was locked… but then whoever it was could have locked it behind them. In all the panic, the guards wouldn't have noticed the noise and they'd have been busy with Mr Vornschawl at first, so they mightn't have checked it straight away,' said Iolanthe, then looked at her friend. 'Do you think that's it?'

Miss Hawthorne leaned forward in excitement. 'I believe that's the answer!' She then sat back again, still grinning. 'So, we are looking for a person with access to the suite, who would not be suspected. It appears the inspector was right, and this is an "inside job".'

Iolanthe smiled at the audible quotation marks but became serious again as they both considered the implications of their deductions. 'It does look that way,' she agreed.

'We must see what Sergeant Benton has to say; he may have more information. He said he would call at ten, either on the phone or on that contraption.' Miss Hawthorne gestured to the radio, drawing another smile from Iolanthe. 'Until then, we may as well go over the files again together.'

'And I'll get my books. If we have found the trigger, the next thing will be working out how to deactivate it.'

Iolanthe left the room and returned a few minutes later with the books. Since her experiences with the gangsters, she'd made a special study of hypnosis, both in hypnotising others and in resisting trances and suggestion. Miss Hawthorne, always keen to broaden her knowledge, had joined her assistant in her studies. Now, they sat quietly together, the books and file pages between them as Miss Hawthorne searched for clues and Iolanthe for a way to break the hypnosis that was causing the hallucinations.

The silence was broken by the telephone bell.

Miss Hawthorne answered. 'Hello? Oh, Sergeant! Yes, it's good to hear you too. Yes, yes, we believe so, yes. But how did... really? Yes, one moment.'

Miss Hawthorne gestured to Iolanthe, who got up from her seat on the bed and came over. The phone didn't have a loudspeaker, but Miss Hawthorne held the receiver between them and Benton's voice came through clearly.

'—and quite a night of it,' he was saying when Iolanthe reached the phone.

'Has there been another hallucination?' asked Iolanthe.

'I'll say!' said Benton. 'Happened just after two. Same as before, as far as I can gather: one minute, all was quiet; the next, he was screaming blue murder. The door was locked. By the time we got in there, whatever it was had gone and he was shaking and couldn't speak for fear. When I spoke to him this morning, he said the visions are getting worse. More figures, and last night they reached out to him with their hands covered in blood.'

'Heavens!' exclaimed Miss Hawthorne.

'Nasty business. Schmitz was right on the spot once we'd broken in. He helped us get him calmed down. I was wondering, could it be part of the hallucination? Would it get worse over time because the person who did it made it that way?'

It was Iolanthe's turn to look thoughtful. 'It's possible; I don't really know,' she said, 'or it could be the stress making it worse. He must be worn out by now.'

'He certainly looked it when I got back yesterday evening,' said Benton.

Miss Hawthorne spoke again. 'Did you find any evidence of what might be causing the palpitations? That must be putting a strain on his health.'

'Possibly.' Benton described his actions with the napkin and dinner trolley. 'The inspector said he would call you this afternoon, assuming he has any results by then.'

'Good. If we can identify the substance, we may be able to counteract it without showing our hand to the enemy, so to speak.'

'And did you say that you've found the trigger?' asked Benton.

'Yes, or, at least, we believe so,' said Miss Hawthorne. She handed the receiver to Iolanthe, who brought Benton up to date with the results of their research. Naturally, Benton then asked if they could stop it happening.

'I think it's possible,' said Iolanthe, 'but I won't know for sure until I try. And I don't know how I'm going to get close enough to do that.'

There was a brief silence at the other end of the line while Benton considered this. Then he said, 'We'll have to get you up here somehow. Maybe talk to the inspector and see if he can wangle it. Oh, half a mo.'

They heard a click as Benton put the receiver to one side, and, in the distance, he could be heard talking to someone. He returned a moment later and said into the phone, 'I'm sorry, sir, I'm due to escort Mr Vornschawl to the conference room. I'll report later.'

Guessing that the other person was in earshot and that they had been temporarily cast in the role of the Brigadier, Miss Hawthorne said goodbye and hung up.

At the manor, Benton replaced the receiver and went to the door, nodding to the guard who stood in the corridor. He'd taken all the precautions he could to keep the call private, from using a direct line and checking for bugs, to locking the door. It was unlikely that the guard had heard anything, but, if he had, it was too late now. Benton had met the guard when he had arrived the previous day, but hadn't got much of an impression of him.

Corporal Brecht was shorter than Benton by at least six

inches. As far as he could judge, the corporal was in his thirties, a stocky, well-built man with curly, dark brown hair and a neatly trimmed beard. Benton didn't want to seem to be interrogating his companion, so after a few pleasantries, the conversation ceased.

When they reached the suite, they found Vornschawl as he had been the previous day: tired, but determined to attend the conference and play his part. He walked between his escorts, stumbling over the front of the lift, but Benton's hand under his elbow stopped him from falling.

'Thank you, Sergeant. It would not do for me to look like an old crock, would it?' he said.

Assuming the question was rhetorical, Benton didn't answer. Instead, he looked ahead at the mirrored lift doors, just in time to catch a curious expression on the face of his temporary colleague. Not hostile certainly but... Benton struggled to put his finger on what it was that bothered him about the expression.

Then he decided to file it away in his memory for later. He would need all his wits about him at the conference.

After speaking to Benton, Miss Hawthorne and Iolanthe gathered what they would need for the day and left the inn for the morning. Miss Hawthorne left a message with the landlord in case Dent should call earlier than expected, then joined Iolanthe who was studying a map of the village. After brief consideration, they took the tourist route around the village, with a few detours.

The church, a Victorian gothic confection, was of limited interest to Miss Hawthorne, who preferred the Norman-style, but they went inside and spent a little while looking at the stained glass and earlier funerary monuments that had been reinstalled after the demolition of the earlier church and its reconstruction in the nineteenth century. After the church, their route took them to the green, which reminded them both of Devil's End and led Miss Hawthorne to reminisce about that most memorable of Beltanes.

After doing a circuit of the green, they made the first of their detours, into a hardware shop. When the hardware shop wasn't able to furnish Iolanthe's needs, the pair called in at a secondhand and junk shop a few doors down. Miss Hawthorne waited outside, trying to appear fascinated with a display of garish Moorcroft pottery in the window, until Iolanthe returned, looking quietly pleased and nodding in answer to her companion's raised eyebrow.

On consulting her watch, Miss Hawthorne suggested lunch might be in order, and, after comparing menus and décor, they decided on a small but inviting looking tearoom. This proved a good choice, and the ladies enjoyed a selection of sandwiches, followed by fruit cake and accompanied by tea. Lunch over, they went back to the inn and took possession of a set of table and chairs outside, so as to be on hand when the inspector rang – and to the disgust of one of the visiting journalists who had his eye on that particular spot to do his crossword and wait for opening time. Ignoring the baleful glare levelled at them by the gentleman, the pair began to pass the time; by reading on Iolanthe's part, and crocheting on Miss Hawthorne's.

The church clock had just struck two when Miss Hawthorne heard her name and looked up to see Dent approaching. He considered pulling up a chair, but, seeing the disgruntled journalist nearby, suggested that they move somewhere more private. A word with the landlord secured the room from the previous evening and the investigators convened to compare notes.

'I'm on my way up to the house and I'm running a bit early, so I thought I'd speak to you in person,' said Dent. 'Always easier to discuss things face-to-face than over the phone.'

'Oh, I agree. May I ask, has there been any report from the laboratory?'

'That's mostly what I came to tell you. The napkin had

traces of a drug used to treat low blood pressure. Because the traces of food and drink were mixed together, we couldn't get an exact fix on which one the drug was concealed in, but the lab boys think it was probably in the coffee – the caffeine would get it into his system more quickly.'

'I see.' Miss Hawthorne steepled her fingers again, deep in thought. 'The effect of the drug seems to have dissipated by the morning; would that be a question of dosage?'

'We believe so,' replied Dent. 'It has to be taken regularly when it's used for treatment, so a relatively small dose would produce a temporary reaction, like the one suffered by Vornschawl. We consulted a medic and he said he thinks the dosing hasn't been going on for long enough to do any permanent damage, but, if it continues there will a risk to his heart.'

'We must find out who's doing this and stop them as soon as we can. Is there anything we can do to counteract its effects?'

'Turns out there is, and that's why I was on my way up to the manor. We don't want the attacker to know we are on to him too soon, so Vornschawl will need to carry on being doped, at least for the time being. Our tame medic has given me something to reduce the effects of the drug, so he can carry on having his dinner, take one of these…' He drew a small glass bottle out of one pocket. '…and pretend to be agitated, but reduce the strain on his heart.'

'Good. And we, or at least Miss Grosvenor, may have found the explanation for these distressing visions.'

Dent listened attentively as Iolanthe explained her conclusions about the hypnosis and the probably trigger for the hallucinations. Finally, he sighed. 'It's beyond me, Miss Grosvenor, but I'll take your word for it. And you think he can be cured?'

Iolanthe bit her bottom lip. 'It should be possible to remove the trigger. Is there anyone you can call on that has experience of hypnosis?'

'Other than yourself? No, so I'm afraid you will need to come with me.'

'Me?' Iolanthe flushed for a moment but recovered herself. 'I mean, if you think…?'

'I do. Do you think you're up to the job?'

A moment's hesitation and then: 'Yes.'

'Perfect. I'll introduce you as one of my plain clothes officers. The tricky part will be persuading the Molvanians to let us talk to Vornschawl alone. I'd like to think we aren't dealing with a widespread conspiracy, but, at the moment, we can't trust anyone, save Sergeant Benton.' Dent stood up. 'I can give you a few minutes to get organised, then we'll need to be off. I'll meet you outside in, say, ten minutes?'

Iolanthe nodded. 'Yes, that's fine. I just need a few things.'

She left the room and Dent looked at Miss Hawthorne.

'Can she do it?' he asked.

'I'm certain she can. Iolanthe has not had the easiest of times lately, but she is a very capable young woman and if she says she can do a thing, we must believe that she can,' said Miss Hawthorne, decidedly.

He was clearly buoyed by this. 'If I need to stay on at the house, I'll get one of the uniformed officers to run her back. Otherwise, I'll drop her off myself.'

Iolanthe reappeared at this point, with a satchel over one shoulder and nodded, rather tremulously, to Dent and Miss Hawthorne.

'All ready? Good,' said Dent.

He led the way out of the inn and towards his car, parked at the edge of the marketplace. He opened the passenger door for Iolanthe and then went round to the driver's side. As he got in, the radio on his dashboard crackled.

'Dent here,' he answered. 'Go ahead, over.'

Miss Hawthorne was too far away to hear the conversation, but she saw Dent's expression grow increasingly serious as he asked terse questions of the person at the other end.

Eventually he replaced his radio receiver and leaned out of the car window. 'Miss Hawthorne? Jump in!'

'I beg your pardon?'

'We need all hands on deck. I reckon you'd pass for a doctor.'

Miss Hawthorne was bewildered by the suggestion but got into the car. As Dent pulled away and drove off at speed, Miss Hawthorne recovered her breath.

'Inspector, I don't wish to distract you,' she asked, then paused as Dent veered suddenly to avoid a cyclist, before carrying on, 'but what exactly is happening and why must I pass for a doctor?'

'I'm sorry to rush you, Miss Hawthorne,' replied Dent, without taking his eyes off the road, 'but we need to get to the manor as soon as we can. Vornschawl has collapsed.'

Discussion had got underway quickly in the conference room that morning. The delegates took their places and began where they had left off the previous day, with a debate on the ratification of trade treaties. The discussion was held mostly in German, which was a shared language of the two states, and the moderator was a representative of the West German government.

Benton, had stationed himself opposite the Molvanian delegates. He didn't try and follow the negotiations. He spoke a little German, but the speed of the conversations and the technical and legal language were beyond him. As far as he could tell, the discussion seemed to be going well; there was none of the tension he would usually have associated with international negotiations. Save for an occasional glance around the room, Benton kept his eyes on Vornschawl and the men either side of him.

Corporal Brecht stood behind Vornschawl. Once again, Benton was vaguely troubled by the man. Something about him that he couldn't quite put his finger on. He looked at Vornschawl who seemed to be struggling to concentrate. He reached for a glass of water and his hand shook as he raised it to his lips. Benton looked at Brecht again. There it was. The expression on the guard's face betrayed no concern for his employer. Instead, he looked... Benton thought for a moment. Yes, that was it: he looked satisfied. Content. Not an expression one would expect a man with his responsibilities to be wearing, particularly at the moment. Benton couldn't condemn a person because they pulled a face, but all the same...

The next moment, all other thoughts were driven from his mind as Vornschawl gasped and fell forward, unconscious, onto the table. Benton moved as if by reflex. He dashed around the table and managed to get himself between the other delegates and Vornschawl.

Brecht was already crouched down. 'He's breathing,' he said.

'Thank goodness,' replied Benton. He put his hands under Vornschawl's arms and raised him a little in the chair. The delegate's head sagged to one side. 'Out cold though. We'd better get him out of here.'

Brecht nodded and, between them, he and Benton carried Vornschawl to the corridor.

The guard on the door jumped as they came through. Benton snapped, 'Don't hang about, man – find a stretcher!'

As the guard departed, the two men laid their burden down on the floor and turned him onto his side to make sure that he was able to breathe unimpeded. The soldier who had been sent for the stretcher soon returned, and he and Brecht carried Vornschawl to the lift.

When they reached the delegates' suite, they met Schmitz, who exclaimed in horror and opened the door for the stretcher bearers to enter and place Vornschawl on the bed. Benton watched for a moment, then ran along the corridor to his room and the radio to contact Dent. When he returned, Vornschawl appeared to be resting comfortably, but had still not regained consciousness. Schmitz was on the telephone, speaking in Molvanian.

Brecht sat by the bed on a chair. He looked round as Benton came in. 'Where did you go?' he asked.

Benton nearly told him to mind his own business, but controlled himself. 'You and the commander had things in hand, so I went to inform the inspector. He's on his way up now.'

'Ha!' Brecht's satisfied expression was replaced with one of spite. 'And a fat lot of use he's been! And UNIT? You didn't manage to stop anything!'

Benton bit his tongue. It wasn't part of his plan to argue. Luckily for him, Schmitz spoke. 'Brecht! You forget yourself,' he blurted out. 'If you have no useful work to do in here, you may guard the door. Go.'

Brecht went out. As he passed, Benton looked at him closely. Was that a flicker of a smile? Or was the paranoia getting to him? Schmitz distracted him from this train of thought.

'I'm sorry, Sergeant,' he said. 'We've all been under stress and the corporal is young and hot-headed.'

'Think nothing of it, sir,' said Benton.

'You are too kind. I'm glad the inspector will be here. In the meantime, I've called the guardroom and asked for them to contact the resident physician. He'll be with us soon.' Indeed, fortunately for them all, the organisers had arranged for a doctor to be on call for the duration of the conference

'Shall I stay here, sir?'

'If you would, Sergeant, I would be most grateful. Corporal Brecht can remain outside, for the time being.'

Schmitz left the room, leaving Benton alone with Vornschawl. Benton loosened the delegate's collar and checked his pulse, which seemed to be slowing. Knowing there was little else he could do, he pulled up a chair and sat by the bed.

Meanwhile in the study, another telephone call was being received.

'What? When?' asked the man.

'This morning at the conference table,' said his contact.

'Is he conscious?'

'Not so far as I know. The doctor has been called – and the police.'

'Good Lord. Looks like we overdid it. Still...' A nasty smile creased the man's face. 'It's an ill wind that blows nobody any good. If it keeps him out of action until the sale goes through, they can have their treaty.'

'And if it doesn't?'

'Then we'll need to take more direct action. How is the UNIT man?'

'As I thought. He suspects nothing.'

'Good. Keep me posted and don't forget: you've got as much to lose as I have if this goes wrong.'

The receiver clicked. The man hung up, then flicked the pages in his desk directory, and dialled a number.

'Yes. Are today's figures in? Yes, I know I did. Come on, man!' There was a pause while the person at the other end left the phone and the man drummed his fingers on the desk. Eventually, the voice at the other end returned. 'Yes? Good. Excellent. No, that's all for today, just put the usual report in. Yes.'

Without pleasantries, the man hung up. He stood up and walked to the window, looking out over the grounds outside with eyes that seemed fixed on something else entirely.

Dent pulled up at the entrance to the manor, got out of his car, and ran up the steps to the entrance. His passengers followed more slowly, shaken by the speed of their journey.

Schmitz was waiting in the atrium. He stepped forward as Dent approached, his hand held out and a worried expression on his face.

'I came as soon as I could,' said Dent. 'How is he?'

'At the moment, sleeping, I think. We've consulted the resident doctor and I have posted men in the corridor. Sergeant Benton remains in attendance.'

'Good, then we won't waste any more time talking.'

‘Indeed—?’ He stopped as Miss Hawthorne and Iolanthe approached.

Dent gave nothing away. ‘This is Detective Constable Grosvenor and Dr Hawthorne,’ he said, briskly. ‘DC Grosvenor is from my own staff and Dr Hawthorne has been engaged as a consultant by the chief constable.’

‘I see. Then if you will please follow me. Hesse!’

Schmitz called to his subordinate and instructed him to guide the inspector’s party to the delegate’s suite, then left the atrium. The visitors followed Corporal Hesse to the lift. Miss Hawthorne was relieved that Schmitz seemed to have taken Dent’s explanation at face value and that an actual doctor had attended the patient.

As they ascended in the lift, Iolanthe caught Miss Hawthorne’s eye and gave a tiny, nervous smile, but no words passed between them. The corporal didn’t seem to be in the mood for conversation, so Dent kept his own counsel until they reached the suite, where he thanked Hesse for his assistance and, with a searching look, requested that the corporal contact him should he have any information to give about the events of the previous days. Hesse nodded, stood briefly to attention, and departed.

Corporal Brecht had been removed from his post outside the door and replaced with two other guards who, when they saw the visitors approach, stood aside to let them enter the suite. Dent knocked on the door, then, hearing a quiet voice from inside asking them to come in, entered, followed by Iolanthe and Miss Hawthorne.

They found Vornschawl sitting up on his bed, with Benton standing by the connecting door to the sitting room, and the conference doctor checking the delegate’s heart with his stethoscope. The doctor ignored the interruption, instead instructing his patient to lean forward before transferring the bell of the stethoscope to the back. After listening to Vornschawl’s heart and breathing, the doctor took off the stethoscope and came to meet the inspector.

'Good to see you, Inspector,' he said, extending his hand.

'Dr Braithwaite.'

In answer to Miss Hawthorne's questioning expression, Dent explained that Dr Braithwaite was a local GP who'd been seconded to the staff of the conference. Dr Braithwaite was a tall, slim man, who, to Benton and Miss Hawthorne's eyes, looked barely old enough to be in practice, with his round, pink-cheeked face and short, fair curls. However, he treated his patient with a quiet professionalism that was instantly reassuring. Dent briefly introduced Miss Hawthorne and Iolanthe, then approached the bed, and asked how Vornschawl was getting on..

Vornschawl smiled thinly. 'Better. The doctor tells me that my pulse has returned to normal, but I believe he still has concerns for my heart?'

The doctor's face became slightly pinker, but he was ready to give an honest opinion. 'From the symptoms Mr Vornschawl has described, and the incident this morning, I would say that his heart has been under considerable strain. I would advise him to consider resting but... I do understand the importance of the situation.'

Dent took the medical report from the police laboratory out of his pocket and showed it to the doctor.

'We believe Mr Vornschawl has been given regular doses of this substance, without his knowledge,' he said.

Dr Braithwaite consulted the report, frowning. After he finished reading, he passed the pages to Vornschawl, who'd held out his hand for them. 'I see,' said the doctor. 'Yes, that would account for the symptoms. This kind of medication in a healthy person would... Well, it would explain a lot. And with the added strain of the hallucinations...'

'Hallucinations?' asked Vornschawl. 'You are certain of that, doctor?'

Dent glanced at Iolanthe, who nodded.

'We believe you may be subject to a form of hypnosis,' said Dent. 'It appears that it's possible to implant a hallucination in the brain of a subject, which is triggered by a word, or even a sound.'

Vornschawl was obviously appalled. 'And can you stop it?'

'We think so. Miss Grosvenor here has some expertise with hypnosis and will try and remove the trigger and the image, if you will allow her?'

Vornschawl sat back against his pillows and let out a long breath. 'Inspector, if it will remove those dreadful visions, I will try anything. I swear, I saw them as clearly as I see you now. I find it hard to believe that they were only in my head – but, please, Miss Grosvenor, do try.'

'Thank you. If you would all please stand back?' Iolanthe looked at the others, who did as instructed. She pulled up a chair and seated herself close to the bed. 'Look at me please, Mr Vornschawl.'

Vornschawl also did as she asked, and Iolanthe went on: 'Now, whatever you hear or see, you must keep looking at me. Do you understand?'

He nodded and Iolanthe gave a tiny gesture to Miss Hawthorne, who was standing out of the view of the delegate. Suddenly, there came a creaking noise. Quiet, but unmistakably the noise of a squeaking hinge.

The effect was instantaneous.

Vornschawl became tense, and his shoulders began to shake.

Iolanthe took his hands in hers and began to speak, calmly.

Her voice was soft, so the words were almost inaudible to the others in the room, but she kept up a constant stream of speech as the delegate's eyes widened and he continued to shiver.

After a couple of minutes – he began to relax. The shoulders first – then the arms – and hands – and finally, his eyelids quivered and drooped – and he fell back against the pillows, apparently asleep. Iolanthe released his hands and let them fall onto the bed covers. She stayed still for a moment, then sighed and stood up.

Dr Braithwaite came forwards and checked Vornschawl's

pulse. He nodded and let the wrist go. 'He's stable,' he said, quietly.

'Good. Thank you, Miss Grosvenor.' Dent shook Iolanthe's hand. 'Will we disturb him if we talk?'

'No, he'll sleep until I wake him.'

'Good. Now, doctor, I must ask you about the drugs. We haven't identified a suspect yet and…'

'I thought you might ask. I cannot, in all conscience, allow him to continue to be drugged. He is a healthy man, for his age, but the strain on the heart has already been considerable and I cannot advise that you expose him to further risk.'

'Thank you for your honesty.' Dent held out his hand. 'I hope we can avoid any further incidents. We've reached an impasse in the investigation in any case and I was going to suggest to Mr Vornschawl that we take steps to force the opposition's hand. Your advice makes this even more necessary.'

Dr Braithwaite shook hands with Dent and left. He turned to Iolanthe. 'Miss Grosvenor, will you wake him, please? Seems a shame, I know, given how disturbed his night have been…'

Iolanthe went over to the bed. She held Vornschawl's left hand and bending close to him, said quietly but clearly, 'Mr Vornschawl, you may wake up now.'

As Iolanthe let go of his hand and stepped back, the delegate's eyelids fluttered and rose. He was momentarily confused, but then as his eyes regained their focus, the confusion left his face.

'Inspector. Miss Grosvenor. Have you…?' He hardly dared ask.

'Yes. You will not see those things again,' said Iolanthe, firmly.

The quiet confidence in her voice seemed to reassure him. 'I cannot thank you enough,' he said. 'What was it that caused them to appear?'

'This.' Miss Hawthorne held up a rusted hinge that

Iolanthe had bought at the junk shop. 'Or something like it. An ordinary sound that would pass unnoticed in your statement.'

Iolanthe stood up, and said 'Of course, it may even be a simple recording. A Dictaphone would be small enough for them to carry around without arousing suspicion. Especially at a conference.'

'Indeed,' Vornschawl considered. 'Well, Miss Grosvenor, I can only thank you again. And now, Inspector, how does your investigation progress. What news do you have for me?'

'Little enough, I'm afraid,' Dent said. 'If I may?' He gestured to a chair and Vornschawl nodded.

'Please, all of you, seat yourselves. Sergeant, if you would be kind enough to fetch chairs from the other room?'

'Yes, sir.'

While Benton opened the connecting door to the next room and went in search of chairs, Dent sat down by the bed and pulled a file from his briefcase. When the entire party was seated, he took some documents from the file and showed them to Vornschawl.

'We've had Interpol and UNIT monitoring political groups who might have wanted to disrupt the conference, or who have a personal grudge against you, but we've come up with very little,' Dent explained. 'It doesn't look as if any of the usual suspects are behind these attacks, or, if they are, they are keeping very quiet about it.'

Vornschawl considered this information. 'It wouldn't be their style to be quiet about such a thing,' he said. 'I know these groups. When they take action, their methods are direct and they are quick to claim responsibility. They wouldn't wish another group to claim their victories.'

'Quite,' Dent agreed. 'That means that we had to look for another motive for the attacks. Were the attacks meant to harm you personally, or was the conference still the target, but for a reason other than to simply disrupt relations between your nations?'

Dent pulled another set of pages from his file. 'Then, instead of looking at who might gain from preventing the treaty being signed, we decided to look at who would *lose* if it went ahead. And that brought us to the question of trade and geography.'

Miss Hawthorne and Iolanthe both looked puzzled at this and Dent turned to them to explain. 'Slokovia is in an unusually difficult position when it comes to exploiting natural resources,' he said. 'The country is rich in a number of highly prized minerals, but the geography of the country makes exports difficult. It's surrounded by mountains on all sides save one, and that is the side that forms the border with Molvania.'

Vornschawl joined in the explanation at this point. 'Until now, the poor relations between our countries have made it almost impossible for companies based in Slokovia to export their goods through Molvania, but now, with this new agreement, they will be able to move across the border with much more ease. Such a thing will not only be of benefit to both our nations, but… Ah, I think I see what you are driving at, Inspector! It may lead to a decrease in price of those resources which are readily available in Molvania, but less so elsewhere.'

Dent nodded. 'Precisely. So, anyone with investments in those areas would see a considerable drop in their profits.'

'But surely, then they would wish the treaty to be abandoned altogether?' mused Vornschawl.

'Possibly. But if they were intending to rid themselves of their investments, they would only need to delay the treaty signing sufficiently to allow them to do that.'

It was Benton's turn to look puzzled. 'But wouldn't they give themselves away?' he asked. 'If they tried to sell off all their shares at once, wouldn't it scare the market?'

'One would think so. But we can assume they would know what they were doing,' said Dent. 'If they'd done it over a long enough space of time, they might have got away with it. My team has been working on trying to trace suspicious stock movements, but it's a lot of ground to cover.'

Vornschawl nodded slowly. 'Indeed, and time is against us,' he said.

'It is. With your permission, sir, I would like to suggest that we take a more direct approach. It will be a risk, but I don't think we can wait any longer,' said Dent.

The delegate sighed. 'I can only place myself at your disposal. What are your plans?'

Schmitz paced up and down his temporary guardroom impatiently. A member of the manor house staff, responsible for clearing tea and coffee cups, opened the door and, seeing the expression on Schmitz's face, thought better of it and swiftly closed the door again.

The telephone bell interrupted Schmitz, mid-circuit.

'Yes, Schmitz here.' He listened for a moment, switched to his own language to say, 'Yes, sir,' and hung up. He left the room quickly, the door banging behind him. Schmitz hurried to the lift and then to the delegate's suite, nodding to the guards outside the door as he went in.

When he entered the room, he found Vornschawl on the telephone. Dent was seated beside the bed, and Benton stood by the wall, gazing stoically at nothing much in particular.

Vornschawl gestured a greeting, then returned to his call. *'Ja, ja, vielen Dank. Bis Morgen.'*

He hung up and smiled at Schmitz, speaking in English for the benefit of Dent and Benton.

'Sir. You are feeling better?' asked Schmitz.

'Much better, thank you. I need you to make some arrangements for me,' said Vornschawl with a smile.

'Yes, sir?'

'I have just spoken to the Slokovian delegation. We will be signing the agreement tomorrow morning.'

'Tomorrow?' Schmitz seemed momentarily startled but recovered himself quickly.

'Yes. On the advice of the doctor, I have decided not to

prolong the negotiations. We are agreed that any further discussion is unnecessary. I shall rest this evening and we'll reconvene at nine tomorrow morning.'

'I understand. When will you require your meal?'

'The doctor has advised that I avoid food for the rest of the day. I have ample water, so a meal will not be required.'

'Sir.'

Benton looked sideways at Schmitz without moving his head. If Schmitz was struggling to adjust to the sudden turn of events, he was hiding it well. But Vornschawl turned his attention to Benton.

'Sergeant, I am indebted to you for your help today. If I might impose on you once more, I would ask that you guard my door again tonight.'

'Of course, sir.'

'Thank you. Then we need detain you no longer at present.'

'Thank you, sir.'

Benton thanked him, stood to attention, and left the room. Once the door had closed behind him, Vornschawl turned back to his head of security. 'And now, Schmitz, I'll need you to inform your men and secure these rooms until the morning.'

'Yes, sir. I will double the guard.'

Dent stood up and extended his hand to Vornschawl. 'I must get back to my headquarters. I'll call with any news we have in the morning.'

Vornschawl thanked him and Dent left through the connecting door to the next room and called to Miss Hawthorne and Iolanthe. Vornschawl exchanged a few more words with Schmitz and then dismissed him before turning on his side and closing his eyes.

Schmitz watched him for a moment, then left to go about his duties.

One of the guards from the corridor escorted Dent and his companions to the lift. On reaching the ground floor, Miss Hawthorne and Iolanthe went out to the car, while Dent spoke to one of the uniformed officers who was on duty in the atrium.

A few moments later, he came over to the car, accompanied by the officer. 'Constable Hawkins will drive you back,' he said. 'I need to have a word with the manager…'

The ladies and the constable got in and he drove them back to the village, at a considerably slower speed than that with which they'd arrived. Dent watched them leave, then turned back to the manor and went back up the steps to the house.

After leaving the delegate's suite, Benton had followed his customary course of action for a night on duty. His first port of call was the hotel bar, to secure a plate of sandwiches, a glass of water, and a flask of strong coffee, which he carried carefully up to his room. It was a bit on the late side to sleep after the meal, but he took off his jacket and sat on the bed with his book, trying to relax as much as he could before his shift began.

A tap at the door distracted him from the novel. Benton looked at his watch. Half past eight. He opened the door to find Schmitz standing in the corridor.

'Sergeant, may I come in?' he asked.

Benton stood aside to let in his unexpected guest. Schmitz walked to the window, then turned. 'I wanted to thank you for your assistance, Sergeant,' he said. 'Our delegation is very grateful to UNIT for their cooperation.'

'Thank you, sir,' said Benton, wondering what was happening. The idea of the head of security visiting him just to thank him seemed unlikely. What was Schmitz up to?

'I hope you have been able to rest sufficiently,' said Schmitz, with concern. 'You must be tired. Do sit down.'

'I… Oh no, sir, I'm quite…' Benton replied, now even more confused.

'Sit. Down.' Schmitz reached into his jacket and drew out a gun. 'And do not think of calling for help.'

Seeing nothing else for it, Benton sat down in a chair.

'Good.' Schmitz reached into his other pocket and pulled out handcuffs, which he used to secure Benton's hands round the back of the chair. He then pulled the curtains, shutting out the last of the daylight and switched on the desk lamp, positioning it so that the light shone directly into his prisoner's face.

'Again,' he said in a smooth, soft voice, 'you must be tired. You are tired, aren't you, Sergeant?'

Benton realised in an instant what was happening. Trying to remember his training, he answered 'yes' in a dull voice, while pushing as hard as he could with his mind against the light and Schmitz's voice.

'Good. Very, very tired. You need to sleep.'

Benton stammered. Nodded. Blinked. Blinked again. Closed his eyes.

'Excellent, Sergeant,' Schmitz's voice was low and soothing. 'You will need to sleep for a long time. Hours. You will not wake until I give you permission. When you wake, you will not remember this meeting, or even why you are here. Do you understand?'

'Yes,' answered Benton, mechanically.

Benton's head drooped onto his shoulder, his breathing slowed, and his eyes remained closed. Schmitz watched him for a few moments, then went behind the chair and removed the handcuffs. Benton sagged in the chair.

Schmitz smiled, pocketed his gun and the handcuffs, and walked quietly to the door. 'Sleep well, Sergeant,' he whispered.

Schmitz went out into the corridor, locking the door behind him. He would be there to open it, so nobody else would know that it had been locked from the outside.

As Schmitz's footsteps retreated down the corridor, Benton opened his eyes. The next moment, he was on his feet and at the door. Finding it locked, he cursed inwardly. He would need to get out without attracting too much attention – he definitely couldn't break the door down without considerable noise.

He had a set of skeleton keys in his 'detective kit', but would any of them would fit and would he have time to find the one that did? There was nothing else for it. Benton fetched the keys from the box in his wardrobe and began to try and fit them in the lock. By a miracle, the third one he tried worked. He threw the keys onto the bed and snatched up his gun, not bothering with the holster.

Benton put his head out of the door and looked both ways: the corridor was clear. He pulled the door closed, then made his way towards the delegate's suite as quickly and quietly as he could.

Schmitz walked coolly along the corridor as if he had every right to be there, as, indeed, he had. He nodded to the guards who were standing outside the door, then turned his key in the lock and went in. The guards relaxed a little, only to be startled moments later by the appearance of Benton, gun drawn, hurrying towards them.

'Did he go in?' he asked.

'Who?' asked one of the guards, his hand going to his hip pocket.

'The commander! Did he go in?' Benton repeated.

'Well, yes, but—?'

Benton tried to get to the door, but the guards drew their weapons.

'Stand back,' said one of them.

'You don't understand; it was him. We've got to get in there!'

'Stand back, Sergeant,' repeated the guard.

Then Benton recognised one of them: Corporal Hesse. 'Corporal! You have to believe me. If we don't get in there…'

At that moment, there was the sound of a shot from the other side of the door. Benton wrenched it open and went in, followed by the guards.

Inside, they found Schmitz sprawled against the wall, blood seeping through his jacket near his right shoulder.

Vornschawl was sitting up in bed, a gun in his hand. Benton went to Schmitz and took the gun from him. Schmitz tried to resist, but feebly. Corporal Hesse removed his tie and bound Schmitz's other hand over his wound. As he did so, the door to the adjoining room opened.

Schmitz laughed, then coughed. 'We do still have the advantage over you.'

'Oh, I'm afraid not, Commander. I met Corporal Brecht and he won't be able to give you his support.' Dent stood in the doorway. He crossed the room to the telephone and made a brief call.

Schmitz's laugh had turned to a stream of cursing.

Vornschawl regarded him with disgust. 'Shut up, Schmitz,' he said, coldly. 'Unless you can explain your behaviour, we do not wish to hear anything from you.'

'Explain?' Schmitz coughed again and spat. 'I was going to be paid so much, I wouldn't have had to spend any more of my life looking after idiot diplomats.'

'Money? That's the only reason?' Vornschawl sounded astonished.

'What better reason could there be?' retorted Schmitz.

The door opened again, to admit three uniformed police officers. Two of them lifted Schmitz to his feet and half-walked, half-carried him outside; the other went into the next room to collect Brecht, who Dent had restrained. Dent then spoke briefly to Vornschawl and the other guards, and left the room accompanied by Benton.

'I'm sorry I couldn't get there quicker, sir,' said Benton.

'Not your fault, Sergeant,' said Dent. 'As it turned out, Mr Vornschawl beat us all to it.'

Three weeks later, Benton, Miss Hawthorne, and Iolanthe gathered in the Brigadier's office to hear the last piece of news related to the case from Inspector Dent.

With Schmitz's influence removed, negotiations had proceeded quickly, and the agreement was signed within a few days. His hope of fortune dashed, Schmitz had seen no reason to stay loyal to his paymaster and had fully confessed. His evidence, supported by investigations by the Fraud Squad, had revealed a wealthy industrialist who had a virtual monopoly on the processing of a mineral in good supply in Slokovia.

'He had been quietly selling off stock, through a number of channels for the past two years,' Dent explained, 'but he was desperate to finish the job.'

'But to attack an innocent man like that?' protested Miss Hawthorne.

'Money does funny things to people. Great amounts of it even more so.' Dent shrugged. 'Look at Schmitz. Unblemished record of service, both in the military and in security.'

'Did he give any more reasons for his conduct?' asked Miss Hawthorne.

'Not really. It seems he had a longstanding grudge about being ordered about by civilians, and pay is never that good, even for the most senior ranks, so when temptation came, he was ready. I know it doesn't seem like a lot, but the money men know how to work on people's feelings. My guess is that he stoked Schmitz's general grievance until he believed he had a personal vendetta against Vornschawl.'

'And it was Schmitz who'd hypnotised Vornschawl?' said the Brigadier.

'Yes, on the journey over. The delegation had travelled in small groups for security and Schmitz managed to get him alone and implant the hallucinations and the trigger before the conference even began.'

'And was he moving the things around in Vornschawl's rooms?' asked Iolanthe.

'Yes,' said Dent. 'It wasn't psychic influence. He was simply shifting things whenever he was in the room. He was in and out all the time and Vornschawl was so tired and confused that he never noticed what Schmitz was up to.'

'And Brecht?' asked Benton.

'He'd served with Schmitz for the longest of any of them. They trusted each other completely and Brecht objected to the treaty. He felt it was a betrayal of his country, so he was easily converted to Schmitz' cause, even without the promise of bribery.'

'I see.' The Brigadier stood up, signalling the end of the meeting, 'Well, thank you, Inspector.'

'Thank you, Brigadier,' said Dent.

Miss Hawthorne also stood up. 'And I must be getting back.' She smiled at the assembled party, shook hands with the inspector, and left.

Dent looked at Iolanthe. 'Aren't you going back with Miss Hawthorne?' he asked.

Iolanthe blushed and opened her mouth to speak, but the Brigadier was before her.

'Ah, Miss Grosvenor is staying on at UNIT. We've offered her a position as a full-time consultant, and, I'm pleased to say, she's accepted.'

'I see! Congratulations, Miss Grosvenor!'

Iolanthe found her voice now and thanked Dent, who departed after shaking hands.

The Brigadier sat down again and got Benton's attention. 'Show Miss Grosvenor to her office please, Sergeant, then send Corporal Scott along to make sure she has all she needs.'

'Yes, sir.' Benton ushered Iolanthe out of the room.

As they walked along the interminable and nondescript corridors of UNIT HQ, Iolanthe tried to remember the route and wondered if she might be given a map, or, at least, a ball of string to find her way out again.

As Benton assured her they were 'nearly there', one of the side doors opened and a tall officer with a rush of dark hair appeared, holding a box file in one hand. He stopped when he saw Benton and his companion approaching.

'Sergeant?' he said.

'Sir. Miss Grosvenor. This is Captain Turner.'

'How do you do?'

Iolanthe shook the captain's hand and smiled. 'Pleased to meet you, Captain Turner,' she said.

Turner withdrew his hand with a puzzled expression. He walked a few steps, then stopped and shook his head as if to clear it. Benton looked at his superior officer, considered asking what the matter was, then thought better of it.

Turner watched them go, bewildered. When he'd shaken Iolanthe's hand, the words, 'Sorry, not interested,' had appeared in his mind as clearly as if they had been spoken. He shook his head again and, recalled to his duties, quickened his pace along the corridor.

Having at last arrived at the room that would be Iolanthe's office, Benton ushered her inside and explained that Corporal Scott would be along shortly to make sure Iolanthe was supplied with everything she needed for her work.

Then, unable to help himself, he asked, 'What did you do to him?'

'I beg your pardon?' said Iolanthe, innocently, but gave in when Benton arched an eyebrow. Iolanthe smiled demurely, though her eyes sparkled. 'Nothing really,' she said, 'I just find it easier if everyone knows where they stand from the beginning.'

As Benton walked away, he began to smile. He'd had some concerns about Iolanthe joining UNIT, though Miss Hawthorne had told him he was worrying over nothing.

He had to admit she'd been right. As usual.

THE MOSELLE MICROFILM MISSION

ᛚᛁᚳᛖᚾᚳᛖ×ᛏᚠ×ᚳᛁᛚᛚ

I

'***IHR BIER***, *Herr* Benton?'

Benton looked up from his book as the waiter put a tall glass down on the table next to him.

'*Danke*,' said Benton, signing the receipt.

'*Bitte sehr*,' said the waiter with a smile.

Benton raised the glass to his lips and took a long draught. This brand of German light beer was a particular favourite of his and it was hard to get in England, so he was making the most of this opportunity. After all, as far as his cover story was concerned, he was supposed to be on holiday. Benton leaned back in his chair and sighed, casting his mind back to the previous week, when he had been summoned to the Brigadier's office.

The summons had come via Corporal Scott, who had called the range and simply said, 'The CO wants you in half an hour.'

Being accustomed to obeying this kind of order without expecting any more explanation, Benton had finished his stint supervising some new recruits and then went back to the main building. When he'd arrived at the office, Benton heard voices from within, so he knocked and waited for permission to enter. After a moment, the door opened and two men came out. One of them was Sir Giles Mulberry, the foreign office representative who'd consulted UNIT in the case of the Molvanian delegate. The other man was unknown to Benton, but something in his bearing and expression made the word 'intelligence' appear in Benton's mind.

As they left, the Brigadier said, 'I really am very sorry, gentlemen, but I'm not at liberty to share details of any ongoing UNIT operations, even if I had them. You are, of course, welcome to contact Geneva.'

'We certainly will,' replied Sir Giles. 'And I will be speaking to the prime minister this evening. In the meantime, I hope you will consider your position. UNIT's presence in this country is based on an understanding that there will be cooperation.'

'And there will,' said the Brigadier, a little wearily, 'but in this case, I really have nothing to share and, even if I had, I would be bound by the conditions of confidentiality imposed by Geneva in the same way as you would in regard to matters of state. Good day, gentlemen.'

Sir Giles had said no more, but it was obvious from his expression that he was far from satisfied with the Brigadier's reply. He and his companion, who remained silent, exchanged meaningful glances and walked off in the direction of the exit. The Brigadier watched them go, then turned to his subordinate.

'There are times, Sergeant, that I wish Her Majesty's Government realised that cooperation doesn't mean sharing all our secrets like schoolgirls on a camping trip.' He sighed, then seemed to pull himself together, and beckoned him inside. 'Please do sit down. I have an assignment for you, and we will need to go through the file.'

'Yes, sir.'

Benton seated himself opposite his commanding officer and waited. The Brigadier sat down and opened the bottom drawer of his desk, drawing out a file, which he passed to Benton.

'Before I start, I should inform you that everything I am about to tell you is in the strictest confidence. This assignment is from the highest authorities in Geneva and will be shared with very few UNIT personnel. And it is certainly not to be shared with any representatives of Her Majesty's government, or the security forces. Do I make myself clear?'

'Yes, sir,' replied Benton. Was this what Sir Giles had been asking about? Had the Brigadier been lying to his visitors? What kind of assignment needed this much confidentiality? And why was UNIT involved?

'Sir, why us? It doesn't sound like a typical UNIT assignment. No invading aliens from outer space or mad scientists.'

'I thought so too. I must admit, Sergeant, I wasn't happy, but the secret nature of our work does give us the advantage. I'd better start from the beginning...' The Brigadier leaned back in his chair. 'A little over a month ago, we received intelligence that a new warhead has been designed by a team of scientists working in a laboratory in East Germany. Details were sketchy at first, but it soon became clear that this new warhead would revolutionise the current surface-to-air missiles in use by the Soviets and would cause a serious imbalance in global security. It might trigger a new arms race, which would be disastrous.'

Benton nodded. He was well aware of the delicate balance of international relations. Lately, there'd been a slight thawing of the Cold War between East and West, but a development like this could set any progress back years, if not decades.

The Brigadier continued: 'As the news began to spread, efforts were made by various governments to either persuade the Soviets to shut down the programme, or to obtain a copy of the blueprints. The first tactics came to nothing; the

Kremlin denied all knowledge of the programme, the warhead, and even the scientists. The second approach seemed to have failed too – until last week, when Geneva got a signal from an agent over there. He'd managed to persuade one of the scientists to pass him photographs of the plans, which he'd reduced onto microfilm.'

'How did he manage to persuade him?'

'It appears that the man in question had a crisis of conscience. He'd been feeling disillusioned for some time and this project was the final straw. Obviously, he couldn't share his feelings with the rest of the team, for his own safety, but, when the agent made contact, he was ready to cooperate. He was of the opinion that either the whole world should have this new weapon, which would mean a stalemate. Or that nobody should.'

'I see. And where's the agent now?'

'Making his way across Europe. The latest update confirmed that he had reached West Germany. This was good news, but, unfortunately the situation has become more complicated.'

The Brigadier held out a hand for the file, which Benton had been skimming through. He fished out a photograph and passed it across to Benton. This showed an aerial shot of what looked like a bomb site. A large building was in ruins, smoke rising from the debris.

Benton looked at the Brigadier, who said, 'We don't know yet what caused the explosion. At the moment, the theory is that it was an accident. Whatever the cause, the laboratory complex has been destroyed, and with it, we think, the plans and prototype of the warhead.'

'Was anyone hurt?'

'Three security guards were badly injured, but nobody was killed. At least, that's the official line. The explosion happened in the early hours of the morning and the staff were in their accommodation at the time.'

'I see. They'll have to start again from scratch.'

'Yes. It also means that, as of this moment, the agent holds the only copy of the blueprints in existence. And that makes his position very dangerous indeed. A number of people will be very keen to get their hands on those blueprints and they won't ask nicely. You can see now why this film must be retrieved by UNIT. No nation can be trusted to hold on to such a thing. The plans could be destroyed, but then if the Soviets rebuild, we'll be back where we started. I believe the plan is to use the film as a bargaining tool to persuade the Soviets to halt production. Be that as it may, we have been tasked with getting hold of the film. What happens to it afterwards won't be our concern.'

'Right, sir,' Benton said. 'Can the agent not deliver it himself? I mean, why do we need to go in and get it?'

'Because time is running out for him. His cover may be blown at any time and he needs to pass on the film in order to escape. If he's recognised and found with it… Well, I wouldn't give much for his chances. But if he can pass it to another agent, one who's unknown to the wider intelligence community, then he stands a better chance of getting away clear and we stand a better chance of getting the film safely into UN hands.'

Benton made no reply to this. He frowned, knowing that what the Brigadier had said about this unnamed agent would apply equally to the UNIT officer once they were in possession of the film.

And that he would be that agent.

The Brigadier watched him, guessing what he was thinking. 'This won't be easy, Benton, but I know we can trust you. You've proved that many times over. We'll be here, day and night for you to contact us, and we will be escorting the UN representative to the rendezvous.'

Benton was silent for a moment longer, seemingly coming to a decision. He knew he should be honoured to be chosen for a mission like this, but he was under no illusion as to the danger.

'Thank you, sir. When do I leave?'

'Tomorrow morning. You'll fly to an airfield here' – the Brigadier pulled a map across his desk and pointed to an area marked 'North Rhine Palatinate' – 'and join a river cruise at Koblenz. The agent will be on the boat, posing as a member of the crew. His photograph is in the file.'

Benton leafed through and found a portrait shot of a man of about thirty, with closely cropped hair and a determined expression. Benton looked at the picture, trying to commit the man's features to memory. He knew that the agent would have changed his appearance, but there was something about the set of the eyes and a slight twist to the upper lip that Benton thought he would remember.

The Brigadier continued, 'He's had some experience working on liners and smaller boats; and the company was short-handed and prepared to take him on without asking too many questions. He's been given your description and will have a code phrase ready. Once he's transferred the film to you, you will either stay on the boat to preserve your cover, or leave it at one of the stopping places. Either way, you'll be expected to rendezvous in Trier by the end of next week. This is the code the agent will be expecting: it's safer for both of you if you don't know his name.'

The Brigadier passed a slip of paper over to Benton, who glanced at it then tucked it into his pocket to memorise properly later on.

'Right, sir. And what's my cover story?'

Much to Benton's surprise, a small smile crossed the Brigadier's lips. 'We've had to give this some thought, as you can imagine. River cruises aren't usually the sort of place for off-duty soldiers, so we had to come up with a reasonable explanation for you being there. A man of your age and profession on his own might attract the wrong kind of attention. But if you were to be on holiday with a relative, say…?'

The Brigadier left the sentence unfinished.

'So it's less *From Russia With Love* and more *Travels With My Aunt?*'

'You could say that.' The Brigadier stood up. 'Well, Benton, I'm sorry to have sprung this on you, but it was rather sprung on me too. You can take the file with you for now but I'll need it back before you leave. Smyth will run you over to Croydon in the taxi tomorrow at seven and Miss Hawthorne will meet you at the airport. I'll brief Corporal Scott this evening. You will communicate either with her or with me directly on these numbers' – he handed over another piece of paper – 'and we will cable the location of the rendezvous in Trier nearer the time. Good luck.'

For the first time Benton could remember, the Brigadier held out his hand. Benton had shaken it and thanked him, before quickly marching to his quarters... He didn't want to let him down. He'd needed to memorise as much of the information as he could, in preparation for the following day.

Benton took another sip of his beer and looked out to the shore.

On either side of the boat rose the Moselle Valley, sheer cliffs in some places, with trees clinging to the rock face; in others, the ground was lower, and houses clustered at the water's edge, the hills behind them covered in vines, producing grapes for the local vineyards. The wide river seemed alive with light as the afternoon sun danced and twinkled on the ripples.

He sighed again and picked up the novel that he had balanced on his knee. As he did so, the sound of approaching footsteps made him look up. 'Hello, Auntie, having a change of scene?'

Miss Hawthorne smiled at her pseudo-nephew. 'You could say that. Mrs Hobson is a somewhat opinionated person and I'm afraid I had to make my excuses and come away or I might've said something unfortunate.'

Benton grinned. Mrs Hobson, an elderly lady of independent means, had taken a liking to Miss Hawthorne and had made more than one attempt to engage her in conversation since they had joined the boat in Koblenz. Miss Hawthorne had finally agreed to take tea with Mrs Hobson, but, from her expression, Benton guessed that she wouldn't be doing that again.

Miss Hawthorne sat down and settled the walking stick she'd brought with her to, as she put it, add verisimilitude to her role. The cover story she and Benton had decided on was that she'd been ill and was travelling as part of convalescence, with her nephew for company and assistance.

Having placed the stick under her chair, Miss Hawthorne set down her handbag and waved to the waiter. 'In any case, why would I want to stay in the saloon, when there is this to enjoy?' She gestured at the view, then turned to the waiter and ordered a small brandy.

Benton raised his eyebrows. 'That bad?'

Miss Hawthorne laughed. 'No, not really. She has a good heart, I think, but she seems to get most of her opinions from newspapers that I wouldn't use for kindling and that makes conversation difficult. Anyway, what have you been up to? Any joy with…'

She paused as the waiter came back with her drink. Once she'd signed for it and the waiter had departed, Benton replied, 'I think so. I reckon I spotted him coming out of the engine room this morning. He's grown a beard and his hair is longer, but I'm pretty sure it's him.'

'Good. And did he see you?'

'Probably. I walked close by him to get to the stairs. I'm hoping he'll make contact soon. This is all lovely, but we're here to do a job and I'd rather be getting on with it.'

His companion sipped her drink and nodded. 'Mm. I agree. In the meantime, however, we may as well make the most of this opportunity. I suspect there will be little time to relax when you have the film.'

'No, you're right. Is that the guidebook? Where are we stopping next?'

Miss Hawthorne took out the cruise schedule and opened the guidebook, placing it on the table so Benton could see it. 'Cochem. It looks charming from the description.'

Miss Hawthorne pointed out some of the sights in the book. Benton, aware that two of their fellow travellers had come over to the rail nearby, looked at the book then said, 'Yes, it does look nice. But you mustn't wear yourself out, Auntie. Perhaps we should pick a couple of places to look at and then see how you feel after that.'

Miss Hawthorne sighed in mock frustration. 'Yes, yes, of course. Well then, shall we see the church and the monastery? I fear I will not be able to tackle the castle – the way looks rather steep – but if you want to go up, I can always wait for you in a café.'

'Don't you worry about me. I can go and see castles any time. Let's do the churches and then have a walk round the old town. It looks nice and there are bound to be places we can stop if you need a sit down.'

'Thank you, John. I'm not quite an old crock yet… but I must admit, I'm more tired than I was expecting to be.'

'There you are then! The doctor did say it might take a little while to get over that flu. You had a nasty dose of it.'

The man and woman at the rail, a husband and wife by the name of Lannis, looked at each other and smiled at the solicitude of the nephew for his aunt. Apparently noticing them for the first time, Miss Hawthorne waved a greeting: 'Hello, what a beautiful afternoon!'

'Yes, indeed,' replied the man. 'I was just saying so to Helen. It doesn't feel like fall at all.'

'No, it could almost be summer,' agreed Miss Hawthorne, 'and the air is so clear, it really is the most delightful way to travel.'

'It certainly beats being cooped up in a plane,' said Helen.

'Goodness yes. You must've had a very long flight. I'm so sorry, I'm so forgetful these days – where did you say you flew from?'

'Williamsburg, Virgina. It took a long time, but it's been worth it. Doug's been researching his family tree and it turns out some of his distant cousins came from the Rhineland. It's been wonderful seeing the places they lived.'

'Oh, but how fascinating!' Miss Hawthorne turned in her seat to face the others. 'That kind of research can be so rewarding. I hope there haven't been any nasty surprises, though.'

'Not so far,' said Doug, grinning. 'But if there are, I'll take it on the chin. You can't choose your family, after all.'

'Very true.'

A bell sounded and Miss Hawthorne looked at her watch. 'Goodness, time has run away from me this afternoon. I must go and freshen up. At least we aren't expected to dress up for dinner, I do find that tiresome.'

'Oh, definitely,' said Helen. 'Don't get me wrong, it's good to change after a day out, but all that putting on long dresses and jewellery for a meal is just a waste of time!'

Doug grinned again. 'Whatever you say, honey. Either way, I want to brush up and shave, so shall we go back down now?'

Helen smiled up at her husband then at Miss Hawthorne and Benton. 'We probably should. See you at dinner?'

'Absolutely,' replied Miss Hawthorne, returning the smile, as Benton stood up and gently helped her to her feet, then handed her her stick. 'Thank you, John. We'd better do the same.'

'Right you are. Have we got everything?' Benton picked up the guidebook and tucked it under his arm. He and Miss Hawthorne walked down the stairs to their cabins, chatting about the scenery and their plans for the next day.

Benton opened the door to his cabin and looked round. At first glance, it appeared that all his belongings were as he had left them. Good. He wasn't expecting any interference this early in the mission, but you never knew. As he stepped forward, a piece of paper crunched under the sole of his shoe.

It must've been pushed underneath his door. He bent down to pick it up, and unfurled it. It was a printed plan of the boat; each of the passengers had been given a copy on embarkation to help them find their way around and there were copies available in holders in the dining room and by the doors to the upper deck. Benton turned it over in his hands, frowning. A cross had been marked on the upper deck, towards the stern, and '23:15 hrs' written beside the cross. There was nothing else written on the plan. To Benton, this looked like a rendezvous. The use of 'hours' suggested a soldier, or else that the person who wrote the note wanted to be absolutely clear and the fact that it was 'hrs' rather than 'uhr' suggested that the writer wasn't German.

Suddenly aware of the time, Benton folded the plan and stuffed it into his trouser pocket, then took off his jacket and went to the tiny bathroom that adjoined his cabin, to get ready for dinner. His preparations completed, Benton went back out to the corridor and knocked softly on Miss Hawthorne's door.

Seeing his serious expression, Miss Hawthorne stood back to let him enter the cabin then closed the door. 'What is it?'

Benton pulled the plan from his pocket and gave it to her. As he had done, Miss Hawthorne turned the paper over.

'It must be from him,' said Benton. 'If it isn't, I can make my excuses and leave, but I can't think who else it would be.'

'No, neither can I. I needn't tell you to take care, but if you aren't back by a quarter to twelve, I will raise the alarm.'

'Thank you.' Benton smiled. 'For now though, we'd better go in to dinner, or people will talk!'

Miss Hawthorne laughed her agreement and led the way out of her cabin.

The dining room was humming with conversation when they entered. Miss Hawthorne was relieved to see that they were not the last; not that she minded, but she would have preferred not to draw any unnecessary attention. As with larger cruise ships, the captain of the Mosel Prinzessin ate with his guests, who took it in turns to sit at his table. On this particular evening, Miss Hawthorne and Benton were among those honoured and they made their way to the table at the head of the room.

Captain Silberstein looked up from his conversation with another passenger to welcome his new guests. 'Mr Benton, Miss Hawthorne, I am glad to see you.'

'Thank you, Captain,' replied Miss Hawthorne as Benton pulled out her chair for her. She thanked him then went on, 'I must say, we're thoroughly enjoying this cruise.'

'I am pleased to hear it,' replied the captain with a warm smile.

Once all his guests were seated and the waiters had begun to serve the starters, the captain turned to Miss Hawthorne. 'So Mrs Rogers tells me you're interested in the local legends.'

Miss Hawthorne briefly nodded towards Mrs Rogers, who was sitting across the table with her husband, a business man from Birmingham. Benton and Miss Hawthorne had shared a table with the Rogers on the previous evening and Miss Hawthorne had found that she and Mrs Rogers shared an interest in legends and mythology. Her interest stemmed partly from her love of opera: an interest in Wagner had sparked an urge to find out more about the stories behind her favourite operas. Miss Hawthorne had made no secret of her interests, though she hadn't shared her personal experiences, for obvious reasons.

Now, she said, 'I am indeed! I'm familiar with our old English legends of course, but I know very little about yours. Mrs Rogers was telling me so many fascinating stories about the Rhine – we wondered if you could tell us more.'

'Well,' replied the captain, 'the one most familiar to me is the story of the Loreley. Have you heard about her?'

'Wasn't she the mermaid?' put in Mrs Rogers. 'The one who lured sailors to their deaths?'

'I thought you said she was a siren,' Mr Rogers put in.

'You told me about her the other day, didn't you? I asked if you were going out looking for mermaids again and you said it was a siren. Not that I know the difference.'

Mrs Rogers shot her husband a distinctly unwifely look, but didn't answer.

The captain ignored the interruption.

'Quite right. She's believed to have been a mortal woman who threw herself into the Rhine when her lover betrayed her. She was transformed and became a siren, or, as you say, mermaid, and she lures sailors to the rocks and their deaths with her song. A rock overlooking the Rhine bears her name to this day.'

Miss Hawthorne had no need to feign her interest: 'The poor young woman. An interesting version of the mermaid legend too.'

'Yes,' replied Mrs Rogers, 'it reminds me of Giselle and the Wilis, pursuing faithless young men.'

'Yes! And then…'

Miss Hawthorne and Mrs Rogers became absorbed in a conversation about the various versions of the legends of vengeful female spirits. Meanwhile, Mr Rogers raised his eyebrows at Sergeant Benton and smiled.

'Off she goes again!' he exclaimed. Then, in answer to Benton's smile, he added, 'Oh, I don't mind really; I'm glad she's got someone to talk to who knows about this stuff. I try to keep up, but it's a mystery to me.'

Benton nodded. 'I know what you mean. It's a bit beyond me, but Aunt Olive is keen. She gave me some books, but I can't get my head round it.'

He stopped, trying not to show that Miss Hawthorne had just kicked him under the table. She might've been talking to Mrs Rogers, but that didn't mean she wasn't paying attention to her surroundings.

Benton smiled to himself and continued to talk to Mr Rogers – or, indeed, 'David, Dave to most people' – about the wholesale paper business, Rogers' line of work.

When the waiters came to change the plates, Benton looked round the room. There were about forty guests in all, mostly couples, with the exception of the formidable Mrs Hobson, a pair of art students, and, of course, himself and Miss Hawthorne.

Benton caught sight of Doug and Helen at another table. Catching his eye, Doug waved and Benton returned the gesture. Since they'd joined the boat, he and Miss Hawthorne had tried to keep a wary eye on their fellow passengers. There were really too many of them for this to be feasible, but there was a quiet watchfulness about Doug Lannis that had caught his attention. It might've been nothing, but Benton knew they couldn't afford to take any chances. If every government with the capability to use the new warheads was after the plans, there was a good chance that they would also have agents on the boat, or, at any rate, in the area.

Benton was brought back from his meditations by a waiter asking if he wanted coffee. Having accepted the offer, Benton turned his attention back to Miss Hawthorne, who had paused in her conversation to drink hers.

'So are we safe from mermaids here?' asked Benton, cheerily.

'I believe so! It appears that the Lorelei limited her activities to the Rhine, but perhaps you should be on the safe side and not follow any strange young women,' replied Miss Hawthorne, returning his teasing with affection.

'I'll keep my wits about me!'

Miss Hawthorne smothered a yawn and looked at her watch.

The captain looked at her with concern. 'I'm sorry, Miss Hawthorne, we've tired you.'

'Oh, not at all! I'm feeling so much better than I was. This cruise has been just the tonic I needed.'

'But you're not quite well yet. We understand.'

'Thank you. I think I had better go to my cabin. I want to be able to enjoy tomorrow. John?'

Benton stood up and helped her up from her chair, offering his arm as an extra support, and they left the room to a chorus of goodnight from the others at the table.

Miss Hawthorne and Benton walked arm in arm to the cabins. After letting herself in, Miss Hawthorne paused in the doorway.

'Are you going back for a bit?'

'I probably should. Keep up appearances. As long as I don't have to listen to another monologue on the paper trade, I should be able to stay awake until eleven.'

Miss Hawthorne grinned. 'Yes, I heard some of that. I'm sure it's fascinating if you are interested in that kind of thing, but…'

Benton suddenly became aware of a fellow passenger strolling along the corridor, so he reverted back to their agreed-upon pretence. 'Anyway, you've got all you need for the night? I'll try not to make too much noise when I come back.'

'Don't worry about me, dear – I shall be quite all right now and I'm sure I'll be fast asleep by the time you get back.'

They bade each other good night, and Benton headed back to the dining room.

In her cabin, Miss Hawthorne changed into her nightclothes, and then brought out a collection of runes, a bag of mint imperials, and objects that assembled into a small transmitter. Taking out her notebook for reference, she began to tap a message out. Having received a confirmation, she disassembled the equipment and put it away, before deciding she would be more comfortable in bed than in the basket chair that was the other option. She got out her crochet, switched off the top light, and settled down under the duvet, using her bedside lamp.

When Benton got back to the dining room, the tables and chairs had been moved to the sides of the room and four couples were attempting a Viennese waltz, some more successfully than others.

Benton watched from the sidelines. Though he would've liked to have joined in, he felt that this wasn't really a situation to be dancing with strangers. Instead, he went to the bar and ordered a coffee with schnapps, then sat down to watch the room, with the guidebook to look at so he wouldn't be caught staring at people.

As the music stopped, Mrs Rogers came over and sat down nearby, while her husband went to the bar.

'Phew! I won't be trying that again in a hurry!' She pulled a handkerchief out of her evening bag and mopped her face. 'An ordinary waltz is bad enough, but that...?'

Benton returned her smile but made no comment. David returned from the bar with two glasses of wine, one of which he passed to his wife.

'That's done you for this evening, hasn't it, love?'

'I think I'll just watch everyone else. John here's got the right idea.'

Her husband pulled up a chair and sat down next to her, then looked at Benton. 'You not tempted to join in?'

'No – at least, not this evening. Besides, I haven't got a partner. I don't want to get into trouble dancing with someone else's girl, do I?'

Mrs Rogers laughed at this rather clumsy gallantry. 'Oh, Dave wouldn't mind. But if you'd rather not... Perhaps tomorrow?'

'Perhaps.' Benton refused to commit himself. For one thing, he wasn't sure that 'Dave' wouldn't object to his wife dancing with strangers; for another, he wanted to make sure he was keeping his attention on his surroundings. That would be tricky on the dance floor.

The music began again at a slower tempo and Mr Rogers stood up and held out a hand to his wife. 'Come on, one more go round for the night.'

'Oh, you're such a bully,' said Mrs Rogers with pretended reluctance. 'See you later, John.'

Benton raised his cup to them as they took to the floor

again. As the couples began to sway to the music, Benton checked his watch. Just after ten. The bar would be closing at eleven and he didn't want to risk the other passengers seeing him making his way up to the deck, so he set down his empty cup and slipped out of the room.

He made his way through the corridors to his cabin, where he collected the novel he'd brought with him and put on a warmer jacket, then went up to the deck. A bench had been put in a spot that was sheltered from the evening breeze and the lights fixed nearby gave plenty of light for reading. Benton sat down, pulled his jacket round him, and opened his book. If anyone asked, he could say he wanted some fresh air before bed. At least one of the other passengers had been troubled with seasickness, so it wouldn't be a stretch for him to say he was feeling a bit groggy too. After one more look at his watch, Benton settled in to wait.

At UNIT, Corporal Scott acknowledged Miss Hawthorne's message. Having finished her signal, she looked down at her notepad, decoding the Morse that she'd just noted down, then picked up the receiver and dialled the Brigadier's direct line.

When he answered, she told him they'd had a message from Theresa – Miss Hawthorne's codename. 'Signal reads, "Contact made, appointment tonight". Signal ends.'

'Thank you, Corporal. Keep me posted.'

Corporal Scott hung up and looked up at the clock. She'd need to wait for news of the 'appointment' before she could finish her shift.

Time for another coffee.

The light of the stars twinkled, waving side to side, blinking and glistening on the surface of the river as Benton waited for his rendezvous.

The bar had closed and some of the other passengers had come up on deck, to smoke or to look at the stars; couples leaning on each other as they stood by the rail. Gradually, the chilly air drove them back inside, with the exception of one man, who stood near the stern, a cigarette between his fingers. Benton looked at his watch. 11.15pm. As casually as he could, he got up from his chair and tucked his book under his arm, then strolled to the stern.

As Benton approached and leaned on the rail next to him, the other man said, quietly, 'I like this time of night – the stars look so close.'

Benton replied, 'Yes, but how many of them are satellites?'

There was a moment's silence. Then the agent held out his hand. 'I'm very glad to see you, Sergeant.'

As the agent turned to face him, Benton could see the shadows under his eyes and the lines between his brows. His hair clung to his forehead, which was damp with sweat, but his hand was steady, as was his voice.

'The feeling's mutual,' said Benton. 'You've got something for me?'

The agent pulled a canister from his pocket and passed it to Benton. 'There's a roll of film in there,' he told him. 'Looks like a normal film. Because it is. Put it in your camera and it'll work. The plans are on microdots on the surface. It'll be useless to anyone who hasn't got the equipment to read them.'

'Right,' replied Benton, pocketing the canister. He held out his hand and the agent shook it again and wished him luck.

'And to you,' said Benton. 'What will you do now?'

'I'll have to stay with the boat for now. It'd look too suspicious if I jumped ship. But we mustn't be seen together again. I'll stick to the engine room and you stick to the passenger side. We'd better get going. You go first. I'll come down in a few minutes.'

'Understood.'

Benton made his way back along the deck and downstairs to the cabins. As he went, Mrs Rogers appeared at the other end of the corridor. She staggered a little as the boat moved in the current, then giggled and waved to Benton. He returned the wave and went on towards his cabin.

*

On deck, the agent lit another cigarette, and stood looking out over the river. His part was finished. Now, he had to maintain his cover until the end of the cruise; if his cover were blown, he wouldn't stand a chance. He blew out a long stream of smoke and threw the end of his cigarette into the water. Time to go back, before anyone started to ask questions.

Benton gave a quiet double knock at Miss Hawthorne's door.

She let him in, neither of them speaking until the door was safely closed and locked. Once she'd turned the latch, Miss Hawthorne waved Benton to the chair and sat down on her bed, then said, quietly, 'Well?'

'Got it.'

Benton took the canister out of his pocket and regaled his story. Miss Hawthorne took the canister and removed the lid.

'He's right. It looks just like an ordinary film. Where will you keep it?'

'I'll follow his advice and put it in my camera for now. I can put another film in here and hide it somewhere, or just have it with me.'

'That sounds like an excellent idea. I'm sure anyone looking for a microfilm wouldn't expect to find it there.'

'I hope not,' said Benton, 'and I hope he can get away now. From the look of him, he hasn't had much sleep lately.'

'I'm not surprised,' she said. 'It must've been a dreadful strain on him. But we'd better get some rest ourselves.'

Benton nodded and got up. 'Will you signal HQ please? And I'll put this in my camera.'

They bid each other good night then Benton slipped out into the corridor.

Miss Hawthorne closed the door behind him and turned the latch, then reassembled her transmitter to send a short message to UNIT.

*

In his cabin, Benton took his camera out of its case and opened the back. He removed the roll of film inside and replaced it with the one that the agent had given him. He placed the first roll in the canister and dropped it into his bag. That was as much as he could do for now; anything else would have to wait. Benton tucked the camera away and began to get ready for bed.

Silence settled over the passenger decks.

II

The following morning was as bright as the previous day had been. The passengers woke to find that the boat had drawn up to the quay at Cochem, ready for them to disembark after breakfast and make the most of their time there. Conversation was muted in the dining room, some of the passengers still feeling the effects of the previous night, so Miss Hawthorne and Benton chatted quietly about the day ahead.

After breakfast, the passengers who were disembarking returned to their cabins to gather their belongings, then congregated on the upper deck. One of the crew took the chain off the gangway and the passengers began to file off.

The captain stood by to wish them a good day, but then turned aside as a member of the crew approached and began to speak to him in an undertone. Miss Hawthorne and Benton exchanged glances as they saw the captain frown and question the man urgently. Under the pretext of helping Miss Hawthorne find her footing on the gangway, Benton paused.

Miss Hawthorne turned and asked, 'Is everything all right, Captain? I do hope there is nothing amiss?'

The captain waved his crewman back and attempted a smile. 'Nothing at all that you need worry about, Miss Hawthorne! Some small matter of personnel. Think nothing of it, I beg you. Enjoy your time in Cochem and we'll see you this afternoon.'

'Oh, I'm glad to hear it,' she said, congenially. 'We've felt so well looked after by you and your crew.'

The captain nodded to her, then turned away as Benton gave Miss Hawthorne his arm to help her down the gangway. The two exchanged another glance, but forbore to comment until they were safely away from their fellow passengers.

Once they were alone, Benton raised his eyebrows and said,'Something's up.'

Miss Hawthorne agreed. 'He was very perturbed. Of course, it could have nothing to do with us, but…'

'If it doesn't, it's a bit of a coincidence.'

'We can hardly question him though,' Miss Hawthorne said, then raised her voice slightly as she noticed the two art students approaching. 'Now, where did we say we would start?'

'The church, then the old town, I think.'

Miss Hawthorne nodded to the students as they passed, and she and Benton set off for the church.

After Koblenz, Cochem proved to be a relatively small city, with most of the main sights within easy walking distance. After visiting the church, Benton and Miss Hawthorne strolled around the cobbled streets of the old town, pausing now and again for Benton to take pictures of the half-timbered buildings. They stopped for lunch at a small café with a view of the fountain that was the focal point of the market square.

Miss Hawthorne was looking at the menu when Benton caught her attention. He leaned over and said quietly, 'The gent over there by the postcard stand. Leather jacket and tan shoulder bag.'

Miss Hawthorne glanced up, trying not to show too much interest. Benton continued, 'He was at HQ with Sir Giles Mulberry.'

'Really? Well, he'd better not see you.'

Benton raised the menu, which was large enough to

conceal his face, and Miss Hawthorne bent to the side of the table, ostensibly to get a phrase book out of her handbag. The man opposite turned the postcard rack, apparently looking at the cards. After a few minutes, he moved off, glancing behind him as he went.

Miss Hawthorne nudged her companion to let him know he'd gone.

Benton, giving a sigh of relief, lowered the menu as the waitress came over to take their order: an omelette for Miss Hawthorne, and spaetzle with a green salad for Benton – who'd discovered a particular liking for the cheesy pasta dish.

Miss Hawthorne looked out across the square. 'Oh, there's Doug Lannis.'

Benton followed her gaze. 'By himself too.'

As Benton spoke, Doug glanced over, and, seeing his fellow passengers, waved, then carried on walking. Miss Hawthorne returned the wave, then looked at her companion.

'I wonder...'

'So do I,' agreed Benton. 'That's the trouble with this job: you start suspecting everyone. He's probably just been to a shop or the bank, and now he's going to meet his wife.'

'Yes, I expect so.'

But the explanation didn't really satisfy either of them. The appearance of Doug, so soon after the departure of the man who'd been at UNIT, seemed too much of a coincidence. There was something about the way the American walked. At first glance, he seemed to be strolling, but there was a purposefulness about his apparently casual progress that made Benton and Miss Hawthorne uneasy.

Before they could discuss it further, however, their food arrived, accompanied by tea served in tall glasses with slices of lemon, at which Benton raised his eyebrows and then sighed again.

Miss Hawthorne smiled sympathetically. 'I'm sorry, Sergeant. You'll have to wait until we get back to the boat for your proper cup of tea.'

'When in Rome and all that… but it's just not the same,' said Benton plaintively.

She consoled Benton by reminding him they both had kettles in their cabins and that he'd brought tea bags with him. Miss Hawthorne resisted the temptation to carry on teasing her companion and turned her attention to her meal. Knowing that coffee and cake would be waiting for them when they returned to the boat, Miss Hawthorne and Benton refused the dessert menu. Benton settled the bill and they continued their walk around the old town until it was time to make their way back to the quay.

Their arrival coincided with that of Doug, reunited with his wife, who was carrying a number of bags, some of which she handed to her husband so she could hold onto the handrail.

She noticed Miss Hawthorne looking her way, and greeted her, asking if she'd had a nice day.

'Yes, most enjoyable,' Miss Hawthorne replied. 'It's a charming place.'

Helen took her bags back from her husband and laughed. 'I know, I'm a walking cliché. But we've got so many nieces and nephews and when they found out we were coming to Europe…' She shrugged.

'Of course, you must keep the family happy!'

'Well, this should keep them amused for a while. Nothing expensive, but those wooden toys they have here are adorable.' She opened one of the bags for Miss Hawthorne to look and the two women moved away, discussing souvenirs and the difficulties of buying gifts for family members who didn't have many interests or hobbies.

Doug grinned at Benton. 'I guess your aunt won't be shopping for you?'

'I'm a bit big for toys these days,' replied Benton.

Doug clapped him on the shoulder with a laugh and the two men followed their companions to the dining room, where an afternoon meal of coffee and a tempting chocolate and vanilla marble loaf cake had been set out. Benton saw

Miss Hawthorne comfortably settled at a table near the window, then went to fetch supplies for both of them, dodging around his fellow diners with surprising grace for a man of his size. He arrived back at the table and carefully deposited the tray he'd been carrying, then lifted off the cups and plates before he sat down.

'Phew! Had a few near misses there!'

The chatter around the room ebbed and flowed, accompanied by the clinking of china and the sloshing of coffee being poured. The sound of a spoon being tapped against a glass brought silence, and the passengers turned in their seats to see the captain standing by the serving table, a serious expression on his face.

'*Meine Damen und Herren,*' he began. 'Ladies and gentlemen. I regret to inform you that there has been an attempt to break into the lockers in the sailors' quarters. I am conducting an investigation and have informed the police. They are permitting us to continue with our journey, but have advised that you all take extra care of your belongings and deposit anything of particular monetary or sentimental value in the safe provided.'

A hubbub arose around the room. Once it had settled a little, the captain continued: 'The crew has been instructed to work in pairs and to report any suspicious behaviour. An officer of the police has come aboard and will be pursuing the investigation while we travel. I would urge you to report anything you see that has aroused your suspicions. I'm sorry that this has happened. I hope most sincerely that you will not be disturbed or inconvenienced. On the advice of the police, we will not be stopping at Bernkastel, but will continue directly to Trier, where you will be at liberty to visit Bernkastel by road. The hotel in Trier has been informed and your rooms will be ready for you when we arrive. Thank you for your attention, I will answer any questions you may have throughout the evening.'

Miss Hawthorne and Benton looked at each other, eyebrows raised.

'Another coincidence?' said Benton.

'I can hardly think so,' replied Miss Hawthorne. 'It looks as if his cover has been blown, poor man, or at least that someone suspects that one of the crew is carrying the film.'

'The captain said an attempt had been made. I wonder how successful it was.'

'Yes, that thought occurred to me. Does whoever it was know that the film is not with the crew? We must be on our guard.'

Benton was watching the other passengers, most of whom were discussing the news with varying levels of alarm. Mrs Hobson had cornered the captain and was gesticulating while her voice rose in squeaks that made Benton think of a series of squibs being let off.

Suddenly, he caught Doug's eye. That gentleman looked over at him calmly for a moment, then looked away.

Benton frowned and Miss Hawthorne, who'd spotted that look, asked, 'What're you thinking, John?'

'I'm thinking that Williamsburg is the closest airport to Langley,' replied Benton.

It took Miss Hawthorne a moment to grasp what he was getting at, but then she frowned in turn. 'But if he was from the CIA, wouldn't they have flown from another airport? Or pretended to have done so?'

'Mm. You'd think so, but perhaps they are doing what we are: telling the truth up to a point.'

'Well, whether he is CIA or not, there's little we can do but to carry on as we'd planned and hope that his interest is benevolent.'

Benton nodded. 'It's getting a bit noisy in here, isn't it, Aunt Olive? Shall we pop outside for a bit?'

'Excellent idea, John.'

Benton stood up and helped Miss Hawthorne up from her chair. She grasped her stick, which had been leaning against the back of the chair, and the pair left the dining room and went up to the deck. It was almost deserted at that time of day, so it was easy for Miss Hawthorne and Benton to find a secluded place to sit. For a few moments, they sat in silence, gazing out over the river, then Benton spoke.

'Something feels wrong.'

Miss Hawthorne looked at him intently. 'How do you mean?'

'Trying to break into the lockers like that. It feels a bit… amateurish?'

'Ah, I see what you mean. Perhaps they were interrupted?'

'Possibly.' He paused, trying to put his feelings into words. 'Unless—'

'Yes?'

'I might be wrong, but… what if the break-in was just for effect? What if whoever did it suspected that a passenger has the film and wanted to scare them? They wouldn't need to actually get into the lockers. They could fake the break-in and then wait for the person with the film to panic.'

Miss Hawthorne considered for a moment, then replied, 'I believe you're right. And think: if all the passengers put valuables and items of personal significance in the safe, surely it would then be easier for the thief to break into it than to search each cabin in turn? We must be dealing with professionals. In which case, they'll surely be able to cope with the sort of safe used on ships of this kind. They're hedging their bets. If the film is with a member of the crew, they'll hope to have frightened them into showing their hand; if it's with a passenger, they'll hope that whoever it is hides the film among their personal effects and puts it in the safe.'

'Right. So what do we do? I could put the camera in the safe. I probably should – it would look odd if I didn't.'

Miss Hawthorne agreed. 'Then we'll have to find another place to conceal the film.'

'Yes, I've got a spare film in my case. I'll put that in the camera.'

'And I can put the transmitter in my handbag.'

'Yes, there's always plenty of room in there!'

Miss Hawthorne returned his smile. 'Well, it's important

to have room for the necessities.' They both knew she'd decided to, for once, leave her crystal ball at home on this occasion.

He glanced over his shoulder as some of the other passengers came up onto the deck for some fresh air before dinner.

Mr and Mrs Rogers emerged from the stairwell, and, seeing Benton looking in their direction, came over. Mrs Rogers drew up a chair and sat down.

'This is all very worrying, isn't it? Knowing there's a thief among us.'

'It is worrying,' acknowledged Benton, 'but it's only for one more night, and there's a policeman onboard now. It sounds like the captain has got things in hand at least. And we'll be putting our things in the safe, like he suggested. It's not ideal, but it's some consolation.'

Mrs Rogers turned to look at her husband, who was standing behind her chair. Mr Rogers sighed. 'Like you say, it's only one more night.'

'Then we'd better go and get our things together for the safe. There's your camera and my jewellery – not much of that, but this isn't a dressing up cruise; and then I suppose the travellers' cheques had better go in too.'

'Better be on the safe side.'

Mr Rogers held out his hand for his wife to lean on as she stood up. As she did so, she turned to Benton. 'Were you going to put your camera in the safe? We can take it down for you if you like, save you some time?'

Benton smiled, but put a hand on the case. 'No, that's okay – I'll take our things down before dinner. Thanks though.'

'Oh, okay. See you at dinner then.'

The couple left and Miss Hawthorne turned to Benton, her eyebrows raised. 'I suppose she could've wanted to save you the trip.'

'Mm. On the other hand… That's the trouble. We can't trust anyone.'

Miss Hawthorne agreed and looked at her watch. 'Shall we also repair to our cabins? 'I believe Aunt Olive might've found today a bit of a strain. Perhaps I will stay in my cabin this evening. That would give us a chance to find a better place to conceal the film and to signal UNIT.'

She reached out a hand and Benton helped her to her feet. 'That sounds like a good idea,' he agreed. 'You've been poorly enough so far for it not to arouse suspicion. If we let them know now, there shouldn't be any bother about having your meal brought to you. Oh, and I can get out of hanging around after dinner because I'll need to keep you company!'

'How touching,' said Miss Hawthorne with a smirk, 'but yes, that sounds reasonable. I'll signal HQ and you can keep an eye and an ear on the others at dinner, then we can pool our resources afterwards.'

They strolled back towards the stairs, Miss Hawthorne leaning heavily on her stick. One of the waiters paused to ask after her health and she smiled and replied that she was feeling tired and was going to rest. When Benton asked if Miss Hawthorne could have her evening meal in her cabin, the waiter readily agreed and called one of his colleagues to make the arrangements.

Once the matter had been settled, the two moved off, with Benton muttering, 'That will help get the word out.'

Having reached the entrance to the lower levels, they went downstairs and along to the cabins. Benton retrieved the films from his case and swapped the microdot film with an unused roll, then put it in the canister that the other roll had come from, writing an earlier date on the sticker on the side to make it look as if he'd used the film some days previously. He slipped the canister into his pocket and put the camera back in the case, then fetched a small folder holding a couple of traveller's cheques out of his case. Having closed and locked his door, Benton knocked for Miss Hawthorne and collected a wallet with a small amount of currency in. Apart from her usual jewellery, Miss Hawthorne had no valuables with her, but she felt she should at least give the impression that she was concerned enough to put something in the safe. Benton joined a queue outside the cabin where the administrative work of the boat took place. He didn't have to wait long. The crew worked efficiently, receiving the valuables, checking them in the presence of the owner, and issuing receipts, before placing the items in the safe.

His task completed, Benton returned to his cabin to freshen up before dinner. He wanted to arrive in good time, so that the absence of Miss Hawthorne wouldn't be so noticeable.

On his way to the dining room, he was passed by a member of the crew, who stumbled and nearly collided with him. He paused and tried to help the man to his feet. To his surprise and alarm, the face that turned to him was that of the agent.

While the man had looked tired when Benton had met him the previous night, now he looked ghastly. His face was pale, his lips almost grey, and his eyes unnaturally bright, the pupils small, as if he'd been staring into a bright light. As Benton reached out to help him up, the man shrank away from him, then pulled himself up with a hand on the wall and stumbled away. Benton looked after him, frowning. He knew the man was under considerable stress and might've been alarmed by the attempt on the lockers, but this looked serious. As he went on to the dining room, Benton debated with himself if he should tell the captain that a passenger looked so ill. In the end, he decided not to; another passenger or a member of the crew might well see the agent and pass on their concerns – he didn't want to put more pressure on the man. Shaking his head, Benton went into the dining room and took his seat.

The dining room was still fairly quiet. Clearly, some passengers had been delayed by their visit to the safe. The Rogers and Lannises arrived not long after Benton and enquired after Miss Hawthorne, so Benton repeated the story that they'd agreed on: that she was tired from the day out and upset by the news of the attempted robbery, so had decided to spend the evening resting. His fellow passengers expressed their sympathies, then turned their attention back to the events of the day.

Benton watched the room from over the rim of his beer glass. Conversation was muted. At some of the tables, people leaned forward, as if concerned they'd be overheard. At others, the passengers seemed less tense and the sound of laughter floated about the general chatter. As the meal progressed, the conversation grew louder and the diners began to relax, warmed by their meal and soothed by wine or beer. Mrs Rogers and Helen became engaged in a debate about the current fashions in women's clothes on either side of the Atlantic, watched with gentle amusement by their husbands. Once the meal was over and coffee had been served, Benton rose from his seat.

'I'm going to check how Aunt Olive is getting on. I'll see you all in the morning.'

His fellow diners expressed their concerns once again; Mrs Rogers even offered to sit with Miss Hawthorne, an offer Benton politely declined.

Benton returned to the cabins and gave his usual knock at Miss Hawthorne's door. She checked through the spy hole, then opened up. Benton entered the cabin and sat down, then turned and smiled when he saw that Miss Hawthorne had turned the kettle on and two cups with tea bags in were stood ready on the dressing table.

'Yes, I thought you could do with a cuppa,' she said. 'How was dinner?'

Benton described the atmosphere of the meal, then told Miss Hawthorne about his encounter with the agent.

'That does sound serious. Could he have been drugged?'

'It's possible – his pupils were tiny. I wasn't expecting him to recognise me in public, but he didn't seem to know where he was at all.'

Miss Hawthorne frowned. 'I'm not sure if you should tell someone. It sounds like he's either very ill, or has been drugged. In either case, he's clearly in danger.'

'If I do that, I risk blowing his cover, though. He wouldn't want to draw attention to himself.'

'Yes, but in this case…? Is there any way you could try and see him without being spotted?'

'I doubt it – the boat isn't big enough for that.' Benton looked down at his hands, then back at Miss Hawthorne. 'If someone has got to him, that means we could be in trouble too. It's a good job we'll be off the boat tomorrow. But do I report him?'

'I honestly don't know. If he is in as bad a way as you describe, surely one of his shipmates will notice? Perhaps we should leave it to them.'

The kettle clicked off. Miss Hawthorne stood up and manoeuvred around Benton to fill up the cups.

Having seated herself again, she went on, 'It seems disloyal not to try and help him, but I don't think we can take the chance.'

A knock at the door cut off whatever Benton had been going to say next. He looked at Miss Hawthorne, who raised her eyebrows and shrugged, then quickly put her legs up on the bed and arranged her pillows behind her back. She nodded and Benton answered the door.

Mrs Rogers was in the corridor. She smiled as she saw Benton and said, 'Oh, I wasn't sure you'd be here. I was just dropping by to see if your aunt wanted anything brought up or needed some company for a bit. How is she feeling now?'

Hearing the question, Miss Hawthorne spoke up. 'Much better, thank you, my dear.'

Benton stood aside so that their unexpected visitor could see Miss Hawthorne sitting on her bed with a blanket covering her legs, her crochet in hand.

'I'm so glad to hear it. Are you sure I can't fetch you anything?'

'Quite sure. It's kind of you to ask, but I'll be fine now. I didn't want to risk spoiling the last few days of the trip.'

'Well, in that case, I'll get back to the bar. See you tomorrow?'

'Yes, if my sleep is undisturbed I shall be at breakfast. John is kindly going to stay with me for now; we might try a game of Scrabble later, but that will be enough excitement for this evening!'

They said good night to Mrs Rogers, and Benton closed the door and turned the latch behind her. 'Bit nosey,' he whispered.

'Yes. Once again, she could just be curious but…'

There was a brief, uneasy silence, then Benton piped up: 'Suppose I'd better get the Scrabble.'

Silence had fallen over the guest quarters as the Mosel Prinzessin sailed on through the night.

Benton had left Miss Hawthorne's cabin shortly before ten and was sleeping comfortably when a sudden noise woke him. He sat up, disorientated. The noise got nearer: the sound of footsteps rushing along the corridor – not running, but staggering. As Benton threw back the bedclothes, there was a bang, as if someone had fallen heavily against the door. Benton got out of bed and reached for his dressing gown. He grabbed the film from the side table and pocketed it. He could hear other doors along the corridor opening and a murmur of voices.

He opened his door a crack and looked out, just in time to see a figure reach the stairs, and, clinging to both banisters, lurch upwards. Opening the door fully, he looked towards his fellow passengers.

Doug had come out into the corridor too and turned to Benton. 'Did you see who it was?' he asked.

Benton shook his head. 'Should we…?'

A crash came from the deck, forcing their hands. The two men ran to the stairs. When they reached the deck, the figure had reached the stern.

It turned – and Benton recognised the agent.

His eyes were wide and his breath came in ragged gasps. He stared at the men as they approached.

Benton said, quietly, in German, 'Don't be alarmed. We're not here to harm you. What's wrong?'

The man looked from one man to the other and said, in English, 'She won't stop. I can't stop her. She keeps asking me, but I won't tell her.'

Benton glanced at Doug. Slowly, they began to move closer. Benton spoke again, in English this time, 'Who is? Who is asking you what? You can tell us; we aren't going to hurt you.'

'No. No. Don't come any closer. She'll get you too. She's stopped now, but she'll come back.'

'Who will?' asked Benton.

'The Lorelei,' the man said, his voice barely audible. He climbed over the rail and stood on the outer edge of the deck. Benton and Doug stopped and Doug held up his hands.

'We've stopped now,' he called. 'We aren't going to come any closer. But you need to tell us who is after you, then we can help.'

His quiet, steady voice seemed to calm the agent a little. He gripped the rail more firmly for a moment.

Then raising his eyes, he gasped. 'No. I can't. I…'

And, before either Benton or Doug could stop him, he jumped into the river.

III

The two men rushed forward, but he had disappeared into the wake. The water was dark and churning, lined with deep cuts of froth from the boat. The man was consumed. But they couldn't give up.

Benton ran for the lifebelt that was secured to the wall and shouted for Doug to keep watching out for the man, then pressed a nearby alarm. A loud bell shrilled and crewmen rushed out onto the deck. The engines spluttered and stopped, and the anchor rattled down.

Doug, who'd kept his eyes on the surface of the water, shouted and pointed – 'There!'

Benton joined him at the rail. He could just see what looked like the agent's head emerge from the water, his arms floating limply on the surface. Benton called out and threw the lifebelt as far as he could in the agent's direction. It landed on the water close to the man's hand… but he made no effort to grasp it.

The captain had issued orders and a lifeboat was lowered. The men at the stern watched as the crew steered against the current, trying to reach the agent as he sank and surfaced again.

The captain came over to the rail and spoke to Benton. 'What happened?'

Benton and Doug regaled the tale to him, and the captain thanked them. 'I must ask you to speak to the police, of course. If you will come with me to the office in a moment.'

It was not a request. The men nodded and sat down on a nearby bench to await their summons.

The lifeboat crew were still trying to reach their fallen crewmate, but the current was against them. At last, one of them was able to reach him with a boat hook and snag the back of his shirt. Balancing carefully, two of the crew drew him closer and then pulled him over the bows. The man at the rudder shouted and waved; the crew turned the lifeboat back towards the cruise ship. The crew on deck were standing by and the lifeboat was raised, then the apparently lifeless body was passed up to the deck.

The ship's doctor, who'd been summoned with the rest of the crew, continued the artificial respiration that had been started in the lifeboat. For what felt to Benton like an eternity, there was no reaction, but suddenly, the agent coughed and retched. The doctor turned him on his side and water mixed with vomit poured out of his mouth. He coughed again, then closed his eyes, breathing heavily.

The man was laid on a stretcher and carried away to the sickbay. Benton and Doug looked at each other in relief.

'Thank God,' said Doug.

Benton gave a sigh of relief. He was a seasoned soldier, but the events of the night had shaken him more than he was ready to admit. The captain, having sent the crew back to their duties and given the signal to restart the engine, came back over to his passengers.

'Gentlemen, if you will come with me now, you can make your statements to the police. We can't hope to speak to this unfortunate man tonight. We'll make all speed to Trier and have him taken to the hospital.'

The two men got up without further comment and followed him down to the office, where a rather startled looking police officer was waiting. Having come aboard to investigate what seemed to be a botched burglary, he was alarmed to find that he was now apparently in charge of a case that could be attempted suicide for reason of insanity. He'd already spoken to some of the passengers and crew, and their descriptions led him to believe that the man in question had been suffering from a serious mental disturbance. He questioned Benton and Lannis politely, then asked them where they would be staying in Trier.

Having made a note of the hotels, he went on, 'From your statements, it seems that this man was attempting to kill himself to escape someone he believed was following him. Would you say that was accurate?'

Benton nodded. 'He mentioned a woman. He didn't give a name, but he said she was asking him something and wouldn't stop.'

'Hmm, well, I can only thank you for your efforts and for raising the alarm. We may need to speak again, but for tonight, I suggest you return to your cabins.'

Doug thanked him, and the pair left the office. Both seemed caught up with thoughts that they couldn't quite put into words.

Benton spoke first. 'Could he have been hallucinating?'

'I suppose. People have been known to hear things as well as see them. It seemed to me, though, that he saw something just before he jumped.'

'Yes, I thought so too.'

Doug sighed. 'Don't suppose it's our business to investigate. But we'd better not say too much to Mrs Rogers. From what her husband tells me, she's so into her legends, she would probably say the Lorelei had moved rivers and started on the Moselle.'

Benton glanced at Doug, but his face was serious. Clearly, Benton wasn't the only one to find Mrs Rogers trying at times. He made no reply to this remark.

They had reached the door of the Doug's cabin, so Benton said goodnight and went on down the corridor. The other doors were closed; perhaps the captain or another officer had been to deliver the news.

Benton saw the light on under Miss Hawthorne's door and tapped gently. Miss Hawthorne was in her dressing gown, her hair in a plait for the night, but she looked as alert as if it were daytime. Neither of them spoke until the cabin door was closed.

Miss Hawthorne explained that the captain had indeed called the passengers to their doors and told them that a member of the crew had fallen overboard, but had been rescued and was receiving medical attention. Anyone who had seen or heard anything earlier in the night would be able to make a statement to the police in the morning, but, for the time being, they were advised to stay in their cabins. Benton supplemented this information with what he'd seen and heard. Miss Hawthorne pulled a notebook out of her bag and began to write down the main points.

Miss Hawthorne looked at him sympathetically. 'I'm sorry, you must be exhausted. I just thought if I could take some notes while it was still clear in your mind…'

'No, that's all right. I doubt I'd get much sleep anyway.'

Benton collapsed into a chair and rubbed a hand across his face. 'He kept saying "she". "She" wouldn't leave him alone. I was wondering, could it be a hallucination? Like with Vornschawl? Could he have been hypnotised?'

'Possibly. From what you said earlier, though, it's

possible he was being drugged. Some drugs do induce aural hallucinations. But I don't know how specific they are; whether the victim would hear the same sounds all the time.'

'Right. So perhaps drugs and what?'

'I don't know. Some kind of suggestion? Although how that would be performed... He was a member of a crew, so it's hard to think of a time when someone might've seen him alone.'

'And he mentioned the Lorelei specifically?'

'Yes, said Benton, yawning. 'Could it be her, the real one? If there is a real one?'

'I don't know,' said Miss Hawthorne, thoughtfully. 'We've seen many strange things, you more than I. But I think it's a bit too much of a coincidence that a legendary siren has decided to attack the one man on this boat on an intelligence mission.'

'Agreed.' Benton nodded slowly and rubbed his face again.

'John, do go to bed,' Miss Hawthorne implored. 'I know you feel like you won't sleep, but at least lie down and read. You look worn out.'

He smiled wearily. 'Okay, Auntie, I'll give it a try.'

Benton returned to his cabin and got into bed.

The events of the night were still running through his head. What had happened to the agent to drive him to such desperation? Who had got to him, and how? Benton turned onto his side to look at his alarm clock and caught sight of the novel he had brought with him. He leaned over to pick it up – it might be worth a try.

The cabin was silent, apart from the ticking of the clock and the quiet rustle of pages being turned. Outside, the river lapped against the hull.

The book fell to the cabin floor. Benton was asleep.

In the cabin next door, Miss Hawthorne had not taken her own advice. She sat up in bed, looking at her notes and trying to make sense of what had happened.

Why had the agent been attacked at this late stage? Nobody appeared to have joined the boat, so why had an existing enemy waited so long to make their move? A sudden thought occurred to her and Miss Hawthorne scribbled a note, then slipped the notebook under her pillow. She laid down and reached to switch off the bedside lamp.

Any further deduction could wait until she'd had a chance to speak to the sergeant.

In the sickbay, the doctor turned from his patient's bedside to greet the captain.

'Sir,' he said, his voice barely above a whisper.

The captain came to stand next to him. 'How is he?' he asked.

'Better than I expected, but still very unwell. The cold of the water has caused severe shock. The sooner we can get him to hospital, the better.'

The captain nodded, frowning. 'Has he regained consciousness?'

'Very briefly. I thought I might have to sedate him, but he's slept naturally, much to my relief.'

'Good. Tell me if there is any change.'

'Of course.'

The captain nodded. He left the sickbay, a serious expression on his face. It was bad enough that a member of the crew had gone overboard, but the circumstances surrounding the incident were unpleasantly mysterious. He would have to hope that the doctor and the police officer on board could get to the bottom of it. Shaking his head, the captain returned to the bridge to brief his subordinates in preparation for the change of watch.

Dr Lindemann watched his patient for a few moments longer, then went to return to his other duties.

A sound from the bed made him turn back. The man had opened his eyes and was looking around. His hands gripped the sheets as he struggled to sit up. The doctor put a hand on his shoulder and pushed him gently, but firmly back down onto the bed.

'It's all right, Hawkins,' the doctor assured him.

The agent was posing as a British sailor. It wasn't unusual for crews to be made up of a variety of nationalities. The agent had got 'Hawkins' from a book he'd loved as a kid. It'd made him feel like an adventurer. Now, all he wanted was home. 'You're safe,' the doctor went on. 'You went overboard but you're safe now.'

'Hawkins' turned his head to face the doctor. 'Safe? Here? Safe?'

'Yes, quite safe. You're not well, but we will take you to the hospital soon and they will help you.'

'Where am I? Not... Not in my berth?' Hawkins tried to sit up again.

'No, you are in the sickbay.'

The ailing agent laid back against the pillows. 'Good. Good,' he muttered, but then he began to struggle again. 'Not there. I can't bear... Her voice... It wouldn't stop...'

Seeing his patient become agitated, the doctor fetched a cup from a nearby trolley. He put his hand behind Hawkin's head and brought the cup to the man's lips. 'Here. Drink. You must rest. You are safe here.'

Hawkins protested, but the doctor persisted and he eventually took a few sips of the drink. The doctor carefully lowered Hawkins' head back onto the pillows and withdrew his hand.

Hawkins looked at him with eyes that were becoming clouded. 'Thanks, doc. You won't... You won't let her...'

His voice faded as the sedative took hold and his eyes closed.

The doctor sighed and put down the cup. He'd hoped that sedation would not be necessary, but it was clear that Hawkins would not have been able to rest otherwise. He checked the man's pulse and made a note on his chart, then turned away from the bed and walked over to his desk.

He'd been told that Hawkins had spoken of hearing a woman's voice, but the presence of that voice seemed to be limited to his berth, which was odd. As far as he was aware, aural hallucinations of this kind followed their victims wherever they went, rather than limiting themselves to specific locations. The doctor sat down at his desk and began to add to the notes he had already made. Early the following morning, the Mosel Prinzessin reached Trier.

Working as quickly and quietly as possible, two ambulance men boarded the boat and removed Hawkins, who was still sleeping off the sedative he'd been given in the night. After hearing the doctor's evidence, the police officer on board, Polizeimeister Braun, had contacted his colleagues in the town and two officers were waiting on the quay, one to escort Hawkins to hospital, the other to help with the investigation.

After the previous night's alarms, many of the passengers slept late. Miss Hawthorne, however, was up at her usual early hour. She decided that, in keeping with her role, she would not be expected to be down to breakfast and that Benton could probably do with being out of the public eye, for the morning at least. So, after checking the corridor, she walked down to the dining room. The waiters and waitresses were still setting out the morning meal when she arrived and Miss Hawthorne managed to request breakfast for two to be brought to her cabin and then get back without being seen by any of her fellow passengers.

That accomplished, she sat down at the dressing table and began to draft a message to UNIT. By the time she'd sent the message, and replied to Corporal Scott's follow-up questions, Miss Hawthorne could hear doors opening and voices in the corridor. She took the transmitter to pieces and stowed it away in her bag, then got up to answer the door to Benton's knock.

Benton looked tired, but smiled when Miss Hawthorne proffered him in, and told him she'd ordered them breakfast already.

Benton sat down in the chair that Miss Hawthorne had just vacated. 'Thank you. I was wondering how I could get away with not answering any questions without being rude.'

'Yes, I thought so. In any case, it would surely be understandable for you not to appear at breakfast, after last night. Our curious fellow passengers will just have to possess their souls in patience for a while.'

Benton grinned. 'Do them good!'

Another knock at the door proved to be a waiter with rolls, pastries, a pot of coffee, and two cups. Benton took the tray and thanked him, then set out breakfast on the dressing table.

Miss Hawthorne sighed with satisfaction as she looked at the spread. 'I won't say I could get used to this kind of breakfast. I miss my breakfast tea and I cannot understand the appeal of cold meats or cheese at this time of the morning. But I have enjoyed having fresh rolls, and the butter and jam are delicious. Now, let us have some coffee, and afterwards, we must try and disentangle the events of last night, at least in part.'

Benton nodded. 'I've been trying make head or tail of it. We can't go asking the captain for evidence, so we won't get the whole story.'

Miss Hawthorne sipped her coffee. 'No, we must just make what we can of what we have.'

'Mm. What time do we have to get off the boat?'

'Half past eleven. The coach is due at about quarter past, I think.'

'Right. We've got a bit of time then. Croissant?'

'Thank you. Now, you say that the man – Did you hear what name he has assumed for this mission?'

'I think I heard someone call him "Hawkins".'

'Ah, then we may as well call him that. Hawkins was

talking about a woman who kept asking him something, but he refused to tell her? Did you get close enough to see his eyes?'

'Not really, but he looked much the same as he did when I saw him earlier. Anyway, the light was in his eyes, so his pupils would have been small in any case.'

'I see. When you met him first, he didn't show any signs of distress? You'd have noticed...?'

Benton set down his coffee cup. 'Yes. I mean, no. I mean, he looked tired and a bit tense, but nowhere near as bad as he was today.'

'So, whatever has happened to him happened very recently.'

'And whatever it is, it's been done by someone on the boat.'

'Must be. Whether she's the main perpetrator or not, a woman's involved.' Miss Hawthorne passed her cup over for a refill and paused while she ate the remainder of her croissant.

While she ate, Benton went on. 'Why now, though?'

Miss Hawthorne frowned as she stirred her coffee. 'I was thinking about that last night. The only explanation I can offer is that the person or persons responsible have only just identified him. They may have had a message that blew his cover, or some other information has come to light. If they joined the cruise knowing only that an agent was on board, but not who he was, that might explain the delay, and also their haste. We're almost at the end of the journey – they have limited time to get the film, so they have resorted to desperate tactics.'

Benton considered. 'Yes, I think you're right. But why torture him like this? Why not just attack him in person and get it over with?' He paused, then continued, 'Oh, unless they weren't sure of him having it on him. If they tried to force him to fetch it for them, it would attract too much attention. Their covers would be blown too.'

Miss Hawthorne nodded enthusiastically. 'It doesn't get

us any closer to how they've been tormenting this unfortunate man, but I believe we now know why. We must leave it up to the police to unravel the rest of the mystery – we can't go any further in investigating that without awkward explanations, and we mustn't risk it.'

'No, I know. Oh well, we'll have to hope the police can sort it out.' Benton looked at his watch. 'We'd better finish off and then start packing. There'll probably be a queue at the office for the safe.'

'Ah, yes,' agreed Miss Hawthorne, 'it's time for the next stage. While you're at the safe, I'll signal to say we're about to leave the boat, then we'll be clear and ready to leave.'

In the dining room, the conversation was even more muted than on the previous evening. The captain had arrived during the meal and had announced that the crewman who'd fallen overboard had been taken to hospital earlier that morning and was in a stable condition. He then reminded the passengers to make sure they retrieved all of their belongings from the safe before leaving the boat.

'Once again, ladies and gentlemen, I must apologise for the disruption and distress that these unpleasant incidents have caused. We wish you a pleasant stay in Trier and a good journey to your homes. Thank you.'

He left to a chilly silence, followed by a sudden hubbub as the passengers discussed his remarks and their plans for the day ahead.

As he had feared, Doug had come in for a good deal of questions, mostly from the inquisitive Mrs Rogers, but he'd fielded them with his habitual politeness. That is, until his wife had firmly insisted that he needed to eat after the night he'd had and that if anyone wanted answers, they should speak to the crew or the police. Mrs Rogers retreated into an offended silence after this, but her husband laughed.

'That's you told then, love!' he said. 'Never mind, I'm sure we'll get all the facts eventually. I must say, it was all news to me; I slept right through, but then I generally do. I have an alarm clock but Caroline had to knock me up this morning too.' He paused, as if expecting questions, but when there were none, went on, 'I snore like an elephant, so we don't share cabins on cruises like this. They're too small and Caroline doesn't get any rest.'

His wife, who'd been finishing her coffee, scowled at him. 'When you've quite finished telling everyone our private arrangements, perhaps you could go and get my things out of the safe? I want to finish packing.'

Mr Rogers looked astonished at this reaction but stood up.

'Yes, okay dear, no need to be like that about it,' he said quietly.

Mrs Rogers put a hand on his sleeve. 'I'm sorry, darling, I'm just tired. You go and get our things and I'll see you at our cabins.'

Placated, he leaned over and kissed the top of her head. He left the room and, after a brief interval, his wife followed.

Doug and Helen looked at each other.

'Well,' said Doug, 'that was unexpected.'

'She got out the wrong side of bed this morning,' agreed Helen.

'Mm. Are you finished, honey? I just want to check and see if there's been a cable for me.'

Helen nodded, and suggested she could get their possessions from the office. He agreed, kissed him on the cheek, and walked out of the dining room. Once in the corridor, he started in the direction of the administrative office, where any communications for passengers would have arrived. At the end of the corridor, however, he looked around him quickly and then went towards the lower deck where the crew was quartered.

Benton had retrieved his and Miss Hawthorne's belongings from the safe and the two companions had packed quickly, as befitted two experienced travellers. They met in the corridor and Benton carried their bags up to the deck and set them down to be loaded onto the coach, then he and his 'aunt' joined their fellow passengers who were taking their first look at Trier from the rails.

A high embankment faced them on the town side of the river, topped with a tree-lined path. Three or four small inns stood side by side near the bridge that spanned the river at that point, leading to the village of Pfälzel and the monument known as the Mariensäule, a column bearing a statue of the Virgin Mary, which stood at the top of a steep, tree covered hill. On the other side of the road to the inns was a large, white building with ornate gables and a steeply pitched roof. Miss Hawthorne identified this from the guidebook as a former monastery, currently used to accommodate students from the university which stood on the outskirts of the town.

A small coach arrived and members of the crew came to carry the luggage down the gangway. Mrs Hobson followed her cases down, keeping up a constant stream of warnings to the imperturbable young sailor who was carrying them. Miss Hawthorne and Benton exchanged amused glances and went over to the gangway to disembark.

The captain was in his usual position and shook their hands warmly.

'Mr Benton, I am so very grateful to you. Were it not for you and Mr Lannis, I fear the worst would have happened.'

'It was the least we could do, really. How is he?'

'The doctor tells me that he's in a stable condition, but he needed to be sedated last night. He had a return of the fear that you spoke of and became agitated.' The captain seemed to realise that he was saying more than he should and stopped. The pair just had trustworthy faces.

Miss Hawthorne put her hand on his sleeve. 'I am so glad to hear that he's recovering. We were both very worried last night, but I'm sure he will receive excellent care at the hospital. We will, of course, be happy to answer any more questions the police may have for us, won't we, John?'

They bid each other adieu, then, as on the previous day,

Miss Hawthorne cautiously negotiated the gangway and the sergeant helped her board the coach.

The hotel was a short drive from the river and Miss Hawthorne looked out with interest as they drove past sections of the Roman wall which had once encircled the ancient town, now fragmented and covered in ivy.

'Amelia would love it here,' she said, referring to her old friend, the archaeologist Professor Amelia Rumford.

The coach turned and pulled up outside the hotel, which was on the intersection of two wide roads, one of which led to the railway station. The passengers got off the coach and stood for a moment, looking across the road at one of the most recognisable and famous of the monuments of Trier, the Porta Nigra. Once a gate to the Roman city, the Porta Nigra had been preserved through the centuries and towered over the paved area in which it stood.

Benton looked up at the age-blackened stonework from which the Porta Nigra took its name and whistled. 'Blimey. That's quite something isn't it?'

'Yes,' replied Miss Hawthorne, 'to see a Roman building standing, rather than a piece of wall or a row of bricks in a field...'

They agreed to go unpack then explore a little. Might as well take advantage of their time here. 'That café over the road looks good,' commented Benton. 'We might even be able to get a good cup of tea.'

After delivering his message at breakfast and before joining his passengers on the deck to say goodbye, the captain had checked with the doctor and two police officers in the sickbay. The doctor elaborated on the brief messages he'd left the previous evening, explaining his concerns after having spoken to Hawkins.

The captain frowned as he listened, then said, 'He seemed frightened to return to his berth?'

'Terrified. It seems that whatever's been tormenting him does so there.'

Polizeimeister Braun spoke up. 'How many other men sleep in the same room?'

'Curiously enough, none,' replied the captain. He went on to explain that, while the boat was fully crewed, there were extra berths for additional personnel at particularly busy times, such as Christmas and New Year, or the peak of the summer season. As Hawkins had joined the crew at the last minute, he'd been assigned a berth in one of the rooms usually set aside for additional crew.

'I was thinking that if someone wanted to make him believe he was going mad, they could do that more easily if he was alone,' suggested Braun. 'May we inspect his sleeping quarters?'

'Of course,' replied the captain, leading the way out of the sickbay.

Hawkins' bunk was in a corner of a room designed to hold six. The tumbled blankets on the top showed where he'd spent the night, until he'd been driven to go up on deck. One of the policemen clambered up onto the bunk and laid down on it, running his hands over the ceiling.

After a few moments, he exclaimed and called for a torch, which his colleague provided. The other men crowded round to look. By its light, they could see two small holes in the ceiling above the bunk.

Braun took a pen from his pocket and poked it into one of the holes. Almost the whole length of the pen disappeared into the hole. He withdrew the pen and got down from the bunk.

The captain looked on, astonished, then asked, 'What does this mean?'

Rather than answering, Braun turned to the doctor. 'Doctor, could some of Hawkins' symptoms have been drug induced?'

The doctor looked thoughtful. 'It's possible, I suppose. What had you in mind?'

'Well,' Braun pointed to the holes, 'if, say, a small tube could be passed through here, to feed a hallucinogen into the room in some form, or some substance that increased the heart rate and caused a feeling of panic…'

He reached up to the bunk and lifted the pillow down. He turned it in his hands, then smelt the pillow case. 'There is something on here…'

The doctor took the pillow and examined it. 'Yes, you're right! I can't identify the scent, but there is definitely something. Look here!'

He held it up and the other men saw a small stain on the surface of the pillowcase.

'And the voice?' asked the captain.

'That could've come through the other hole. Another tube, or a small recording device…'

The doctor looked up at the ceiling, considering. Finally he said, 'You could be right. But why would anyone do such a thing?'

A new voice made them all turn round. Doug stood framed in the doorway.

In German, he said, 'I believe I may be able to help you with that.'

IV

Having checked in and unpacked, Miss Hawthorne and Benton had set off to explore Trier. Their first stop was the Porta Nigra and Benton climbed the narrow stone steps to look out at the view. He waved to Miss Hawthorne, who returned the wave, then greeted Rogers who had followed them over the road.

'It's stunning,' said Mr Rogers, 'but you wouldn't catch me climbing up there.'

'No, John is much more energetic than I am,' agreed Miss Hawthorne. She looked up towards Benton again, but he vanished from view as he went back to the stairs.

Mrs Rogers' mind was on their fellow passengers. 'Did you see the Lannises? They must've been late getting off the boat – I don't think I saw them on the coach.'

'Oh,' Miss Hawthorne was surprised by this news, but feigned disinterest. 'I can't say I noticed particularly. I expect we'll see them later.'

Having been rebuffed, Mrs Rogers again retreated into an offended silence. Miss Hawthorne smiled to herself as the couple walked away. She had no time for gossips.

Benton rejoined her at this point Miss Hawthorne explained, 'The inquisitive Mrs Rogers was asking about Mr and Mrs Lannis. She says they were delayed in leaving the boat.'

'Really? Can't say I noticed.'

'You were with Mr Lannis last night. What was your impression?'

Benton thought carefully before answering. 'Doug was certainly calm under pressure. He seemed genuinely surprised by the state Hawkins was in though. If he was putting that on, he's a very good actor.'

'I see. Then perhaps we can discard him from the list of suspects for the attack on Hawkins.'

'I'd think so. That doesn't necessarily mean he isn't after the film.'

A couple from the boat walked by, so Miss Hawthorne suggested she and her 'nephew' get some refreshments. She led the way over to an ice cream parlour with a frontage of large windows and art nouveau style metalwork. Benton joined her as she looked at the menu outside.

'We can certainly get tea here, though I must admit the hot chocolate looks very tempting, as do the cakes and… what on earth can that be?' She pointed at the section of the menu that listed ice cream sundaes and read, 'Spaghettieis?'

'Oh, yes, one of the lads told me about that,' replied Benton. 'It's ice cream that looks like spaghetti, with strawberry sauce on top and a bit of white chocolate to look like cheese.'

'How very odd. Why would anyone invent such a thing?'

'I suppose it's like climbing Everest – if you have to ask

why, you wouldn't understand the answer!'

Feeling that there was no adequate reply to this, Miss Hawthorne merely smiled and shook her head. Benton held the door open for her and they went into the café, where they were met by a welcoming waitress, who showed them to a table near the window and left them with the menus. Miss Hawthorne took her guidebook out of her bag and placed it on the table, completing the picture of a pair of British holiday-makers having a mid-morning treat. Benton resisted the lure of spaghettieis and ordered a coffee and a slice of cheesecake; Miss Hawthorne had the same, but with hot chocolate, which arrived with a topping of whipped cream.

'One couldn't have this every day,' she said, as Benton tucked into his cheesecake, 'but once in a while won't hurt, I suppose.'

Miss Hawthorne turned suddenly to look more closely through the window. Benton put down his fork and leaned forward.

'Over there...' She pointed. 'Outside the bookshop. Isn't that the man we saw in Cochem?'

Benton followed her gaze. 'Yes, it's him. He's followed us here.'

'Are we to assume he's working with British intelligence? You did see him with Sir Giles at UNIT HQ?' Benton nodded and frowned, so Miss Hawthorne prompted, 'But...?'

'I don't know. It's odd. You'd think if MI5 or MI6 wanted someone to get hold of the film, they'd have tracked Hawkins and put someone on the boat, rather than have him following along behind. Although we don't know when he got here; I guess he might've been here before us. He could be here officially. I mean, that's the most likely explanation...'

Miss Hawthorne looked at Benton quizzically, then said, 'You should never ignore your intuition, Sergeant. If it's telling you that there's something wrong here, then you should listen to it. After all, intuition is partly the voice of your experience.'

Benton looked over at the man again, and then shrugged. 'We

should try and steer clear of him, whoever he's working for.'

The waitress showed some more customers to a nearby table and Benton changed the topic of conversation. By the time he and Miss Hawthorne next looked out for the man, he'd gone.

'Where would you like to go next? The cathedral is just off the main marketplace. It's a shame there isn't a market today, but you can't have everything. It says here…' He consulted the guidebook. '…that the cathedral has a relic believed to be the robe Christ wore at his crucifixion.'

'Really? How extraordinary!' Miss Hawthorne looked at the book. 'So I see. I always found the preservation of parts of the dead rather ghoulish, but I've never heard of such a large and, er, complete relic. Ah, but it says here it's kept behind the high altar and only brought out at festivals. That would make sense. I cannot think that it's really what it purports to be, but strange things happen.'

They could both attest to that.

Brigadier Lethbridge-Stewart looked over the signals from his agents with a serious expression. Clearly, he'd been right to assume that more than one agency would be looking for the microfilm, but the attack on Hawkins was disturbing. Theft of the microfilm might be expected, but that approach suggested a ruthlessness that made the Brigadier decidedly uneasy. He was relieved that Benton and Miss Hawthorne had arrived safely in Trier, but there was still enough time before the rendezvous for something to go wrong.

The Brigadier looked at his watch. Time to go. He was due to meet the UN representative at the airfield, then they would fly together to Luxembourg and travel across the border into Germany.

The Brigadier pressed a button on his intercom. After a moment, a voice replied. 'Sir?'

'Corporal Scott, my office; quick as you can.'

A few moments later, there was a knock at the door and Corporal Scott entered.

'Corporal, here is the rendezvous signal. Cable to Sergeant Benton at his hotel as soon as you can.'

'Yes, sir.'

The cable was in code, but any passing reader would have assumed that it was a message regarding the progress of a house sale. Corporal Scott saluted and left the office, then returned to the communications room to arrange for the cable to be sent from a number that wouldn't be identified as UNIT.

Shortly afterwards the Brigadier put his head round the door of the communications room.

The Brigadier ran down the steps to his car. The driver had been briefed and drove away as soon as his CO had fastened his seat belt.

Miss Hawthorne and Benton emerged from the cathedral and into the sunlight. They had admired the exterior of the building, built on the site of the Roman Emperor Constantine's summer palace, and built using many of the materials from the original building. The walls were high, and the towers increased the height of the building still further, as it dwarfed the surrounding settlements. Inside, pillars reached up to the vaulted ceiling. The two visitors sat down to get a proper look at the vaulting above and then made a circuit of the structure, looking in the many side chapels and queuing behind the high altar for a glimpse of the precious robe. The cathedral treasury provided a further diversion, though it contained rather too many reliquaries for Miss Hawthorne's taste. Outside, Benton handed the guidebook to his companion, so he could take a photograph of the ornate carving that surrounded the main door.

Miss Hawthorne shivered and moved further away from the shadow of the building. Benton glanced at her. 'Bit chilly in there.'

'Yes,' she agreed. 'Beautiful, and the shade would be welcome in the summer, but a little cool for this time of year.'

Benton put his camera back in its case and offered his

arm to Miss Hawthorne. 'Maybe we can find something warm for lunch – soup or something would be nice.'

'That's an excellent idea. Oh…' Miss Hawthorne paused and gave a gentle wave as Doug and Helen approached.

Benton smiled in greeting, but his smile faded at Doug's serious expression.

The American held out his hand, as if meeting Benton for the first time and said, 'Sergeant Benton, we need to talk.'

Benton hesitated, but then shook hands. 'Where?'

Doug looked around, then pointed to a restaurant nearby, which had tables and chairs outside. 'How about over there?'

Miss Hawthorne looked at Doug and asked, 'What's happened?'

Doug paused, then said, 'You two are working together? Of course you are. How did I miss that?'

Benton's expression darkened. 'I think it's time we heard a bit more about you, as you seem to know all about me. Shall we?'

He held out his hand towards the restaurant. Helen took her husband's arm and he led the way. Once they'd been shown to a table and drinks had been ordered, Benton looked at Doug.

'So, Mr Lannis – Is it Mr Lannis?'

'Douglas George Lannis, Central Intelligence Agency.'

Benton looked at the woman he had thought of as Helen Lannis.

She picked up the hint: 'I really am Helen Lannis too. Just along for the cover story, with strict instructions to run for cover if things get nasty.'

'I see. And the CIA is here because…?'

'I'm here to help make sure the UN gets that film, as, I guess, are you.'

Benton hid his surprise at this answer, but Miss Hawthorne did not. 'Really?' she asked. 'And are you aware of the identity of the agent who brought it on board.'

'The unfortunate Mr Hawkins?'

'But you didn't approach him?'

'No, at least, not until I had to. I'm here to observe and to protect the film and the person carrying it. My government might be tempted to get a leg up in the arms race, but the agency is not going to risk an escalation of hostilities.'

Benton considered. He was tempted to trust Doug, who had, after all, joined him in trying to save Hawkins, but he was cautious. He decided to open up a little. 'And we know that Hawkins doesn't have it any more.'

Miss Hawthorne glanced at Benton from behind her menu. Guessing his tactics, she said nothing, but waited for Doug to reply.

'No, he doesn't. I asked him if he could tell me who he gave it to, but of course, he won't split.'

'You spoke to him?' asked Miss Hawthorne in surprise.

'I've just come from the hospital. I'd been thinking since last night that Hawkins looked familiar, then I remembered we met in Romania last year on assignment. I went to see if he remembered me and if he'd open up a bit, give me something to work with. But he couldn't, beyond saying that he'd handed off the film to another agent a couple of nights ago.'

'Did he say who it was?' asked Miss Hawthorne, trying to sound genuinely curious, rather than nervous.

'No. He's trying to protect whoever it is, of course, I can understand that, especially after all he's been through.'

Turning the question away from the identity of the 'agent,' Benton asked, 'Have the police worked out what happened to him to make him want to go overboard?'

'They think he was drugged through a hole in the ceiling above his bunk, then either someone spoke to him, or they played a recording. The police are working on identifying the drug, but it looks like it was dripped through a tube onto his pillow and he inhaled it in his sleep.'

'Was the voice familiar to him?' asked Miss Hawthorne.

Doug waited for a server to walk past, then explained, 'Says he didn't recognise it, but that doesn't mean much. Says it was a woman's voice though. He would've been dazed from the drug and from being half-asleep, and, like I say, it could have been a recording.'

'So it might not have been a woman at all.'

'Guess not. But whoever they are, they're clearly very well prepared. So whoever has the film now had better watch out.'

Doug shot a glance at Benton, but Benton's face was expressionless. Doug sighed. 'Look. I know you don't trust me. No reason why you should. But if you've got that film, or if you know who has, tell them to watch their backs. I'll do my best, but we're up against ruthless and resourceful people.'

Benton asked, 'Did they find out who was in the cabin above?'

'That cabin was supposed to be unoccupied, according to the passenger manifest. When I left, the police were checking the lock to see if it'd been picked or if the person who was in there had a key.'

Benton was about to speak again, when Miss Hawthorne put in, 'Mr Lannis, were you following someone in Cochem?'

Lannis looked taken aback by the bluntness of her question, but then laughed. 'Not much gets past you, Miss Hawthorne. Yes, a man by the name of Verney. He's been tracking the cruise since Koblenz. He's MI6.'

Benton sensed some hesitation in the reply and asked, 'But?'

'Yes, Sergeant, there is a "but". I would've assumed that MI6 were party to the same information that we were. They might not be able to identify the agent – pure coincidence that Hawkins and I know each other – but I would've thought for sure they would have put someone on the boat. Why was he following on land? Did he have a colleague or colleagues on the boat, and, if not, how would he know what was happening? I may be wrong, but something about that setup smells funky to me.'

'You think he might be playing a lone hand?' asked Benton.

'Maybe. I don't know. I don't want to damn him on suspicion alone. The best we can do is stay alert and hope the handover goes smoothly. The UN hasn't shared the location with us, but I'm here to help, so if you get in touch with the agent, you let them know they can call on me.'

Again, the sideways glance at Benton once more went unrewarded.

The waiter arrived with a loaded tray and the fellow travellers shelved the serious topic of conversation and enjoyed bowls of creamy soup, filled with chopped vegetables and seasoned meatballs, with crusty bread on the side. While they ate, the conversation was kept on lighter matters, as they compared notes on the various sights they'd seen, and hoped to see during their visit. The restaurant terrace was filling up, and all four members of the cruise party wanted to avoid the risk of being overheard.

After some good-natured arguing, the gentlemen of the party split the bill between them and Miss Hawthorne and Benton headed off in the direction of the Lutheran Basilica, and the Lannises turned back towards the market place.

As they walked, Helen asked her husband, 'Do you think they believed you?'

The CIA man frowned. 'I don't know. They're hard to read. I hope so. I guess we'll just have to wait and see.'

Benton and Miss Hawthorne decided against going into the Basilica and instead walked on to the garden of the Kurfürstlichen Palast, an expanse of neatly manicured lawns punctuated by pools and rose beds, and surrounded by paths and clipped hedges. These presented themselves in front of an extraordinary pink and white confection of a building that, as Miss Hawthorne remarked, appeared to be made out of sugar rather than bricks and mortar. The companions walked round the paths, talking in low voices, but trying not to appear too concerned.

As they paused by the largest of the pools, Miss Hawthorne asked, 'Do you believe him?'

'I want to – he seems to be here for the right reasons, and he did help with Hawkins, but… No, I don't think we can risk it. I think we've given him as much as we can.'

Miss Hawthorne sighed. 'I agree. It would be comforting to think we could take him into our confidence, but we dare not. What do you make of his pursuit of Verney?'

'I'm not sure about that either. He could've been trying to find out what he was up to, I suppose.'

Their discussion was particularly pertinent. Benton paused and put a hand on Miss Hawthorne's arm. Verney, if that was his name, had come from behind a hedge and was walking towards them, a determined expression on his face.

Miss Hawthorne gripped the handle of her walking stick and was about to step forward, but realised that wouldn't be in character, so looked up at Benton. He gently moved her behind him and drew himself up to his full height.

Verney gave a bitter smile as he neared them. 'Well, I can see someone has got to you. Lannis, was it?'

Benton said, quietly, 'I don't know what you mean. What do you want?'

Verney held out his hand. After a brief hesitation, Benton shook it.

'Thomas Verney, MI6. I know you've spoken to Mr Lannis. I don't know what he's told you, but whatever it was, I advise you to take it with a large measure of salt.'

Miss Hawthorne said, 'And why should we give you any more credit than we give him?'

Verney looked at her as if seeing her for the first time. 'So you're Miss Hawthorne. I can't really give you a reason, except that I'm telling the truth and he… may not be as honest as he looks. But if you've decided to disbelieve me, I can't help you.'

He turned away, but Benton asked, 'Why are you here?'

'Come off it!' Verney was suddenly angry. 'You know why I'm here. And I know why you're here. To get that microfilm and make sure it doesn't fall into the wrong hands!'

Benton remained cool. 'And the right hands would be yours?'

There was something fierce and steely behind Verney's eyes. They held each other's gaze for a moment.

Then, as suddenly as Verney's anger had risen, it was gone. He shrugged. 'No. As it happens. Much as the minister would like us to have the warheads, we've been overruled. I'm here to offer support and assistance, should it be necessary. Now we understand one another, I need to know if the film is safe.'

Benton said calmly, 'As far as I know.'

'Really. What have you done with it?'

'I haven't done anything with it.'

'Are you saying you haven't got it? Come on, man, I'm on your side.' Verney was growing frustrated again.

Benton, his face expressionless, said, 'I'm not at liberty to say, sir. You must know I can't disclose any details of a UNIT operation, even to friendly agencies.'

Verney turned away in disgust. Looking back, he said, 'Well, if that's how you want it. I might have known you'd just parrot the same nonsense as Lethbridge-Stewart. You're in a very dangerous position, Sergeant. You need to choose your friends carefully.' He paused, then said, 'I can see you've made up your mind. Don't forget, if the UNIT mission fails, it will be your responsibility. You and that absurd, stiff-necked throwback in London. Consider yourself warned.'

Verney turned back and walked away.

Miss Hawthorne put her hand through Benton's arm and asked with unusual timidity, 'John?'

'I'm okay. I think that might've been a threat, don't you?'

She nodded. 'If he really is here to help, he has a funny way of ingratiating himself.'

'Yes. I was about to ask him why he wasn't on the boat, or if he had a colleague reporting to him, but now didn't seem the right time to ask.'

Benton squeezed Miss Hawthorne's arm tenderly. The pair determined to go back and check if they've got any messages. Miss Hawthorne, though, was somewhat absentminded; concerned for her, Benton asked what was going through her mind.

'I was just wondering... I noticed a sign to the hospital on the way from the hotel. Perhaps we could call in and enquire after Mr Hawkins.'

Benton was silent for a moment, then said, 'And check if our friend Doug was telling the truth about going there?'

'Well, I don't imagine we would be allowed to see Hawkins. Indeed, I wouldn't wish to – it would only cause him more stress and the poor man has been through enough. But if we could perhaps ascertain if he had any other visitors today...'

'It's worth a try.'

By this point, they had arrived back at the Porta Nigra. The hotel was just over the road from them; the sign to the hospital pointed to the left.

'Hotel or hospital first?' asked Benton. 'It's still early yet; the signal might not have come through.'

'Hospital, then,' said Miss Hawthorne, taking a tourist map from her bag. 'I believe if we cut through here.' She pointed to a side road that branched away from the Porta Nigra, almost parallel to the main road. 'We can reach the hospital without needing to go past the hotel. If someone we know is in the bar they might see us through the window.'

The pair made their way back across from the Porta Nigra and took the side road, past a small cinema and snack bar, and on down a leafy, tree-lined street. The hospital was in a cul-de-sac off this street, well hidden from the road behind high hedges. Miss Hawthorne and Benton consulted the signs around the entrance and made their way to the reception. Benton's German was functional rather than fluent, but he managed to make the purpose of their visit clear to the man at the desk, who, after looking searchingly at both Benton and his companion, gestured to a row of seats near the door and picked up the telephone receiver.

About ten minutes passed, then a uniformed police officer came from the corridor that led to the lifts. Benton recognised Polizeimeister Braun, and stood up to greet him. Braun approached with a frown, which lifted a little when he saw who was waiting for him.

'Mr Benton! Frau Hawthorne! How may I help you?'

Miss Hawthorne explained that they'd been concerned about Hawkins since he'd been taken from the boat, and, as they were near the hospital, had decided to call in and see if there had been any improvement in his condition.

'We didn't mean to trouble you, Herr Braun,' she said, earnestly. 'I'm sorry we have caused you any inconvenience.'

Braun could see nothing but polite enquiry in her expression. He frowned again, as if considering how much he could say, then gestured for the twosome to sit down and took a seat next to Miss Hawthorne.

'The doctors are confident that Hawkins will recover his physical health,' he said. 'He received a severe shock, and swallowed some river water, which is worrying, but he's been given antibiotic medication and the signs are good.'

'Oh, I am relieved to hear that,' said Miss Hawthorne. 'But you said his physical health. Please don't answer if you can't tell us, but...'

'I may tell you a little, I think. Mr Benton did, after all, help to save Hawkins. When he arrived at the hospital, he was calm, and it was hoped that the change of environment would help him to stay so. However, just after lunchtime, he became suddenly disturbed – to such an extent that the doctor was obliged to sedate him. He has remained in this state until now. When he wakes, he will be assessed by a psychiatrist.'

'The poor man,' said Miss Hawthorne. Then, almost to herself, 'I wonder what it was that set him off again.'

Benton replied, 'Yes, poor chap. I suppose it could have been anything, though: a sound; someone who looked familiar; maybe one of the doctors or nurses might've reminded him. He won't have had any visitors, of course, so it can't have been that.'

Braun nodded, not noticing the hook that Benton had drawn in front of him. 'No. He's certainly not had visitors. We have his room under guard: only hospital and police personnel may enter. Today, he's been seen only by the doctors, nurses – Oh, and I believe an orderly who came to clean the floor of the room, about midday…' He trailed off.

Benton and Miss Hawthorne avoided each other's eyes, but they both guessed that Braun had had the same thought as they had. After a moment's silence, Braun stood up and turned away, speaking quietly and urgently into his radio.

He then turned back and said, 'I'm afraid I must ask you to leave now. I would be grateful if you would keep all this information to yourselves.'

Benton, seeing that the time for subterfuge had passed, at least where Braun was concerned, replied, 'You have our word.'

Braun looked searchingly at Benton, then held out his hand. The two men shook hands, then Braun walked quickly back towards the lift.

Benton and Miss Hawthorne left the hospital with concerned expressions. Once they'd gone through the main gates and were on the road back to the hotel, Benton said, 'So Lannis was lying. Unless he was the orderly.'

'Yes,' agreed Miss Hawthorne, 'and whoever that orderly was upset Hawkins so much that he relapsed. This can't have been a chance similarity; somebody deliberately impersonated a member of staff to get to him.'

'But did they want to question him, or silence him?' asked Benton.

'They didn't kill him, so I suppose we must assume they

were intending to question him. In a way, his collapse has worked in their favour. For as long as he's sedated, he will not be able to answer Mr Braun's questions. And in such a large and busy hospital, it will be difficult to trace the path of the intruder.'

Benton grunted in agreement, then took Miss Hawthorne's hand and tucked it through his arm. Miss Hawthorne looked at him in surprise, but then noticed Mr and Mrs Rogers on the other side of the road and understood. Apparently noticing them for the first time, she waved to the couple, who returned it and carried on.

Before long, Benton and Miss Hawthorne arrived back at the hotel, and the latter went to sit in the lounge, while Benton checked at the reception desk for messages. While waiting for the receptionist to check, Benton noticed Helen and greeted her as she came up to the desk.

'Hello, you've called it a day too?'

'Oh, yes. We've done quite enough for one day. Now,' she stood alongside Benton and spoke to another of the reception staff, 'I need some stamps for these.' She reached across the desk and held out three postcards as the other receptionist came back with a slip of paper in his hand.

'Mr Benton, we have this message for you. Will there be a reply?'

Benton looked at the paper briefly, as if the contents were expected and said, 'No, that's fine. Thank you.'

Helen finished paying for her stamps and came alongside him as he walked back towards the lounge. 'Not bad news, I hope?' she enquired.

'Not at all. My mother is trying to sell her house and my sister and I are handling the paperwork. My sister just cabled to give me an update.'

'Ah, I see. Not that it's any of my business really.'

'No, that's okay. Ideally, I'd be there, but things moved on a bit more quickly than we were expecting.'

'Well I hope she'll be happy in her new home. She's lucky to have her children to look after her.'

'Thank you,' said Benton, then, as he sat down next to Miss Hawthorne, he said, 'Liz cabled – mother's had two offers.'

'Oh good!' said Miss Hawthorne, 'That will be a great relief to her.'

Benton nodded, folded the cable, and put it in his pocket. He picked up his coffee cup and the two companions sat in silence for a few moments, then Benton put down his cup, and said, 'I'd better go and make sure my shirt doesn't need ironing. Wouldn't want to show you up at dinner!'

Miss Hawthorne laughed. 'I'm sure there's no chance of that, John, but I suppose this hotel is a little more formal than the boat.'

Benton made his way to the lift and up to the second floor. As he turned the key in the door of his room, he felt a slight resistance in the lock, and bent down to inspect it. He straightened up with a grim expression, opened the door, and went in.

Inside, everything seemed to be in place, but Benton checked the position of all his belongings, even down to the tube of toothpaste in the bathroom. Having made a thorough inspection of his room, Benton sat down at the dressing table and took out the cable form and a small notebook. This contained the decryption key to the code, disguised as a series of addresses. He reread the cable, decoding it in his head, then put the form in the ashtray on the dressing table and set light to it. He watched it as it burned, then crushed the fragments of ash with the end of his pen, tipped them into the bathroom basin, and turned on the tap.

A final thought occurring to him, he fetched the stool from the bathroom and stood on it to inspect the ceiling light, then checked the bedside and desk lamps. He tucked his notebook away in his pocket and left the room, locking the door carefully. In the lift, he tried to adjust his expression, and managed to smile at a member of the hotel staff who greeted him when he emerged on the ground floor.

Miss Hawthorne turned in her seat as Benton approached. 'That didn't take long!'

'No, it was fine. But I remembered you said you wanted to do your postcards before dinner. Do you want to do them here, or back upstairs?'

Miss Hawthorne had not, in fact, mentioned postcards, but her experience of working with Benton meant she didn't hesitate before replying. 'Oh, so I did. Thank you, John. I think I'll come up – I left my address book in my case.'

As they walked together to the lift, Mrs Rogers joined them. They exchanged some pleasantries about long walks and last minute postcards, then Mrs Rogers went into her room, giving Miss Hawthorne and Benton chance to share what he'd found.

'Someone's been in my room,' he regaled. 'They were very careful, but a couple of things weren't quite right, and the lock's been interfered with.'

'They didn't take anything?'

'There wasn't anything to find, really. I had it all with me.'

'And you were wise to. I wonder if I've had visitors as well.'

When they reached Miss Hawthorne's door, Benton bent down and looked at the lock, then took the key and turned it.

He nodded. 'Yes, same as mine.'

Miss Hawthorne said nothing, but went inside. As Benton had done, she checked all her belongings.

When she returned from looking over the bathroom, Benton had brought his notebook out and showed her a page where he'd written, 'Bugs.'

Miss Hawthorne nodded and sat down at the dressing table. Taking the notebook from Benton, she wrote, 'Rendezvous?'

Benton's turn: 'Palace gardens, eighty-thirty pm.'

He thought whoever was listening in would get suspicious before too long, so they needed to use this to their advantage. He said aloud, 'It looks like someone might've been in my room, but I've had a good look and I don't think anything's missing. Perhaps they were just trying their luck, like on the boat.'

Miss Hawthorne replied, 'Whoever they are, they don't seem to have been in here – at least not yet.'

While she spoke, she wrote, 'What will you do? You'll be followed.'

Benton nodded. He said aloud, 'Good, I hoped they wouldn't have. The rendezvous is at nine tonight, so I'll leave straight after dinner. That'll give me time to lose anyone who comes after me.'

'That could be tricky. Where do you need to go?'

Miss Hawthorne took the notebook and scribbled, 'Then I go instead? What will happen when they find out?'

'Here, look' said Benton, pausing as if to take out the guidebook. 'It's on the other side of the river, so I'll be a bit exposed crossing the bridge. But the other side will be dark and it looks like there's quite a bit of cover from the trees on the way up the hill.'

'I see. And will it be quiet up there at that time?'

Benton had taken the notebook back. He returned it, having written, 'We'll risk it. You go to the garden, fetch CO – come get me if I haven't come back.'

Miss Hawthorne frowned as she considered, and Benton said, 'I think it should be. I hear it's the local spot for courting couples, but the weather forecast isn't good for later, so hopefully that'll put them off.'

'Ah, but you will take care?' replied Miss Hawthorne, looking intently into his eyes so she knew this part was meant. She gave the notebook back with her answer: 'We'll be with you as soon as we can.'

Benton smiled as he read her habitual warning and nodded.

'I'll be careful. And now, I suppose we'd better get ready for dinner. See you outside in about half an hour?'

'I suppose we must,' said Miss Hawthorne, 'See you soon, John.'

Benton went to his room to prepare himself. As with the cable, he burned the pages from the notebook and then flushed the ashes away. There were more this time, but he couldn't run the risk of their notes being found. He changed, then met Miss Hawthorne in the corridor, and they went down to the dining room together. The meal passed uneventfully, as might've been expected: most of the conversation was taken up with what the diners had been doing and the sights they'd seen during the day. After coffee, the diners dispersed, some to the bar, others to the casino in the basement of the hotel, and others still to their rooms. Miss Hawthorne and Benton similarly returned to their rooms to get ready for the night ahead.

Benton changed back into the casual clothes he'd worn during the day, covered by a dark coat, and put the bag containing his camera and films over his shoulder. Miss Hawthorne had fetched her crochet and a shawl. As before, they met in the corridor. In the lift down, Miss Hawthorne put her hand in Benton's and they wished each other good luck.

Benton saw Miss Hawthorne settled in the lounge, then left, laughing as she told him not to stay out too late. Having watched Benton go, Miss Hawthorne sighed, took up her crochet, and ordered a coffee with schnapps. If she was going to be involved in any action, and it seemed that she was, she wanted a drink first.

She hadn't had much of her coffee when she was joined by Mrs Rogers.

'Hello!' she exclaimed, sitting down nearby. 'Has he gone and left you?'

Miss Hawthorne smiled and replied, 'He wanted to take some pictures of the town at night. I've no idea how he would do that, but apparently he can "lengthen the exposure", whatever that means. And where is David?'

'Oh, he's at the casino. I'm not interested in all that nonsense, so I've left him to it.' Apparently struck by an idea, she went on, 'It's a bit dingy down here. Why don't we go up to my room for a bit? I've got some coffee and tea – we could have a little party of our own.'

Mrs Rogers began to hum. A simple repeated phrase, over and over.

She leaned forward and looked directly into Miss Hawthorne's eyes. 'You'd like to come, wouldn't you? It's too noisy for you down here. You want to get away from the noise.' Her voice was lilting yet intense.

As the Master had discovered at Devil's End, Miss Hawthorne was resistant to hypnosis, but that didn't mean she couldn't tell when someone was trying it on her. She opened her eyes wider and said, as expressionless as she could, 'Yes. It's too noisy. I want to get away from it all.'

'Good,' said Mrs Rogers. 'You will come with me.'

V

Benton walked briskly, but not too fast, along the road towards the river. He hoped he hadn't been too obvious in describing the Mariensäule: it wouldn't do for his enemies to feel they had been handed the location on a plate, as that might make them suspicious.

He stopped for a moment and checked to see if he was being followed. Not yet – at least, not as far as he could tell. But then, if they'd identified the fake rendezvous, they might be waiting for him.

Benton reached the bridge, close to where the boat had moored when they arrived. Looking at the hill on the other side of the river, he began to wish he'd chosen somewhere a little less elevated, but it had to be somewhere far enough away from the actual rendezvous to make it difficult for the opposition. He paused again, then crossed the bridge and began to walk up the steep road to the monument.

When the hotel lift reached the second floor, Mrs Rogers led Miss Hawthorne into her room. She instructed her captive to sit, which she did, still with the same blank look in her eyes.

Mrs Rogers locked the door behind them.

Bending down to look in Miss Hawthorne's eyes, she said, 'You are tired. You want to lay down and sleep. You want to sleep for a long time.'

'Yes.'

Mrs Rogers turned away to pull down the sheet and blankets that covered the bed. At that moment, Miss Hawthorne jumped from her seat and struck her captor on the back of the head with the weighted handle of her stick. Mrs Rogers fell forward onto the bed – and lay face down and motionless.

Miss Hawthorne turned the other woman over and checked her pulse and breathing, then moved her so that her head was on the pillow and she would appear to be sleeping. She drew the bedclothes up to Mrs Roger's neck and tucked them firmly under the edge of the mattress, so that, even if she did come round, she would have some difficulty getting out.

Miss Hawthorne checked her watch. No time to lose.

Taking her stick, she left the room, hung the 'Do Not Disturb' sign on the handle, then locked the door and slipped the key into her pocket. She ran the short distance along the corridor to her room and went in.

Her preparations were brief. She put on her cloak before leaving the hotel, using a side exit to reduce the chance of her being spotted. A few drops of rain started to fall as she crossed the road behind the Porta Nigra, but Miss Hawthorne was accustomed to being outside in all weathers, so she put up the hood of her cloak and rushed towards the palace.

*

Benton reached the top of the hill and went to the edge of the plateau to look at the view. He could see all of Trier spread out before him, lights twinkling. Some of the buildings were spot lit and he could see the grand cathedral clearly against the darkness. Far below, the river wound in inky curves beneath the bridges.

He was about to turn back to look at the monument behind him when he heard footsteps and felt the cold metal of a gun barrel at the back of his neck.

A voice, familiar, but not immediately recognisable, said, 'Hands.'

Benton raised his hands.

'Good. Turn around.'

He did so, his captor moving to stay behind him. 'Give me the bag.'

Benton took the camera bag off his shoulder and held it out. His next instruction was simply to walk, which he did, until he was level with the monument in the wooded area that surrounded it.

'Turn around. Now step back.'

Benton obeyed and found himself with his back against a tree trunk. A second person seized his wrists from behind the tree and tied them with rope around the trunk, then put a bag made of dark-coloured material over Benton's head.

As he stood, he felt his pockets being searched with a quiet efficiency that confirmed the impression that he was dealing with professionals. There was silence, punctuated by the sound of the camera being opened and the quiet popping noise of the film canister lids being removed. The contents of Benton's pockets didn't occupy his captors for long, but Benton had put as many films as he could in his camera bag, so as to force his enemies to spend time checking them. Through the cloth he could see flashes of light, possibly from a torch being used to look at them all.

Eventually, a second voice spoke. 'It's not here.'

'It must be!'

'No. None of these is the one. He hasn't got it.'

Benton tried to concentrate on the voices. The first was male, and had an English accent. The second was lighter and might belong to a woman.

Suddenly, he found himself squinting as the bag was removed from his head and a torch shone directly in his face.

The male voice said, 'Where's the film? Don't pretend you don't know.'

Benton said nothing – no use lying now, so his best strategy seemed to be keeping schtum – then gasped as he was punched in the stomach.

The voice spoke again. 'Where is it?!

Again, Benton remained silent. Another blow landed and he strained forward, coughing. The person with the torch stepped back. As the light receded, Benton could see two figures clad in dark clothing, one slightly taller than the other. The taller figure stepped forwards.

'We don't have a lot of time, Sergeant Benton... and neither do you. I'd advise you to tell us where the film is. You've hidden it, haven't you? Somewhere on the way here?'

Benton braced himself for another blow, but none came. Instead, the second figure spoke. He hadn't been sure, but, without the muffling effect of the bag, Benton could definitely identify this voice as female.

'You obviously don't care about your own safety, but you might consider Miss Hawthorne's.' The woman came closer, lowered her voice, and said, 'Our colleague has got her. She's safe – for now.'

Silence. The woman stepped back with an impatient exclamation and gestured to her colleague who came forward and struck Benton across the face. Benton turned his head and spat, but still said nothing. He hoped that Miss Hawthorne had managed to evade capture by whoever had tried to secure her. He had faith in her.

The woman had pulled a radio from her pocket and

walked to the edge of the plateau, speaking softly but urgently. Benton strained his ears to try and hear what was being said but couldn't make out the words. It was clear, though, that the caller was not getting any replies.

The woman shook her head to her colleague. They were aiming for subterfuge, but Benton could tell something had gone wrong with their little plan. They covered this with some manhandling: the man grabbed Benton's hair and pulled his head back against the tree trunk.

'For now though, you've got our full attention. Now. Where's the film?'

Benton said nothing. The man let go of his hair and Benton leaned forward again, coughing once more. If Miss Hawthorne had escaped, that meant he needed to keep these two occupied for as long as he could, to give her a chance to get to the rendezvous.

Benton coughed again, then asked, 'Who do you work for?'

The male agent looked at him, eyed him up and down, considering this little soldier out of his depth. 'We're in the supply and logistics business. We supply and deliver information to the highest bidder, and, in this case, the bids have been very high.'

Ah. Freelancers.

And these remarks had given Benton a chance to identify the speaker. He thought for a moment. *If I give away that I knew who my attackers are, they will probably kill me.* On the other hand, it didn't sound as if he had much of a chance anyway; he might as well keep them talking a bit longer. It would give Miss Hawthorne more of a chance.

He said, 'So not MI6 after all.'

The slap he received made Benton's ears ring. Verney stepped back and said, 'Oh, very clever. You've done it now.'

The woman looked at the luminous dial of her watch. 'There isn't time,' she said. 'Shut him up and help me search. He must've hidden it somewhere round here.'

Verney grabbed Benton's handkerchief off the ground –

it must have fallen there when his pockets were emptied – and stuffed it in Benton's mouth. Then he joined his colleague in the search around the base of the monument. Benton leaned his head back against the tree and waited.

Eventually, the woman gave another exclamation. 'I don't know what he's done with it. Ask him again.'

Verney returned and pulled the handkerchief out of Benton's mouth.

'Well, Sergeant? Have you changed your mind? Your friends should be on their way here soon and if you won't tell us where the film is, we'll make sure you can't tell them either. What's it to be?'

Benton spotted the woman coming over to him too, so asked, 'Hmm, well, what does the CIA think?'

Helen laughed. 'Oh, I've got nothing to do with them. Dear dutiful Douglas may be an agent, but I'm certainly not.' She looked at Verney. 'UNIT should be here by now. Even if they've been delayed, they won't be long. We'd better finish here and split.'

She went to the edge of the plateau and looked down to the road. She seemed lost in thought for a moment, then ran over to the tree and grabbed Benton's chin, turning his head towards her. 'It's a diversion, isn't it? You got us up here while your old witch was doing your job for you. You never had the film here at all!'

Benton simply smiled.

Helen watched him for a moment, then called to Verney and the two of them retreated to the edge of the plateau, talking in low voices. Their conversation took no more than a couple of minutes, but when they turned back, Helen cried out in amazement.

Benton had vanished.

The palace gardens was a scene from a sinister fairy tale, the light from the lampposts casting shadows from the hedges, the flowers closed, and the fountains stilled for the night.

The statues of lions that stood by the hedges looked as if they might jump down from their pedestals at any moment and prowl along the path.

Miss Hawthorne paused on the palace steps to draw breath, then walked down the path to the farthest pool. She stood still by the rose bed and waited.

There was a rustling sound, and Brigadier Lethbridge-Stewart stepped out from behind a hedge, accompanied by another officer, unknown to Miss Hawthorne, and followed by three men in suits. A detachment of UNIT troops stood at a distance, enclosing the pool and the people nearest to it.

The Brigadier came forward. 'Miss Hawthorne? Where…?' He stopped himself. 'You have the film.'

It was a statement, not a question: the Brigadier knew her well enough by now. Indeed, Miss Hawthorne took the canister out of her pocket and passed it to the Brigadier. The Brigadier opened the canister and moved into the light, drawing a magnifier from his pocket.

He inspected the film, then nodded and gave the film to one of the suited men. 'This is it, sir.'

'Thank you, Brigadier.'

The man turned to his companions. 'Well, gentlemen. We are agreed?'

The other two men nodded, and the first took a lighter out of his pocket. A soldier stepped forward with a camera and took a photograph as the man set fire to the film, then dropped it onto the gravel and watched as it burned. When it had been destroyed, the soldier with the camera took another photograph of the ground where it had been.

The men shook hands with each other, then with the Brigadier and the other officer, then left, accompanied by two soldiers.

The Brigadier turned to Miss Hawthorne. 'Thank you, Miss Hawthorne. May I introduce Brigadegeneral Holz?'

Miss Hawthorne shook hands with the Brigadegeneral quickly, then said, 'Brigadier. Sergeant Benton—'

'I was about to ask. I assume as you're here, Benton is in trouble again.'

'He went up to the Mariensäule, on the other side of the river, to decoy the enemy agents. As I was able to get here, we must assume he was successful.'

The Brigadier looked to his colleague. 'You know this place?'

'Yes,' said Holz, calling out an order to his troops, who moved out from the garden to a nearby road where jeeps were parked.

Miss Hawthorne got into the lead jeep with the officers and the vehicles roared away and were soon crossing the bridge.

They slowed and climbed the hill more quietly, but, a little over halfway up, the Brigadier signalled to stop.

'We can't risk being heard,' he explained. 'We'll go on foot from here.'

His opposite number agreed, and got out a map, shining his torch on it. 'I say we should close on them from both sides: one group from this path here, and the other from the road, here.'

The Brigadier nodded, then asked, 'Miss Hawthorne, are you coming with us?' But he already knew the answer.

'Naturally, Brigadier,' replied Miss Hawthorne. 'If they're holding the sergeant by the Monument, might I suggest that I cut through the trees here?' She pointed at the map.

'Very well,' replied the Brigadier.

The Brigadegeneral raised his eyebrows, but said nothing. He had heard too much about Lethbridge-Stewart to doubt his methods. Instead, he issued the order to his men and joined the group that would be advancing from the other path.

Miss Hawthorne walked with the Brigadier's squad until they were nearly at the top, then she turned off and vanished into the trees, swallowed by the darkness. The Brigadier paused, then signalled to his men, and they continued up the hill. As Miss Hawthorne walked, she twisted the handle of her walking stick and pulled out a short knife.

As she neared the monument, Miss Hawthorne heard voices. She crouched down and moved forward more slowly, being careful to make no sound. The spotlight on the monument dazzled her for a moment, but she was able to make out a tree with rope around it and see Benton's hands.

Miss Hawthorne whispered, 'John,' and closed her hand briefly over Benton's fingers. She quietly cut through the rope with her knife. Benton stayed in position until his captors turned away, then moved quickly around the tree and into the darkness behind.

Two moments later, Verney and Helen turned back, but they could do nothing. The next moment, the plateau was flooded with torchlight and shouts filled the air as the UNIT troops converged.

Verney tried to make a run for it into the trees, but Benton sprang from his hiding place and tackled him, holding him down and pulling the gun from his hand. Two soldiers came over and relieved the sergeant of his prisoner.

Benton stood up, slowly, to greet his commanding officer. 'Sir.'

The Brigadier looked Benton up and down, and coolly asked, 'All right, Sergeant Benton?'

'Yes, sir.'

'Now, Miss Hawthorne, you said on the way that there was some mopping up to do at the hotel?'

'Well, I may not have put it quite like that,' said Miss Hawthorne. 'But yes, there is at least one more conspirator to secure. And Mr Lannis…?'

Benton spoke up. 'Helen said he doesn't know anything about this. I don't know if that's true, though.'

The Brigadier muttered a thoughtful 'hmm' then spoke briefly to the Brigadegeneral.

As they all headed back to the jeeps, at the foot of the hill, the Brigadegeneral and some of his troops turned off to go to the barracks with their prisoners, while the Brigadier and his agents carried on across the bridge, accompanied by the remaining UNIT soldiers.

When they arrived at the hotel, they found Mr Rogers berating the manager and Doug making an urgent and agitated telephone call. The men had returned from the casino to find that their wives had not, as they'd been told, gone out for cocktails together.

Mrs Rogers had regained consciousness, but had been unable to get out of her bed, never mind out of her room. A guest in a neighbouring room had heard her shouts and summoned a member of hotels staff who'd released her. Her irate husband was demanding an explanation from the bewildered manager while the lady in question sat sobbing ostentatiously in an arm chair nearby.

The Brigadier looked to Miss Hawthorne with an eyebrow raised. Miss Hawthorne took a great deal of pleasure in seeing Mrs Rogers like this, but allowed herself only a brief smirk and a shrug to Lethbridge-Stewart. The latter gestured to two of his men, who lifted Mrs Rogers to her feet and led her, protesting loudly, out of the hotel.

On seeing this, Mr Rogers turned his attention away from the manager and towards the Brigadier. 'You there!' he berated, full of sound and fury. 'What do you think you're doing? That's my wife! I can't get a word of sense out of anybody in this godforsaken country! What is happening?'

The Brigadier looked calmly at Mr Rogers and said in a quiet and level voice, 'Mr Rogers. Your wife has been arrested on suspicion of being part of a criminal conspiracy, involving espionage, attempted theft, kidnapping, and the infliction of psychological torture. She'll be afforded all the legal rights of representation available to her, but, for the time being, I suggest you moderate your voice – unless you wish the facts of the matter to be broadcast throughout the hotel.'

The poor man stood there, mouth agog, sweat pearling on his brow. 'Arrested? But she… It must be a mistake!'

Something about the calm certainty of the Brigadier caused the colour to drain from Mr Roger's face. He sat down in the armchair that his wife had recently been forced to vacate and wiped his hand across his forehead.

The Brigadier looked down at him and said, dryly, ' I think we should have a little chat. And once Mr Lannis has finished his phone call…'

He looked across the lobby to where Doug had just hung up and was staring at the wall as if it held an explanation to the events that had just taken place.

At the other end of the reception desk, Miss Hawthorne, ever practical, had demanded a bowl of water and a first aid kit and was gently cleaning Benton's bruised face. The manager, distressed that his hotel foyer seemed to be turning into a cross between an incident room and a dressing station, nervously approached the Brigadier and suggested that he might move to one of the hotel's conference rooms to carry on his conversation. The Brigadier, with an ironical smile, agreed and joined the manager in manoeuvring the two husbands out of the foyer.

Once they were safely installed in the conference room and brandy had been ordered, Lethbridge-Stewart returned to the foyer to speak to his agents.

Benton stood up as his commanding officer approached. The Brigadier said, 'I know I promised you an explanation, Miss Hawthorne, but I suggest we wait until the morning. I may be some time with Messrs Lannis and Rogers.'

'I doubt I would take in even half of the facts now, regardless,' she said. 'And Sergeant Benton…'

The Brigadier cut in, 'Yes, get cleaned up and go to bed, Benton. Debrief can wait. Your transport will be here at ten am.'

'Yes, sir. Thank you.'

They bade each other good night, and Miss Hawthorne

hooked Benton's arm around her shoulders to keep him steady. They headed towards the lift together. The Brigadier smiled as he watched them, then his face became serious again as he turned towards the conference room.

His long night was about to become even longer.

VI

The following morning, Benton and Miss Hawthorne had breakfast in their rooms, then packed and were ready with their luggage when a jeep arrived outside the hotel. They were surprised to discover that Braun was also a passenger. He greeted them warmly and explained that he was going to the UNIT barracks to exchange information relating to the case, but said nothing more. On arrival the three visitors were greeted by Brigadegeneral Holz and escorted to a conference room where Brigadier Lethbridge-Stewart was waiting.

When they were all assembled, the Brigadier stood up and cleared his throat.

'This won't be a very detailed briefing: we've a little over an hour before our flight, but I wanted to pool the information we've collected and fill in some of the missing pieces. Firstly, as Miss Hawthorne and Holz witnessed, the microfilm was destroyed. This was the result of an agreement that's been brokered urgently over the last week – that the Soviet government would agree to cease attempts to restart development of the warheads, provided the microfilm was destroyed in front of witnesses. It's hoped that this might be the start of real progress towards thawing the Cold War, but we will have to wait and see.'

The Brigadier paused, and Miss Hawthorne could see that he was unconvinced. 'And now, Polizeimeister, I gather you've news for us too.'

'Thank you, Brigadier.' Braun took Lethbridge-Stewart's place at the head of the table. 'Our laboratory has determined that the substance found on Hawkins' pillow was a hallucinogenic drug. It would've increased his heart rate and caused distortion of vision and hearing. We've not identified the voice that spoke to him, but we believe it to have been Mrs Rogers. She had the opportunity to gain access to the empty cabin and she was seen in the corridors alone. This is, of course, circumstantial evidence, but we hope, when Hawkins has recovered sufficiently to ask him identify her. The doctors have advised that we cannot attempt this at present, however; his health is still too fragile.'

Miss Hawthorne asked, 'Have you any idea what caused them to attack him when they did? And how did they get the equipment? Surely she didn't bring it with her?'

Braun considered her question. 'We believe that the equipment was supplied by the man known as Verney,' he said. 'He was in contact with his fellow conspirators on the boat and would've had the opportunity to purchase the necessary tools and the drug. He could then have arranged for these to be collected, or passed them to one of the women during a shore trip, assuming they were able to leave their husbands, or at least distract them. As to the timing, again, we have no real evidence to confirm, at least at present ...'

The Brigadier said, 'I can clarify that.' He stood up again as Braun looked at him in surprise.

'I'm sorry to take you by surprise, Herr Braun,' he went on, 'but this morning, I was brought the news that Caroline Rogers wished to make a statement. Whether this is an attempt to extricate herself from the charges against her, or revenge on her co-conspirators for leaving her to the tender mercies of Miss Hawthorne, who, she had been led to believe, would be easily dealt with...' He paused and Benton grinned. 'Well,' he went on, 'we don't know. Nor do we know how accurate her statement is, but it does clear up some of the questions.

'According to Mrs Rogers, the attack on Hawkins was triggered by his meeting Sergeant Benton. Mrs Rogers and Mrs Lannis had been trying to identify Hawkins, but, though they knew he was among the crew, they hadn't been able to single him out. When she saw you coming back from the deck, Mrs Rogers went up and saw Hawkins standing alone at the stern. This persuaded her that Hawkins must be the agent. Mrs Lannis had persuaded her husband to check your background and once your connection to UNIT was established, it was decided to try and keep an eye on you. When she saw you that night, she deduced that you had been speaking to Hawkins to persuade him to surrender the microfilm, as, indeed, Lannis had been planning to do.'

Benton snorted. 'So much for seeing it safely in UN hands.'

'Is that what he told you? I believe the CIA also intended to destroy the film, but they were foiled by Hawkins passing it on to Sergeant Benton. Only we knew that Hawkins was going to transfer the film; the other agencies, and the conspirators, believed that he was intending to carry it to Trier himself, hence their attempts to persuade him to reveal its location and, incidentally, to cause him to become sufficiently unstable that nobody would believe him when he tried to tell them what had happened. Which was very nearly the case.'

'How cruel,' said Miss Hawthorne, tutting and shaking her head.

'Following Hawkins' accident, and the attack on him at the hospital,' the Brigadier continued, 'the conspirators believed that he had, in fact, passed the film onto someone else, and turned their attention to Benton.'

Miss Hawthorne asked, 'Why did Mr Lannis lie about seeing Hawkins at the hospital?'

'This came up last night,' replied the Brigadier. 'He said that he thought it might persuade Sergeant Benton to cooperate with him. In point of fact, he had worked with Hawkins in Romania, but he hadn't seen him for years and hadn't recognised him until it was too late, so to speak.'

'So who was the mysterious orderly?'

'That was Verney,' put in Braun. 'Witnesses have

described seeing a man of his description dressed as an orderly in that part of the hospital, close to the time of the attack. We believe he had with him a recording of the voice that had spoken to Hawkins and set it playing, while he cleaned the room and pretended to hear nothing.'

'Not only did this attack set Hawkins' recovery back, but it also confirmed to the conspirators that he had passed on the film,' said the Brigadier. 'He didn't say who to, but he repeatedly told them he hadn't got it any more, and that was enough for them.'

'So when we saw Verney…?' asked Benton.

'He would've come from the hospital, but Lannis had not.'

'I see.' Benton thought for a moment then suggested, 'And they bugged our rooms and thought they'd get the film off me at the Mariensäule.'

'Indeed. Their first hope was that you would surrender the film to Lannis. Had you done that, Mrs Lannis would've had a comparatively easy job of stealing it. But you weren't persuaded by Verney, so they had to try more direct action, either to find out where the film was hidden or to take it from you.'

Benton was silent at the memory of the previous evening and Miss Hawthorne went on where he had left off. 'And they would've succeeded, had Sergeant Benton not found the recording devices. But who are these people? How did they come to be working together?'

The Brigadier turned a page in his file. 'There's a relationship between two of them that was, so to speak, hidden in plain sight. You remember that Herr Braun referred to the "man known as Verney"? MI6 are understandably reluctant to release details of their personnel, but we know that Verney's name is, in fact, Thomas Jeffrey. Mrs Rogers' maiden name was also Jeffrey. Verney's sister.'

Miss Hawthorne gasped. 'Heavens! And Helen Lannis?'

'When she told you that she was nothing to do with the CIA, she wasn't being quite honest,' Lethbridge-Stewart explained. 'She'd worked in intelligence but had resigned when she married Douglas Lannis. One of her last operations had brought her into contact with Verney – or rather, Jeffrey. It's hard to say exactly why they embarked on a career in crime together. I doubt we'll get a straight answer out of any of them. My suspicion is that the motive was largely financial, together with wanting revenge on the intelligence community, or, at least, to get one over on the organisations that Jeffrey and Mrs Lannis felt ill-used by. Mrs Rogers told me that her brother felt he'd been sidelined, and that his expertise was being ignored, and Mrs Lannis felt she had been forced into resigning and missed the excitement of field work. When Jeffrey decided to start his business on the side, so to speak, his sister was easily persuaded to join him. She has expensive tastes that not even her husband's income can support, and she was keen of what she saw as a bit of adventure. She also sympathised with her brother and made his grudge against MI6 her own.

'Jeffery remembered working with Mrs Lannis and used his connections in MI6 to find out her circumstances. When he found that she'd resigned from the CIA and had her own axe to grind, he persuaded her to join him and Mrs Rogers in their new enterprise. At first, they operated on a relatively small scale, selling information from either MI6 or the CIA. Mrs Lannis used her former connections to get access to files that she shouldn't have been anywhere near, and worked on her husband to persuade him to involve her in cases, as his cover, that brought her closer to sources that might prove profitable for her and her business partners.

'That kind of thing can't go on for long without questions being asked, though, and people in high places were beginning to sit up and take notice. This being the case, when Jeffrey learned that a microfilm of international importance was in the open, he was unable to resist the chance of securing a payment large enough to keep him and his conspirators comfortable for a number of years, if not the rest of their lives. And believe me, had they been successful, they would've been able to name their price.'

Benton frowned. 'How did they know the film would be on the boat?' he asked. 'You didn't tell MI6, sir, so how would they have found out?'

'Caroline Rogers says that Sir Giles Mulberry was given the intelligence through a former colleague and that the CIA received it from an agent in Kiel,' the Brigadier went on. 'Whether or not this is true remains to be seen, but the foreign office will need to conduct a thorough investigation to find out. If it is true, it'll mean serious consequences for Sir Giles, because, instead of dealing with MI6 directly, he passed the information on to Jeffrey, who then persuaded him to communicate only with him. I find it hard to believe that a diplomat as experienced as Sir Giles would fall for such a scheme – it may be that Jeffrey and his sister are protecting another source, but, be that as it may, both Jeffrey and the CIA found out that Hawkins was on the boat.

'Douglas Lannis was sent because of his proficiency in German and his experience of working in the region. And also because he and his wife could easily pass for tourists. Had he not been assigned, his wife would have urged him to seek the assignment. Jeffrey took leave of absence from MI6 and Mrs Rogers persuaded her husband to buy her the cruise as a belated anniversary gift. I'm sure you're aware of how manipulative she can be...' He looked pointedly at Miss Hawthorne.

'Her interest in German culture is quite genuine, I gather,' he continued, 'so it was a relatively easy matter to persuade him to indulge her wishes. He'd arranged to be away from work for a week, but they had made no firm plans, so, when Jeffrey contacted his sister, she was able to join him. With the two women on board, Jeffrey decided not to try and get onto the boat, but to support them via land. He travelled between hostels and met one or the other of them on their shore visits, and, as he was in the same country, it was a relatively easy matter to arrange contact by telephone if necessary.'

Benton had been thinking. 'And was it her voice? Was she the Lorelei?'

'Yes,' said the Brigadier. He took a tape recorder from his pocket. 'This is where her statement became… well, I'll play it to you and you must make your own judgements.'

He pressed play and the assembled company heard his voice, then that of Mrs Rogers.

'What did you say to him?' asked the Brigadier on the tape.

'I sang to him,' replied Mrs Rogers, in a light dreamy voice. 'I sang him her song. I changed the words, but it was her song. She taught it to me.'

'Who?'

'The Lorelei. They say she only stays on the Rhine, but that isn't true. I went to find her. David said I was mermaid hunting. Fool. He doesn't know. Nobody knows but me. I found her and she taught me her song.'

The Brigadier looked round the table. 'And that is all Mrs Rogers had to say. Had Hawkins still had the film in his possession when the conspirators identified him, I wouldn't have given much for his chances, or for the success of the mission. But, thanks to his actions and the actions of Sergeant Benton and Miss Hawthorne, the conspiracy has failed.'

He gathered up his files, ready to conclude. 'And now, if you'll excuse us, due to leave for the airfield shortly. Once I'm back at headquarters, I'll contact you all to finalise our statements. Good day to you, gentlemen.'

The Brigadier left, followed by Miss Hawthorne and Benton.

A jeep was waiting to take them to the airfield, where a small plane had been chartered to fly them back home.

There was too much noise in the interior of the plane for conversation, so Miss Hawthorne took out her crochet.

She looked down at the landscape, now far below them. Had Mrs Rogers really met a siren, and learned her deadly song? Miss Hawthorne sighed. She supposed that it didn't really matter; the criminals had been caught and the mission completed. But she did wonder. Miss Hawthorne looked at the dark curves of the river and tried to imagine what might lurk beneath its glassy surface.

The Brigadier smiled as he watched her working away and his grin broadened when he saw that, despite the racket from the engines, Sergeant Benton was fast asleep. And snoring. Oh yes, he could still hear that...

THE SHAKING OF LOWER BUDWORTHY

ᛏᚻᛖᚱᛖ×ᛁᛋ×ᛗᚨᚷᛁᚳ×ᛁᚾ×ᚦᛖ×ᚹᚨᚱᛚᛞ×ᚨᚠᛏᛖᚱ×ᚨᛚᛚ

ARNOLD GOODWIN, landlord of *The Royal Oak* in Lower Budworthy, whistled to himself as he closed up for the night. It was a fine, clear evening, and the full moon glowed through the windows and gleamed on the glasses above the bar. Mr Goodwin checked the front door one last time then, still whistling, went through to the back room.

As he did so, a low, rumbling sound began, apparently coming from the cellar. The landlord swore under his breath and hurried to the cellar door, unlocking it with frantic haste and running down the steps without bothering to turn on the light. The sound was louder down there, the rumbling amplified by the empty barrels that stood ready to be collected by the brewery. Goodwin turned on the light and made a quick round of the cellar, checking for leaks in the couplings that connected the barrels in use to the taps above.

As he moved back towards the steps, the rumbling grew even louder, and the floor seemed to shake under his feet. An empty barrel wobbled, then fell, missing him by inches. Goodwin jumped out of the way and swore aloud, then ran back up the steps to the bar.

Grabbing the telephone receiver so hastily it fell from his hand (which did nothing to improve his mood), he dialled a number from memory and when he got an answer, didn't give the person at the other end a chance to speak.

'When are you going to find out what the hell is going on here?' he shouted into the handset. 'What? Of course I'm not drunk! I've nearly been killed by one of my own ruddy barrels, that's what!'

The voice at the other end was interrupted in mid-sentence by the landlord. 'Don't give me that! You could investigate it if you wanted to. The truth is, you're afraid! You're as superstitious as those old biddies at the tearoom. What? I should think you *are* sorry.'

Goodwin paused to draw breath as the recipient of his tirade spoke again. This seemed to calm him a bit, and he spoke more slowly. 'Right. Yes, of course. No, no, I'm sorry. Flew off the handle. Blasted barrel coming down. Look. Can't you at least call county and ask them? Of course, they won't – they know you're by yourself here, don't they? All right. Yes, yes, see you tomorrow...'

Goodwin hung up and then stood for a moment, staring at the telephone. Now the moment had passed and the adrenalin had subsided, he felt slightly ashamed of himself. Ordinarily, he got on well enough with the local constable whose ear he had just bent, but the incident in the cellar had pushed him over the edge. He walked behind the bar once more and made his way to his rooms upstairs. His bedtime preparations completed, he switched off the last of the lights and *The Royal Oak* was in darkness.

At the rectory, Reverend Edmund Stott had also been disturbed by the tremors. And, like the landlord, he'd been moved to make a telephone call, albeit in a less emotional manner.

'I hoped you would still be out and about. Did you manage to spot—? Magnificent. Pardon? Oh, of course. Yes, it's happening again. No, I know, but really, Bryce is out of his depth. Well, yes. Of course, I'll trust your judgement completely... That would be a great relief. Yes, goodbye.'

*

In his study, Sir James Trevor, chief constable, put the receiver back in its cradle and sighed. He couldn't blame Stott. The tremors were getting more frequent and had, thus far, defied explanation. The village constable, usually reliable, really was out of his depth and the man sent from the geology department of the nearest university had been unable to account for the disturbances, though he'd made some suggestions. If the phenomena were natural, then it wasn't really a police matter; more a case for the local council. But the chief constable didn't hold out much hope for assistance from that quarter.

Then there was the question of the research facility that had opened the previous year and was still treated with suspicion by many of the locals. Really it would be better if…

Ah. Yes. A neutral party. His mind made up, Sir James went up to bed. He'd call in the morning.

Brigadier Lethbridge-Stewart opened the door of his office and called to the soldier who'd just walked past. 'Sergeant Benton!'

'Sir?'

'A word with you.'

Benton entered the office and was surprised, but not startled, to see Miss Hawthorne sitting opposite the Brigadier's desk. She stood up as he entered and held out her hand.

'Sergeant.'

'Good to see you, Miss Hawthorne.' It was a shared sentiment: they'd become good friends in the comparatively short time they'd known each other. The feeling was mutual. During the time they had worked together, they had become firm friends. After facing mythical beasts and villainous humans, a real trust and respect had grown between them.

The Brigadier gestured to an empty chair, then sat down

himself. Turning a file on his desk so that Miss Hawthorne and Benton could see the contents, he started at the beginning.

'I've had a call from Sir James Trevor, chief constable of South Somerset. He'd like us to look into some disturbances at a place called Lower Budworthy.' The Brigadier raised his eyebrows, but his auditors both shook their heads. 'No, well, I hadn't heard of it either. Hardly surprising – it's a small place. Here, near the coast.' He took a map from under the folder and pointed to the location.

'I see.' Miss Hawthorne bent forward to get a better look. 'It looks quite remote.'

'It is. One of those places with one bus a week to the nearest town. All right if you want a quiet life, or at least it *was*. About three months ago, the villagers started reporting strange noises that seemed to be coming from underground, followed by tremors.'

'Heavens! Earthquakes?'

'That's what they thought at first. It's unusual in that area, but not unheard of. But the authorities called in a geologist who told them that whatever it was, it wasn't earthquakes.'

'Did they suggest any other possibilities?'

'Only one: the tremors might be caused by rockfalls in caves nearby.'

'Ah, and are there a lot of these caves?'

'Turns out there are. Whole area's riddled with them. See here…' He pulled out another map, this time showing the network of caves that lay under the village and extended to the coast. 'This is the village, and these caves run right underneath it.'

Benton pointed to the first map, to a large building just outside the village. 'What's this place, sir?'

'That, Sergeant, is the Institute of Energy Resource Research. Opened a year and seven months ago, dedicated to researching for alternatives to fossil fuels. Solar power, that kind of thing. The sort of stuff Miss Grant would've loved.'

'I don't suppose it could be them causing this… disturbance?'

'It seems unlikely, given that their research doesn't involve drilling, but as we know, anything is possible and they may be up to more than they're letting on. We've seen that before. Whatever they're up to, they've managed to upset the locals – not surprising in a small place.'

Miss Hawthorne looked up from the plan of the caves. 'Is there a village policeman?'

'Yes. Policeman singular. Capable enough, I think, but rather out of his element with this kind of thing. Sir James thinks, and I agree, that given the bad feeling between the villagers and the research establishment – and the lack of an obvious explanation for the tremors – it would be better if a neutral agency led the investigation. Which means you two.'

Miss Hawthorne tried to hide her delight. (Benton, on the other hand, was visibly enthused.) Instead, Miss Hawthorne asked, 'Has there been any recent exploration of the caves?'

'Not as far as Sir James knows. The whole area was declared unsafe about twenty years ago and the main entrances closed off. Of course, that's not to say that people haven't been going down there but there hasn't been any official exploration. It's a pity, because I would've said they were the most likely place to start looking.'

'I agree. But if they are really too dangerous, we shouldn't run the risk. The system looks fascinating though; it extends so far in from the coast…'

Miss Hawthorne returned to her examination of the map and Benton took the opportunity to ask a question that had been bothering him. 'Will we be… going as *us*? I mean as UNIT?'

'Not exactly,' replied Lethbridge-Stewart. 'A neutral agency is one thing, but we don't want to alarm the locals. Or scare off any villains. The chief constable knows, of course, and he will share as much information as he sees fit with the county HQ, but for the time being, you'll be researchers, with a vague connection with the University of London. I've cleared it with them, so they will vouch for you should anyone enquire.' The Brigadier looked at his watch. 'Speaking of which, you've got a briefing with Sergeant Beacham in the workshop. He'll show you all the kit you'll need to take with you.'

'Right, sir.'

Benton stood up, as did Miss Hawthorne. The Brigadier closed the file and handed it to his subordinate.

'Good luck. Stay in contact. And don't run any unnecessary risks in those caves.'

'We will certainly try not to!' retorted Miss Hawthorne, 'If we should need to go down into the caves, we'll be taking all precautions.'

The Brigadier's curiosity got the better of him. 'Are you an experienced caver, Miss Hawthorne?' he asked.

'Oh, I haven't done any for years, but I did do a bit of potholing in my younger days.'

Benton would've given a large part of his salary to see his commanding officer's expression at this revelation, but he didn't dare look. Instead, he kept his eyes carefully fixed on the opposite wall as the Brigadier coughed, then recovered himself.

'Well, let's hope you won't need too many of those skills,' he said.

Following a visit to Sergeant Beacham – who gave them a thorough briefing on the geological equipment they'd be taking with them – Benton went to his quarters to pack and Miss Hawthorne went to the canteen to wait for him, and to chat to Corporal Scott and Iolanthe. The pair were taking a short, but very welcome, coffee break. Miss Hawthorne had always known Iolanthe would be a hard and vigilant worker; it was a joy to see her fitting in at UNIT so admirably.

Benton arrived before long, and he and Miss Hawthorne

made their way to the garages, where a concerned-looking Beacham was overseeing the loading of his equipment into a small van.

Benton smiled. 'All ready, Sergeant?' he asked, cheerfully.

'Mm.' Beacham passed Benton the keys to the van, his expression still worried. 'Do look after this equipment, Benton. You're sure you remember how to use it?'

Miss Hawthorne laid a comforting hand on Beacham's arm, causing him to jump slightly. 'Don't worry, Sergeant,' she said, trying to ease his mind, 'we'll take good care of it. We've got your guidance written down. We'll have it back safe and sound; you'll see.'

Beacham grunted something that might've been an affirmative and left the garage.

Miss Hawthorne looked at Benton. 'Is he quite well?'

'Yeah, he's mostly all right. He doesn't go out in the field that much, so I suppose sending any of his precious kit out makes him nervous.'

'Ah, I see.' Miss Hawthorne got into the passenger seat and unfolded a map. 'Well, Sergeant, if we're going to get to Somerset before nightfall, we'd better be on our way.'

Benton started the engine and the van pulled out of the garage.

It was early evening when the van pulled up outside the vicarage, where Miss Hawthorne and Benton had been offered accommodation. The vicarage was a gaunt, rambling building, in which the current incumbent rather rattled around. Rev Stott was a tall, slim man in his early sixties. He bounded down the front steps of the vicarage with the energy of a much younger man and held out his hand to his guests.

'Welcome! I'm so glad you're here. Thank you so much for coming all this way.' He shook hands, first with Miss Hawthorne and then with Benton. 'Come in, come in. Let me take your luggage. Is this all?'

'Thank you, sir, I'll take this one,' replied Benton, picking up the case that held his gun and ammunition. 'I'll just make sure the van is locked and the rest of the stuff can stay here.'

'Just as you like. This way!'

'It's very good of you to have us,' said Miss Hawthorne.

'My pleasure, Miss Hawthorne. It was I who contacted the chief constable, so it was the least I could do to put you up. We don't have much in the way of accommodation in the village and I have far too many spare rooms so…' He shrugged.

The priest led the way up the front steps and into the house. Inside, the décor reflected the Victorian exterior, with a few modernisations. The tiled floor of the hall led to the study, parlour, and dining room, with a kitchen in the rear. Upstairs were bedrooms and a bathroom.

When Miss Hawthorne exclaimed at the sight of the massive enamelled, claw-footed bathtub, its owner sighed. 'It's a museum piece,' explained Rev Stott. 'It takes enough water to float the Queen Mary, but parish funds are tight, and the Diocese can't fund a replacement so…'

They continued onto their modest but warm and comforting rooms.

Once Miss Hawthorne and Benton had unpacked, they joined their host in the dining room, where he was setting the table for dinner.

'I don't entirely do this myself. My… housekeeper, I suppose you might say – at least, the lady who cleans the house and cooks my dinner – has left us a casserole in the oven, so you won't have to suffer my rather undergraduate culinary skills.'

He left the room and his guests smiled wryly at each other, both of them thinking that their host's enthusiasm, while touching, might also have reflected the fact that he didn't get many visitors. Before either of them could voice this thought aloud, Rev Stott returned, carrying a large dish from which a savoury smell was emanating. This was followed by two smaller dishes containing potatoes and vegetables.

While they ate, Rev Stott expanded on the information that had been given by the file. 'The first occurrence was three months ago. It wasn't felt by the whole village; just the houses on the right side and the pub. The next was stronger and more sustained. It began on the right, as before, then spread across the village from one side to the other.'

'Has there been much damage?' asked Benton.

'Not material damage,' he went on. 'The tremors haven't been strong enough to damage buildings; at least not as far as we know, barring a few loose tiles coming off, but the landlord of *The Royal Oak* has had some trouble with barrels shaking loose in the cellar and other people have had ornaments and the like broken. In fact, I myself…' He got up and went out of the room, returning a few moments later with a cardboard box.

Rev Stott moved his empty dinner plate to one side and set the box down on the table. Miss Hawthorne and Benton stood up to look. Inside were what appeared to be fragments of unusually thick glass.

Rev Stott sighed. 'That's what's left of a crystal fruit bowl, given to me by my great aunt Mavis. When the tremor struck yesterday, it was close to the edge of the parlour table and the vibrations carried it off the table and onto the floor.'

'Was it a family piece?' asked Miss Hawthorne.

'No, by no means. To be frank, it was hideous and I'm glad to have an excuse not to have it on display. But it is most unnerving to see household objects moving around by themselves and on a fairly regular basis.'

'I wanted to ask you about that,' put in Benton. 'In the file, it says that the tremors are becoming more frequent?'

'Indeed! For the first few weeks, there was one every two days; now, there's one a day.'

'And always at the same time?'

'Give or take a few minutes. Which seems suspicious. I know that the geyser in Yellowstone Park, for example, goes off at regular intervals, but I would've expected earth tremors to be more... sporadic?'

There was a pause while his guests considered this. Miss Hawthorne was about to ask another question when her host held up his hand.

'Before we go any further with the discussion, I suggest we move to the parlour. You go and make yourselves comfortable and I'll clear up in here and bring the coffee,' he said. Benton attempted to join in with clearing the table, but Rev Stott held up a hand and implored, 'No, I insist! I have few enough guests as it is, so you must allow me to spoil the few that I have, whatever their reason for coming.'

Benton and Miss Hawthorne exchanged a glance, then, seeing it was pointless to argue, made their way to the next room, where remnants of the vicarage's Victorian past rubbed shoulders with a motley collection of more modern furniture, including the table that had been the perch of the ill-fated fruit bowl. They were soon joined by their host, carrying a coffee pot and cups on a tray.

Once his guests had been served, Rev Stott poured himself a coffee and sat down. 'Now, where were we?'

Miss Hawthorne stirred her coffee and reminded him: 'You were telling us about the timing of the tremors; how they seemed to be at regular intervals.'

'Ah, yes. The early occurrences seemed random. The first was, I believe, at about eight in the evening?' Rev Stott looked over at Benton, who had the UNIT file open on his knee.

'Well remembered,' said Benton, checking the file. 'And since then... well, the first week, they were at eight and then at nine; the second week was a bit later and now they're... at quarter to eleven every night?'

'That seems right. I admit that I have very little knowledge of geological matters, but the regularity does seem *odd.*'

'I agree,' said Miss Hawthorne, 'unless they're linked to another natural phenomenon that occurs regularly.'

Benton looked puzzled. 'How do you mean?'

'Well, the map shows the caves run to the coast, here,' she explained, putting her finger on the point where the caves opened in the cliffs. 'I wondered if perhaps the movement of the water at high tide could've contributed to the tremors. Connected, perhaps, with some instability of the cave walls?'

'I'm afraid it can't be that,' replied Rev Stott. 'Though it is an excellent suggestion. Yet the tremors coincide with low tide.'

'Ah, then that settles that. Now, about the sound itself?'

'Assuming it happens again later on, you'll hear it for yourselves! There is certainly rumbling, but nothing that I would associate with the sound of falling rocks. Then there's the movement. It begins at the same point every time and then moves in a definite route under the village.'

Miss Hawthorne sighed impatiently. 'I wish we could have a look in the caves. I feel sure that the key to the matter lies there. Is there no way of gaining access?'

'I fear not. The cliff entrance is accessible around low tide but both that and the other entrances were fitted with fences and gates, secured some years ago.'

'Hmm. I'd still like to see the entrances – perhaps tomorrow? Though with low tide being so late, will we be able to get to the beach safely?'

'Oh yes, the path is clear and not too steep,' replied Rev Stott. 'The tide is at its lowest at around eleven, but we should be able to go down a little earlier. Did you bring torches with you?'

'We did. Thank you, Reverend.'

Benton looked at his watch. 'With your permission, I'd like to start setting up for later on. There isn't much equipment, but it'll take a while to prepare.'

'Of course, Sergeant. Anything you need. Can I help you bring it in?'

'Oh! Well, if it's not to much trouble...?'

The two men went out to the van and returned a few moments later carrying the equipment that Beacham had given them to record and measure the tremors.

After a careful half hour spent reading and rereading Beacham's exhaustive instructions and tinkering, the portable seismometer was ready. Benton walked around it cautiously, noting the movement of the needle as his feet touched the floor.

'Phew!' said Benton with a sigh. 'I reckon that's ready to go now.'

While they waited for the tremors to start, Rev Stott diverted his guests with lively accounts of the history of the local area. For a small place, Lower Budworthy seemed to have had more than its fair share of action. The treacherous sea and coastline had caused a number of shipwrecks and led to the construction of a lighthouse a short distance from the village.

And, as in many coastal communities, there were stories of smuggling. Rev Stott told these tales with particular relish.

'Yes, many families tell tales of their relatives outwitting the revenue men,' he enthused, 'or their great-great grandfather knowing a man who knew a man who could get the finest brandy or cloth, no questions asked.'

'How fascinating!' Miss Hawthorne was keenly interested. 'But if the coast is so treacherous, how did they bring the goods ashore?'

'I have it on good authority that they used the caves.'

Miss Hawthorne was thrilled by the suggestion. 'Really!'

'With the entrance only accessible at low tides, they had to be careful, but it was possible to run a shallow-bottomed boat to the beach and bring contraband in. They'd then either store it in the caves, or bring it up the cliff path. I believe that some of the gangs may have gone further in and used the caves as tunnels to bring the goods up further from the coast.'

'How fascinating. And when did the smuggling stop?'

'The historical accounts aren't clear, but the caves were first closed off at the end of the nineteenth century, and there have been significant collapses since then, so I suspect that, if there was still smuggling going on, they would've had to have found another route.'

Miss Hawthorne seemed disappointed in this. Oh, she did love the adventure of it all. Recognising his kin, Rev Stott grinned, and continued, 'The old legends still persist though. Like the smuggler who was killed in a rock fall and whose vengeful spirit haunts the caves – that sort of thing.'

'Ah, yes, those kinds of legends have a habit of lingering.'

'I'll say!' he exclaimed, sounding more like a schoolboy. 'Only the other day I had a parishioner tell me, quite seriously, that the tremors were the spirits of smugglers being hauled away to be executed by the customs men!'

'Heavens!'

'He swore that he could hear their voices. He also told me he saw what he described as "Jack-o'-lanterns" on the beach, and men with strange clothing.' Rev Stott looked at his guests and smiled. "I would give his story slightly more credence if he hadn't been so well refreshed when I spoke to him!'

He broke off and jumped up from his chair. 'There it is!'

Miss Hawthorne and Benton could feel it too, the floor vibrating under their feet. With it came the noise, a distant rumbling that grew steadily louder, and then faded again, the strength of the vibration matching the volume of the sound.

The coffee cups trembled on the tray.

A photo frame was shaken off the windowsill.

In the distance, a car alarm sounded its tinny distress call.

Once the sound and movement had ceased, Benton, Miss Hawthorne, and Rev Stott went over to the seismometer. The needle had traced a jagged line on the paper, the zigzags increasing in height and frequency as the strength of the tremor increased, then decreasing again as it passed. Miss Hawthorne held down the lever that released the paper and Benton carefully removed the roll, then spread the paper out on a table so they could look at it more easily.

They considered it in silence for a moment.

'It looks… regular?' said Benton.

'I agree. Look at this.' Miss Hawthorne indicated the point where the tremor increased. 'And here, where it begins to fade. It's at almost exactly the same frequency.'

'So, are we thinking it's mechanical?'

'Must be. I can't think of a natural phenomenon that would produce such a result, nor such an even sound.'

Miss Hawthorne turned to the pages of sample readings they had been given during the briefing. 'This one, for an earthquake, is really erratic.'

'Mm, so,' suggested Benton, 'someone is up to something, using some kind of machinery, and, presumably, in the caves. And you're right about the sound. It was much too even to be natural.'

'But if the caves are in such a dangerous condition, what can they be doing down there?'

Benton was about to reply when the telephone rang. He and Miss Hawthorne had momentarily forgotten that they weren't alone.

Rev Stott rushed off and answered it in the study. After a few moments, he appeared in the doorway of the dining room, where the seismometer had been set up.

'I'm sorry, Sergeant. I need your help.'

'What's happened?'

'There's been an accident. Goodwin, at the pub. I've had a call to tell me that he's been crushed by barrels. He's trapped. The doctor is out on a call, so they rang me. I've had some first aid training, but I could use another pair of hands to help me free him…'

He didn't need to say any more. Benton followed him down the hall to the front door, where Rev Stott paused to collect a first aid kit. Benton checked to see if they'd need to take the van, but Rev Stott assured him that it would be quicker to walk anyway. Rev Stott then turned back to Miss Hawthorne and told her not to wait up, warning her they might be some time if they had to wait for the doctor too.

'Is there anything I can do?' asked Miss Hawthorne.

'No, the people at the pub have left a message for the doctor and phoned for an ambulance.'

Miss Hawthorne nodded and waved them off, then went back inside. She was tempted to disobey Rev Stott and sit up, but it had been a long day: she'd accomplish nothing by tiring herself out. Nonetheless, she was determined to listen out for his and Benton's return.

The two men made their way down from the vicarage to the pub, following a path that wound between the houses and avoided the main road through the village. The night was dark, but Rev Stott had picked up a torch with his first aid kit, and the route was familiar to him.

When they arrived at the pub, a small group of people had gathered outside. At the centre of the group was a young woman, who came forward when she saw the vicar.

'Oh, Mr Stott!' she said.

'How is he, Virginia?' asked Rev Stott.

'I don't know, they won't let me go down. Dave Bryce and George are there – they said I should stay up here.'

'We'll do all we can. The doctor will be here as soon as he gets word and an ambulance is on the way,' said Rev Stott, a voice for calm in the hubbub. Indeed, his commanding presence meant the crowd turned his way. He looked around and singled out a woman who was standing nearby, and went on, 'Dorothy, why don't you take Virginia home and have a cup of tea with her. And the rest of you: there's no need for you all to wait here.'

He broke off, but the edge to his voice gave the villagers the hint. The woman – Dorothy – put her arm around the shoulders of the younger woman, who shook her off impatiently, but allowed herself to be led away; the others began to move away, albeit reluctantly.

Rev Stott watched them for a moment, then led the way into the pub. 'Really,' he muttered, 'I suppose one must forgive their curiosity, but…'

'Was that the landlord's wife?' asked Benton.

'No, his daughter. She lives next door. She's the one who called me. Apparently Bryce, the village bobby, was passing and saw a light on in the pub. When he looked through the window, he saw the cellar door open and went and called Virginia who let him in. Then he and her husband went down…'

By this time, they had reached the cellar. Looking down from the steps, Benton could see a man lying on his back on the floor, partly concealed by barrels. Standing nearby were a short, round-faced man in police uniform and a younger chap who he took to be Virginia's husband. They were engaged in trying to shift one of the barrels that had trapped the poor publican. The men looked up at the newcomers and said breathy hellos to Rev Stott.

'George, Bryce, how is he?'

'Still out cold,' said George, as he unsuccessfully tried to heave the barrel off his father-in-law. 'Must've hit his head on the floor when he fell.'

Benton joined George, helping him shift the first of the barrels. George looked at him questioningly but said nothing. Seeing this, Rev Stott merely said, 'Oh, this is Mr Benton,' and left it at that for the time being.

Rev Stott asked Bryce to go and guard the main door and watch for the doctor and ambulance; the constable departed with alacrity.

While Benton and George began to carefully lift the barrels away and stand them safely at a distance, the vicar knelt down next to the landlord and began a gentle and cautious examination for injuries. As he looked closely at Goodwin's head, his softly fingers running over the skull, his face darkened. Catching the change of expression, Benton spoke to George, partly to distract him from his father-in-law's injuries, but also to keep his mind on the task in hand.

'Right, Mr…?'

'Vincent. George Vincent.'

'Steady as she goes with this one, Mr Vincent, then we're nearly there.'

They lifted the barrel, exposing Goodwin's legs. His right leg seemed as normal, but the left was crushed and splayed out at an unnatural angle.

George gulped.

'Just keep your eye on the barrel, Mr Vincent – that's it.'

Benton's calm voice helped George tear his eyes away and refocus. The two men carried the barrel and set it down safely with the others.

George wiped his forehead with his sleeve. 'I don't understand it. He's so careful. And after the last time…'

'Yes?' asked Benton, trying not to sound too curious.

'Well, he told Ginny he was going to rope them together. One had come loose yesterday and nearly hit him, so he said he was going to make extra sure they'd be safe.'

'Ah, I see.'

'And for all of them to fall, this must be the strongest earthquake we've had yet.'

Benton was examining the area of the floor where the barrels had been stored. His eye was caught by a length of twine and he bent to pick it up. As he did so, he suddenly froze and said in a carefully level voice, 'Mr Vincent, supposing you go upstairs and tell PC Bryce we've got the area cleared.' Fortunately, they could hear a murmur of voices upstairs, so Benton added, 'That could be the doctor now.'

As the landlord's son-in-law ran up the stairs, Benton turned to the Rev Stott, the piece of rope in his hand. What he was about to say was interrupted by the arrival of the doctor, followed by two ambulance men carrying a stretcher. Benton turned away again and quickly dropped the rope.

Rev Stott got up from his place by Goodwin's still unconscious body and greeted the local physician. 'Dr Elphick.'

'Stott. Good to see you. Has he come to?'

'Not yet. We haven't moved him. George and Mr Benton…' Rev Stott indicated Benton, who exchanged nods with the doctor. '…took great care moving the barrels, so I hope we've managed to avoid hurting him. Apart from the leg, there's two injuries to the head.'

They both bent down and the vicar carefully indicated the area. Dr Elphick met Stott's eyes.

'Ah, I see. Interesting. Very well.' He turned to the medics and ordered, 'That leg needs a splint and he'll need a support on his neck before we get moving.' He stood aside to let the men get to work. Benton joined him and Rev Stott at the bottom of the stairs.

'Who found him?' asked the doctor.

'Bryce, or rather, Bryce and Vincent.'

'I see. Hmm, if he gets over the concussion, we may hope to pull him through, but that leg will need surgery.'

Shaking his head, Dr Elphick followed his colleagues as they carried their burden carefully up the stairs and out of the pub. Benton and Rev Stott followed them in silence.

Outside, the vicar exchanged a few words with George, then led Benton back to the vicarage. Rev Stott opened the front door quietly and headed to the study without turning on the hall light. Once inside, he fetched a decanter and poured two brandies, one of which he passed to Benton, then sat down behind his desk.

Benton took a seat on the other side of the desk and the two men sat in silence for a moment. Having taken a sip of his drink, Benton asked, 'What did you find?'

'You saw then? I hoped my face wasn't giving me away.'

At that moment, there was a gentle tap at the door, which opened to reveal Miss Hawthorne.

'I heard you come in.'

Rev Stott fetched another chair and poured out a brandy for Miss Hawthorne, which she accepted gratefully. 'I was about to tell Sergeant Benton,' he explained. 'There was an injury that… worries me.'

'Oh?'

Rev Stott leaned forward, his chin on his hands. 'According to what Bryce and Vincent said, and how we found him, I'd have expected him to have hit the back of his head on the floor when he fell,' he said. 'But there was a swelling over his left ear – it was beginning to bruise – and I cannot, for the life of me work out how he could have sustained that injury when he fell, or after he was trapped.'

'You believe he was attacked?'

'I wish I could think otherwise, but I can't. Sergeant Benton found something in the cellar too.'

Benton nodded and put down his glass. 'Mr Vincent told me that Mr Goodwin had roped the barrels together, after he was nearly hit by one of them yesterday, but there wasn't any rope round the barrels when we got there. Then I did find some, thrown in the back behind the other barrels. The end had been frayed a bit, but it had been cut through.'

Rev Stott laid his head in his hands. 'So,' he said, gloomily, 'one of my parishioners has tried to murder another.'

Miss Hawthorne and Benton were silent at this. For a minute or two, nobody spoke, and they avoided each other's eyes. Eventually, Miss Hawthorne asked, tentatively, 'Has he any enemies?'

'Enemies? I don't think so. He has a hot temper, but it's the kind that blows up then blows over. I think mostly people just put up with him exploding every now and again. He told me he'd been shouting at Bryce last night for not investigating the tremors, but, by the next day, he'd sought him out to apologise.'

'I see.'

Rev Stott put down his empty glass and sighed. 'Whatever has happened, we still need to rest,' he said. 'I'll call the Vincents tomorrow morning. Until then, there's little to be done.'

Breakfast the following morning was a subdued affair.

Rev Stott was obviously disturbed by the events of the previous night, so Miss Hawthorne and Benton, tired by their journey and the late night themselves, left him to his thoughts. A phone call to the Vincents, which established that Mr Goodwin had regained consciousness and that the operation to set his leg had been a success, brought some relief, but there was a cloud hanging over the vicarage which Miss Hawthorne and Benton could do nothing to dispel. Rev Stott was determined to assist his visitors, however, and after giving them the news from the hospital, asked what they had planned for the day.

Miss Hawthorne was studying the map. 'This research station, Reverend – have you ever been inside?'

'No. There was an open day shortly after it opened, but I missed it.'

'Are visits permitted?'

'I wouldn't say they were encouraged… but on the other hand, there's been no actual hostility from the staff. In fact, there's been very little from them at all. It was expected that the workers would become part of the community here, but they appear to be entirely self-contained. I believe Bryce calls in now and again, but for the most part, they keep themselves to themselves and have deliveries of food and equipment.'

Miss Hawthorne exchanged glances with Benton, who nodded, and the latter said, 'In that case, we'll have a look, from a distance at least, and closer to if we can.'

'I wish you luck. Mrs Hobson has made some sandwiches, so you won't need to come back for lunch.'

'Ah, thank you, then we'll be on our way.'

The investigators gathered their kit for the day quickly. Benton, after a moment's consideration, leaving his gun behind, in case they managed to get into the research centre and had to pass through security. They left their host attempting to bury himself in work, the study window open but the door locked.

Miss Hawthorne looked at the window and sighed. They both made their way down the drive. 'It's been a great shock to him,' she said.

Benton agreed. 'He thought he knew these people, but now…? Once you've fought off Axons and giant maggots and dinosaurs, I guess you become accustomed to the strange, the supernatural. We've dealt with so many strange alien things, you almost forget the everyday horrors. And knowing someone you trust can betray you absolutely… It shakes you to your core. Makes you question everything and everyone. Even your friends. Especially your friends.'

Miss Hawthorne nodded, sadly, and put a gentle hand on his shoulder. 'Quite, John,' she said, and paused, giving him time. Then: 'But there's still a lot of good in this world. In this universe. Come on. Chin up.'

The path from the village took them out onto the moorland that surrounded it on three sides. The sunlight was bright, and a refreshing breeze stirred the heather and pulled wisps of Miss Hawthorne's hair loose to wave around her face. A ten-minute walk brought them within sight of the research centre.

A massive, three-bladed wind turbine towered above the buildings, which, with their small, evenly spaced windows and white walls, had the appearance of temporary demountable buildings stacked on top of each other. The centre was surrounded by a high fence, topped with rolls of barbed wire.

'Hmm,' said Benton, looking at the fence through binoculars, 'nobody's getting over that fence in a hurry.' He lowered his gaze from the top of the fence, and spotted a uniformed figure patrolling the buildings. 'There's a security guard too. And he's armed. Doesn't seem likely they'll let us in for a visit.'

'We can but try. But even if we do get in, it's unlikely that they'll show us anything conclusive.'

'Mmm. My word. They must have some equipment in there – look at the size of that generator!'

Benton passed the binoculars to Miss Hawthorne and pointed.

'Ah, yes, I see,' she said. 'Surely that cannot be powered by one turbine? I know very little of such things but… Oh!'

At that moment, a lorry pulled out from behind the generator and drove along the inside of the fence towards the front of the research centre.

'An oil driven generator?'

'So much for not using fossil fuels!'

'Indeed. Shall we move on? We don't want to be seen paying too much attention to the place.'

Benton agreed and asked where they were heading next. Miss Hawthorne picked up the map, and said, 'According to this, there should be an opening from one of the caves about a hundred yards west of here.'

'West it is, then.'

Miss Hawthorne returned the binoculars to Benton, who hung them round his neck, then folded the map to a more manageable size.

They reached the opening before long and both crouched down to look. The opening was scarcely bigger than a rabbit hole, but an iron grille had been placed over it, with a small warning notice attached.

Benton shifted slightly to get a closer look. 'I don't think people are getting in through this one.'

'Certainly not.'

'Wait a minute, do you feel that?'

Miss Hawthorne leaned closer, then stepped back, a startled look on her face. 'A definite breeze! Is it cooled air from the caves or…?'

'I'd say it's ventilation. It's too steady for a breeze. Whatever is going on here, it looks like the caves are back in use, and they've had an upgrade.'

'In which case, I'll be very interested to see the opening

on the beach. But that must wait for low tide.' Miss Hawthorne stood up, and went on, 'Shall we have lunch now? I'd prefer to eat before we approach the researchers in their den.'

A patch of higher ground surrounding the vent provided a suitable place to eat and Mrs Hobson's sandwiches proved to be of the same quality as her cooking of the previous night. After packing away the sandwich wrappers in his shoulder bag, Benton stood up and helped Miss Hawthorne to her feet.

'Thank you. And now to try and effect an entry!'

Benton led the way down the hill towards the road that led to the research centre. The entrance was as forbidding up close as the side had been from a distance. A gate was let into the fence, also topped in barbed wire, and a security guard stood inside. Unlike his colleague, he didn't appear to be armed, but his expression didn't encourage friendly conversation.

Ignoring his forbidding aspect, Miss Hawthorne approached the gate and addressed the guard in her breeziest manner: 'Good afternoon! My colleague and I were wondering if we could arrange an appointment to visit. My name is Hawthorne and we...'

'I'm sorry, no visitors.'

'Oh, what a shame. We weren't expecting to be let in immediately. We wouldn't want to interrupt this vital work. Could we perhaps come tomorrow? We're in the neighbourhood for a few more days.'

'No. No visitors.'

'At all? Ah. Oh well. I'm sorry to have troubled you. May I give you my card at least?'

The guard grudgingly accepted the pasteboard square and tucked it into his pocket. As he did so, a phone rang close at hand. The guard went into a hut that stood next to the gate and took the call, watching Benton and Miss Hawthorne through the window as he did so.

The call over, he came out of the hut and, to Miss

Hawthorne's surprise, unlocked the padlock holding the gate closed.

'Come in.'

'Oh, how very kind. I… John?'

Benton followed her inside, casting a thoughtful glance towards the security camera mounted on the gate. If he and Miss Hawthorne wanted to have a look inside the research centre, it appeared that someone in the centre also wanted to have a look at them.

As he and Miss Hawthorne waited inside the gate, two figures approached. One wore a suit and had a rectangular badge on his lapel. The other, Benton realised, he recognised from the previous night. It was Constable Bryce. The man in the suit walked up to Miss Hawthorne and offered his hand.

Bryce seemed not to see the other visitors. He brushed past Benton and made his way quickly out of the gate, picking up his bike from where he'd leant it against the fence and riding away at speed. Benton watched him go with a curious expression on his face. Then he became aware that he was being introduced.

'… and this is my colleague, John Benton.'

'How do you do? Ian Wiveliscombe, I'm the director here.'

'Pleased to meet you.'

'Now, how may I help you?'

'We're here for a few days to measure the earth tremors and report to our college. One of our colleagues in the department of ecology mentioned the work you're doing here, and we couldn't resist the opportunity to see if you would let us in, even for a brief look!'

'I think I can give you that. Our laboratories are off limits, of course.'

'Oh, naturally.'

'But if you would like to come to my office, I can give you an idea of the scope of our operations and what we hope to achieve.'

The pair thanked him, and the director led the way down the central drive to the largest of the office buildings. As he scanned a card to enter the building, Benton took a few steps towards the structure on the other side of the path.

'Mr Benton, this way please.'

'Sorry. I got distracted for a moment.'

'I wouldn't advise you to wander off. We've pretty tight security here.'

The director opened the door and ushered his unexpected guests inside, Benton exchanging a meaning glance with Miss Hawthorne. Clearly, the centre employees were not above a few gentle threats to visitors.

Their host led them along a featureless corridor, punctuated with identical doors, to a staircase. On the first floor, Benton and Miss Hawthorne entered a large but sparsely furnished office. A desk stood near the window, enabling its owner to have a view of the path below. A round table surrounded by metal-framed chairs stood on the other side of the room, and one of the walls was covered with cutaway drawings of the turbine and other pieces of equipment. A monitor, set into the surface of the desk, gave an explanation of the director's knowledge of their presence.

Benton, in keeping with his newly adopted absentmindedness, wandered over to the window. The director motioned to Miss Hawthorne to sit down at the round table and was about to join Benton when Miss Hawthorne spoke.

'John! Do come and sit down. You must excuse him, Mr – ah –'

'Wiveliscombe.'

Miss Hawthorne paused. 'Indeed. He's a very competent geologist but he does have a tendency to get distracted at times.'

Benton, looking suitably abashed, came away from the window and sat down. The director relaxed a little and began to give what was obviously a well-rehearsed speech about sustainable energy resources, including solar, tidal, and wind power, the last of which was the focus of the research centre at Lower Budworthy. Having given his introduction, the director then invited his guests to look at some of the diagrams on display.

The pair had been primed by Beacham, so Miss Hawthorne and Benton had questions ready, which their host appeared happy to answer. After this, the director apologised profusely, but said he had a meeting in a few minutes' time and would have to ask them to leave.

Miss Hawthorne smiled understandingly and held out her hand. 'We wouldn't dream of imposing on you any longer. This has really been a most interesting visit.'

'I'm glad to hear it. I'll just get one of my men to show you out.'

Wiveliscombe pressed a button on his desk and spoke to his secretary. A few minutes later, a tall, heavily-built security guard came to the office and was instructed to escort Miss Hawthorne and Benton to the gate.

'Goodbye,' Miss Hawthorne said, 'and thank you. Do come on, John!'

Benton was still looking at the technical drawings, so turned and apologised, keeping up appearances.

The guard led the way quickly through the buildings and down the drive, then saw his charges out of the gate and closed it behind them with a vigour that caused Miss Hawthorne to remark, 'And stay out!'

'He was chosen for effect, eh?' said Benton as they walked back to the village.

'I should say so. Did you notice anything else?'

'Apart from their work not being particularly new?'

'It was exactly what Beacham told us about – that kind of research has been going on for years.'

'Miss Grant was always on about it too. I noticed that Bryce looked scared out of his wits when he left.'

'Really? That *is* interesting.'

'And there was something about one of the buildings as

well, but I'll need to check the maps first...' Benton refused to be drawn on his theory about the buildings. Instead, he suggested they return to the vicarage before anyone from the centre came to make sure they weren't hanging about. Miss Hawthorne saw the sense in this, and they set off.

Once he was sure his visitors had left, the man who had introduced himself as Wiveliscombe made a phone call.

'I've seen Bryce. He's falling to pieces. You'll have to do something. No, he's very much your problem I should think...'

'I'll see what I can do.'

'You better had. And we had those two from UNIT nosing around.'

'What? You let them in?'

'It seemed less suspicious than keeping them out. I think they swallowed the story, but they could be a nuisance if they're going to be hanging around much longer.'

'How long do you need?'

'A week at the most. The last consignments are almost complete.'

'Good. Leave Bryce and UNIT to me.'

'I intend to. I wouldn't underestimate them though. That big fellow looked like he would be handy with his fists.'

'We might be able to deal with Bryce and your UNIT guy all in one go. Kill two birds.'

The person at the other end hung up abruptly. The director put the phone down and shuddered. His partner was efficient, but sometimes brutally so. All things considered, he would really prefer not to know what they had in mind for Constable Bryce and Mr Benton.

Trying to distract himself, he picked up the phone again and dialled.

'Yes, Mr Brookes?'

'Progress report.'

'All going smoothly. We'll be ready to move the last load by Thursday.'

Wiveliscombe – or, indeed, Brookes – hung up and turned his chair to look out of the window. All they needed was a few more days. Blasted UNIT interfering. Oh well, they would be taken care of.

When Miss Hawthorne and Benton arrived back at the vicarage, Rev Stott had emerged from his study and was having a late lunch in the parlour. He questioned his visitors eagerly about the research centre and snorted with laughter when Benton mentioned the name of the director.

'Really! Look, here.' Rev Stott pointed to a village on the map of Somerset. 'That's Wiveliscombe. If he wanted to choose an alias, you would have thought he'd have chosen a less obvious one.

Benton agreed that it did sound a bit odd. Miss Hawthorne, meanwhile, was looking at the plan of the caves, and asked, 'Sergeant, what did you mean when you said you needed to check the maps?'

'Oh, right, yes,' he said, and pulled a sheet of blank paper towards him. He drew a quick sketch of the centre as he had seen it, pointed with his pencil, and explained, 'The building over here looks as if it's over the mouth of a cave. See?' He took the plan from Miss Hawthorne and put it side by side with his drawing.

'So it does!'

'I can't believe they would do that unless they were using the cave for something – otherwise, that'd be the last place you'd want to build.'

'And with what we know about the ventilation…'

'Ventilation?' asked Rev Stott, bemused. He'd half-expected a story about Miss Hawthorne rushing through ventilation shafts to get in.

Miss Hawthorne explained their discovery on the moor. Rev Stott leaned forward and rested his chin on his hands again, his expression torn between confusion and curiosity, then said,'I've been living in this village for thirty years. I thought I knew Lower Budworthy and its inhabitants. Now I'm beginning to wonder if I know anything at all!'

Miss Hawthorne placed a sympathetic hand on his arm. 'I do understand.' Thinking that Rev Stott was, perhaps, not ready to hear about her personal experience of vengeful aliens at Devil's End, she left it at that.

Bringing her companions back to the matter in hand, she took out her notebook and prepared to compile the evidence.

'So,' she began, 'we have a research centre that appears to do little or no research, but has a large and powerful generator. One of the buildings is on the site of an entrance to the caves, and at least some of the caves seem to have been fitted out with a ventilation system.'

'And the village has been disturbed with a mechanical noise and vibration, which I think we have to connect with the centre,' added Benton.

'Agreed. Plus, we've now established that the director of the centre is using a pseudonym.' Miss Hawthorne looked at her list, and concluded: 'As I see it, this leaves us with the following questions: firstly, what is going on at the research centre? Secondly, how far does the conspiracy extend? And thirdly, can the attack on Mr Goodwin be connected with the activity at the centre?'

Benton looked thoughtful, and said, 'We can't answer the first question yet – not until we've had a look in the caves, or a closer look at the centre, which won't be easy. As far as the second one goes, I reckon that Bryce is definitely involved, even if he's just looking the other way while the others get up to whatever it is they are doing.'

'Sergeant!' protested Rev Stott.

'I'm sorry, but I can't see a way round it. We saw him leaving the centre, looking scared out of his wits, and you said he went there regularly. Then there's the attack on Mr Goodwin. The day after he gave Bryce an earful about him not investigating the tremors, he's attacked. And Bryce is first on the scene.'

'But the door? He needed George Vincent to let him in.'

'That's what he said. Supposing Goodwin let him in earlier on, Bryce attacks him, hits him on the head, maybe with his truncheon, tips the barrels over him, and then lets himself out, locking the door behind him, ready to raise the alarm later on…'

Rev Stott shook his head. 'I can't believe it,' he said, yet his face belied his words. 'I wouldn't have thought for a moment he'd be capable of such a thing.'

Miss Hawthorne spoke quietly. 'I'm sorry we've distressed you, Reverend, but I believe Sergeant Benton is right. From what you've told us, I don't think Bryce was acting of his own accord. He must be under some malign influence from the people at the centre.'

Rev Stott sighed. 'I still don't want to believe it, but I fear you are correct. What is our next course of action?'

Miss Hawthorne considered. 'I suggest that we keep our plan to look at the caves tonight at low tide and see what information is to be gained there. If we can get sufficient evidence, we can pass that to the county police and let them take over.'

'And Bryce?'

Miss Hawthorne acknowledged that this was a particularly difficult question, but before she could say any more, she was interrupted by the telephone bell. Rev Stott hurried to answer it and returned a few moments later, looking both puzzled and worried.

'It's Bryce,' he explained. 'He wouldn't give his name, but I recognised his voice. He insists on speaking to you, Sergeant.'

Benton went to the study without a word. When he returned, he looked even more concerned and had a piece of paper in one hand. Miss Hawthorne raised her eyebrows as he came in and simply waited for the explanation.

'He wants to talk. But only to me. He wants to meet me tonight.' He consulted the note in his hand. 'Where the coast path meets the Upper Budworthy Road. And I'm to come alone.'

Miss Hawthorne frowned. 'I don't like it, John. Insisting you go alone... It could be a trap.'

'I don't like it either, but I'll have to chance it. I can't miss the chance to talk to him. You'll have to do the caves without me, if I meet him at ten.'

'We'll manage,' said Rev Stott unexpectedly. Miss Hawthorne and Benton looked at him in surprise. 'Well, of course I'm coming into the caves! Assuming we *can* get in, that is.'

Miss Hawthorne relaxed a little and smiled. 'Thank you. And, Sergeant, if you aren't back by the time we return, I shall call UNIT and the chief constable.'

'I'll do the same for you.'

Miss Hawthorne gathered up her notes and bid them adieu: she intended to head to the garden and collate a report. She suggested the three come together later on before they headed their separate ways that evening. Benton and Rev Stott shared a warm smile as she left the room.

'Well, I did little enough of my sermon this morning,' said Rev Stott, getting up himself, 'I suppose I should make another effort.'

'And I'll sort out my equipment for this evening.'

Rev Stott decided not to enquire what this 'equipment' was as he had a shrewd idea that he wouldn't like the answer. Instead, he went back to his study.

Benton went up to his bedroom, where he cleaned and loaded his gun, then checked the batteries in his torch. That done, he sat on his bed to read the novel he'd brought with him until it was time for dinner.

Dinner was a quiet meal, as the diners were all preoccupied with what was to come later that evening. After the meal they separated again, Miss Hawthorne to her room to crochet and consult the plan of the caves; Benton to work out the best route to his rendezvous, and possible escape routes in case of an ambush; and Rev Stott to his study to prepare for evening prayer the following day – and wonder what on earth he'd got himself into.

At half past nine, they reconvened in the study. Miss Hawthorne, to her fellow investigators' considerable surprise, was wearing overalls and carrying two hard hats, one of which she passed to Rev Stott. Neither of the gents asked where she'd got them from. Benton was dressed in dark clothes, so as not to draw attention to himself. He carried a torch in one hand and a slight distortion of the fabric of his jacket under one arm showed that he was armed.

Rev Stott led the way to the main road and then to the cliff path. Torches weren't really necessary in the bright moonlight, and the party made quick progress along the edge of the cliff, until they reached a point where the path split, part of it going down towards the sea, the other carrying on along the clifftop.

'Good luck, Sergeant,' said Rev Stott. 'Straight along for another two-hundred yards or so and you'll be able to see the road.'

Benton thanked him, wished them both good luck, and continued to walk along the upper path. Miss Hawthorne looked after him for a moment, then sighed.

'Well, Reverend, let's get on.'

'This way, Miss Hawthorne. It's quite smooth but there's the occasional rough patch, so take care.'

Rev Stott led the way, proceeding cautiously and shining his torch on the path to show up any uneven ground.

After about ten minutes, he and Miss Hawthorne had reached the beach. The sand was damp from the retreating tide and their footprints disappeared behind them as they walked to the cave mouth.

Rev Stott began talking to his companion, showing her the gate – then stopped suddenly. Even in the torchlight, Miss Hawthorne could see his astonishment – as he put his hand on the gate, and, at his touch, it swung silently open.

Miss Hawthorne moved her torch to shine just inside the entrance. A thick chain and padlock were piled to one side. She looked questioningly at Rev Stott, then, without waiting for an answer, went through the gate. After a moment's hesitation, Rev Stott followed her.

The opening of the cave was dark, but, after a few yards, there was a glow of light. Miss Hawthorne turned off her torch. Not daring to speak, she beckoned to her new friend. They crept along the natural corridor, until they reached the source of the light: there were electric lamps, mounted on the walls at intervals. Between the lamps were square boxes connected to broad tubing, which Miss Hawthorne recognised as the ventilation system she and the sergeant had encountered from above.

The floor of the cave was almost artificially smooth, save for two parallel grooves, about four feet apart, that ran along the length of it.

The two explorers walked a little further, following the lights and the grooves in the floor, until they reached a point where a smaller cave branched off from the main one. Suddenly, voices could be heard and a faint rumbling noise shook the cave wall. Rev Stott pulled Miss Hawthorne into the smaller cave and they flattened themselves against the rocky wall as the sound grew louder. The voices stopped, but the rumbling got louder and louder and *louder* until a vehicle of sorts appeared, accompanied by two men in dark overalls. The vehicle was composed of five wooden crates mounted on metal frames, with small metal wheels underneath, linked together to form a train. A battery pack was mounted on the frame of the front crate, and connecting cables showed that the entire contrivance was powered by electricity. One of the men carried a bulky remote control, with which he seemed to be regulating the speed of the train; the other carried a tool bag. Both men wore heavy, insulated gloves.

From their hiding place, Miss Hawthorne and Rev Stott

watched the train of crates go by. Once it had passed and the sound had faded, they crept out into the main cave.

Rev Stott looked at his companion and mouthed, 'What do we do now?'

'Follow them? We need to get out again and there are some gaps in the wall, should we need to conceal ourselves. The alternative is to wait here until they come back, but by then, the gate will probably be secured and there's no guarantee that we'll be able to open it. Not to mention that we may learn what's in those crates.'

With that, Miss Hawthorne set off, back the way they had come, and Rev Stott, after a brief hesitation, followed her. They made their way cautiously back down the corridor, staying close to the wall and making as little noise as possible. The corridor curved as they neared the entrance, and Miss Hawthorne stopped and peered cautiously around the corner.

A boat was pulled up on the sand outside the cave, shallow-bottomed, but strongly built. Two men were carrying a crate, using ropes as handles. When she saw them, Miss Hawthorne suppressed a gasp. While the men from the tunnel were clad in modern overalls and gloves, these men were dressed in loose shirts and breeches, with scarves on their heads and heeled boots on their feet.

Miss Hawthorne ducked back around the corner. Unless the men moved away, they were trapped. If the gate was closed on them and they were unable to open it, they'd be at the mercy of the tide, or of the research centre's guards at the other end of the tunnel. Rev Stott, who shared her concern, looked at her questioningly, but she shook her head.

At that moment, one of the men in the tunnel called to the sailors in a low voice: 'Oi! Hurry it up, you two – we've got to get moving.'

One of the sailors turned and spat derisively. 'Huh! You give us a hand and we'll be done quicker.'

The man in the tunnel swore, but spoke to his mate, and,

between them, they lifted one of the freed crates and began to carry it towards the boat. For a moment, the coast was clear.

Miss Hawthorne and Rev Stott slipped out of the gate and dashed for a rocky outcrop at the foot of the cliff, where they could conceal themselves until the men had gone. When the final crate was loaded, the men from tunnel closed and padlocked the gate and disappeared into the caves; one of the sailors shoved the boat off the sand and then jumped aboard. His shipmate started the outboard motor and the boat headed out to sea.

When the beach was finally deserted, Rev Stott came out from behind the rocks, and said, 'I think we have the place to ourselves again.'

'I'm very glad to hear it. Well, we know that smuggling is still very much alive in Lower Budworthy.'

'Yes, and that my parishioner wasn't telling tall tales!' Rev Stott laughed, softly. 'I suppose that their disguise is to make sure that anyone who sees them will not be believed. I must say that it worked in my case.'

'Oh yes,' Miss Hawthorne agreed, 'there was nothing ghostly about those men, but from a distance, and after a few drinks, one might easily think otherwise.'

Rev Stott's mind turned to the contents of the crates 'What could be in those crates? They looked heavy.'

'For the time being, we'd better leave that aside. We've seen the criminals at work and that will do for now. How long before the tide turns?'

Rev Stott looked at the luminous dial of his watch. 'About another half hour – plenty of time for us to get up the path.'

'Then let us not delay: I want to get back and make sure that Sergeant Benton has returned safely.'

Rev Stott led the way to the bottom of the path and they climbed back up. Clouds now covered the moon and a breeze had sprung up, catching at their hair and clothes as they climbed.

At the top of the path, Miss Hawthorne stopped.

'Do you hear that?' she asked.

In the distance: the faint sound of a siren.

She set off quickly across the moor. Rev Stott caught up with her after she had gone a few yards, and checked in, 'You don't think—?'

'I don't know. I believe that siren came from the village, so it may have nothing to do with Sergeant Benton; nevertheless, I'll be much happier when we know he's safe.'

When Benton left his companions at the top of the cliff, he walked briskly along the path in the direction he'd plotted on the map. The moon gave ample light for him to follow the way and he was glad not to have to use his torch and risk the light attracting attention.

After the two-hundred yards mentioned by Rev Stott, he saw the Upper Budworthy Road crossing the moor to join the cliff path, and quickened his pace.

Benton had almost reached the rendezvous point when he heard the unmistakable sound of a shot, close at hand. He dropped to the ground, then, when the shot was followed by silence, crawled forward, his gun in his hand. Just ahead, he could see a glow that looked like torchlight. As he got closer, the sergeant saw a torch on the ground, the light showing the shape of a body lying next to it. Benton got up into a crouch and, keeping low, moved closer to the body. By the light of the torch, he could see that it was the body of a man, dressed in a police uniform. Benton's heart seemed to spring into his throat. The man was lying on his back, his eyes staring sightlessly at the sky.

It was Constable Bryce. His face was contorted in an expression of shock and the round, dark hole above his left eye showed where the fatal bullet had struck. Benton shifted slightly to examine the wound.

At that moment a bright light shone from close at hand and a voice shouted: 'Stay where you are!'

Benton turned, blinking in the light. The voice came again: 'Put the gun down!'

Benton lowered his gun slowly to the ground and raised his hands. The next moment, he was hauled to his feet, his arms held behind him. Glancing over his shoulder, he could see that he was being held by policemen – or, at least by men in police uniform.

The owner of voice approached. Squinting in the torch light, Benton could make out a man in plain clothes, slim, but well built, with an angular, high cheek-boned face, dark brows, and dark curly hair. The man turned the full beam of his torch into Benton's face, making the sergeant wince and close his eyes.

'Take him to the van. We'll get his story at the station. There's no use in struggling, Sergeant, you'll only make it worse for yourself.'

Benton tried to push forwards towards the plain clothes man but was restrained by the officers holding him.

'I didn't shoot him,' he explained. 'I heard the shot, and I came. You can see, I haven't fired. Check my gun!'

The man picked up Benton's gun from the ground with a gloved hand and opened the chamber.

'So you haven't. Well...'

Extending his arm, the man fired one shot into the ground.

'Now you have.'

Benton was silent with horror. The man pulled a bag from his pocket and dropped the gun into it, then passed the bag to another uniformed officer who had just arrived.

'Dig that bullet out, Briggs, and then make sure everything's ready for the pathologist.'

'Sir.'

'And now, Sergeant,' said the man, with a malicious smile, 'let's get you safely put away for the night.'

Shocked and bewildered by the turn of events, Benton was hustled down to the road, handcuffed, and put in the back of a police van. One of the constables got into the back and sat opposite his prisoner; the other got into the driving seat. The plain clothes man banged on the hood and the driver started the engine. They drove quickly towards the village, with lights flashing, but no siren until they reached the main road. The streets were empty at that time of night, but the sound of the siren brought some of the inhabitants to their windows and some bedroom lights were switched on as they went by.

When the van reached the police station, Benton was taken out and led inside. The station was a small one, with a front office and interview room on the ground floor and cells in the basement. The constable who'd driven the van entered Benton's details in a ledger, then escorted him downstairs, where his handcuffs were removed, and he was shoved unceremoniously into a cell. As the key turned in the lock. Benton sat down on the edge of the bed – the cell's only furniture – and put his head in his hands. His mind raced as he tried to make sense of what had just happened.

He had been set up. That much was very clear. And so had Bryce. Perhaps whoever was responsible had decided to solve two problems at once. Benton shuddered. He was clearly in the hands of real police officers; they wouldn't have brought him here otherwise, and yet… The picture of the plain clothes man firing his gun swam before his eyes. He looked up as the hatch in the door was pulled aside and the plain clothes man looked through.

'Comfortable? I don't suppose you'd care to tell us where your friends are this evening? I tried to call to let them know where you were, but they don't seem to be at home.'

Benton remained silent, so the man spoke again: 'Perhaps you'll feel more like talking in the morning. Sleep well.'

He was about to close the hatch when Benton asked, 'Who are you?'

'How rude of me. I quite forgot. I'm Inspector Gibson, South Somerset Constabulary.'

Light dawned.

'That's how you knew who I was.'

'I was informed of your activities by the chief constable.

At first, I let you amuse yourselves, but when you started to be a nuisance, I had to take action. Poor Bryce really wasn't up to the job. His nerves were all to pieces.'

'So you killed him?'

'No, Sergeant Benton. *You did.* Now, I suggest you get some rest, and we'll talk again in the morning. Goodnight.'

With that, Gibson closed the flap and flicked a switch beside the cell door, plunging the interior into darkness. As there was nothing else for it, Benton laid down on the bed and closed his eyes. He didn't think he would sleep, but, worn out by the shock and the speed of events, he did.

When Miss Hawthorne and Rev Stott reached the vicarage, the house was in darkness. The latter opened the door and turned on the light, checking on the key hook to see if the spare key he'd given the sergeant was there. He turned back to Miss Hawthorne and shook his head. Miss Hawthorne ran up the stairs and knocked on Benton's bedroom door, then opened it.

She came slowly back down again and noted, 'He isn't here.'

'Perhaps he and Bryce went somewhere together, or Bryce gave him some clue he had to follow up on straight away.'

Miss Hawthorne nodded slowly, pushing back at the tendrils of panic starting to weave through her mind. 'Perhaps.'

Rev Stott opened the door to the study, and said, 'We must wait for news. Come in and have a brandy while we do.'

His guest smiled wanly. 'Thank you. I dare say it's silly of me to worry: he's a trained soldier, after all, but – '

The telephone rang, making them both jump. Rev Stott ran into the study and picked up the receiver, Miss Hawthorne following him.

'Vicarage, Reverend Stott speaking. Yes. Yes,' he said, then went silent for a few seconds while the caller spoke. 'I…

I beg your pardon? He… Yes, yes, Inspector. Goodbye.'

He put down the receiver and looked at Miss Hawthorne.

'Constable Bryce has been found dead. He'd been shot. Sergeant Benton has been arrested for his murder.'

The colour drained from Miss Hawthorne's already pale face.

'Where have they taken him?'

'To the police station in the village, I believe. Inspector Gibson called me from there, at any rate.'

'I don't believe it. Murder? There must be some mistake. Or foul play.'

Rev Stott sat down beside her. 'If there is, we'll find it out.'

Then a thought occurred to her.

'I must call UNIT!' she said. 'The Brigadier must know.'

Rev Stott handed Miss Hawthorne the receiver and quietly left the room, leaving her to make what he knew would be a difficult call.

The Brigadier had been working late and was about to leave the office when Miss Hawthorne's call came through.

'Lethbridge-Stewart. Hello, Miss Hawthorne. What? *What?!*'

He listened intently as Miss Hawthorne gave him as much information as she had.

'I'll call the chief constable first thing in the morning. We'll get this sorted out. I suppose you don't… No, of course I'm not suggesting… No, Miss Hawthorne. And the caves?'

Miss Hawthorne recovered herself a little and reported what she and Rev Stott had discovered.

'Smuggling, eh?' the Brigadier said. 'Very well. Stay where you are. I'll call you as soon as I have any news. Yes, goodnight, Miss Hawthorne.'

Benton was woken the next morning by a loud knocking on the door of his cell, followed by the hatch being drawn back, and a small tray, with a plate of toast and mug of tea on it being thrust through the opening.

Benton got up and limped across to the door, his muscles stiff from the previous night's exertions and the hardness of the bed. He took the tray and the hatch slammed shut. So, they were going to feed him, at least. He sat down on the bed and put the tray down next to him. It wasn't much of a meal, but it lifted his spirits a little and made him feel a bit more himself.

He wondered if the Brigadier knew. Probably. Miss Hawthorne had likely phoned him.

Miss Hawthorne... If Gibson was prepared to frame him for murder, he wouldn't stop at much. Characteristically, Benton's concern was more for the safety of his colleagues, rather than himself and he hoped that the Brigadier would send reinforcements or get Miss Hawthorne safely away before anything could happen to her.

Frowning, he finished his breakfast and put the tray on the floor, then swung his legs onto the bed and laid down. There wasn't anything he could do but wait and see, so he might as well rest while he could.

The Brigadier hadn't waited long before calling the chief constable. At six in the morning, he was in his office and waiting for his call to be answered, drumming his fingers impatiently on the desk.

After what felt like an eternity to the Brigadier, Sir James' voice came quietly over the line.

'Brigadier?'

The Brigadier didn't beat about the bush.

'Sir James. My sergeant has been arrested. Can you explain to me how this happened?'

The chief constable sighed. 'Constable Bryce is dead. Sergeant Benton was found alone at the scene with his gun drawn, and was taken into custody.'

'Has he made a statement?'

'Not yet.'

'Who was responsible for the arrest?'

'Inspector Gibson of the South Somerset Force. I'd informed him of UNIT's presence in the area so he could cooperate if necessary.'

The Brigadier snorted. 'Cooperate!' Then he controlled himself – with some difficulty – and went on: 'I'm sorry, Sir James. You have my condolences for the death of Constable Bryce, of course, but Sergeant Benton is my concern.'

'I quite understand.'

'So what happened?'

'I don't have all the details, but I gather from Gibson that Bryce had arranged to meet Benton, a struggle took place, and Bryce was shot at close range. A bullet was recovered from the scene and one round is missing from Benton's gun. It looks bad for your man, Brigadier.'

'What possible reason would he have to shoot Bryce?'

The chief constable began to lose patience. 'I don't know. I only spoke briefly to Gibson last night. He told me there was a struggle; it may have been self defence.'

The Brigadier had been thinking. 'This Gibson – he was very much on the spot wasn't he?'

'What are you implying?'

'Oh, nothing, nothing at all. I was merely wondering how he and his men came to be in exactly the right place at exactly the right time to arrest my sergeant.'

Another sigh came from the other end of the line. 'They were on their way to arrest Bryce,' explained Sir James. 'We have been concerned about his conduct for a while, and Gibson tells me that evidence had come to light suggesting that he was involved in the attack on Arthur Goodwin. Gibson and his men were driving to the village when they heard the shot on the moor and stopped to investigate.'

'Really?' asked the Brigadier in his flattest voice. 'You'll pardon me, Sir James, but that sounds like too much of a coincidence. I want to speak to Sergeant Benton. I take it your inspector will arrange that.'

'You're implying that Gibson is somehow involved?'

'I can hardly think otherwise, can I? But, leaving that aside, I'm Sergeant Benton's commanding officer, and, as such, I am entitled to have contact with him. May I also remind you, Sir James, that it was you who requested our assistance with this investigation, which could've been undertaken by your own officers? That alone suggests to me that you have doubts about your force, even if you won't admit it to an outsider.'

There was a long silence, finally broken by Sir James. 'Very well. Yes. I'd had concerns about the investigations into the tremors. The lack of results was suspicious and Bryce had been behaving erratically, but I didn't imagine that Gibson...'

'Well, you'll have to imagine it now. I refuse to believe that a competent inspector would be unaware of a major smuggling operation in his county.'

'Smuggling?'

'Yes. My most recent report from the field confirms it. The research centre is a cover operation for smuggling through the caves.'

'My God.'

'Quite. The question is, what are you going to do about it?'

Sir James started stammering, then regained control of himself. 'What am I...? You'll have to give me time. I can't interfere with the arrest, but I'll get you your call. As for the rest...? If Gibson is implicated, how many of his officers are also involved? And how much do the smugglers know about the investigation?'

'My suspicion is that they've arrested Benton, not only to get him out of the way, but also to question him about the investigation.'

'I... I must have time to think.'

'Don't be too long about it, Sir James. And get me that call.'

The Brigadier hung up and gazed into space for a

moment. He had been shaken by the news of Benton's arrest, but the clouds had begun to clear. What he needed now was action, but he had to wait for news from the chief constable.

The Brigadier reached for the telephone again. Was it too early to call Miss Hawthorne? Probably not. Lethbridge-Stewart smiled wryly as he dialled.

The call was answered by Rev Stott after a short interval.

'Rev Stott? Brigadier Lethbridge-Stewart here. Is Miss Hawthorne available?'

'Yes, of course. One moment.'

A pause, and then Miss Hawthorne's voice was heard at the other end of the line. 'Brigadier? What news?'

'I've spoken to the chief constable. He's going to arrange for me to speak to Sergeant Benton.'

'That's something, at least.'

'Yes, not much, but we'll have to be satisfied with that for the time being. It's clear that Benton has been the victim of a conspiracy; the police evidence and the circumstances of his arrest are much too convenient for my liking.'

'I cannot believe he is guilty.'

'Neither can I, but, unfortunately, what we believe is neither here nor there. The evidence is against him.'

'Then what can we do?'

The Brigadier was sad to report that they could do very little for now. But he promised to keep her updated with news, then advised, 'In the meantime, Miss Hawthorne, I'd advise you not to venture too far afield. You've given us evidence of the smuggling operation and Rev Stott has corroborated it. There's no need for you to put yourself at risk. Understood?'

She agreed, and the two bade each other goodbye.

In his cell, Benton had fallen into an uneasy doze. He opened his eyes as the cell door opened.

A uniformed constable stood in the doorway, a gun in his hand. He stood back and gestured to the room beyond. 'Out.'

Benton stood up and moved slowly out of the cell, keeping his eyes on the man with the gun. A table stood in the centre of the room – bare, save for a telephone.

Gibson was seated on one side and indicated the empty chair on the other side with his hand. 'Sit down, Sergeant. You'll excuse the precautions; we don't often have prisoners who are trained in combat.'

Seeing nothing else for it, Benton sat down. Gibson passed a sheet of paper across the table. 'Your statement. Here.'

He pushed a pen towards Benton. Benton glanced at the page, then pushed it away. 'I'm not signing that.'

'Why not?'

'Because it's not true.'

Gibson smiled thinly, and said, 'We have your gun. And your bullet. If you decide not to confess, it'll be our word against yours. Who do you think will be believed? An undercover representative of a shadowy military outfit, or the local police, pillars of the community?'

Forgetting the armed guard, Benton lunged across the table. Instantly, two men grabbed him and forced him back into his chair.

'Dear me,' said Gibson, brushing his jacket, 'I can see how your temper might get the better of you. So you won't sign?'

The telephone on Gibson's side of the table rang. Gibson shushed Benton and picked up the handset. 'Yes? Yes, put him through.'

Gibson turned back to where Benton was sitting, still held by the two constables. 'A call for you, Sergeant.' Benton began to struggle, so the inspector told his underlings to hold him steady. 'Really, Sergeant, you aren't helping yourself. Ah, yes, that's better.'

The guard with the gun produced handcuffs and fastened Benton's wrists to the back of the chair. Gibson waited for a moment, then brought the receiver round and held it up to Benton's ear.

'Benton, are you there?'

The Brigadier's voice was the most welcome sound his sergeant could have heard.

'Yes, sir.'

'Listen, Benton, we won't have long. We're going to get you out of there, but you'll need to bear with us. How are they treating you?'

'Well, enough,' replied Benton, feeling that, with a gun to his head and surrounded by uniformed thugs, he could hardly say otherwise. Then, because he needed to say it aloud: 'Sir, whatever they say, I didn't kill him.'

'I know, Sergeant. I know. Hang in there. We'll get you out.'

'I think that's long enough,' said Gibson, replacing the receiver. 'And now, Sergeant, how about making all our lives easier and signing your statement?'

'No.'

Gibson eyed him up and down for a second or two. Then he gestured to the guards, who opened the handcuffs and removed them from the chair, then pulled the sergeant to his feet and escorted him back to the cell.

Gibson left the room and went upstairs to the desk, where one of his men was on the telephone. Seeing his superior officer, the constable held out the receiver, and the inspector took it.

'That you, Gibson? Brookes here.'

'Yes, what is it?'

'We've got ahead of schedule. The men managed to get a double load out last night so we're ready to start dismantling.'

'Excellent.'

'Did you… solve our problem?'

'Part of it. I'm about to go and get us some insurance. How would you feel about having a guest for a while?'

He didn't wait for a response.

*

At the vicarage, Miss Hawthorne was doing her best to wait for the Brigadier to call. She had finished a written report of the events of the previous evening and taken her crochet to the garden. But, despite her usual patience, she couldn't stop looking at her watch.

Eventually, Miss Hawthorne decided that a short walk might clear her head a little. She needn't go far; just along the road and back. Miss Hawthorne went back through the house to find her host. She met him in the hall, bag in hand.

'I'm sorry, Miss Hawthorne, but I have to go and see one of my parishioners. She's been ill for some time and I've just had a call to say that her condition is serious.'

'I quite understand, I was going to go for a stroll – not far, just for some fresh air.'

Rev Stott nodded, understandingly. 'Of course,' he said, 'take my key; you'll be back before I am. I'll see you later and perhaps we'll have had better news by then.'

Miss Hawthorne thanked him, took the key, and followed her host out of the house. Rev Stott set off towards the centre of the village and Miss Hawthorne towards the moors.

The day was fine once again, and the fresh breeze and the beauty of her surroundings lifted her spirits a little. At first, Miss Hawthorne followed the main road, then she turned aside and began to walk over the moor.

A sudden noise made her look back. The research centre gates were open and a heavy goods lorry was pulling out onto the road. Miss Hawthorne stood and watched as the first lorry was followed by a second. What was happening? More from habit than from the hope of seeing anything, she had brought the binoculars with her.

She walked on, close to the place from where she and Benton had observed the generator and the oil lorry, and raised the binoculars. A lorry was parked outside one of the buildings – possibly the one which had been built over the cave mouth – and men in overalls were walking backwards and forwards, loading what looked like pieces of mechanical and electrical equipment into the back of it.

Miss Hawthorne dropped the binoculars on their strap and made her way quickly back to the vicarage. Once inside, she ran to the study and dialled the number for UNIT HQ.

'Corporal Scott? This is Olive Hawthorne. Is the Brigadier there?'

'Yes, Miss Hawthorne, he's here – actually, he was about to call you.'

A pause, and then: 'Lethbridge-Stewart. That you, Miss Hawthorne?'

'Brigadier. The research centre is being dismantled! There are men loading equipment into lorries and—'

Miss Hawthorne broke off, suddenly and the Brigadier heard a scuffling sound in the distance.

'Miss Hawthorne? Are you there? *Miss Hawthorne*?'

There was a moment's silence, then a male voice came over the line.

'I'm afraid not, Brigadier. Miss Hawthorne is... indisposed at present.'

The Brigadier made an educated guess. 'Gibson?'

'Now. Listen carefully. We have both your agents. You know what's happened to Sergeant Benton. We're taking Miss Hawthorne somewhere for a bit of peace and quiet for a while, so we can finish our work. Should you make any attempt to interrupt our work, or to rescue your agents, or mount any kind of attack, that peace and quiet will become permanent. Do I make myself clear?'

'Perfectly,' replied the Brigadier in a low, growling voice.

'Good. Don't try and contact us. We'll find you when we're ready.'

Gibson hung up and turned to Miss Hawthorne. She was being held by one of his men, who had a hand over her mouth.

She glared at Gibson, who smiled.

'Dear me, it seems that Sergeant Benton isn't the only

one with a temper,' said Gibson. 'Bring her along. Don't think about calling for help, Miss Hawthorne – there really isn't anyone around to hear you.'

At his words, she was hustled out of the house and into the back of the police van. She couldn't see where they were going, but her sense of direction told her that the research centre was the likely destination.

At UNIT HQ, the Brigadier slammed the receiver back in the cradle and stood up, bristling with anger. He walked to the window, then back to his desk, possible courses of action running through his mind.

The idea of leaving the criminals to get away repelled him, as did the idea of abandoning Sergeant Benton and Miss Hawthorne – yet mounting a large scale attack was clearly out of the question.

Once again, his fingers drummed on the desktop as he thought. *Gibson. How many officers are working with him? Could any of the police in the area be trusted? Was it checkmate?*

Suddenly, a light came into the Brigadier's eyes that his enemies would do well to fear.

He picked up the receiver and dialled an internal number.

'Hello?'

'Miss Grosvenor. My office. Quick as you can.'

Not waiting to hear her reply, the Brigadier hung up and then dialled again, this time an external number. 'Sir James? Lethbridge-Stewart here. I'm going to need your assistance...'

Benton looked at his watch. Nearly five. He hadn't been given any food since breakfast, which, he assumed, meant either that his captors were hoping he would sign the statement on the promise of a meal, or that they'd forgotten about him. The latter, he admitted, didn't seem likely.

A sudden noise outside made him sit up. The cell door was thick, but he could hear the sound of footsteps running down the stairs. Preparing to defend himself if necessary, Benton got up from the bed and backed into a corner of the cell.

He heard a commotion, followed by a familiar voice call:

'Benton?'

'Sir!'

'Get out of there, man! What are you waiting for?'

Benton came out of the cell and found the Brigadier, and, to his surprise, Iolanthe waiting for him.

The Brigadier smiled as Benton emerged from the cell. 'There you are, Benton. Are you okay?'

'Yes, sir, I—'

Anything else he might've said was forgotten as Iolanthe ran forward and threw her arms round him. The Brigadier had had an idea for a while now that Iolanthe saw Benton as a sort of adopted elder brother and the strength of the hug she was currently giving the sergeant confirmed that impression.

'John!' she cried.

'Steady on, kid. I'm all right.'

Benton returned the hug, then gently disengaged himself, and turned to his superior. 'What's the plan, sir?'

'They've got Miss Hawthorne,' he informed the sergeant, grimly. Benton went to say something, but the Brigadier stilled him with a hand in the air. 'I'm not entirely sure where, but our best guess is either at the research centre or in those wretched caves. The research centre – or some of it, at least – is being dismantled, so if we want to stand any chance of getting to her and catching those swines, we'll need to act quickly.'

'Yes, sir. Just... *us*?'

'For now, yes. The chief constable is bringing in reinforcements from outside the county, but we can't risk a large show of force while Miss Hawthorne is still in their hands.'

'Right.'

'You'll need this,' the Brigadier said, passing Benton a holster and gun. 'We'll see about getting your own one back later on. We'd better get moving. I want to stop off at the vicarage so Miss Grosvenor can get the radio set up to coordinate operations.'

The Brigadier led the way up the stairs. Benton stopped in surprise at the sight of the constable, who'd been left on guard, dancing like Mick Jagger, then shot a sideways glance at Iolanthe, who blushed a little.

They got into the Brigadier's car, which was parked outside, and set off at speed towards the vicarage. Nearby, another guard was in the process of taking the final penalty in the World Cup final.

Benton smirked.

The Brigadier glanced at his sergeant. 'When was the last time you had something to eat?'

'Early this morning, sir.'

'Food in the glove box. Help yourself.'

'Thank you, sir.'

Benton opened the glove box and found a bag containing sandwiches and a currant bun, which he quickly devoured.

A few minutes later, they reached the vicarage and the Brigadier jumped out of the car and strode purposefully to the front door. His knock was answered by Rev Stott, looking deeply troubled.

The call to his parishioner had been a decoy. He'd reached her house to find her in excellent spirits and bewildered at the idea that she was at death's door. When he got back, he'd found the vicarage door open and Miss Hawthorne gone.

Benton stayed in the car while Iolanthe followed Rev Stott and the Brigadier into the house, the latter having fetched a portable two-way radio from the car.

'I am so very sorry,' murmured Rev Stott. 'I wish I had been here.'

'Don't apologise, Reverend – chances are, there wouldn't

have been anything you could've done.'

'If I can help in any way...?'

'You can stay here with Miss Grosvenor and monitor communications with her. I'm expecting the chief constable to be in contact shortly. You'll need to relay any information he may give you to us in the field.'

'And Sergeant Benton?'

'Safe and well,' the Brigadier said, and Rev Stott gave a sigh of relief. 'All ready, Miss Grosvenor?'

Iolanthe, who had been setting up the radio, nodded. 'All ready, sir.'

'Good, you'll hear from us shortly.'

Rev Stott wished them good luck, and the Brigadier ran back to his car and drove away. Rev Stott went back into the house. If nothing else, he could keep Miss Grosvenor supplied with cups of tea.

As the Brigadier's car neared the research centre, the radio crackled.

'Answer that, would you, Sergeant?'

'Greyhound four, over?'

'Greyhound four, this is trap five.' Iolanthe's voice sounded oddly distorted by the radio 'We have news from the CC. Over.'

'That was fast. Go ahead. Over.'

'News follows: reinforcements secured, expected time of arrival approximately... twenty minutes from now. Over.'

'Thank you, trap five. Understood, over.'

'Good luck, greyhound. Out.'

The Brigadier pulled into the side of the road and stopped.

'We'd better walk from here – no point in announcing our arrival by driving up to the gates.'

The two men got out of the car and began to walk towards the research centre. Benton pointed out the security camera at one side of the gate, and they made a detour to stay out of its range, then waited.

A few moments later, one of the lorries spotted by Miss

Hawthorne drew up inside. The security guard opened the gate as the lorry inched forwards. The driver paused to check for oncoming traffic, so the Brigadier and Benton ran forward and through the gate, the lorry concealing them from both the camera and the guard.

Once inside the complex, they paused in a corner behind a stack of empty crates.

'Right, Sergeant, you've been here before. Where are they likely to be holding her?'

Benton looked around the corner of the crates. They were surrounded by piles of wood, metal, and electrical parts, some of which were being loaded into another lorry by a small group of men. Benton could just about see a figure he took to be Inspector Gibson, standing by the entrance to what he mentally termed the 'cave building'.

The only building that seemed to be untouched by the chaos and general destruction was the main building, where he and Miss Hawthorne had been taken.

He pointed it out to the Brigadier. 'Over there, sir. Director's office. It's out of the way and they can watch the security cameras from there.'

'Lead the way, Sergeant.'

Benton did so, staying close to the walls and doing his best to keep out of the way of any CCTV. The door of the office building stood open, and the two men made their way upstairs. A uniformed constable stood outside the door to the director's office. The soldiers approached silently, their boots muffled by the carpet. At the last minute, the guard turned in their direction, but – too late.

Benton lunged forward and dealt him a blow to the jaw that made his head rebound off the wall. His body slid down to the floor.

The Brigadier looked down at the unconscious man and raised his eyebrows. 'Well, I'm glad you've got that out of your system, Benton.'

Benton grinned briefly, then became serious again as the

Brigadier stood back from the door and gave a whispered count down from five. At one, Benton put his shoulder to the door and pushed. It gave way on his second try, and the two men charged through the doorway and came to a sudden halt inside.

Brookes was seated at his desk, seemingly frozen in the act of turning his chair towards the door. The Brigadier ran over to the desk and put his gun against Brooke's temple.

'Where is she?' he growled.

Brookes pointed silently to the other side of the office.

Miss Hawthorne was seated on one of the metal framed chairs, her wrists tied to the frame and a scarf obscuring the lower half of her face.

Benton was by her side in an instant, pulling the scarf off her mouth and cutting through the cords that secured her wrists with his penknife.

Once her arms were freed, Benton helped her gently to her feet and offered his arm for support. Miss Hawthorne smiled at him. 'Thank you, John. Rescuing your damsel in distress yet again!'

'You're welcome.' Benton smiled and gave her a quick hug. 'Let's get you out of here.' There was no time for dillydallying. They walked back across the office, where the Brigadier had secured his prisoner.

'All safe, sir.'

'Glad to see you, Miss Hawthorne.'

'And I you, Brigadier!'

'What do you think, sir? Shall we make a run for it?'

The sound of engines outside drew them to the window. Two police cars and a large van raced through the gate and screeched to a halt on the central path. Armed officers piled out of the back of the van and, given a signal from a senior officer who was standing by one of the cars, they fanned out and began a steady progress through the complex, the workers fleeing before them, the renegade policemen opening fire.

'I think, Sergeant, that we'll be better off up here for the time being.'

Benton grunted in agreement, then pointed to a figure who was approaching the building, apparently unnoticed. 'Sir, look – Gibson.'

'Stay here with Miss Hawthorne, Benton,' said the Brigadier, then, when his sergeant went to object, he added, 'That's an order, Sergeant.'

'Yes, sir,' said Benton, trying and failing to hide his disappointment.

The Brigadier hid a smile as he left the room: as far as he was concerned, Benton had had quite enough action for one mission – not that he was going to tell him that.

Staying close to the wall, the Brigadier made his way quickly down the stairs and out of the building.

Outside, the chief constable's reinforcements had encircled the front of the building over the cave mouth. Shots had been fired from within, so the police had fallen back and were sheltering behind a ring of crates and other detritus.

The officer in charge, Inspector Bruce, had taken cover behind a pile of scrap metal and was in hasty conference with his second in command.

'Derwent, take five men. Go round to the back. We'll draw their fire.'

'Sir.'

Derwent looked across and caught the eyes of a group of officers nearby. 'Okay, you lot, with me!'

The men signalled their understanding and, ducking low behind the crates, made their way towards the building. As he saw them leave, Bruce gave the order to give them covering fire. Immediately, shots came from inside the building. The officers outside didn't try to advance, but kept up a steady barrage on the entrance, dodging in and out from behind their defensive barrier.

A sudden yell came from behind a pile of oil drums and plastic sheeting and one of the men dashed over to help his colleague who was trying to stem the blood flowing from a wound in his shoulder. A shout came from inside the building, followed by silence and, outside, a yell – '*cease fire!*'

Then the doors opened fully and the men inside came out in silence, their hands above their heads, followed by Derwent and his men.

The cleanup operation began. Ambulances arrived to take the wounded for treatment, either to the hospital or to the medical wing of the county prison. Uninjured prisoners were taken in vans to local headquarters, where the chief constable was overseeing operations.

Pausing to take stock, Bruce looked at Sergeant Derwent and asked, 'Where's Gibson? Did anyone see him? Check the vans, quickly!'

Gibson had almost reached the front gate, when the sound of a footstep behind made him stop. He turned, quickly, but could see nobody.

Gibson let out a long breath. He was getting jumpy. Not too far now though: he had a forged passport in his pocket and his share of the profits was on the way to a bank account in his new name. Soon this place would be behind him, and with any luck, buried in the rubble.

The noise again.

Damn it. Again.

They'd promised the quakes would stop. But it seemed like the earth had other plans.

Then, the noise again.

Another tremor rolled beneath his feet: small, but sharp, like something deep underground had stirred. Gibson paused, listening. For weeks now, the ground had shifted and groaned. At first, it had been useful, terrifying the locals, scattering suspicion. But now it was unpredictable. Dangerous. He froze, turning just as a nearby outhouse gave a groan and crumpled, its roof caving in with a hollow thud, swallowed by the rising dust. When he turned around, there was a soldier staring at him. Gun drawn. A look of cold rage in his eyes.

'Inspector Gibson,' said the Brigadier. 'We haven't met.'

Gibson's lips drew back from his teeth in a mirthless smile. 'Trying to frighten me? You wouldn't shoot an unarmed police officer, would you?'

'Probably not,' replied the Brigadier evenly.

He holstered his weapon. There was a moment's pause. Then the Brigadier stepped forward, calmly, and punched Gibson in the face.

Gibson fell back, gasping, clutching at his bleeding nose. The Brigadier pulled a pair of handcuffs from his belt and knelt down to secure his prisoner.

As he did so, he leaned forward and whispered in Gibson's ear. 'Really, this is much more satisfying anyway.'

He then stood up, pulling Gibson up with him and led Gibson back through the complex to hand him over to Bruce.

Sergeant Derwent put Gibson in one of the cars and gave him a handkerchief to stem the flow of blood from his nose. The Brigadier led the way up to the director's office, where Brookes was added to the list of those detained, and Miss Hawthorne and Sergeant Benton could make their way out and back to the vicarage.

After an emotional reunion with Iolanthe, Miss Hawthorne was ordered to rest by Rev Stott, supported by the Brigadier and Benton. She argued, but gave way in the end and went upstairs on the understanding that she be called as soon as there was any news. The rest of the party sat in the parlour talking over the action of the afternoon and filling in gaps in each other's knowledge.

It was close to nine in the evening when the chief constable arrived. Miss Hawthorne had come down for dinner and was sitting with the others when Sir James was ushered in by his old friend.

'I thought I'd come and give you an update. I owe you all that much after helping to root out the nest of vipers in county HQ.'

Miss Hawthorne spoke first. 'Have they confessed?'

'Some of them have started to talk,' he replied. 'Some of them are still loyal to Gibson, curse him. The men from the research centre have been a little more communicative, particularly as we've recovered all their equipment and timetables, which should allow us to track their distribution network.'

'And what was it? I mean, what were they moving in those crates?'

'Currency. Forged coins and notes. They had a whole printing operation set up in the cave under that research building, powered by that monstrous generator. We found a box full of the stuff. Nothing high value, but enough to cause serious problems if it got into circulation.'

'So the caves had been prepared while the forgeries were being produced?'

'Yes. The main run you explored had already been hollowed out by some Edwardian entrepreneurs. Brookes and his men picked up where they left off. They installed the lights and ventilation systems. The quakes started when they began tunnelling far beneath the bedrock. We found the machinery stashed away in one of the lower cave, quietly humming, still active. It's a good thing we got to it when we did, or the whole place might've come down around our ears.'

'Oh, I see,' said Miss Hawthorne, adjusting her shawl. 'So the tremors were deliberate? A clever distraction.'

'Clever, yes, but criminally reckless,' replied the Brigadier darkly. 'Those tremors weren't just a diversion, Miss Hawthorne. Another few days of digging and they wouldn't have needed an escape plan. They'd have destroyed half of Lower Budworthy.'

Rev Stott looked up in surprise. 'Ingenious… But I knew nothing of these enterprising Edwardians,' he said. 'How is it that they had been so completely forgotten?'

'Hard to say,' replied Sir James. 'The money fell through, of course, and there were doubts over the safety of the project. Then there were some rock falls in the side caves and the whole thing was shut down and the gate closed again.

When Brookes and his crew were prospecting for a location with concealed access to the sea, they checked the caves themselves and found they had little work to do. They chose to move the currency by boat to try and avoid detection on the roads, I believe. The cargo would be split and moved in small boats to a number of small ports and marinas around the country and sent out from there. Luckily for us, we managed to find a lot of their distribution list intact. They were planning to burn it all in the cave, but the access hatch became jammed during the fight so they couldn't get down there, either to destroy their records or to escape.'

The Brigadier, who had been enjoying a glass of Rev Stott's brandy, asked, 'Who was behind it? Gibson? Or was he just the enforcer?'

'Brookes was the brains behind the operation. Though I believe he gave you some nonsense pseudonym. Somewhere local – Huish or Milverton or—?'

'Wiveliscombe,' put in Miss Hawthorne.

'Ah, yes, Wiveliscombe,' said Sir James, smiling wearily. 'Well, Gibson came in as a partner. Now we've had a proper look at his record, he's been running a number of scams under our noses for years with his gang at county HQ. This was to be his last big pay-off. He had a fake passport, and was planning to go to Spain and live off his ill-gotten gains.'

'And Bryce?'

Sir James sighed. 'Poor Bryce. I feel I've let him down badly. Gibson was blackmailing him, in effect. Bryce was being paid to turn a blind eye to the goings-on at the centre, but was feeling increasingly uneasy. When Goodwin began to kick up a stink about the tremors, Gibson bullied Bryce into attacking him. Gibson told Bryce that he was in too deep to back down and that Goodwin needed to be put out of the way. After the attack, his nerves really started to go and he appealed to Gibson, who promised to cut him loose if he would do one last thing…'

Benton cut in: 'Meet me on the cliff path.'

'Precisely. The man had no idea he was going to his death.'

Silence fell, until the chief constable shifted uncomfortably in his chair, then reached down into the briefcase he'd brought with him and took out Benton's gun.

'Ah, Sergeant, your property.'

Benton took the gun without a word.

'Obviously,' Sir James assured him, 'the charges against you have been wiped from the record.'

'Thank you, sir,' said Benton in an expressionless voice.

Rev Stott sensed the awkward atmosphere in the room, so thanked the chief constable for coming and offered to show him out. Sir James departed, to general thanks, and, when Stott returned, the others were discussing plans for their departure the following day.

Genuinely disappointed at losing his guests so soon, but aware of their many commitments, not to mention that he'd see at least some of them again soon when they returned to pay their respects to Bryce, Rev Stott thanked them for their help once more. He further offered to accommodate any of them should they wish to come back and visit 'under happier circumstances'.

Benton considered the offer, then replied, 'To be honest, I'll be glad to be back in the city for a bit. I know the countryside is meant to be the place for peace and relaxation, but it never works out that way for me.'

The Brigadier, smiling to himself, softened his subordinate's words with thanks to their host, then he and the sergeant turned to their maps to plot their routes –

To Devil's End.

To UNIT HQ.

And, Benton hoped, to a bit of peace and quiet.

MISS HAWTHORNE'S GUIDE TO RUNIC TRANSLATION

AH, I see you're looking to do a bit of investigating of your own! Good for you. I'm sure you've spotted the runic letters at the start of each of our missives. These are Old Norse, the stuff of legends.

But the runes you find scattered here and there are a little complicated. For one thing, not every letter exists in futhark – that is, the runic alphabet – so some are doubled up to cater for the tastes of you and I.

A and O, for example, are both represented by the same character.

And spaces are represented with another letter, i.e. ×

While there are numerous dialects, we shall concern ourselves with the Anglo-Saxon Futhark. In fact, the runes you find hereabouts, sent by the gods and used extensively in magic, are adapted to the modern mind. Whereas traditional runes are phonetic, those you find in this extensive report of the investigations of myself and Sergeant Benton are spelled out so that even the good Brigadier wouldn't get too frustrated.

So, as I said to him when leaving the fellow to translate some of my reports: good luck. I'm sure you'll do splendidly.

A B C D E F G H I J K L M N O P Q R S T U V W X Y Z

ACKNOWLEDGEMENTS

I wish to express my gratitude to the following people:

To the late Mervyn Haisman, Henry Lincoln, Barry Letts, and Robert Sloman, for creating such vivid and memorable characters, and to their Estates, for allowing me to write new adventures for them.

To Shaun Russell at Candy Jar for accepting my work, and to Philip Bates for editing it. My thanks to you both for your support and kindness to a very inexperienced author during the publication process.

To the late Damaris Hayman, for her inimitable performance as Miss Hawthorne.

Finally, to John Levene, for embodying Sergeant Benton on screen, for his enthusiasm for my stories, and for his diligence on their behalf. When I gave him a copy of Sergeant Benton and Miss Hawthorne's adventures during the *Day at Devil's End*, I did not imagine that we would end up here, with the publication of a book!